The Hunger To Look Younger

*To Joan Barrow Roy
Blessings.

Skip Klein*

The Hunger To Look Younger

A Novel

Skip Klein

iUniverse, Inc.
New York Lincoln Shanghai

The Hunger To Look Younger

Copyright © 2007 by Skip Klein

All rights reserved. No part of this book may be used or reproduced by any means, graphic, electronic, or mechanical, including photocopying, recording, taping or by any information storage retrieval system without the written permission of the publisher except in the case of brief quotations embodied in critical articles and reviews.

iUniverse books may be ordered through booksellers or by contacting:

iUniverse
2021 Pine Lake Road, Suite 100
Lincoln, NE 68512
www.iuniverse.com
1-800-Authors (1-800-288-4677)

Because of the dynamic nature of the Internet, any Web addresses or links contained in this book may have changed since publication and may no longer be valid.

This is a work of fiction. All of the characters, names, incidents, organizations, and dialogue in this novel are either the products of the author's imagination or are used fictitiously.

ISBN: 978-0-595-46737-2 (pbk)
ISBN: 978-0-595-91032-8 (ebk)

Printed in the United States of America

Dedicated to:

My Mother for trying so hard to teach me something.

My Grandmother for teaching me not to ever give up.

My much older sister, Marilyn, for being a life long friend.

My deceased wife, Liz, for sticking with me for forty four years and presenting me with four great children.

My current wife, the lovely Miss Ellie, for putting up with all my nonsense.

My old high school classmate, Betty Robbins Bouchard, for her endless patience and encouragement. God rest her.

Mary Cole, who got me started on this journey in the first place.

Gina Joseph, for her boundless editorial assistance.

Chip and Miss Ellie were sitting on the veranda of her Condo in Coral Creek, Florida. It was an unusually warm day for this time of year. However, there was a soft, gentle breeze wafting through the palms. *Very pleasant,* he thought. *Certainly beats the frozen temperatures they left behind in Michigan.* They we're enjoying the scenery and enjoying each other's companionship.

This was all new to Chip. He had never been to Florida before. In fact Miss Ellie was new to Chip, too. Both, now in their seventies, and both, widowed a number of years ago, they were married only a month ago after a one year, long distance courtship. When he finally got up enough nerve, to ask her if she would like to get married, her reply was, "Sure, I don't have anything better to do."

A long distance relationship, when, you're over seventy, is a lot different than when you're a teenager. You really don't have time to discover each other's little quirks. It's sufficient to find out that the two of you are compatible.

So here he sat, in South Florida, taking it all in. In addition to the palm trees and the flowering shrubs he noticed the entire complex was rimmed with hedges about four feet tall. They were exquisitely pruned, preened and pampered.

Chip thought to himself. *If anyone would have told me ten years ago, that I would be living down here in this fair y tale land with this lovely but mysterious woman, I would have laughed at them. But who was this Miss Ellie anyway? And how could she possible afford this resort type living? Interesting, very interesting, she really was mysterious, yet no more so than the rest of the inhabitants of this land of eternal youth. She would rise very early and be gone by 6:30 every morning. Walking, she said, but where? There wasn't a store within ten miles, another mystery.*

He often sat on the veranda smoking while she was out walking. That was the only place she allowed him to smoke. (Never in the house, oh no, no, no.) But he didn't mind. The veranda was part of the second story suite and afforded a good view of the walking paths as well as a large share of the complex. From his perch, he could keep track of who was coming and going.

He soon started to identify them as: "The Wanderers"; "Grouch Face"; or "Antsy Pants". It became kind of a game. *I wonder where they're going or where they've been,* He would ask himself. One evening, after dinner and toward dusk, he inquired about a well rounded, blond he had seen a few times.

"Oh, that's my neighbor, Barbara. She's originally from Connecticut, "said Miss Ellie.

He immediately tagged her: 'Babs, the Blond Bombshell from Bristol'.

Why was she only seen at dusk? Did she have some kind of an aversion to the sun? Very interesting! She was supposed to be a writer. However, he never met anyone that read anything she wrote. So why so many trips to the same place all the time-like Rome, Brussels, London and especially Paris, all cities with large populations? Could she be an undercover agent for the FBI or CIA, or maybe a double agent? It appeared very interesting and very mysterious. Chip pondered the possibilities.

From his second floor coop he had a bird's eye view of all the flora and fauna like the ten different varieties of palm trees and the flowers in every hue of the rainbow. And don't forget the hedges that are clipped, trimmed and preened to look like a picture out of Better Homes and Gardens.

As Chip sat there, admiring the scene in this fantasy world, puffing on his last cigarette, (it was always going to be the last, well maybe tomorrow) he noticed the black Cadillac several times. *Who were these people with the New Jersey license plates?* Quite by chance, he happened to be out of cigarettes again. And also quite by chance he saw this tiny little thing get out of the black Cadillac smoking a cigarette. He had been buying cigarettes two for a quarter from a multitude of people, so he thought to himself *Why not?*

"Excuse me, could I buy two cigarettes from you for a quarter?" Chip asked.

"No," she said, "But I'll give them to you."

"I can't let you do that. See, if I buy a pack, I smoke a pack. If I only buy two, I only smoke two until someone else comes along that smokes. I'm cutting back-trying to quit." Chip explained.

"Oh, what can I say?" she said. (He found out later this was her favorite expression, said with a Northeast accent, in a manner of speech that he calls sliding. Whaat can eye say; can you hear that in your mind?)

"Thanks a lot. My name is Chip. And you are?"

Anita she says, "And this is my husband Sam."

So now he knew 'Alluring Anita' and 'Sexy Sam'. (I'll explain the 'Sexy Sam' part later.) Nice folks, who Chip thought he should get to know better.

Chip had learned the two-for-a-quarter scam back home. He stopped at his favorite gas station one day only to realize there were young people working there. Now he had nothing against young people, but sometimes they couldn't add or subtract too well. Several times he had to explain that two-for-a-quarter was equivalent to the cost of a pack. He even joked that the employment application should have a line on it that says new employees had to sell the old guy two for a quarter. Some of the sharper ones kidded when they saw him coming.

"Here comes two-for-a-quarter," they'd announce.

Another time, as he was strolling along the Florida path, he noticed a dark complexioned man heading toward him, smoking a cigarette.

"You don't happen to have a couple of cigarettes, do you?" he asked.

Chip could tell the guy wasn't a native North American but what happened next really floored him. The man, tall, bronze skin, nicely dressed, extended his right hand to shake Chips.

"I'm fine, thank you" he said, and kept on walking.

I guess you meet all kinds down here in the sunny south, thought Chip.

In her attempt to make him feel more comfortable, Miss Ellie introduced him to several other condo occupants. 'Antsy Pants', it turned out, was interesting. It seemed like he left every two hours or so, was gone for an hour and then returned only to leave again in another two hours. Strange behavior too, as he would pull up across the parking lot as close to the hedges as possible, get out, and just kind of stand there.

I hope he's not doing what I think he's doing, thought Chip. *Not here, in broad daylight, in front of the building.*

Some of the other occupants were also pretty interesting. They would ride their two wheel bikes around pretending to check to see if the cars that were parked really belonged there. Miss Ellie called them, 'Condo Commandoes.' Trucks were strictly forbidden. But one guy, Tiny Tim, did have a golf cart. He was supposedly watching for illegal fishermen along the many canals. Tiny Tim seemed to be more interested in the growth of the hedges than he was in any illegal fishermen.

ARTHUR & MILLIE

One of the other couples he met was Arthur and Millie. (No story would be complete without a king and a mermaid, right?) So now we have "King Arthur" and "Millie the Mermaid". Millie earned her name the hard way. She can't swim but looks great in a bathing suit! So why not tab her, 'The Mermaid'?

"King Arthur" looks the part, like he was a king during the time of the round table and the knights. About six foot four, well proportioned, with a stern expression; he was befitting the mold of a king in the days of yore. However, initial impressions were deceiving. He had a gracious smile and a gregarious personality. In a younger life he was a wine merchant, which required him to taste wines with his customers. No wonder he was happy. His old stomping grounds covered New York and New Jersey. And boy did he know New York City.

"I still made frequent trips back there-for old time's sake." he said.

Arthur couldn't walk like he used to. There was a strange gait to his meanderings as though he was leaning to the left all the time. At first Chip thought it had something to do with his driving habits in New York. However, a left always seemed to point toward the hedges. (Very strange, indeed.)

KENNY DEE

One day Chip decided he needed a haircut. He had heard about an Italian singing barber in one of the many strip malls. Chip was entering the barber shop when out comes Kenny Dee.

Kenny was the peripatetic druggist 'snow bird' from the North Country with twinkling eyes, a slight paunch, and a slow, easy way of talking that almost made you think he was a native. The most ubiquitous person Chip had ever met.

"What the hell are you doing down here? I haven't seen you in years. When did you get down here? Where are you staying?" he would say, and on and on.

"Let's have a beer," said Chip.

"Okay, I'll meet you across the street after your haircut." Kenny replied.

It had been thirty years or more since they had last seen each other so they talked and talked and talked. Kenny, it seems, had wanderlust and had sold his business, left his wife, and hit the road. As you may imagine, Kenny Dee was a druggist of the old school, before the days of the over the counter remedies, when a druggist used the pestle and board and little beakers to mix cure all potions. The itinerant 'chemist', (I use that word loosely) could sell his services almost anywhere.

A very dim light began to shine in Chip's head. (I think I'd better keep this in mind. There are too many coincidences here.)

The weather was hot and sticky. The barber was old and grumpy. When he was through chopping Kenny's hair, the barber took an old-fashioned whiskbroom and took a casual swipe at the loose hair on the back of his neck. More of it fell down his neck and back than hit the floor.

As they sat in the bar drinking warm beer and eating stale old bread stick dipped in Salsa sauce, Kenny kept squirming on the bar stool.

"For God's sake, will you sit still? You're making me dizzy with your twisting and turning. What the hell's the matter with you?" said Chip.

"That damn barber shoved all the hair down my neck. I'm never going back there again. I think I'll let my hair grow long enough to have one of those Chinese pigtails. Then I can have it done in a salon," said Kenny.

"Oh, that would be cute, very cute," said Chip.

Chip later learned from one of the other residents that Kenny Dee was indeed a doctor. Not an operating type doctor but a doctor of chemical science or something. He had the sheepskin to prove it. The other guy said he saw it.

(Oh sure, so now he has a quack doctorates degree from some mail order house in Vienna.) It did however seem to impress everyone else. Chip knew better. He had known this character for too long.

SKEETER

And then there was Skeeter. Just about the most happy-go-lucky guy; on the face of the earth. He didn't live in the condo. No one seemed to know where he lived or where he came from. He was kind of a jack-of-all-trades but master of none. In fact he wasn't good at any. But most people paid him to do odd jobs because he was always so happy and so much fun to have around.

Skeeter was an odd little guy. There was a light spring to his step because he seemed to bounce on the balls of his feet. You never knew what to expect. Sometimes he was seen in bib overalls, one strap hanging loose. Another time it may be in someone's old gym shorts, the short kind, and a Hard Rock T shirt. His favorite outfit was the one that made him look like Pee Wee Herman or Mr. Bean. He loved it. He was weird but very well liked.

Every time you met him he would have some little story to tell. Or he would spring a limerick on you. For instance, one day Chip bumped into him at the mall.

"Hi Joe, whaddya know? Just got back from the burlesque show." said Skeeter.

Or other times he would break into song for no apparent reason:

"My gals a corker

She's a New Yorker

I buy her everything to keep her in style.

She's got a pair of hips

Just like two battle ships

Oh boy, that's where my money goes."

And on and on the parody would continue.

THE POOL

There was something strange going on here but Chip just couldn't put his finger on it. He would keep his eyes and ears open and on occasion he would notice various people head for the pool. That's a whole different story, the pool crowd. Some of these ladies shouldn't be wearing those skimpy little bathing suits. In fact some of them shouldn't wear bathing suits at all. And those beer guzzling, hanging over the belt, wannabe Schwartzeneggers, shouldn't expose themselves to the public either.

All that aside, Chip wondered why he never saw anyone in the pool or no one ever looked wet while walking back home.

One day, feeling braver than usual, he put on his trunks, sucked in his gut and headed for the pool. There is a small clubhouse that you must go through to enter the pool. Security ya' know. Once inside the clubhouse he saw several people sitting around little patio tables, stuffing stuff into cellophane zip lock bags. Some of the contents were white and some was green.

What's going on here? Chip thought he recognized the white packages. *But green?* Back in the corner, kind of away from everyone else, sat Kenny Dee. *Aha!* The light flashed in Skip's head. Dee sat there chain smoking one cigarette after another with a very happy smile on his face. Even more unusual were the four people sitting at another table, all in dry bathing suits, packing the little envelopes in neat little shoe boxes.

What the—? Chip exited quickly. Since he wasn't a regular at the pool, he doubted that anyone even noticed him and Dee sure couldn't see that far. Chip had to find out a lot more before he revealed himself to anyone else.

From his vantage point Chip could see almost everything in the village. He happened to notice Dee was coming and going more often. That was very strange because he didn't even live in this village.

What kind of business could possibly bring him here so often?

Chip decided right then and there that Dee might have some of the answers that he was looking for. How to go about finding out was another question. As so often happens with the elderly, the light flashed in his minds eye. *Aha,* he thought. *I remember how that old lush could put away the beer. He didn't do too badly in the bar a month ago either. Invite him out for beer.*

They met at the same bar as before, across the street from the chopper hair guy. Chip thought it was called 'The Flamingo Express.'

Geez, this place is kind of sleazy! he thought as he pulled his 5 foot 3 frame up on a lopsided stool. The air was stale, almost putrid and the cigarette butts hadn't been swept up from the night before.

"What'll it be?" he was asked.

"A cold Coors" said Chip.

"Seltzer water," says Dee.

Oh man, thought Chip, *this isn't going as planned!*

Chip asked, "What's with the seltzer water?" as he watched Dee extract a small zip lock bag from his blue jean pocket.

"Well, I can't order a glass of just plain water in a joint like this can I?" said Dee.

"Why not?" said Chip.

"Cripes, first of all that ugly bar tender would kick my butt out, and secondly, I need it to take my medication," replied Dee.

"What's the medication for?" asked Chip

"A variety of things," said Ken. "I'll be okay in about five minutes."

Chip thought to himself, *I've seen little packages of stuff like that before.*

"So what have you been up to?" he inquired.

"Not much", says Dee, "Just been hanging out, picking up a buck here and there."

"That's cool," said Chip. "I wondered how you were making a living down here, what with you being a 'Doctor of Chemistry' and all."

"Oh, you heard about the sheepskin, eh? What a hoot. And at my age," said Ken.

"Yeah, well I wouldn't brag about it and sure as hell wouldn't display it anywhere," said Chip.

"Don't intend to. But you can call me Doc, if you like," said Dee.

"Fine with me," Chip said. "Hey, enough of the seltzer stuff, how about a beer, Doc?"

"Okay, I haven't had one in a long time," said Doc.

What Chip didn't know was that Doc wasn't supposed to drink any kind of alcoholic beverage at all. It only took about four gulps when old Doc gets very loquacious. Soon he was inquiring about 'Babs. The Blond Bombshell from Bristol.' (Connecticut, that is.)

"Is she like married or attached? How old is she? What does she do for a living? Come on man, lay it on me," said Doc.

So Chip filled him in as much as he could. After all he didn't know her too well either. Doc seemed to be especially interested in her trips to the continent.

Chip couldn't help but wonder about that. He realized, too, that Doc was rattling on pretty good. Eventually Chip asked about Doc's medication.

"I can't tell ya' about that, but man, it's good," said Doc.

"What do you take it for?" asked Chip.

"Just about everything, we call it Floragra, but don't tell anyone," said Doc.

"I never heard of it. Where do you get it?" inquired Chip.

"Right in your village, you big dummy," replied Doc.

"Come on, there aren't any stores even close to my village," said Chip.

"In your own clubhouse, turkey brain," said Chip.

(Wow-the beer & Floragra combo was really working no!)

"Tell me more, my Doctoral friend," said Chip.

Chip figured it wouldn't hurt to butter him up a little. So Doc really spilled his guts.

"Those beautiful hedges that you think are so pruned, preened and trimmed to the nth degrees are really a medical miracle. Ponce de Leon never found the fountain of youth but we did," he said.

"Whose we?" asked Chip.

"The group in your complex, you Flamingo flea." replied Doc.

Doc explained that either "Sexy Sam" or "King Arthur", he couldn't remember which, had a bad bee sting:

"He stumbled against the hedges and voila, the sting was gone. Then another member had those old age brown spots all over her hands. Liver spots, they call them. She was out pruning the hedges when she accidentally dropped the shears into the bush. She reached in to retrieve them. However, when she pulled her hands out the spots were gone. She could hardly contain herself. She had to tell someone. Along came 'Alluring Anita', the cigarette smoker, but of course who would believe such a story? It was only a couple of days later when 'Alluring Anita' dropped an ash on 'Sexy Sam'. Damn! He must have yelled. She was so upset she didn't know what to do. God, he must have been hurting. Then she remembered the story about the hedge leaves. She rushed outside, grabbed a handful of leaves and quickly held them on the burn. It was awkward trying to hold them on his legs, what with Sam jumping all around. But alas, it worked. The pain was gone almost instantly. Then as one person told another and that person told another, the word was spread. We've really got something here but what?" asked Doc.

'King Arthur'', remember him? The wine taster from New York had talked to Doc at the clubhouse about analyzing some new wine he heard about.

"Sure, for a couple of bucks," Doc said.

He couldn't complete the analysis all at once so they met several times for Doc to give him progress reports. During one of the sessions, 'King Arthur' mentioned the story about his neighbor 'Sexy Sam', relieving the pain of a leg burn with the leaves off some hedges. Doc didn't believe the story for one minute. 'King Arthur' was so insistent, he told Doc to talk to Sam himself. Doc (always with a nose for making a buck) said, "Sure, why not?"

Meanwhile, Babs had returned from yet another trip to Paris. She told Chip she had seen The Chancy de Elias and The Church of the North Dame. It sounded pretty French to him so he believed her story about being in Paris. Chip also noticed that she was wearing a cute little tam on her head, a hanky type thing around her neck, a black and white horizontal striped light blouse, a very short, shiny skirt and of course high heel shoes with ankle straps which were now back in style.

What's not to believe? He thought. *If Doc saw her like this there's no telling what would happen.* Chip was nursing his beer all the while Doc kept ordering more Seltzer water. Only now he was getting fancy. He added a lime twist before putting in the Floragra.

But he was happy. Man was he happy! The happier he got the more he talked. He explained that he was the official 'chemist' hired by the handful of condo owners who knew the 'secret of the shrubs'. *Have another Seltzer and tell me more,* thought Skip.

"Well," Doc said, "this discovery was strictly by accident."

He recalled the stories of the brown spots, the bee sting and the ash burn.

"We don't know why this works but it does. They hired me to find out why. So far I don't have a clue. My only guess is that it has something to do with folic acid. The mysterious part is that it's only growing in front of two buildings although the same hedges appear all through the complex. Hell, all over Florida! I've heard rumors that Hurricane Andrew flooded those two areas pretty badly while the water quickly ran off the rest of the complex. There may; have been something either washed into the soil or dropped by the wind. We don't know and we don't care. What we're concerned about is whether or not the next hurricane will extricate it away as quickly as it came. And this is only the beginning. We have barely tapped the potential. Chip, old buddy, I'm telling ya', like the U.S. Marines, we just need a few good men," said Doc.

"Okay," cries Chip. "Count me in!"

As they left the bar and their eyes adjusted to the bright Florida sunshine, they saw the barber heading toward the bar. "I need a quicker picker upper," he remarked, as he went flying by them.

Doc was still pumped up from his seltzer Floragra combo when he returned to the little clubhouse. He was all for doing the lab test to find out what this stuff was good for. What he didn't know was that it was bingo night. The place was jammed with bingo players. There was no prize money but no one cared. They were just there for the camaraderie. He thought it was strange that they're all drinking seltzer water. His beakers, test tubes, jars and bottles were strewn all over the place. *What the hell happened, another hurricane,* thought a poor Doctor Dee. The forlorn druggist was so dejected he went home and went to bed. It was only nine o'clock!

Ellie went back to Michigan with Chip to tie up some loose ends on some business transactions. They were gone for about five or six weeks.

They returned to Florida only to find that 'Sexy Sam' and the 'Alluring Anita' had returned to New Jersey, while, at the same time, 'King Arthur' and 'Millie the Mermaid' had gone back to New York. Chip couldn't blame them, as it gets pretty hot and humid in Florida during the summer months. Doctor Kenny Dee was nowhere around either. Everything seemed to be going to hell.

What am I going to do, Chip thought. *This is the opportunity of a lifetime and it's slipping away.* The next couple of days he sat on the veranda, smoking one cigarette after another. One day he saw a familiar figure, good old Skeeter. He had almost forgotten about him.

"Hey, Skeet, come on up here. I'll buy ya' a beer," said Chip.

Skeeter took the steps two a time, he was so glad to see them back.

Skeeter came in rather cautiously, what with the highly polished ceramic tile in the foyer and all. He started to remove his sneakers but fumbled a little as he remembered the holes in his socks.

"Never mind," said Chip, "just get in here."

He was already popping the top on a cold Coors before Skeeter got to the veranda.

"Here's to ya Buddy, what's new?" said Skeeter.

Skeeter started to run off at the mouth like he was a rabid dog or something. He went on about how hot and dry it's been and how that it was ruining the orange crop, how the water level in the canals was so low that the marine life was disappearing, and how even the alligators were coming ashore in search of food like birds, dogs or small children. (At least that's what he said he heard someone say.)

"Whoa, whoa, whoa," bellowed Chip. "That's not what I want to hear. Where is everybody, especially Kenny Dee?"

"New Jersey, New York, Ohio, Iowa," says Skeet.

"Yeh, but what about Dee, Doctor Dee?" asked Chip.

"Oh, he's at the Uni-vers-a-tee upstate somewhere," replied Skeet. "Ya'll been gone for four-five weeks. I forgot about it."

"What the hell is he doing up there, chasing the co-eds around?" asked Chip.

"No Chip, you know he's too old for that. The last time I saw him chasing anything was the 'Buxum Blond from Bristol' and he didn't catch her either. Anyways he told me he was taking a 6-week crash course in Bo-ton-ic-al chem-is-tree or somethin' like that. He should be home next week," explained Skeet.

"Thanks, Skeet, that's what I wanted to know. Hate to see you rush off but here, take a beer for the road," offered Chip.

"Okee-dokee," Skeet drawled.

Chip had a whole week before Doc came back. Maybe he should have used that time to get something organized. The gears in his head never stopped turning. They slipped a little once in awhile but never stopped turning. If this Floragra stuff was as good as it sounds they would have to be organized.

He started to make a list of the occupants of the two buildings. He would enlist Miss Ellie's help. *Didn't she have a roster of some kind?* He thought. *Of course she did. Let's see now, there's the Goldberg's, the Dimaggio's, the Cohen's, the Benute's and the Yung Sen's. The Yung Sens, how did they get in here? This was beginning to sound like a United Nations venture. He couldn't see too much help here but then you never know.* Chip hadn't realized how astute 'Sexy Sam' and 'King Arthur' were either, until recently.

Damn, I wish they'd get back here! he thought.

As he sat on the veranda, sipping a Mai Tai and puffing on yet another cigarette, he noticed the yard maintenance crew trimming the grass and cultivating the flowerbeds. It dawned on him, that he had seen them trimming the hedges in front of other parts of the complex but never this one. *That's why the lady with the disappearing liver spots dropped the shears in the bush; they prefer to trim their own!*

He went down to talk to them.

"Habla Angles?" he stammered.

"Hell yeh, we are Americano too" said the taller one.

The conversation revealed Manual Monegra was from Puerto Rico and Ramon Rodriguez was of Nicaraguan parentage. *Nice guys could be useful,* thought Chip who asked if they knew what the hedges were called.

"Hell, yes, man, that's Florida agriculture," replied Ramon.

Chip blinked his eyes. *So that's where Kenny Dee got the name. Doc had invented his own name and why not? After all, it was only in front of these two build-*

ings. *We don't care what anybody else calls it. And if it was good enough for Doc, it was good enough for Chip.* He could see it on the letterhead; THE FLORIDA AGRICULTURAL CO.… or better yet, FLORAGRA.com.

THE BEGINNING

"King Arthur" and his 'Mermaid' had gone back to New York City and environs. As he made the rounds of some of his old customers, they kept saying: *My God, you two look great. What's the secret?*

"No secret, must be that Florida Living," chimed in Millie.

'Alluring Anita' and Sam had migrated back to New Jersey but since Sam had worked in the Philadelphia area for so many years they thought a little side trip was in order, as they visited with old friends and neighbors they kept hearing, "My God, you two look great. What's the secret?"

"No secret-must be that Florida living," chimed in Anita.

Obviously none of them were going to divulge 'the secret of the hedges.'

LOIS

Chip was pondering his dilemma when he saw Miss Ellie, The 'Merry Maid from Michigan' returning from one of her frequent jaunts around the two mile circle. She paused to say hello to a resident Chip had never seen before. Curiosity overcame him so he went downstairs to check it out. Ellie introduced him.

"This is my new devoted husband, Chip and this is Lois Clawhammer." She said.

"So pleased to meet you," Miss Ellie replied.

"Likewise, I'm sure," said Chip.

In the ensuing conversation he learned that she was a widow, was very pleasant and upbeat, had some time on her hands, and was a part time bookkeeper for a florist company. *How incredible can this be?* He mused. *A bookkeeper right here in our midst.* It was easy for Chip to be nice to this lady (and she was a lady). However after the bookkeeper revelation, Chip really laid on the charm. He immediately dubbed her 'The 'The Lovely Lois'.'

"Lois, I am so pleased to meet you," he said. "I'm sure we will be seeing you again."

"The Lovely Lois" had already turned toward her building as Chip turned to Miss Ellie.

"I really like that lady and I think I can convince her to be our treasurer," he remarked.

In the next couple of days not much happened. The weather was hot and sticky. (Thank God the automatic sprinklers were keeping the hedges green.) Chip made frequent forays toward the pool but stayed clear of the clubhouse. He was really casing the joint, so to speak, to find out how the occupants of the two buildings kept 'the secret of hedges' from the rest of the compound. It was simple. They just yelled: *"It's filled beyond capacity!"* as they locked the door and as several of them quickly swan-dived, jack-knifed, or belly-flopped, into the pool just to make it look good. Chip thought to himself, *this would be a good group to work with. They might be old but by golly they were quick and alert.*

Doc arrived back in town within a day or two of "Sexy Sam", "Alluring Anita", "King Arthur" and "Millie the Mermaid". (Things were looking up.) The first order of business was to coral Kenny Dee to find out if he had learned enough to be useful. They again met at the Flamingo Express. Reluctantly, Doc had straight Seltzer water with no additives. He had experienced some remorse at spilling his guts the last time they met.

"Well, Kenny Baby, you aren't being very obstreperous today," Chip chirped. "Come on now; tell me what you learned at the big University. What about the powder I saw people stuffing into zip lock bags?"

"Oh that was nothing; these dumdums didn't know how to blend it. They thought they really had something. I convinced them they really needed me," replied Doc.

Doc gave him a devilish wink.

"So what did you find out? Can you turn the hedges into a powder or an ointment or a liquid?" asked Chip.

"At least a liquid and a powder but I'm not sure of an ointment," replied Kenny.

"And what makes it such a miracle product?" said Chip.

"No one knows. We tried every experiment imaginable but no luck. It's some kind of a quirk of nature but who cares as long as it's safe. And so far there haven't been any problems," said Doc.

After a few more seltzers and a couple more beers, Chip finally decided to lay his cards on the table.

"Doc, as I see it," talking directly into Doc's face. "Now that you know how to make something of those miraculous little leaves, we have a virtual gold mine here. BUT ... we need to get organized. First, we have to protect 'the secret of the bushes' from the rest of our village and any outsiders that get too nosy. What I'm saying is, we need around the clock surveillance. This can mostly be done by hidden cameras, closed circuit TV and a back up alarm system. Do you agree?"

"Jeez, Chip. I never thought of anyone stealing hedge leaves," said Doc, kind of wistfully.

Then Chip said, "Well, I've given it a lot of thought and we sure don't want to miss out on a good thing. Think back a little, you Lunk Head! Remember what happened after Hurricane Andrew? Every crook, every scam artist, every TV network in the world flooded this area. Once the world finds out about Floragra, they'll be all over the place like a swarm of locust. Have another seltzer; only this time put some of your powder in it so you sharpen up. You're brain is acting old right now."

"Okey-dokey," Kenny said, who could always use a little extra lift.

"Where can we go that's large enough to hold all the residents for a secret meeting?" Chip inquired,

"The clubhouse, naturally," replied Kenny.

"No, no, no. A, it's too small for all of us at one time. And B, it's too obvious," said Chip.

"Okay, how about the back room of Taco Loco, or behind the peacock cages at South Winds Park? No one would realize we weren't looking at the birds," said Doc.

The peacock thing sounded good. Chip put a notice in everyone's box that the meeting was extremely important to every resident of those two buildings. (Amazingly, every single one that was back in town showed up. Also, amazingly, not a one of them had ever been to the peacock park before.) They OOH'd and AAH'd over the green and blues and golds of the fantails. In fact Chip had a terrible time getting their attention.

Once under way he explained his mad plan. He called on Doc to tell them how these little leaves could be turned into a powder, or an ointment or a liquid. Doc wasn't used to expounding in front of a group, so he blundered along for a while.

"Never mind all that stuff, tell us about the money," yelled Mrs. Goldberg.

"Yes, how about the money, honey," came a cry from the rear.

Chip stood up again, "We'll get to that shortly," he said. "We need to set up some officers to run this thing, any volunteers?"

"Not till we know about the moolah," one guy said.

"All right, already," barked Chip. "May I suggest the "The Lovely Lois" as our Treasurer? She has experience keeping books for a florist."

"Okay, let's hear it for Lois," someone yelled.

"Good, now we're getting somewhere," Chip said, "and Doctor Kenny Dee will be our resident chemist. And to save time and haggling, this is the slate of officers I think you should elect," Chip explained.

He then produced the following list for review:

Treasurer	The 'The Lovely Lois'
Distribution Mgr.	'King Arthur'
Recording Secretary,	'Millie the Mermaid'
Manufacturing Mgr.	'Sexy Sam'
Personnel Mgr.	'Alluring Anita'
Expediter Mgr.	'Tee Shot Tom'
Public Relations	Beauteous Bev
Local Advertising	Lonely Lucille
Security Mgr.	Sly Eli
Security Deputies	Bert & Gert
Legal Eagle	'Lean Jean'

"Are there any objections? If not, I suggest one vote on the entire slate," said Chip.

"Wait a minute," a voice from the crowd spoke. "What about a general manager and his assistant? And I want to know the qualifications of some of these people. And when do we get around to the money?"

Just about then Skeeter wandered toward the front of group.

"We want Chip! We want Chip! We want Chip!" he chanted.

The crowd quickly fell in with his lead: "We all, want Chip!" they blurted.

Surprise of all surprises, Chip went on to be General Manager. He immediately appointed The 'Merry Maid from Michigan' as his assistant. The slate was voted in lock, stock, and barrel.

One of the 'elder elders' spoke up very weakly, "Mr. Chip, now that you have a funny title and you're going to guide us through this venture, we can't keep calling you Chip," she squeaked. "Do you have a last name?"

"Well yes," he replied. "It's Dale, Chip N. Dale."

He could see it already: *FROM THE DESK OF CHIP & DALE ... Cool.*

"You see, I was the first born on either side of the family. My Grandpa Fred had been a sailor on the Great Lakes, when they still used sails. When he first saw me he said, 'Well, there's a Chip off the old block and tackle. The name stuck and I've been Chip ever since," explained Chip.

Chip went on to explain to the assembled multitude, that he, the resident chemist, and the treasurer would be getting together, to figure out the cost of production, distribution, etc. before they could establish a selling price, This in turn, would determine how much each one would earn. He was about to end the meeting when it occurred to him that there was one last item that needed to be covered.

"Folks," he said, "none of us has anything invested yet. So, in order to keep it that way, we must have absolute secrecy. Does everyone understand?"

"Yes we do," the crowd responded weakly.

"You can't tell anyone; not your relatives; not your kids; not your grandchildren. Not anyone. Do you all understand?" he said.

This time, in reply, it sounded more like a group of Marines yelling "YES SIR!" to the First Sergeant.

The meeting was adjourned amid hugs, high fives and general all around happiness. Chip asked Doc, the resident chemist, and the "The Lovely Lois", the new treasurer, to hang back for a minute. Doc noticed that the "The Lovely Lois" looked lovelier than usual in a crisp, clean looking pink polka dot blouse with plain white shorts on and sock less strap sandals. She caught him eyeing her up.

"Just forget whatever your thinking," she snapped. "First of all, you can't afford me because there's no money in the treasury yet. And secondly, we have some serious business to discuss."

Doc got the message. (This one was all business.) Of course, Miss Ellie, who was Chip's wife, had to stay behind to get a ride home. She could have told Doc not to mess with the "The Lovely Lois".

The Food Fight

During this little side bar meeting, Doctor Kenny Dee explained that it wouldn't take too much to get started. Of course they couldn't make too much Floragra to start with, but that was okay because they needed to experiment to find its most beneficial uses. They knew about the brown spots, the bee stings and the cigarette burns but what else could this miracle hedge be used for?

Doc went on to explain that if he had a couple of pounds of fresh cut leaves, several Tupperware bowls, maybe four dozen Popsicle sticks, and about a dozen KFC chicken buckets (washed out) he could get started. Oh yea. A gallon of bleach too, to make it as opaque as possible.

The next day, the phones in the complex were ringing like a 911 center. The 'Merry Maid from Michigan' and the "The Lovely Lois" kept repeating the same message over and over again: *Free Kentucky Fried chicken in the clubhouse, tonight at six o'clock. Bring a Popsicle on a stick and carry it in a Tupperware bowl, if you don't mind.*

The giddy crowd arrived promptly at 6 o'clock. They all agreed what a great idea it was to have a picnic in the clubhouse. Now what? Someone spoke up saying that because we forgot to bring silverware we would have to eat the chicken hand fed, so to speak. They gleefully popped the tops off the buckets and dug in.

"I haven't had this much fun since my senior class picnic and that was fifty years ago," one of them remarked.

However, since this was a group of senior citizens (a hateful term) they tended to be a little sloppy. There was chicken on their blouses, chicken on their shorts, chicken on shirts and chicken on pants. What a mess! At one point, 'Sexy Sam' had to duck as a drumstick went flying by. He saw the perpetrator laughing as he picked up a wing and winged it. Soon there were bones and partial carcasses flying all over the place. Talk about a food fight. *And these are people I want to be in business with?* Chip thought to himself. Someone with a brainstorm blew a whistle.

"Everyone in the pool" he yelled over the clamor. (Would you believe it, every single one except "Millie the Mermaid", who can't swim jumped in fully clothed-shoes and all?)

"I can't swim," said Millie.

"That's OK," somebody yelled, "Your boobs are big enough that you'll float."

So she jumped in!

After about ten minutes of spitting, sputtering and choking, they dragged themselves out. What a sight! Clothes disheveled, shoes squishing and hair dripping like an old rag mop While walking through the clubhouse, someone piped up: *Oh crap, we forgot the Popsicles! That's alright, drink the melted stuff out of the bowls, but be sure to save the sticks because Doc needs them."* another noted. And so ended, the best pool party, picnic and food fight that any of them had been in for a long, long time. The next day several of the "gofers" cleaned up the buckets, the sticks and the bowls. Doc was in business.

Meanwhile, 'Marvelous Marilyn of Milford Michigan' was monkeying with her modem. Chip's much older sister was marvelous for several reasons. Number one: She could still get around on her own and still breathe at the same time. Number two: She was jumping into the next millennium with her new computer. It didn't compute much but she had Email, the Internet, and at least a thousand different games. Not surprising that she caught on so fast having been head teller at several banks in the southwest and recently retired from a real estate title company.

"Learn all you can, Sis. We'll soon have you contacting the whole world," Chip advised. Chip asked, via E-mail, if she could do a newsletter.

"*P-e-a-c-e of cake,*" she wrote. Giving him doubts of her spelling skills. "*Tell me what you need.*" she added.

THE FIRST EXPERIMENT

Before six o'clock the next morning, Doc Kenny Dee was in the clubhouse chomping at the bit to get started. He had even showered and put pharmaceutical type clothes on. (In reality it was just a smock over his tee shirt and blue jeans.) But for the itinerant druggist this was a major change.

At 6:08 A.M., Chip's phone rang. He didn't bother to answer because he knew Miss Ellie was already up preparing for her usual walk.

Doc practically screamed into the earpiece, "I ain't got a blender, not even; a hand mixer!" *The Merry Maid kicked Chip in the rump,* explained the phone call and told him he better get up and leave.

Chip scrounged up an old blender and headed for the clubhouse. On the way, he passed several other residents of the village that were not occupants of the two 'special buildings.' One even questioned where he was going with a blender at this time of the morning.

"Just going to mix up some alligator eggs," he flipped, as he briskly walked away.

This little encounter alerted him to two things. One, he'd better get the security set up. And two, he could conceal more if he drove, which he preferred since he wasn't much of a walker anyhow.

Doc Kenny was ecstatic for the chance to finally get started. The first several handfuls of leaves blended quite well using high speed. However as a green, mush, the concoction didn't look too inviting. (Would you want to rub it on your body?)

He poured the mixture into a KFC tub and added a half-cup of bleach. The chlorophyll green was just rising to the top when the door opened. *Damn,* thought Doc Kenny, *an intruder.* Just then Babs, (The Blond Bombshell from Bristol, Connecticut, that is) stepped into the room. The skin tight, shiny short shorts and the halter-top were almost more than Doc Kenny could handle.

"What ya' doin'?" she asked.

"Oh just blending," Doc mumbled, as the sweat began to bead on his partially baldhead and was about to drop onto his glasses.

"So where have you been? You almost missed all the excitement," he said.

"I just got in from Venice," she said.

Doc was struggling to handle this encounter, what with the appearance and now the kittenish cooing. Chip, on the other hand, wondered if she really had been to Venice. Babs went on to tell them that she saw the Tivoli Bridge, had a ride in a Gondola and saw The Place of the Doge. It all sounded pretty Venetian to them! They believed her and when you look like that, what's not to believe?

She suddenly blurted out, "What's that running all over the floor?"

"Shit!" they said in stereo.

The bleach was too much for the cardboard buckets, having eaten a hole right through it. Babs grabbed the broom but the concoction quickly shriveled it to whisk broom size. Chip grabbed a mop, only to be holding an empty handle within 30 seconds. Doc pulled a hose in from the shower room. He hung a makeshift sign on the door:

CLOSED: DUE TO DISINFECTING

They washed the mess down the drain and headed for the local pub while the place dried out. Chip decided he better sit between Babs and the Doc. He was afraid Doc would get too carried away, and then the whole Magilla would be down the drain. Chip as usual ordered a beer. Doc ordered two Seltzers, one for himself and one for her, which he obligingly sprinkled with his miraculous powder.

"Oooh, that's good" she purred.

Good thing I'm sitting between them. Chip thought.

They filled her in on the great 'secret of the shrubs,' explained she was gone too often to be elected to an office and asked how strong her contacts were on 'The Continent.' As she had so often explained to anyone that would listen, it didn't cost her anything. The companies that hired her paid her transportation. She met enough 'Gentlemen' that she never had to pay for anything else. She impishly said she usually came back with more money and a larger wardrobe than when she left.

Chip just raised one eyebrow while Doc sighed, "Oh really?"

Enough of this, thought Chip. They disbanded for the evening, each going their separate ways.

The failure of the initial experiment did not deter Doc. At 6:30 A.M. the next morning he was back at the clubhouse. He hurriedly hung a DO NOT DIS-

TURB sign on the doorknob that he had filched from a Hilton something or other. Now, even Chip couldn't get in nor, Babs, for that matter. He definitely didn't want to be interrupted. Out came the old blender and instead of Popsicle sticks and KFC buckets, he used genuine silver plated spoons swirled in the Tupperware. He didn't need a Bunsen burner but wouldn't it make it look more like a real laboratory? After trying three different wall plugs, Doc was fed up with the damn blender. He abruptly kicked it against the wall. (Yawee-it worked!) He picked it up without unplugging it. The first batch was strained through the Picker Upper paper towel. Holy cow, the green was gone. The remaining liquid was almost clear. Now what?

Doc picked up his cell phone to dial Chip. The inter-condo number was 1,2,3,4. *Who are we for?* he thought to himself.

"Chipper, get down here with "Tee Shot Tom", our expeditor, and "Sexy Sam", our manufacturing director," said Kenny.

As the three of them rounded the corner near the pool and the clubhouse, a squadron of turkey hawks flew over them. Yep, you guessed it, PLOP.

"Shit!" the trio sang out.

Doc was frantically waiting at the door.

"Come on in you idiots. Take a small amount of this in your hand, rub it in your hair, and then rinse your head off in the pool shower," he said.

(The effect was immediate. Shazam! Clean as a whistle!)

Chips internal light clicked on: "WOW-Head N Floragra, what a great shampoo!

"Wait a minute!" Doc screamed. "Let's not jump into anything."

He went on to explain how he came up with the clear liquid.

"What are they supposed to do with it now?" they asked.

"That's why I called you Lunkheads. Now, Mr. Manufacturing manager, how do you propose to package this stuff? And you, Mr. Expediting manager should get together with him to figure it out," said Doc.

Chip chimed in, "I've given it some thought so let me throw this at you. If we want to sell it for insect bites and minor burns, we could use those little bottles with a brush in them like the finger nail polish stuff. Or for larger quantities, maybe we could scrounge up some of those old half pint milk bottles, the kind with the large mouth."

"No, no, no" said Sam. "We don't know how much of this stuff we're going to have."

"Remember," piped up Tom, "we only have the hedges in front of the two buildings on which the 'goofy dust' was blown in from the Bermuda Triangle during hurricane Andrew."

"Yea, but" said Chip "the more you trim it, the more it grows. It rejuvenates itself."

"Hold it right there," yelled Doc. "That gives me another idea. I have to figure a way to make it into a paste. Thanks Chip for the thought. I know you would come in handy sooner or later."

As he was removing his professional looking smock, he suggested they better figure out what to do with the first batch and where the hell are all the gofers needed to clean the place up.

"After all," he said, "Other residents might want to use the clubhouse and the pool, and we sure don't need them nosing around."

Chip picked up the cell phone. Very quickly a half dozen folks showed up. The blender went into one truck, the Tupperware in another and the spoons were shoved into a purse to be washed and cleaned at home. They had fashioned a funnel from a piece of newspaper and drained the liquid into a brown Mrs. Butterworth syrup bottle. (That shouldn't attract too much attention.)

"I'll take charge of that," Chip yelled as jumped up and knocked over a chair.

THE CHEW WA-WA

Doc giggled, "What the hell, it's only syrup."

As the temperature escalated and the humidity climbed faster than a monkey up a tree 'other' residents of the complex wanted to use the pool. They had to suspend their operation for a couple of days. Skeeter showed up one day, out of nowhere as usual, with the cutest little dog you ever did see. He didn't even have a leash, just a plain old piece of string around his neck. Everyone in the group of 6 or 7 people standing around in the shade of a giant palm tree, wanted to know what kind of dog it was and did it have a name?

"It's a chew wa-wa, a female type, so I call her Belle Taco," said Skeeter. "Sort of like the ones in the commercials."

Little itsy bitsy Belle Taco soon became the mascot for the whole group. They actually fought over who was to keep her over night. As Skeeter became more perturbed, he told them no way they could keep the dog. Over emphasizing a Latin accent, he said: "Chew can't keep her. Chew would feed her dog food, banana splits and Aunt Chulatas. Chew only eats Tacos, so I keep him, I mean her."

"*Okay Skeet, don't get your Freehatas to the boiling point*", they replied.

They all took turns holding Belle Taco while Skeeter cooled down. They finally got around to handing her to Chip who as he cradled her gently said, he needed to be excused with the dog for a minute. He then took off for his condo. When he returned, "Lean Jean" asked why he had left.

"I just thought she needed a drink and to be wetted down to cool off," he answered, as he handed the soaking wet dog to the next one.

No one gave it a second thought, thinking how nice it was for Chip to be so considerate. They seemed to have forgotten that Chip was in possession of the Mrs. Buttersworth bottle with the Floragra mixture. No wonder the poor little thing was wet. Chip had doused it liberally with the clear liquid. Looked like water to everyone else.

That evening, as they laid side by side in the king size bed with huge pink and purple flowered sheets, Miss Ellie was feeling more amorous than usual.

"Do you wanna?" she asked.

"Not tonight Hawney, I got things on my mind," replied Chip.

"Oh, like what?" she said.

"Like what did I do to that little dog today? Did I kill it or what?" said Chip.

He filled her in on the dousing.

No wonder he's not in the mood. Skeeter will shoot him, she thought.

"Good night, dear," she said.

However, Chip didn't sleep well that night. He tossed and turned. Finally he got up to have a cigarette out on the terrace. *I shouldn't have done that. What the hell's the matter with me,* he repeated to himself over and over again

It was almost daylight when the 'Merry Maid from Michigan' got up for her morning 'movements walk,' that is. Chip was on his way back to bed.

"See ya' in a little while," she said, exiting out the door.

The morning seemed to drag on and on. Miss Ellie returned from her two-mile jaunt, refreshed and ready for anything.

"Nope," Chip nodded. He decided to stroll outside to see what was happening.

Just then Skeeter came walking around the corner with an entirely different dog.

"Where's Belle Taco?" inquired Chip.

"Right here," said Skeeter.

"No, can't be. Belle Taco was a tiny little hairless Chihuahua. This mutt is three times bigger and has all that curly white dog hair," cried Chip.

Skeeter was humming: *How much is that doggie in the window?*

"Chip you scoundrel, look what you did to my dog. I even had to change her name to 'Fifi Taco' because now she's a French poodle," exclaimed Skeeter.

"Hand her over," said Chip.

Fifi Belle, or whatever her name was, recognized Chip instantly, as she lapped his face.

"I can't believe it," Chip said in awe. "Let's go find Doc."

Doc was just pulling in when he saw them.

"Where the hell did you find that mutt?" he questioned

"I didn't find nuthin'," Skeet said. "Chip did this to my Chew-wa-wa."

Doc grabbed her for a closer look. "Like man, I can't believe it."

"Do you two know what this means?" he gasped.

"No" said Skeeter.

"No" said Chip.

"It means Floragra grows hair! It may grow other things too but we need more experimenting. Right now let's be content with hair," said Doc.

"Just think," he said excitedly, "brown spot removal, insect sting relief, burn medication and now corrective hair growth. Truly, miraculous, and we still haven't made it into a cream."

Skeeter and Chip stood there with their mouths at half-mast.

"King Arthur" and "Millie the Mermaid" had returned from their summer vacation. They were on their way out to brunch when they saw the group in front of their building.

"What a cute little poodle," says Millie.

"It's a Chihuahua," says Skeeter.

"Harumph!" gargled Arthur. "I know a French poodle when I see one."

"But you don't see one," said Chip who then brought them up to date, including dousing the dog.

"So I see," said Arthur, rather royally.

'Lucy the Lip' (so named because her lips were so sensuous) and the "The Lovely Lois" who had been listening from one of the lower patios, wanted to know if the new hair could be dyed like their gray hair. Or could it be curled? Or if necessary, straightened? *What if you accidentally dropped some, would it grow hair where you didn't want it,* they inquired?

"For Gods sake, give me a break," yelled Doc. "We just discovered this an hour ago. We need to do more research."

Chip chimed in, "Don't tell anyone, no one, and nobody. Understand?"

Doc said to Chip, "I'm exhausted from all the excitement. Let's go have a beer."

As they sat in The Flamingo Express, Doc said he thought they were making great strides. He was ready to experiment making the cream but he was becoming concerned about security and the fact that there was too much gathering out in public. Chip agreed and vowed to check into it immediately. Doc thought maybe they needed a secret code to communicate in, if Chip or the security people could come up with one. He said he felt much better now and felt like getting back to work in the clubhouse if he could get in without attracting too much attention. After they split up, Chip went to see 'Ely the Deadeye'.

"Can we have a secure security meeting with Bert and his wife, Gert?" said Chip.

"Sure, let's just walk over there," replied Ely.

Ely knocked at the door. Bert peeped through the peephole. He undid the hasp, loosened the dead bolt, turned the safety lock, removed the chair and softly said: "Come on in."

They entered timidly.

"Bert, where's your wife, Gert?" said Ely.

"In the laundry room, ironing a shirt, "replied Bert.

Bert was still in his Jammies, the ones with the orange and black stripes. As they talked, he slipped on his khaki cargo pants and looked around for his V necked tee shirt.

"Hey Gert, where's my shirt?" he said.

"It's in the wash, with my skirt. Put on a sweater-it shouldn't hurt," she replied.

As Gert entered the room, a beeper went off to let her know the laundry room was secured. The twosome learned that Bert had retired from the CIA, the FBI, the ADC or one of those alphabetical government agencies. They asked Bert if he had given the security problem any thought. Bert thought he had a couple of good ideas. He proceeded to explain they should install at least four cameras strategically placed at each end of the hedge, one focused on the clubhouse and one at the corner of the rear building.

"Why the rear building?" they asked.

"To catch anyone sneaking around where they don't belong," he replied.

"Won't the cameras in the hedges be a give away or at least attract attention?" asked Ely.

"Not if we conceal them in the hedges and camouflage them like the Army does," said Bert.

They all agreed it was a good start. Gert asked Bert where the monitor should be.

"I believe we need three of them, one in our house, one at Ely's and one at Chips," he explained.

Chip brought up Doc's concern about the meetings out in front of the rest of the complex and with a suggestion of a communicating code. Bert and Gert said to give them sometime they would come up with a rhyme. Suddenly, Bert blurted out:

"If you're a friend, say Hi Ho. If you're a foe, get lost Moe."

Chip thought they could do better than that.

THE WEATHER FORCAST

It was at approximately this point in time when Chip really began to worry about the abundance of the miracle hedges. *If we lose these hedges*, he thought to himself, *we are out of business, dead in the water, DOA, ____out of luck*. He decided they needed someone to keep an eye on the weather. Should there be any hint of a new hurricane developing, they would strip the hedges right down to the roots.

He thought Mrs. Goldberg might be a good choice. After all, she rarely left her apartment, electing to spend ten or twelve hours a day watching television. He stopped by to see her.

"Hi, Mrs. Goldberg, how've you been?" asked Chip.

"Don't call me Mrs. Goldberg, I hate that. and I feel lousy. I got the miseries all over," was her reply.

"May I come in?" Chip asked.

"Sure, just for a minute. What do you want?"

Chip explained the need for someone to frequently monitor the weather and let him know immediately of any impending storms. She thought she could handle that.

"Do I get paid for it?" she asked.

"No, but you haven't kicked in anything yet either," said Chip.

As 'King Arthur' and Millie got into their Crown Imperial (isn't that appropriate?) they could see "Sly Ely" breaking up the crowd. Bert and Gert were heading for the flea market. After spending several hours they managed to scrounge up four video camcorders. It wasn't exactly high tech closed circuit type security cameras, but they would have to suffice. Bert told Gert they would set their monitor up in the spare bedroom. She agreed they could watch in four-hour shifts. She was to take the first shift. He didn't mention that the monitor was an old 13 inch black and white. After two hours, she complained she didn't see anything but a black screen.

Bert said, "Good, that's the way we want it."

Chip hooked his up on the veranda because that's where he spent most of his time. He and Miss Ellie weren't going to set there and stare at an empty screen. No siree. He had a twenty-five inch color with remote control sitting right along side of it. That would work out just fine.

'Ely the Deadeye,' along with his wife, the 'Audacious Audrey', outsmarted them all. (He wasn't security manager for nothing.) He had the camera on the far end of the hedges and the camera at the rear corner of the building hooked up to his apartment. How did he do it? He had a giant 72-inch screen with picture in a picture. In fact he had a different picture in each corner and the main screen was still larger than most TV screens. (Talk about security.)

BABS AND DOC

In the meantime, Doc Kenny Dee (shifty character that he was) had picked Chips pocket for the clubhouse keys. The first chance he got he had a spare key made. Now he could come and go as he pleased. He left the original key lying on the steps where Chip would find it and think he had dropped it.

Along about midnight Doc thought he would try his new key. *Surely there wouldn't be anyone around to see him at that time of night,* he thought.

The key worked fine. He only had one light on so as not to attract too much attention. He was just getting everything in place to start experimenting with a cream base when the door opened. In stepped Babs, 'The Blond Bombshell from Bristol' (Connecticut, that is). In the semi-darkness, Doc was afraid to trust his eyes. Here stood the slinkiest, sexiest, cut high over the hip, shiny blue Spandex bathing suit he had ever seen.

He spit and sputtered a little.

"Hi there" he said drooling heavily, "what are you doing here this time of night?"

"What does it look like silly? I came down for a swim. I just hate the crowds of old people during the day," replied Babs.

"Oh so do I," he muttered condescendingly.

"Want to join me?" she said.

"No, I don't think so," he said choking a little." I have work to do, and besides I don't have a suit with me."

"Don't be silly," she squeaked. "I don't leave this on. That's one of the pleasures of swimming this time of night."

"Thanks anyhow," he gulped. He thought his Adams Apple was going to break right through his wattle.

She was inching past him very slowly as she was dropping a strap off of one shoulder. Doc noticed the sparkling blue of the bathing suit matched the sparkling blue of her mischievous eyes. The blond hair and the total package, was almost more than he could stand.

"Go right ahead. Don't let me stop you," he said, gasping for air.

Moments later he heard the shower turn off and a gentle splash in the pool. The restraint was almost unbearable as he peeked around the corner. (If he was bold enough to steal a key, he was bold enough to steal a peek.)

"Oh, Myyy God," he whispered to himself. The damn bathing suit was lying on the shower room floor. *What the hell! Why not? It's too late to start an experiment now anyhow.* He said convincing himself to join in.

Daylight was just dawning as 'The 'Merry Maid from Michigan" came out for her usual early morning stroll.

"It's kind of early for you to be taking a swim," she said, approaching Babs.

"I really needed it badly," replied Babs as she literally dragged herself along the sidewalk.

Doc was sound asleep huddled in a corner when Chip entered the clubhouse.

What the ... thought Chip.

"For God's sake, get some clothes on," he yelled.

Doc was about to nod off again when Chip grabbed him by the shoulders, shook him mightily and bellowed at him to get his clothes on. Chip asked Doc what he had learned during the night since it appeared he had been there for a length of time.

"I learned a lot, but not about Floragra." Doc replied.

"Then I would suggest you get with it Buddy. You have a hell of a lot of people depending on you," Chip chirped again.

Chip had brought a thermos of coffee, which he tried to get Doc to drink. Chip didn't know Doc had swallowed a lot of the pool water. Chip left the good doctor playing with his beaker. Doc had retrieved the Mrs. Butterworth bottle and proceeded to carefully pour the contents into a Tupperware bowl. First, he tried mixing in a clear gelatin product. The blender had a nice gentle whir to it. However, the stuff congealed and jiggled all over the place, fun but not practical. Then he tried some dry wall taping mix. *That wouldn't jiggle*, he thought. It didn't. It just got stiff as a board. He just had to find a way to make a cream or a salve or at least a lotion. (You wouldn't want to rub dry wall stuff on your body!) *As a cream, it wouldn't have to be clear,* he thought to himself. *Hey, I got it. Why not confectioners, 10 X powdered sugar? Of course, why didn't think of that before?* So he borrowed 'Tiny Tim's' golf cart. Of course he didn't tell Tim about it. Chip saw him scooter off to the nearest store.

Bert, being a retired big city cop, had been thinking about the communications problem. He thought of different things he had seen where guys talked to each other without really talking. The movie *Stalag l7* came to mind as well as the jokers from the old TV series Hogan's Heroes. *Nah, Ely wouldn't go for any of that.* In fact, Ely had suggested running a wire from his place to Bert & Gert's, to Chips, and then to the clubhouse. Clean Campbell soup cans made a great microphone on the end of a wire. *That wouldn't hardly, attract any attention, would it? One could just see that strung out in the neatly groomed, classy resort type setting?*

Bert finally remembered the old police system walkie-talkies. *What a great idea!* He thought. So he and Gert were going to the nearest Toys R Us store. (They couldn't afford much remember?)

"No Gert, you better stay here and keep an eye on the monitor. I don't trust that Ely to pay attention," said Bert who made a dash for the car. (Well for him it was a dash.)

Just then old 'Antsy Pants' came out of his place and inquired where Bert was going. After Bert told him, he said:

"Great, I'll go with you, been there many times. I know right where it is."

Ely's wife, 'Audacious Audrey', answered the phone when Gert called him to tell him she had to go to the bathroom and would he please watch his monitor.

"Sure. No problem, I'll tell him," Audrey said.

Ely was still on the phone when Gert walked over to tell him he could hang up now. She told him of Bert's idea and that he was on his way to Toys R Us.

"Damn!" Ely swore. "I wish he would have told me. I love to go there."

Chip hadn't heard from Mrs. Goldberg (don't call her that) since he appointed her the official weather person. He stopped by her condo.

"Mrs. Goldberg, I haven't heard from you," said Chip.

"What was I suppose to do, hop down to your place on my walker?" she spouted.

"Why didn't you just call me?" asked Chip.

"I don't have a phone, I'm retired, and I live on Social Security. I can't afford a phone," she explained.

"Oh, for God's sake, why didn't you say so in the first place?" said Chip.

"You didn't ask," was her retort.

"Well then, we'll get you a walkie-talkie," Chip replied.

"That would be nice. You're such a nice boy," said Mrs. Goldberg.

As he was on his way back home, Chip saw Doc disgorging himself from the back seat of a local taxi. His face was radish red, the sweat pouring off his brow onto his coke bottle glasses, his jaw set firm as an immovable old rusted vise. He elected to get out of the cab on the street side of the hedges so he wouldn't attract any attention. He headed directly for the Dale's residence, his baggy Dockers swaying as he walked. His hair was rumpled from riding in the back seat while the driver had his window open. One sock was down and one sock was up, on the same side as the untied shoelace. Frankly, he was a mess!

"What the hell happened to you?" inquired Chip. "I thought you were in the club house laboratory?"

Doc told him about his 10X sugar idea and the need to run to the store on 'Tiny Tim's' golf cart.

"I could use some help, damn it!" Doc was swearing more now than he ever did.

"Slow down, pal, here, have a beer," Chip said." What the hell happened to you?"

Doc started by saying Chip wouldn't 'believe it.' He was pulled over by the police and given a ticket.

"Can you believe it, and me, a Doctor of Pharmacology? How humiliating! And it's all Tiny Tim's fault," said Doc.

"How so?" asked Chip.

"Get-t-t this," Doc stammered.

"Here's what the stupid cop wrote up," he said, handing Chip a piece of paper.

Chip read the list.

1. *No license on the vehicle*

2. *No valid Florida Drivers license.*

3. *Unauthorized vehicle on the highway.*

4. *Impeding traffic.*

5. *Illegal left turn.*

6. *No lights on the vehicle.*

7. *No horn.*

8. *No turn signals.*

9. *No stop lights.*

"And for good measure, the cop added, #10, no windshield wipers! Wait till I get my hands on Tim, the idiot," exclaimed Doc.

Chip was just calming him down when Skeeter came careening around the corner in the golf cart with Belle Taco under a seat belt alongside of him.

"How did you get it back?" Doc and Chip chimed together.

(As previously mentioned, Skeeter's elevator didn't always go to the top floor.)

"I saw it in front of the police station. It looked just like Tiny's. So I took it," he said with a smile. (Skeet, so proud of himself.)

"Oh,—." said Doc. "Now I'll be charged for a stolen vehicle, too unless of course, they trace it to Tiny."

He went on to explain what he called a kangaroo court was held by a so called Justice of the Peace, under a huge palm tree, alongside the park, where the cool breezes blew over a pond and ruffled the feathers of the flamingos.

"So the JP says three hundred dollars or thirty days," says Doc. "What was I supposed to do Chip? I got work to do, being the head pharmacist and all."

"What did you do?" asked Chip.

Doc kind of guffawed a little, "I didn't have three hundred dollars so I gave him a stolen credit card that I had picked up some time ago."

"Good for you, Doc," sang Skeeter. "I guess you showed them."

Since Doc still didn't get the l0X sugar, Chip asked 'The 'Merry Maid from Michigan" to hop in her little Ford Contour to pick some up.

"But for crying out loud, mind the traffic laws!" he added.

When he returned, Bert found Gert very inert with her eyes at half-mast, starring at the blankety-blank monitor.

"Whatcha' doin' Hon?" he asked.

"Huh, what, where, who's there?" she screamed as she bounded out of her chair.

"Don't worry Gertrude, I wouldn't intrude," says Bert. "I got the walkie-talkies. Why don't you take one over to Chips and one to Ely's? Then we can try them out."

"Okey, Dokey, Bert Baby. Only next time at least ring the bell so you don't scare the ba-jeebers out of me," said Gertrude.

"Sly Ely" saw her coming. He asked "Audacious Audrey" to answer the door as he was trying to stay cool by leaving his pants off. Audrey handed the phones, without wires, to Ely who was standing behind the door. Being Chief of Security, he knew how to use these things.

"Security two, this is Security one," says Ely

"Bert, here." answers Bert.

"For an ex-cop, you sure are dumb," says Ely. "You're supposed to say: Security two here."

"We're not a police force," replies Bert.

"But we are on the air waves and there is a certain protocol to be followed," Ely says. "Don't you understand protocol?"

"Yea, but, who cares?" retorts Bert.

"Hang up now," says Ely. "I'm going to raise Chip."

"Me too," says Bert.

"Chip, it's me, Ely"

"Me too," adds Bert.

Chip replies, "Don't you guys know anything about protocol? This is: Security Three. Do you read me?"

"Gotcha", says Ely.

"Me too," says Bert.

Chip concluded he couldn't take much more of this, so he signed off. and headed back to the clubhouse to see if Miss Ellie made it back with the confectioner sugar. She made it back all right. She was covered from head to toe with white powder. Doc was so anxious to see how it worked that he had everything running; the blenders, the mixers, the bowls, the fan, and stuff were flying all over. Chip rushed in and unplugged everything.

"Hey, what the hell are you doing?" yelled Doc.

"My God, Doc, look at this place. It looks more like a bakery than a club house," said Chip. "Let's get organized."

Chip wanted to know how many pounds of leaves it took to make a quart of liquid. Doc didn't know. Nor did he know how much bleach to a quart: nor how much sugar to add to the liquid to make it into a paste? "Don't know," was all Doc could say.

"Okay, that's it," cried Chip. "You are the most disorganized person I've ever met. Don't do anything else until I return with 'Sexy Sam'. He is the manufacturing manager, you know?"

They returned in about fifteen minutes during which time Miss Ellie cleaned up the bulk of the mess. Chip told 'Sexy Sam' that he was to take charge.

"Give him anything he wants but keep track of everything. And I mean everything. If it will help, we'll get our treasurer, the 'The Lovely Lois', to help you keep the records straight," said Chip.

Doc, Sam and Miss Ellie spent all afternoon experimenting with so much of this or so much of that. No matter what they tried it always came out looking and tasting like the icing on a hot cross bun. Finally Sam said they should call it a day adding that his stomach was getting squeamish.

Miss Ellie was reporting back to Chip when he asked her if she would like to go out for dinner.

"Are you nuts?" she screamed. "I've been drinking, gulping, tasting and swallowing Confectioner's 10X sugar, bleach and Floragra juice all afternoon. No thank you!"

Chip suggested pizza sounded good. She agreed.

Just as they were leaving, Bert and Gert pulled up on the two-seated bike they had acquired for police patrol duty.

"Wait, wait," they puffed out breathlessly, partly from pedaling the bike and partly from excitement. "The surveillance camera showed a figure all dressed in white going in and out of the club house. We rushed right over to see if it was a Klu Kluxer."

"Slow down, catch your breath," said Miss Ellie (The Merry Maid) "Doc got carried away with the sugar and had it flying all over. It was only I covered with sugar powder."

"Well thank God for that," they said in unison. (Which seemed appropriate in that they were on a bicycle built for two!)

While walking back to their quarters to freshen up before going out for dinner, Chip heard some squealing on his walkie-talkie.

"This is security three, come in," he announced.

"Yea, this is 'Moldie Mrs. Goldberg', you know, an Oldie but Goodie." replied Mrs. Goldberg.

"Yes, Mrs. Goldberg, what's up?" asked Chip.

She went on like a long lost friend. She has been watching the weather every hour on the hour on channel 82.

"'Windy Willy' was really cute," she remarked. "He had on a different suit every day. The latest one was a single-breasted pin stripe. Not like the pin stripes in the old James Cagney gangster movies. And his shirts were the new style solid dark colors with contrasting solid color ties. Man he was cute!"

She also said she found out that they didn't call him Windy because he was a weatherman, but because he talked so much.

Chip finally cut in, "What about the weather?"

She said she didn't pay any attention to it because she was busy watching 'Windy Willy'.

"Then why did you call?" asked Chip.

"Just to see if I could operate this thing. 10-4, good buddy," she added, and then hung up.

That night Chip was restless. It was all in front of him. The hedges were a miracle. Time was running out before the next hurricane season started. The potential was endless. Yet they couldn't develop it. *Think, think, think,* he thought. *The answer is right there, in front of us. We don't need to be brain surgeons we don't need to be chemist, not even pharmacist. Think petroleum. Oil? That won't work. Think petroleum. Gasoline? To volatile-won't work. Think petroleum.*

"That's it," he screamed. "Eureka, Hoover, or whatever. I've got it!"

"What, what?" asked Miss Ellie.

"Petroleum, that's what," yelled Chip.

He went on to tell her, "It's safe, it's non-toxic, it's smooth, it's plentiful, it's cheap and it's almost colorless."

He tried to call Doc at the clubhouse. As usual, the line was busy. No great athlete, Chip, but he set a record racing to the club house on his short, stubby, little legs.

"Doc, where the hell are you?" he yelled. "I got it. I got it!"

5hrs He was so excited he almost burst a blood vessel. He completely forgot about the need for secrecy and security

"Quiet down, you idiot!" replied Doc.

"What you got is jungle fever," someone in the pool says.

Doc was sunning himself in a lounge chair since with this many people around, he couldn't very well do any experimenting. Doc had never seen Chip like this before. He didn't even get this excited when he made amorous advances to the 'Merry Maid from Michigan'.

"Come on Miss Ellie said, and get your clothes on," said Doc. "We're going for a beer."

"Okey-dokey," agreed Chip.

Again they headed for the Flamingo Express. On the way, Chip toyed with Doc's head.

"I got it," he said.

"You got what?" queried Doc.

"Just think jelly," replied Chip

"Are you thinking of Floragra jelly?" asks Doc. "Who the hell would want to rub strawberry jelly all over themselves?"

Such a Smart Alec, thought Chip, who then replied, "Think of the slogan: Rub jelly on your belly. Sounds great, doesn't it?"

"No, it doesn't, you Schmucker brain," retorted Doc.

Once inside the bar Chip got serious. He ordered a Pina Colada while Doc ordered his usual Seltzer water, with just one drop of the elixir in it

"Now listen up, chemistry head," said Chip. "How about using a petroleum jelly for a cream base, anything wrong with that, Beaker Breath?"

"It won't work, too sticky," said Doc.

"You're the pharmacist here, not me. Can't we cut it with something?" asked Chip.

"I don't know. Water runs off of it and you sure couldn't use milk, wine or beer," said Doc." Let me call my colleagues at the University."

Chip decided that in the meantime, they should have another meeting. Miss Ellie, his ever, able assistant, made all the phone calls.

The only question came from Bert." Should I bring Gert?"

"Yes," she replied.

"Who will mind the monitors?" asked Bert.

"Leave it up to Skeeter," she said.

So Bert yelled to Gert to tell Skeeter to put on a shirt and get over there.

They convened at the South Wind Park. Only this time the peacocks were nowhere around. The meeting got off to a good start. Chip gave them a progress report. As he spoke the crowd got more excited. Especially when he told them Doc was on the verge of a break thru in making an ointment.

"However," he went on to say, "We have one small problem."

The groans were most audible. He turned the meeting over to "The Lovely Lois" since she was the official treasurer. As she stood up, dressed in a white pinafore with big yellow and red flowers on it, there was mild applause and even a few hoorays. You could sense the group was waiting for the other shoe to fall, so to speak. Lois read the crowd like a stand up comedian. Normally smooth and loquacious, she decided to hit them between the eyes and get it over with.

"Frankly, we're broke," she said.

The cries went up immediately, "That figures."

"Yea, where's the money?" they asked.

Lois majestically raised her arms.

"Now wait a cotton picking' minute!" she said. "You haven't received any money because you haven't spent any money except for fried chicken and popsicles."

"Hey, that was great. Let's do it again," someone yelled out.

Lois went on, "It takes money to make money. Therefore, we will have to levy a fee. Let's call it a surcharge like some theatres or sporting events does."

She continued, "We all just got a raise in our Social Security payments, so let's put that money to work. Your board thinks it can get by for the small sum of one hundred dollars apiece.

"Does that include the chicken?" she heard.

"Now if each of you will just sign this pledge card, I'll be around to pick up your checks tomorrow," she explained.

After all the pledges were turned in, (wouldn't you know it, Mrs. Goldberg gave her an IOU) the meeting was adjourned. It was turning dark by the time Chip and Miss Ellie got back to the clubhouse. They were anxious to find out how Doc was doing with the petroleum jelly. Doc sat in the corner, in the dark, rubbing his temples.

"How's it going, my pharmaceutical friend?" asked Chip.

"Terrible," he grunted

"Poor baby, what's the matter?" Miss Ellie said.

Doc replied that he had tried a dozen different combinations to make the Vaseline into a smooth cream but nothing worked. Chip suggested that maybe 'King Arthur' could help. After all, he is a scholarly type.

As they were mulling all this over, Skeeter suddenly appeared-wearing a skirt, white with pink flamingoes.

"What the hell is that?" they asked.

"Well Bert and Gert told me to put on a skirt in order to watch the monitors," he answered.

"Skeet, you better get a hearing aid like the rest of us. Bert said shirt. Like with armholes and buttons down the front. Not a split skirt with buttons down the side. What are ya' trying to do, compete with the Blond Bombshell?" said Chip.

Skeeter giggled and they all had a good laugh.

'King Arthur' and 'Millie the Mermaid' were lounging in their royal purple lounging robes (as befits a couple of dubious royal stature) when Doc, Chip & Miss Ellie arrived. On the way they bumped into "Sly Ely' the Deadeye' and 'Audacious Audrey'.

"We're headed that way so we'll go with you," they chimed.

They rang the bell and as the door opened

Chip said "Hi," Doc said "Hi," and the others joined in "Hi."

'King Arthur', in his deeply resonant voice, intoned "Good afternoon gentlemen, and ladies too. We're just having a little afternoon repast. Please come in and join us."

As they devoured the Brie cheese, the Carr wafers and the Chateau Rothschild 1982, they explained their plight to His Highness.

Doc babbled, "We're in a bind, I have nothing on my mind. Come on Art, You're smart. Give us a start."

Arthur agreed with all of the above and related that as he understood it they had all of the ingredients except the cream was not a cream; it was more like axle grease.

"Simple enough, you Simpletons," Arthur said. "I have a dozen or so cream, ointments or salves in my medicine cabinet. Let's compare them for the most common ingredients. Then we can try that."

They decided mineral oil; paraffin, white petroleum and purified water would probably do the trick. As it was an unusually warm day, even for Florida, the clubhouse and the pool were crowded with 'others', as the group referred to them. So they all decided to go out for the early bird specials. Each couple went their own way. Doc and Skeeter headed for the local hang out. Alligator Alley, this one was called.

The Smoother

Skeeter was telling Doc how his poor little 'Chew wa wa' seemed to be so confused lately. She didn't know if she was supposed to be a French femme fatal or a Spanish Flamenco teaser. He explained how he had taken her to dog grooming shop to have her clipped down to her skin so that maybe she could regain her identity.

Doc was just telling him to put a muzzle on himself so that he could concentrate on the Floragra problem, when Skeeter said "But Doc, I just want you to know that stuff really grows hair."

"We already know that Skeet' but we have to find out what else it can do," replied Doc.

"Yeah but what you don't know is that it's a "smoother" too." Skeet said.

"What do you mean, a 'smoother?'" Skeeter replied. "I mean my dog doesn't have a wrinkle on its body. Even the babe in the pooch parlor noticed it after she clipped all the hair off. But I kept the secret. I didn't tell her how Chip doused the dog with the stuff from the Butterworth bottle."

"Good for you" snapped Doc. "Now shut up for awhile."

"Okey dokey," said Skeeter.

As the others returned two by two and meandered toward the clubhouse, they were confronted by a large sign on the door: *DO NOT ENTER-EXPLOSIVES*. They rather deduced what was going on, they retreated into the night to leave Doc alone.

About midnight Chip couldn't stand it any longer. He had to know what was happening. He picked up the old Walkie-talkie from World War II.

"This is security, one. Come in Doc," said Chip

"Security one, this is Bert. How are you doing?" came the reply.

"What kind of security is this you moron? Get off the phone," ordered Chip.

"I'm not on the phone," said Bert.

"Well then get off of whatever you're on and go to bed," said Chip.

Chip said he just wanted to know how it was going and if there was anything he could do to help.

Finally Doc answered, laconically, "No, I don't think so. I'm so tired right now that I can't hold my head up. I think I'll just curl up in a corner. See ya' in the morning."

Chip heard the phone click. He thought he might as well hit the hay himself. It was a fretful rest, however. He kept seeing hurricanes in his sleep; devastating, destroying, annihilating, demolishing that short row of beautiful hedges. (The kind of hedges that might make him rich.) He tossed, twisted and turned.

Finally Miss Ellie, 'The 'Merry Maid from Michigan',' said. "Take me now and get it out of your system or go to the other bedroom." She thought he wanted to be *frisky* but had no idea what torment he was going through.

Chip glanced at the GE clock radio on the nightstand. It was only 5:30 A.M.

"Sorry honey. I love ya' but I can't. I got things to do," he said.

He threw on some old shorts, a striped t-shirt, some worn out flip-flops and headed for the clubhouse. He wanted to wake Doc before the snowbirds arrived at the pool.

He quietly opened the door. He didn't know if Babs, 'The Blond Bombshell,' was there or not, but he certainly didn't want to disturb them, if she was. Chip was aghast at what he saw. The place was a mess. Paper towels, napkins and tissues were strewn about like a tornado hit a paper factory. There were cardboard cartons and glass containers all over the place. As his eyes adjusted to the early morning hues, they rested on the object in the corner. There was Doctor Kenny Dee slumped over a white, round table, similar to the type one used to see in the old soda parlors, with the wire back chairs. *Oh no*, Chip thought to himself. *This can't be happening. Dear God, please tell me this isn't happening.* His mind was racing. His feet were racing as he made his way through the mess to the corner. Doc was slumped over with his head buried in a pile of crumpled paper towels. Chip took his pulse. *Well at least he had one, and not bad either for a guy his age.* Chip tapped him on the shoulder, nothing. *Oh, my God! He's worse than I thought,* thought Chip. Chip put his hand on Doc's shoulder to give him a good nudge … still. nothing. Standing behind him, Chip put both hands on Doc's shoulders and pulled him back into a sitting position. When he finally came to, Doc was abrupt.

"What the hell are you doing?" he grumbled.

"Doc, look at you. What the hell happened here?" chirped Chip.

"And what did you do to your face? My God, I can't believe it," Chip said looking awestruck.

"Look at you!" he kept repeating over and over again.

"Look at what? I don't have a mirror, you invader of my dreams," replied Doc.

"Doc, you don't have a wrinkle or a crease on your entire face," Chip exhorted.

"You look twenty years younger. Just look at you, I can't believe it."

Upon closer examination Chip could still see the weather lined cracks on the back of Doc's neck check marked like a migrant worker who has spent most of his life outdoors, probably due to Doc's, itinerant life style. Doc explained how he had been up all night with the blenders going, the test tubes brewing and the beakers breaking in the microwave.

"Fine, fine," yelled Chip "but what about your face? What happened?"

"I'm not sure," Doc mumbled." The last batch I made seemed to be the right consistency, almost like a fine face cream. So I rubbed it on just to see how it felt. Then I fell asleep"

"With your face buried in a pile of use paper towel," chimed Chip.

Chip called Miss Ellie to round up a gaggle of 'go-fers' to get the place cleaned up before the 'Easterners' showed up at the pool. Ellie immediately called Lucille because she had a mobile. Lucille then rounded up Beautious Bev, Quaint Camille, The Wondering Wanderers, and several other eager participants. They had the place ship shape just as the first snowbirds arrived. Lucille and Camille were especially helpful.

In the meantime, Chip had shepherded most of the officers of the Florida Agriculture Co. into his apartment. The group was chattering away, the questions and the excitement were boiling over. Doc was the center of attention. Chip let them rattle on for ten or fifteen minutes. He asked Doc to bring them up to date, which he did. But he could not explain what happened to his face, or his hands, for that matter. They were as smooth as butter.

"Geez Doc, you look wonderful," one of the ladies squealed.

Chip chimed in, "Doc seems to have found the right formula. We'll need 2 to 3 days to see if his skin stays smooth or turns back into a prune."

The omnipresent Skeeter piped up, "I told you it was a smoother. Remember what it did to my dog?"

"That's right, Skeet, we forgot about that," said Chip.

It was decided that because there were so many different managers that none of them had the time for any additional duties. What they needed now was a good expediter, someone who could cut through the red tape, and get things going NOW.

They all agreed that "Tee Shot Tom'," who had been some kind of labor negotiator during his working days, was the right man for the job. If only they could keep him off the golf links, for a while.

Lucille, on her mobile, tried to call 'Tee Shot Tom'. But 'The Beauteous Bev' bellowed, in her New York accent, *"He ain't heah. He's golfing or something."*

"Tell him to call Chip as soon as he gets in." she replied.

"Yeah, OK."

The next day dawned as beautiful as could be. The temperature was expected to hit ninety degrees. However the humidity was still a tepid eighty percent. The hedges, those beautiful hedges, would show in all their glory. Mint green was the best description. Chip prayed, as thou' talking to the hedges, *hang in there, baby we need you.*

Slowly the little group came awake. Some showered and shaved only to find the same old puss in the mirror. The ladies de-wrinkled or pancaked or did whatever else they do in the morning, but the face in the mirror hadn't changed. It looked the same as it did yesterday, or the day before, or even the day before that. One by one or two by two they showed up at Chip and Ellie's door. And it wasn't even eight o'clock yet. Miss Ellie had learned by now to make a full pot of coffee in the 35-cup coffee maker. She knew it would be gone by noon, which is about the time they all started to switch to something more stimulating. The conversation took several different turns, depending on its originator. But ultimately they all came back to the same theme. They wanted to look like Doc. Not that they wanted to look like Doc but they wanted their skin to do what Doc's did. (You know-like look younger.)

"You will," promised Chip. "In about a week, but we have a lot of work to do in the meantime."

Tom stopped by about nine o'clock.

"What's up Doc?" he said.

"Very funny, very funny, you hare breath," piped Doc.

Bodies were milling about, some coming, and some going some just hanging out waiting for something to happen. They explained to 'Tee Shot Tom' the duties of an expediter, why they needed one and the reasons they thought he was the right person for the job.

"Not to worry, worry warts. I can handle it in between tournaments. In fact I have made numerous contacts on the golf links that might come in handy," Tom said swiftly.

"However," Chip warned, "secrecy is of the utmost."

"Okey, dokey," was his reply as it was the standard answer with this elder clique, even though Tom was at least fifteen years younger than most.

Chip finally felt relieved. For the first time in weeks, he felt things were working out okay. As he relaxed he realized he hadn't paid much attention to the 'Merry Maid', Miss Ellie. She still had on her Japanese Kimono. She looked very seductive.

"Want a 'Morner'?" he whispered.

"What's a Morner?" she asked.

"That's sooner than a 'Nooner'," he replied. "Like do you want to fool around?"

"No way, Jose, I got things to do and places to go," she said impishly and then quipped "That's what you've been saying for two weeks," as she headed for her room to put on some day clothes. About ten minutes later she was going out the door.

"See ya' later, alligator," she sang out.

Chip hadn't heard from Mrs. Goldberg recently. He picked up the Walkie-talkie.

"Yeah, Moldie Mrs. Goldberg, here," she answered.

"Mrs. Goldberg, it's security three here," said Chip

"What the hell is security three?" she questioned.

"How's the weather looking?" Chip asked.

"Stick your head out the door and check it yourself," she snorted.

Chip asked, "Have you been watching 'Windy Willy' the weather man?"

"Oh, yes," she almost sighed. "Did you see the suit he had on today? He's so handsome."

"What about the weather forecast?" Chip asked.

"Nothing much, it's the same old Florida weather day in and day out," she said.

"Thanks, Mrs. Goldberg," he said.

"Don't ever call me that," she hung up

'Tee Shot Tom', threw himself into this new assignment with gusto. He needed to learn as much about the hedges as he could. He wondered what their botanical name was. He called the Florida State agricultural department for that. Next he needed to find out how mineral oil was shipped. *Was it quarts, gallons or barrels? How about paraffin? Was it by the ounce, the pound or in blocks? White petroleum was a real challenge. Where to start? Purified water was no problem. Every supermarket in the country was selling some form of it.*

Tee Shot decided he needed to confer with Doctor Dee.

"Doc, I need a shopping list. How much of each do you need and how much will it make?" asked Tom. "Write out a prescription if that's the way you want to do it, sort of like you're doctoring a sick elephant."

Tom next contacted 'Sexy Sam' who was, after all, manufacturing manager.

"Sam, we'll need something larger than a food processor to mix this stuff. See what you can come up with that's quick and cheap," said Tom.

Tom met Chip on the sidewalk in front of the building.

"We gotta' talk," he said, "You, me and Doc."

They met once more at the Flamingo Express. Tom wasn't impressed.

"This place ain't exactly a country club. What a dump," he remarked.

"Yeah," responded Doc. "But the guy across the street gives great hair cuts."

"How the hell would you know, with the mop you got on your head?" sniped Tom.

Chip intervened, "Let's get down to business. We're losing time."

Tee Shot injected that he thought packaging would be the biggest problem. They discussed the possibilities. Paper was out. Cardboard was not much better. Glass was expensive and very breakable. They agreed on tubes, but what kind? Chip reminded the other two that they still wanted to maintain secrecy. Therefore, they couldn't just hire a packaging agent

"Let's sleep on it for tonight," he suggested, and they agreed.

THE SHACK.

Tom wasn't referred to as 'Tee Shot Tom' for nothing. An avid golfer, he played every course within a two-hour drive. He sat with 'Beauteous Bev' having a beer and lamenting that this expediter thing was really cutting into his playing time.

"I wish I was on the ninth hole somewhere right now," he said to her.

As he mulled over some of the ninth holes he had played, something was nagging at his memory. *What was the matter with him?* His mind was trying to recall something associated with golf but he couldn't get focused. Suddenly, a light in his brain came on. (Like a Ford having a better idea.)

"That's it Bev, my buxom beauty, why didn't I think of that before?" Tom exclaimed.

"Don't ask me. I don't know what you thought of." she replied.

He proceeded to tell her that, while waiting for some elder snow birds to either get moving or get out of the way, he saw an old shack in the distance, just off the ninth tee at South Winds Park. (I wonder?)

They hopped in the restored Jaguar and headed out to the park. On closer examination he determined that while the shack was old, it still looked serviceable. On further investigation and putting out a lot of inquiries, he discovered the shack was left over from World War Two and had been part of a bombing practice field. (This didn't say much for the accuracy of our flyboys.) The U.S. Government still owned the shack but no one alive could remember ever seeing anyone near it.

The twosome made a beeline back to the Dale's place. Chip and Ellie were having a Margarita on the veranda when they arrived.

"Come on up and join us," hailed Chip.

When they related the story about the shack Chip asked, "What do we need that for?"

"Don't you see? It's out of the way. No one knows about it. We could do anything we wanted. Complete privacy. And it's FREE!"

"What do you mean free?" said Chip.

"Well why not?" said Tom. "What are they going to do, send someone from Washington to investigate? All we got to do is get in."

"I can see your reasoning now. Good work Tom. And you too, Beauteous One," said Chip.

Chip quickly rounded up Doc, Bert and 'Sexy Sam' to run out to see the place. (Skeeter just happened to ride along.)

"Oh goodie, I just love surprises," he squawked.

The golf cart was slightly overloaded as they took the back roads to the park. A winding gravel road led right to the door. There were pock marked bomb craters, overgrown now with saw grass, on both sides of the trail. But none were near the shack. After they unfolded from the golf cart they trampled the weeds down around the perimeter. They excitedly circled the outside. *Looked pretty solid for as old as it was but how about the inside?* Chip thought. There was a rusted old Army padlock on the door.

"We don't want to break the door in and be accused of destroying government property," said Chip.

Skeeter chuckled as he said, "Don't sweat the shack, Jack. Just stand back."

He proceeded to empty his pocket of a large blank key and a triangular file. Within five minutes, they were all inside

"Skeeter, where did you learn that trick?" asked Doc.

"My father showed me that before they took him off to prison," he replied.

"Geez, this place hasn't been used in years," exclaimed Bert.

"Not since World War Two," said 'Tee Shot Tom'. "I checked it out."

There was only the one door and no windows. Visibility was almost zero. The always-alert Bert had a pen light in the pocket of his shirt. They found a brittle, old yellow, newspaper on the floor dated Dec. 7, 1941, a couple of holey Army blankets, a dry canteen, two cans of C-rations and a used condom. (Apparently the shack had been used for more than bombing practice.) *No wonder it was still standing-it probably wasn't even on a flight chart,* thought Tom. There were several old wooden crates stacked in one corner. No one had thought to bring any tools since this was strictly an exploratory trip. Cracking them open would have to wait for another time. Doc thought the place would serve their purpose just fine but he noted that the only problem was, it didn't have electricity.

"Not for long," said Tom.

The next day, Tom, always the expediter, came up with a very old kerosene table lamp and a ceiling hung lamp off an old whaling ship. Doc was upset; explaining that working in the shack was one thing but hanging lamps was a little too much, besides there was a need other then for electric lights.

"It would be nice to plug the mixers, blenders, etcetera into something," said Doc. Speaking of blenders, what happened to the king size mixer you were going to come up with? And if you found one what do we plug it into?"

'Tee Shot Tom' was momentarily set back, "I'm working on it, okay already?"

Chip was going to have to keep Doc. happy for a little while longer.

JOLTIN JOE & BOBBIN BOBBIE

Ellie and Chip were just saying they hadn't seen or heard from 'Joltin' Joe' and 'Bobbin' Bobbie', in about six months. They looked up from their afternoon Margaritas just in time to see the candy apple red, 1936 Ford coupe coming around the corner.

Chip let out a yell, "WOW!"

The Ford was magnificently restored. Not quite back to original. (But who would know?) They greeted the couple with handshakes and hugs.

"Come in please. Have a Margarita," said Ellie.

As they sat on the veranda sipping their beverages, the conversation got around to the car.

"That's incredible Joe. I always knew you were a mechanical genius but how did you ever get a wheel chair lift in the rumble seat?" asked Chip.

"A lot of trial and error," replied Joe "Once I got the hinging figured out, the rest was easy."

Chip chimed in, "I remember when you first bought that thing in 1946. Some returning GI got his mustering out pay and wanted something bigger and faster. I'm glad to see you still have the big sixteen-inch white wall tires on it. They look like new. Where'd you ever come up with those?"

"Some old guy had them stashed away in an old aircraft hangar in Arizona," replied Joe. "They've never been in snow, and it's so dry in Arizona, they're like preserved."

"I see you had the moon shaped hubcaps chrome plated. Cool. By the time you add the chrome beauty rings, you don't see much of the wheel itself. And the fender skirts are classy," remarked Chip.

"Yeah, they are cool," said Joe. "But you know what I miss? Those big dummy super chargers coming out of the hood that was really cool. Remember why I got rid of them? You might recall that the 21-stud engine burned oil like it had a direct hose to Saudi Arabia. So every time I added oil, which was quite frequently, I had to disconnect the super chargers from the side-opening hood. What a pain."

"What ever happened to the naked lady gear shift knob or the knuckle busting steering wheel knob?" inquired Chip.

"Oh, Bobbie wouldn't let me keep those," replied Joe sheepishly.

"Good for her," piped up Miss Ellie.

They conjured up memories and rehashed old times for quite a spell until finally Joe says:

"What have you guys been up to?"

Chip jumped in before Ellie had a chance.

"I'm glad you're here, Joe. With your mechanical background and your knowledge of electricity and computer stuff maybe you can help solve a problem or two," said Chip, who then laid out the whole nine yards at how they discovered the miracle hedges, all about the bee story, the cigarette burn, the disappearing brown spots, the hair on the dog and now 'The Smoother.' Bobbie and Joe agreed that it was an incredible story.

"So what's the problem? You're on top of the world," said Joe.

Chip pointed out that the group had to move out of the clubhouse because there were too many suspicious people around. He explained about 'Tee Shot Tom's discovery of the shack and also that it didn't have electricity.

"WAPFOO!" cried Joe.

"WAPFOO! yourself," recanted Chip. "What the hell does that mean?"

Joe replied, "That means: We Are Paid For Overcoming Obstacles. Let's go see the place."

As they opened the car door, Joe pushed a button under the dashboard. The rumble seat sprang open a big arm with a strap like a car seat belt and a sturdy hook swiveled to the rear of the car. With a hand held device that resembled a portable phone, Joe lowered the strap, hooked it onto Bobbie's 'Little Rascal Scooter' and gently positioned her for the ride to the park. The other three including Ellie, Chip and Joe, squeezed into the front seat.

"Open the wind wings if you want to hear something special," said Joe, as he switched on the radio. Static free FM sound blasted through the interior.

"How'd you do that? There wasn't FM radio in 1936," said Chip.

"That was easy. I have a portable AM/FM taped in behind the Ford Script Radio. The FM antennas are built into the glass of the wind wing glass vents. Now listen to this," Joe said.

He flicked another switch. This time the smooth sounds of Glen Miller's Moonlight Serenade filled the airways.

"Holy crap, Joe, how?" exclaimed Chip.

"Easy," boasted Joe. "The CD is concealed in the glove box with just enough room behind the clock on the glove box door."

"Amazing," said Chip. "I also seemed to remember that the Squirt soft drink company had a cartoon character that you had on the front fenders just in front of the running boards."

"Yeah, I had to remove them when I redid the car," said Joe.

They had parked quite a ways from the shack, as 'Joltin Joe' didn't want to scratch the car in the underbrush.

"What about Bobbie?" questioned Ellie, with concern.

"Not to worry," said Joe.

The car slowed and was stopped by the converted hydraulic brakes. Joe again pushed the button, the swing arm came up, he latched the hook on the scooter and Bobbie was gently placed on the ground.

"We'll never get her through this thicket," exclaimed Ellie.

"Not to worry," said Joe.

He had fashioned two hedge clippers in the form of a V on front of the Rascal. A flip of a switch and they operated off the power take off. (Nothing like clipping along!) As they neared the shack they saw the golf cart on the far side, partially hidden from view. Sure enough, there was 'Tee Shot Tom' and Skeeter unloading a bulky looking piece of equipment. After the introductions were made, Skeeter piped up:

"Hi Joe, what do ya' know?"

Chip asked what the monstrosity was that they were unloading

"A portable generator," replied Tom.

"There ya'go," said Joe. "You're worries are over."

"Where did you ever come up with that thing?" inquired Ellie.

"I remembered that after Hurricane Andrew, everyone went nuts for generators. I figured that after the novelty wore off and they sat around in the way most of the time that a lot of people would get rid of them. Thanks to good old Skeeter here, we found this one at the local dump," explained Tom

"Yea, Skeeter! Skeeter yelled.

The four guys finally got the cumbersome thing out of the golf cart and on to the ground. Chip asked if anyone had brought any extra gas to try it out.

"No," said Tom. "We came straight from the dump."

"Incidentally," said Chip. "I didn't notice any tire tracks on the way in here and we didn't see the golf cart hidden behind the shack."

"Not only am I an expediter but a sneaky one at that. Remember, I told you I spotted this old shack from the ninth hole at the golf course? Skeet and I came in that way. We drove off the ninth hole, stopping a couple of times as though we were looking for a stray ball. I'm sure no one was the wiser," boasted Tom.

They carried the generator inside the shack. As Joe and Bobbie looked around they asked what was in the wooden crates.

"No one knows yet," was Chip's response." We haven't had time to pry them open and we still don't have the tools to do it."

"Not to worry," said Joe once again.

He hustled back to the '36 Ford with the other guys right behind him. Tom and Skeeter were dying to see it anyhow. After using the secret combination to open the doors and pop open the rumble seat, Joe pushed one more concealed button. Lo and behold, the back of the front seat rolled up like an accordion pleated shade to expose an assortment of tools that might be necessary to make repairs should the old flivver break down while on the road. The socket wrenches, crescent wrenches, pliers, screwdrivers, etc. were each held in place by a small pocket and a Velcro strap. The fiberboard backing was painted gray to match the upholstering but each tool was outlined in black in its appropriate place. Not a rattle in the bunch, yet so clean and neat like they had never been used, (which they hadn't.)

"Here's a full one gallon gas can and a hand operated siphon so you don't have to swallow any in case you need more," said Joe. "And here's a handy little pinch bar to pry open those wooden crates."

"Joe, you're a Godsend," said Chip

"Yeah, sure, now let's go see if we can get that thing started," replied Joe.

Skeeter pulled the starter cord while Tom finagled the controls. The rusty old contraption spit and sputtered a few times.

"Here, I'll fix that," exclaimed Joe as he gave it a swift kick.

Skeeter pulled again. Shazam! It started.

Luckily, Joe had a trouble light with 25 feet of cord. It illuminated the shack quite well, thank you.

"Wait till Doc sees this," said Chip. "This generator has four outlets so he can have light and still plug in the blenders or whatever."

. Miss Ellie had sort of straightened the place up and even shook out the old Army blankets. The joint looked almost habitable. Chip was anxious to see what was in the wooden crates. He was just about to try opening the first one when Joe took over.

"I'll do that," he said. "It may be pretty stubborn after all these years. Besides I don't want you to break the pry bar, I may need it to remove one of those moon hub caps." (He didn't want to come right out and say he was bigger and stronger than Chip.)

It took a little gruntin' and groanin' but the first one kind of squawked as the nails were torn loose. *"Well, what is it?"* they all chimed.

Chip reached in to extract one of the small jars with the white contents. No one had a clue. Especially since the jar had a metal stick or handle protruding out the top. There were no labels, so the contents were a mystery.

"What do you think? Should we open one?" said Chip.

"NO, NO, NO!" cried Ellie. "Suppose it's some kind of World War II bomb, or a form of germ warfare? Or it might even explode. We should get Bobbin' Bobbie out of here first. In fact we should all get out of here and wait for Doctor Dee to examine it."

They all agreed it was an excellent idea and proceeded to lock the shack up.

On the drive back to the complex Chip thanked Joe for all his help. He also asked whatever happened to the white pussy cat that sat in the rear window of the '36 that was wired to the after market turn signals and that blinked an eye for a right or left turn?

"I hated to give it up," explained Joe. "But it was over fifty years old and pretty shabby. Besides, I couldn't use it with Bobbie back there on her Rascal. Not only that, but I put in a roll down window so she and I could talk back and forth."

When they got back to the complex, Joe and Bobbie stayed just long enough to have a cup of coffee. Then they left on the road to another adventure.

THE BOTTLES

Chip immediately called Doc on the walkie-talkie.

"Security one here. Come in Doc," he said.

Doc answered laconically as usual, "Yeah, what?"

"Doc, we got good news and maybe some bad news," announced Chip.

He filled Doc in on the generator and the electric power as the good news. The bad news could be the peculiar jars they found in the wooden crates.

"We need your expertise before going any further," said Chip.

"Okey, dokey," Doc replied.

To avoid detection or arouse too much suspicion in the community, they decided to borrow Bert and Gert's bicycle built for two.

"Hey, where are you goin' with our bike?" asked Bert.

"Cool it, Bert baby, just don't call the cops," Chip yelled over his shoulder.

As soon as they entered the shack, Doc took a bottle out of a carton. He examined it upside down, left, right and all around. Chip stood in the open doorway, just in case.

"I just gotta' open it," Doc said slyly. "Stand back, it could blow."

And as he waved it around majestically, Chip crouched, ready to drop to the ground and cover his head.

"Ready? 1-2-3," counted Doc.

Chip was sweating and began to shake.

"Aha," yelled Doc. "Just as I thought."

"Thought what?" asked Chip. "Tell me, you idiot."

"It's plain old school room paste. See the little paste brush inside? That's the handle sticking through the top," said Doc, with a smile.

"Oh, my God!" exclaimed Chip. "You dirty rat. You knew it all the time."

"Sure. Even a pharmacist can play games once in a while," remarked Doc.

Upon closer scrutinizing, they found that all the wooden crates contained the same thing. They wondered what the hell the Air Force was doing with cases of school paste. Doc thought he had the answer.

"Remember what 'Tee Shot Tom' said about this place? That it had been part of an Army Air Force bombing training center? I believe the guys that were in charge of this one never pasted the bull's eyes on the roof. That explains why the paste is still here and, in fact, why the shack is still here. No one has ever bothered it because it was supposed to have been blown up years ago," said Doc.

"I'll buy that one," said Chip.

"Further more," chimed Doc, "this solves our packaging problem. Wash the paste out. Use the bottles, brushes and all. What a great discovery, the whole place has been. We'll have to thank Tee Shot when we get back."

"Don't bother. He gets thanked enough from Beauteous Bev," noted Chip.

That only left one big problem that they could think of and that was a mixer of some kind bigger than a portable beater.

When they returned to the compound good old Tom who was resting on the doorstep with a weird looking drum sitting on his lap greeted them. He explained that it was a lapidary drum or a rock polisher used to polish stones

"I don't think it's big enough for our needs," said Doc.

Tom told then that he had thought of a clothes dryer, but since they didn't have either a 220-volt outlet, or any gas, that was out. But not to worry he said he would expedite something yet.

THE LOGO

"Alluring Anita" and "Audacious Audrey" hadn't been too involved, as yet. Both were craft oriented, talented ladies with time on their hands. Sitting on Audrey's veranda, sipping a home made Cappuccino, while watching the buzzards soar in the wild blue; they decided they should experiment with some color combinations for the new Florida Agricultural Senior Association, or FASA, as they called it. They got out dozens of pieces of construction paper in a myriad of colors. They tried combinations of hot pink with iridescent fuchsia, maroons on grays and blacks on whites. They tried triangles, circles, oblongs and rectangles. After hours of trials and error, they concluded the company's colors should be Flamingo Pink and Sunshine Yellow with a dash of Passionate Purple. *Very Floridian*, they thought.

The logo they concocted was unique, indeed. Picture, if you can, a circle of Sunshine Yellow, a Flamingo Pink triangle, whose apex ended in the center of the circle, a Passionate Purple zigzag line cutting diagonally through the circle, yet not touching the triangle. The bottom of the logo had a wavy line; more like saw teeth than waves, accented in mint green. They were just finishing up and were admiring their creation when Chip and 'Sexy Sam' walked in.

"What have you girls been up to?" Chip asked. (He still called them girls even though they were both over seventy. He said it made them feel good.)

"Just look at this," they replied excitedly.

"S'plane it to me. I don't understand it," said Sam.

'Alluring Anita' pointed out that the yellow circle was the sun, the sustenance of all life on earth; the triangle represented the mystical or magical powers of the hedges.

"Okay, but what are those other dumb things?" asked Chip.

'Audacious Audrey' took umbrage with that attitude.

She loudly said, "They aren't dumb, you're the dumb ones! Now pay attention."

She went on to explain that the purple zigzag was like a thunderbolt of lightning. It signified the rejuvenation of life.

"After all, this is the logo for the new, miraculous Floragra, which we know can rejuvenate anybody," she explained. "And the mint green ripples, on the bottom depict the hedges themselves. Isn't it a great combination?"

The boy's had to agree that it was pretty unique and certainly colorful.

"We'll show it at the next meeting and take a vote on it," suggested Chip.

In the meantime, while all this was going on, Doc wasn't letting the saw grass grow under his feet either. He had become acquainted with 'Wishbone Willy,' so nicknamed because the upper part of his chest protruded immensely due to an injury he suffered during the big war and 'Perky Penny' at a local V.F.W. club. Doc recalled Wishbone talking about his 1987 Plymouth mini-van that he called his SOV (as opposed to the more current craze of SUV's) when someone asked what kind of vehicle he was driving, he would reply *"My SOV, that Same Old Vehicle!"* Of course, everyone would chuckle and guffaw because that's what Wishbone expected. There weren't many vans or pick up trucks in the immediate area. After all, most of these folks were well beyond child hauling years or hauling anything for that matter.

Doc recalled that Willy didn't live too far away, only nine or ten units. So he had trotted (he really couldn't trot much, his trotting days were over) down there one day. Greetings and curtsies were exchanged out on the sidewalk. It was another warm day in southern Florida. Doc couldn't help but notice that Perky Penny had on a polka dot halter-top, some old-fashioned short shorts and sandals with just enough heels to accentuate the contour of her legs. Pretty nice, he thought, especially for a woman her age. He envisioned 'Babs, the Blond Bombshell from Bristol', (Connecticut that is) in an outfit like that. He wondered to himself why he hadn't seen Babs for a while. He collected his thoughts and proceeded to ask Willy if he could borrow the mini-van for a couple of hours. He figured Willy would say yes, which he did. Doc hustled back to the complex at 25MPH's. He didn't need another scuffle with the not too friendly Florida police. Doc recruited Bert and Skeeter to go with him to the shack. Bert hadn't been there yet and his first utterance was:

"Wow, I can't wait for Gert to see this place and all the dirt!"

Doc told Bert to stay alert; after all they were on a secret mission.

"What might that be? asked Bert.

"Load those crates in the van. Then we need to make a quick get-away," said Doc.

Bert saw a beat up old windsock lying in the corner. Probably another reason the shack was still standing. Some doughboy was supposed to hang it on the roof to help the bombardier figure the wind direction. Skeeter thought the whole thing was exciting, like an episode from NYPD Blue. Bert grumbled that there must be at least fifty cases there. The mini-van was loaded amidst huffs and puffs. The threesome headed back to the complex where they encountered Chip at the front entrance.

"Now what?" questioned Doc.

"Discreetly give a box or two to each of our people and instruct them to flush the paste out of the jars and sterilize them in the dishwasher," instructed Doc, who then asked if anyone had seen Babs lately.

"She's been laundering her lingerie in London lately," lamented Lucille.

"That's easy for you to say," said Doc.

DOC & BABS

He was just turning the corner to return the mini-van, when who should he see heading for the pool but good old Babs. The one piece, backless, phosphorescent Jonquil bathing suit revealed everything that needed to be revealed, and almost more than Doc could stand.

"Hey, wanna' go for a short spin?" he said hopefully.

On the way to Wishbone Willy's, Doc asked her if she had heard of the shack.

"No, why don't you tell me about it?" she said.

"Better than that, I can show it to you, if you're game," stated Doc.

"Why not," Babs replied, "I don't have anything better to do."

She literally poured herself into the front seat bending over enough for Doc to get an eyeful. (She had enough for two eyefuls!)

"Nice to see you again and I do mean see you," he gulped.

She flicked her eyelashes quipping, "Same here."

The sun was just descending as they entered the shack.

"There really isn't a whole lot to see but this is where it's happening," explained Doc.

"I don't see much or much happening either," was her throaty response

Doc noticed she shivered a little. The bathing suit was pretty skimpy. He offered her one of the thermo blankets.

"Gee, thanks. You're so thoughtful," she said

"Yeah, sure," replied Doc. "Do you want a cold beer?"

"Where you going to get a cold beer," Babs said, "you don't have a refrigerator."

"Oh yes I do. I have a small portable one hidden in one of those wooden crates that we didn't have room for in the van," said Doc.

He told her this was working out great. Since the generator, appropriated by 'Tee Shot Tom', had four outlets, he could even have a TV or radio on when he wanted it. The little refrigerator was so small that he could have the beer cold in about ten minutes. With that said, he turned on the old Emerson radio that he had scrounged from someone. It was always tuned to the same station, an oldies but goodies thing. Doc never got out of the big band era. The mellow tones of Glen Miller's "Moonlight Serenade" wafted through the air.

"Wanna' dance?" he offered.

"Sure, why not?" Babs replied.

As he started to put his arm around her waist he said: "The blanket kind of gets in the way."

"Well, it's kind of itchy, too," she replied.

"Take it off," he said kind of sheepishly

"What, the blanket?" she asked.

"No, the whole outfit, then I'll take off my pharmaceutical clothes and there won't be any itching," Doc suggested.

"You're so clever, Doc," she purred.

The radio continued to play the soft strains of the haunting melody. There wasn't a whole lot of room to dance in the little ram-shackled shack, so they did more swaying than anything. Like the old days of "Swing and sway with Sammy Kaye". The music was hypnotizing as only Glen Miller could play it. The dance was sensuous. And Babs was seductive, Doc didn't want to perspire but he couldn't stop the little beads that were forming on his forehead.

"Oh, my God," he thought to himself. "What did I ever do to deserve this?"

The floor in the old shack was pretty uneven. Doc was just going to take her into a dip movement when he tripped-accidentally or otherwise-and pulled her down with him. They conveniently fell on the army blanket, which Doc had strategically placed on the floor.

"You sly devil," she cooed.

She was ready. Doc was ready. They were just getting down to the nitty-gritty when Doc heard a strange noise outside. His ardor dropped quickly as he reached for his pants while he threw the bathing suit to her. He quickly doused the light and very slowly opened the door. He stood there, breathless. She stood behind him also breathless, but for other reasons.

"There's no one out there," said Babs. "Come on baby cakes, let's bump and grind."

"Put the damn suit on and try to behave yourself," ordered Doc.

She retreated to a corner with a very pouty lip. Doc saw something moving around the corner and it was heading right for him. He questioned himself, *Where's the damn security when you need them? What can I use for defense, a beer bottle?* Just then 'Tee Shot Tom', with Skeeter trailing behind, came through the now closed door.

"What the ____?" blurts Tom. "Doc, is that you?"

"Yes, it's me," answered Doc, "and I'm not alone. What the hell are you two doing here?"

"Likewise," spits out Tom.

Doc said he was showing Babs around the shack, which just then stepped out of the shadows wearing only that fantastic suit. She did, however, have a blanket thrown lightly around her shoulders.

Tom whispered to Doc, "You were showing her more than the shack, you devil."

Skeeter piped up, "Is she cold?"

Doc regained enough composure to ask why they were there. Tom told him the story of how he had found an old cement mixer at the dump. They had been chipping cement all afternoon and now it was as clean as a whistle. They waited till this time of night to be less conspicuous.

"Not only that," interrupted Skeeter, "but I fixed up an old wash machine motor so as it will run on 'lectricity off the gen-er-ator and ya' won't have to buy gas for it."

(He sounded a little bit like Forrest Gump at times.)

Doc let out a yell, "Wow, that's great guys! Wow, thanks a lot." He then added in a lower tone, "Even if you did ruin a great evening."

The two alley pickers left with out a word to Babs. After they left, she sauntered up to Doc in a very provocative manner.

"Well Doc, do you want to do any more experimenting?" asked Babs.

"Night tonight honey, I have a cement mixer of a headache or a headache of a cement mixer or something like that," remarked Doc.

THE CONCOCTION

The next few days were harried. The little group hustled back and forth like a colony of ants. The bowls, the beakers, the beaters, the Popsicle sticks and the now clean paste jars were all shuttled to the shack. Someone had come up with a couple of old doors, which Doc sat on top of a couple of the wooden crates to form work counters. When Doc was finally satisfied that all the junk was there that needed to be there, he ordered everyone out. Doc requested that only Chip, "Sexy Sam", the manufacturing manager, "Tee Shot Tom", the expediter, "The Lovely Lois", the treasurer and Miss Ellie, the 'Merry Maid from Michigan', remain behind.

No sooner had the last one exited, than Doc explained he thought Lois and Ellie should keep records of how much of this or how much of that, they were using, primarily to establish cost. He thought Sam and Tom could help him get started, especially with the cement mixer and that Chip could keep an eye on the whole thing so there weren't too many screw ups. Doc didn't think they needed the cement mixer right away. He wanted the first run to be enough so that every member of the group could have a jar full for their own personal use. And besides, they had purchased most of the ingredients from local super markets, so it could be replaced.

Miss Ellie and 'The Lovely Lois' recorded:

10 lbs. of cocoa butter

8 quarts of mineral oil

10 jars of white petroleum jelly

3 cases=24 bottles of purified water

5-30 gallon rubbish bags of hedge leaves

6 gal. of bleach.

The big experiment was about to begin. Doc asked Chip to feed the leaves into the blender to emulsify them and then pour that mixture into the Tupperware bowls. The next step was to add the bleach, which would extract the green color. In the meantime "Sexy Sam" was melting the wax in an old electric percolator while "Tee Shot Tom" was pouring the mineral oil and the purified water into the old washtub. The washtub had a few dents in it but Doc couldn't find any leaks so it would do just fine for now. The petroleum jelly didn't need much dissolving so the crock-pot was set on low.

"Oh nuts," said Doc.

"What's nuts?" asked Lois.

"We should have Bert here with this camera to record this epic moment for posterity. You know, like Edison discovering the light bulb," suggested Doc.

"C'est la vie," exclaimed Miss Ellie. "Well, *That's Life*" as Frank Sinatra was wont to sing.

As soon as the foliage was dechlorophyllized and blended, the remaining mush was dumped into the washtub

"Add some of that wax," ordered Doc.

"Okey, dokey," says Sam.

"Now, the petrol jelly," he said.

"Okey, dokey," says Tom.

"Okay, we got it all in there. Now start mixing!" yelled Doc.

"With what?" they all asked at the same time.

"Ya' want us to jump in the tub and mix it with our feet like they do to make wine?" said Tom.

"Don't be stupid-this is a fine body cream, we've got to be hygienic," said Doc

Just then good old Skeeter showed up driving his motorcycle with the Chew-wa-wa sitting in the sidecar.

"Whatcha' doin'?" he asked as he stumbled through the rickety old door.

Doc replied that they were trying to figure out how to mix this washtub full of stuff.

"Oh, the smoother stuff?" asked Skeet. "Why don't you use a paddle?"

"We don't have a paddle," said Chip.

"I do," replied Skeeter. "I got a canoe paddle."

"Where, in your back pocket?" asked Doc.

"No, silly, in my sidecar," replied Skeeter.

There was just no sense in trying to figure out Skeeter, no sir, just no sense. Skeeter brought the canoe paddle in and as he walked in front of Doc said:

"I want to do it first. It is my paddle, ya' know."

"No problem, Bubba, go right ahead," replied Doc.

Instead of using the standard canoe paddle grip and twirling it in the center of the mixture, Skeeter grasped the paddle with one hand above the other, as though he wanted to strangle it. He then proceeded to march around the washtub singing: *Round and round the mulberry bush.* The rest of the group just howled with laughter. (Where was Bert with the camera when you needed him?) They let him go for about five minutes when Doc persuaded him to let someone else have some fun. But fun it wasn't. Each one present took a turn at mixing the goop. Slowly, ever so slowly … it started to blend together. Doc kept encouraging them not to give up. It would work he kept repeating. The two ladies finally exclaimed that they quit. Their cake mixing days were over a long time ago. This was ridiculous. Chip calmed them down, (for a while at least.) He then sent Skeeter for some new recruits. It wasn't long when the ubiquitous Skeeter returned with an entourage the likes of 'Gorgeous George' of wrestling fame. There was Bert and Gert of course they were followed in by "King Arthur" and "Millie the Mermaid", who in turn were followed by "Audacious Audrey" and 'Ely the Deadeye.' Then came Camille with Lucille at the wheel. The last arrivals were 'Charmin Carmen' and "Lean Jean' the Legal Queen.' Chip was afraid that this was too much activity and that they were attracting too much attention. He asked the original group to return home, all except Doc. (And would they please get some of these extra cars out of here?) After the entire hubbub died down, Doc explained what he needed them to do. Lucille, who is of Italian decent, said she could stomp it down faster with her feet then they could with a paddle. That idea was quickly vetoed. "King Arthur", the organizer, spoke up first:

"We need a plan here," said Arthur. "Let's try this."

He positioned four people, opposite each other, on four sides of the washtub.

"Lucille, you swish the paddle a quarter of the way and hand it to Camille," he instructed. "Camille will swish it a quarter of the way and hand it to Bert. Bert does his quarter and passes it to Gert. That way, not one person is doing all the work and it should go much faster."

They tried it. The first time wasn't so good. They needed a little practice. After all, even runners in a relay race, practice handing off the baton. They tried holding the canoe paddle up out of the mixture to get the passing better. The next time, with the paddle in the mixture, they only dropped it in once. After a few more tries they began to get the system.

"I knew it would work!" bellowed Arthur. "But it does seem to be slow; we'll be here all night." "Yeh, ya gotta get some rhythm baby," said "Audacious Audrey" to Lucille, as she performed a little dance step.

She motioned to "Sly Ely" to join her. They started to hum: *Dum-dum-dum, da-dum, dumpty dum, da dum.* It almost sounded like: *Row, row; row your boat, gently down the stream.* The rest of the group chimed in. No one cared if you were Soprano or Bass. (Just sing it out, baby!) The mixing went very well after that. ('Thank you very much' as Elvis would say.) Doc thought it looked pretty good. If he wanted a cream, leave it alone. If he wanted a lotion, add a little more mineral oil or purified water. If he wanted a salve, a little more paraffin wax would do the trick. For now anyway, he thought, The 'Floragra Smoother', should remain a cream.

"Ok, we've gotten this far, what's next?" asked Arthur, who was really beginning to get with it.

They sat around yakking for a few minutes, excited that they were finally going to try the miraculous Floragra for themselves. They were just in the process of telling Doc he should make some more liquid stuff. (Man that really works great!)

"Just a drop a day keeps the doctor away," piped up 'Perky Penny', who had been languishing in a corner so she wouldn't have to work the paddle.

"What a great slogan," said Doc. "We'll have to remember that."

Just then the door opened with a bang.

"Take cover, it's a raid," someone yelled.

But it was only little Belle Taco, the Chew-wa-wa. They knew Skeeter couldn't be far behind. Sure enough, he wasn't. When asked where he'd been, he replied he was up on the roof putting up the windsock.

"But why?" asked Doc.

"Don't you' want to know how the wind blows?" he asked.

(Good old Skeeter. You never knew what he was thinking or going to do.)

Someone asked him how his little dog was doing?

"Just fine," he replied. "Look how smooth she is since Chip poured that stuff on her"

They all gathered around because they hadn't seen Belle Taco since Skeeter had her clipped.

"That's just incredible. That's as smooth as a baby's bottom," they remarked.

"But she aint no baby, she's pretty old for a Chew-wa-wa," Skeeter responded.

"That just makes it that more incredible," said Arthur.

"Millie the Mermaid" said she would like to look like that. Not like the dog but with skin that smooth. Bert and Gert thought they could use a beer before the filling process began. Bert asked Skeeter to jump on his motorcycle and go get a six-pack.

"Don't have to," said Skeet, "got some right here."

Doc started to sputter as Skeeter headed for the wooden case hidden in the corner with the little refrigerator in it. Skeeter pulled out two six-packs of Coors.

"How did you know they were there?" Doc asked.

"I made the key for the front door in the first place. Don't-cha' remember?" replied Skeeter.

They had enough spoons and knives to fill the jars. (After all, this was just for their personal consumption. They weren't in full-scale production yet.)

They split into pairs and all knelt down around the washtub. One person held the jar while their partner dipped a spoonful out of the tub. The jar holder person would skim any excess off the top with a Popsicle stick, shove the lid with the paste brush attached, into the mixture, give a couple of twists and just like magic, there were the first jars of official "Floragra TM". (They really didn't have it trade marked but they thought it would scare the competition off). The group was extremely jubilant on the way home.

NEW VIBRANCE

"Tee Shot Tom", the avid golfer, always checked the next day's weather. *Force of habit,* he would say. He bumped into Chip, around sundown, the next evening.

"Did you see Stormy Weather on channel 101 report the storm that's brewing off the coast?" Tom asked.

"No, what about it?" asked Chip.

"She looks great!" replied Tom.

"For Gods sake, I thought we were talking about the weather," chirped Chip.

"We are.' Stormy Weather', the cute little weathercaster, haven't you seen her?" said Tom, who went on: "About five foot two with eyes of blue? When she walks out with that blue mini skirt on and the blue see-through blouse that gives you a peek at the blue bra, Va-va-vaboom, know what I mean?"

"Yes, I know what you mean, but what about the weather? I told you before if there was another hurricane stirring up, we would have to muster all hands to strip the hedges while we have time!" Chip emphatically verbalized.

Tom responded that there weren't any hurricanes in the forecast, just one hell of a storm.

"Check out Stormy Weather to see for yourself. Vava-voom!" he added.

Obviously, the next day was not going to be your typical Florida sunshine variety at least not the morning. A good share of the happy little group spent the morning playing Dominoes, twelves at that. The rain let up shortly after noon. Chip and Ellie decided to make some house calls to see how it was going with the

Floragra. "Sexy Sam" and "Alluring Anita" were bopping around like teenagers. Sam, especially, looked twenty years younger. (FANTASTIC!) "King Arthur" and "Millie the Mermaid" were all dressed up to go out to lunch. Arthur had straightened up and had increased his walking stride considerably. *Just amazing and in only one day,* thought Chip. The "The Lovely Lois' never looked lovelier; most of the so-called, 'crows-feet' around her eyes were gone. The wrinkle or two around her mouth were completely smoothed out. (Just, incredible!) Bert and Gert were doing pretty well, too. Bert's sagging jowls were tightening up nicely.

"How about that," Chip said to Miss Ellie 'The Merry Maid from Michigan', "and in only one day?"

They hadn't seen Doc or Skeeter yet but were sure they would soon. Just then "Tee Shot Tom" and 'Beauteous Bev', came around the corner. Tom looked very collegiate wearing his white saddle shoe type golf shoes, white, over the ankle socks, Coral pink shorts and V-necked yellow tee shirt. 'Beauteous Bev' never looked more beautiful. Even her lips were beginning to smooth out and the skin, which was loose under her arms, was beginning to constrict. (Truly, incredible!) Chip and Miss Ellie did not hear a single complaint. Although they hadn't seen everyone yet, they were sure the results were no less miraculous. How do you describe such happiness, such elation, and such jubilation? Never mind the 'Fountain of Youth', they had the secret of the 'Shrubs-FLORAGRA'! Chip looked at Miss Ellie for the first time that day. And this time, <u>he really looked at her.</u>

"My God," he said, "what happened to your wattle?"

"Why, what's the matter?" she replied.

"It's gone, disappeared, vamoosed!" Chip said.

Chip parodied to her, "You wonder where your wattle went, when you stroke your chin with Floragent."

He touched her. He stroked her cheeks. He caressed her chin. It sent chills up and down her spine. *What a sensational thing, the Floragra was! She didn't have many wrinkles to begin with but now she looked absolutely radiant.*

"Wanna' go back to our pad?" he asked.

"Maybe later," she said.

MRS. GOLDBERG.

Mrs. Goldberg was standing in her doorway as they approached. (Well, she wasn't just standing there. She was actually posing for anyone that wanted to look.) She stood almost erect. She got out of the wheel chair that morning feeling like a new person. She still had the cane; however it was lying on the doorstep. As erect as she could be, considering everything she had been through, she threw her shoulders back and had her chest thrust out.

"My Lord, Mrs. Goldberg, look at you!" exclaimed Miss Ellie.

"Yes," she cried out.

"Just look at me now, baby. My breasts have shrunk from a 42 long to a 38 short!" she added, almost shouting it out.

Chip chimed in, "But Mrs. Goldberg *(I know, don't call you that)* the Floragra is supposed to be a face cream like a vanishing cream."

"From now on, you can call me anything you want," said Mrs. Goldberg.

She went on to explain that she was putting some on her face before going to bed last night and she accidentally dropped some down her front. Instead of getting up to wash it off, she decided to just rub it in. *After all, it shouldn't hurt* she thought. She went on how she usually has to drag herself out of bed every morning but not this morning.

"Oh no, not this morning!" she exclaimed.

She explained that where before she usually just splashed a little water on her face and puts her teeth in, this morning she felt good enough to get up and shower. It wasn't until she was suds'n herself that she noticed her breasts.

"Isn't it just wonderful, Chip, you dear boy? Just look at me now. Who needs a Wonder Bra when they have wonderful Floragra?" she said excitedly.

Miss Ellie looked at 'Mrs. Goldberg', then at Chip. Chip looked at 'Mrs. Goldberg', then at Miss Ellie. They walked away shaking their heads.

"Keep an eye on the weather," Chip yelled over his shoulder.

THE SENTRIES

Mr. & Mrs. Dale were setting out on the veranda having a lunch of Campbell's chicken noodle soup, a few cheese and crackers and a cool glass of lemonade. Chip was deep in thought, staring off into the wild blue yonder. A soft ocean breeze barely rippled his hair. Miss Ellie broke the silence:

"What's the matter, honey?" she asked.

"Not much," he replied. "I was just thinking of how we could get a quantity of leaves off those bushes without making them look bare. Doc had mentioned that he had used up the supply he had at the shack."

Chip had already determined that they didn't want to use the regular clippers because they damaged too many leaves and they were noisy. He finally decided that if they wore gloves, they could pull the leaves by stripping each branch. Then if the stem was sticking out, they could cut it off with a scissors or pruning shears. Miss Ellie, "The 'Merry Maid from Michigan'" interrupted:

"That doesn't sound like a good idea, they would never be able to rejuvenate then," she suggested.

"You're right, as usual, 'Esmerelda'," said Chip. "We'll just have to be more selective: a few off the bottom, some from the middle, and as the barber says, a little off the top. That way no one will notice any difference. Thank you, honey. You always come up with a good idea."

Chip called "Sexy Sam" on the walkie-talkie to ask if he and the "Alluring Anita" could meet him by the bushes, say around 10:00 P.M. He told Sam to wear gloves and be quiet. He then called "King Arthur" and "Millie the Mermaid".

"Meet me by the bushes at 10:00 P.M." he instructed. "Bring gloves and be quiet. We don't want to attract any attention."

They converged at exactly 10:00. Chip wearing truckers driving gloves while Miss Ellie had several 30-gallon trash bags under her arm.

"Did you all bring gloves?" asked Chip.

"Yep, here is mine," piped up Anita, as she thrust both hands out wearing oven mittens. They all laughed as silently as they could. Chip explained what he wanted them to do.

"We need to fill at least two of these 30 gallon trash bags," said Chip. "But try not to leave too many bare spots."

They tackled the assignment with gusto. 'Sexy Sam" even started to whistle, "Hi ho, hi ho, it's off to work we go." When he saw "King Arthur" hold up his right hand to signal the stop sign.

"I'm sorry, I forgot," whispered Sam.

They filled the two bags in about a half hour. The hedges didn't look any the worse for wear. They all retreated to their individual apartments for a good nights sleep.

The next day dawned with yet another beautiful Florida sunrise. Chip was extricating the bags from the back seat of his Volkswagen Beatle when Doc, Skeeter and "Tee Shot Tom" pulled up. They had stopped at the local super market to pick up some more purified water and two six-packs of Coors. Skeeter was just unlocking the old Army padlock when two figures jumped out of the brush behind the shack.

"Don't shoot!" yelled Skeeter. "I ain't got any money."

Doc and Tom both threw their hands up.

"What do you want? What's going on?" asked Skeeter.

"It's us," they replied, "Corporal Bert and Private Gert."

The trio couldn't believe their eyes. They could make out Bert okay; he at least looked the part. He explained that he found a whole army outfit lying in the weeds. He was wearing an army fatigue uniform, complete with combat boots, splashed with pale yellow, orange and browns. They figure some GI must have left them there during World War II. Gert had applied the paint to make it look like camouflage. *And what about the private?* They thought privately. That was another story. She was wearing a painter's smock covered by the necessary colors, a pair of Bert's old dungarees, splashed appropriately, and a pair of old fashioned over the ankles tennis shoes. (Not sneakers, like everyone has now.) In addition to the already ridiculous outfit, she had her face streaked with brown paint and black streaks, which she had applied with her eyebrow pencil. The real topper was the helmet. She had glued an elastic strip on to two sides of a Tupperware bowl, which was also artistically adorned. The elastic was supposed to suffice as a chinstrap. However, since the Floragra had tightened up so much of her loose skin, the strap kept slipping and would catch her under the nose. The payoff was the sprigs of weeds she had tucked behind each ear. The guys started to giggle as they stood there assessing her appearance.

"Don't laugh!" she commanded like a drill sergeant. "It must have worked because you three yo-yo's didn't see us."

They all agreed that even the U.S. Army would be proud of this surveillance team. With that said, they all entered the shack to have a beer.

THE FLEA MARKET

Lucille was just fixing a meal when she heard her phone peal. It was Chip.

"What do you want? She practically screamed into the phone.

"Would you be kind enough to take Mrs. Goldberg shopping?" he asked.

"I'm just fixing veal for my meal. But I could do it later, gator," she added.

"Fine, I'll send her down," said Chip

Mrs. Goldberg arrived at Lucille's about fifteen minutes later, dressed in her Sunday best

"I need a deal, Lucille. Let's go to the flea market," said Mrs. Goldberg.

"Where's your walker, ya' don't think I'm gonna' carry you, do ya'?" yelled Lucille, who may have been a little hard of hearing, which would account for her high volume.

"I don't use the walker any more since I got this Floragra stuff from Chip," Mrs. Goldberg responded.

"I didn't know it was that good," said Lucille.

"Oh yes, just rub it on your legs. Makes you feel younger all over," explained Mrs. Goldberg.

Mrs. Goldberg didn't even need help getting into the car. They headed for the flea market. The flea market was nothing like the 'Old Kasbah'. This place was huge, clean, well lit, and the vendors only hawked new goods. (None of that used recycled stuff here.) As they entered the flow of the throng, Lucille asked what they were looking for.

"Bra's," exclaimed Molly. "Now that I've gone from 44long to 38short, I need some new bra's."

Lucille asked how that had happened. So Mrs. Goldberg went through the story again about dropping the Floragra down her front and not wanting to get up to wash it off. Lucille said she was using hers on her face only because she didn't know if she would get any more. Mrs. Goldberg assured her there would be plenty as long as they didn't have another hurricane

Mrs. Goldberg was feeling young and youthful. She didn't want any of those back braces bras with the thick straps and five hooks like she used to wear. They moved from one lingerie booth to another. The prices ranged anywhere from $4.95 to $9.95.

Mrs. Goldberg said, "Lucille, find me a deal."

Lucille saw a sign announcing: "Victoria's Lingerie Wardrobe".

"Let's try that one," she suggested.

Apparently they had stumbled onto the right place. The lone clerk behind the counter, with a New York City twang'y accent, asked what they were looking for. Mrs. Goldberg replied she wanted something young and youthful, something that would hold her up and point her out. She wanted to be noticed. The clerk nestled:

"Boy, have you come to the right place. We just got in a new line called "*Stick "em up*". Man, they are great! And we have an introductory offer, buy three, and get one free."

Mrs. Goldberg was ecstatic. She ordered a pink one, a robin egg blue and one called: "Nude". She had her mind set on the free one, a black, under cut, wire number with no straps.

"How much is costing?" Mrs. Goldberg inquired.

"Only $14.95 each, for brand new exclusive merchandises your not going to find in a dime store," the clerk said.

"Couldn't you maybe make it for me a little cut rate?" asked Mrs. Goldberg.

"It's already cut rate. You're gonna' get a free one, ain'tcha'?" replied the clerk.

"Yeah, but I know you people from New York. You got it all figured in the price all ready," from Mrs. Goldberg.

"Okay lady, how about $9.95 each?" replied the clerk.

"Includes the free one yet?" asked Mrs. Goldberg.

"Of course," she answered.

While getting out her credit card, Mrs. Goldberg mentioned that she never thought she would be buying these types of flopper stoppers when she was in her seventies.

The NYC clerk gasped, "You don't look a day over forty seven. If you're a senior, you're entitled to an additional 10% discount. I'll have trouble explaining it to the boss though."

So for approximately twenty-seven bucks, Mrs. Goldberg had four new bras. She was happy as a model on the cover of Sports Illustrated. She couldn't wait to get home to try them on.

On the way out, Lucille said, "I thought you needed me to get you a deal?"

Production

The main cogs of this wheel, mainly Doc, Chip, "Sexy Sam", and "Tee Shot Tom", had gathered at the shack to contemplate the next phase. Doc expressed that he thought they had enough raw material on hand, to make a large batch. He said if they could get the generator revved up, the cement mixer would be just fine. The only problem he could see was getting it out of the mixer and into the little paste bottles. They decided shovels were too big and they would spill too much. Spooning it out would take forever. Soup ladles might work, if they weren't too big.

"Sexy Sam" chimed in, "I'm the manufacturing manager. Let me work on this production problem for a while. We need to devise an assembly line."

That evening, Sam and the "Alluring Anita" went to a fast food hamburger joint for a nutritious meal. Sam was curious about how they got from raw hamburger to the customer in two to three minutes. He stood there watching while waiting to order. He thought he grasped the routine. A pre-formed patty was taken out of the cooler to be cooked. Another person sets out a bun. The next guy sprays mustard on the bun. Then another person does the ketchup. The pickle person does his thing. By that time the burger is almost annihilated under intense heat. It's thrown on the bun. Somebody slaps the top of the bun on it while another guy is waiting to wrap it. Total elapsed time, 2 minutes and 37 seconds! (Of course they weren't real busy that night either.) Sam watched the tote board in front of the building, 1,009,008,031. He was impressed. *That's what we need*, he thought to himself, *a production line.*

That night "Sexy Sam" didn't want to go to bed even though "Alluring Anita" was more alluring and adorable then ever. He was too anxious to start on his project to think of anything else, yet alone sleep. He started doodling on paper. His line of thought was that the cement mixer full of the various compounds was more than they could handle. If only Doc could reduce the quantities by half or even a quarter, they would be much better off. He doodled, he dabbled and he scribbled. Finally, the whole process was taking shape in his mind. *By golly, I think that will work,* he thought to himself. By 3:00 A.M. he was satisfied as he stretched out on the sofa for some shuteye.

Sam reasoned that as head pharmacist, it was Doc's responsibility to get the correct proportions of everything into the cement mixer. From there, he or Chip would take over. The concoction would be tipped out of the mixer into a very large funnel, which in turn, emptied into a much smaller funnel. The small funnel allowed just enough mixture to drop through a short length of downspout into a section of a vacuum cleaner hose, which reduced the forward motion enough to empty into a child's sand bucket without overloading it. The sand bucket had had a hole drilled through the bottom, which allowed enough of the mixture to be deposited on the loading platform of a Lionel Train sand loader. The sand loader raised it high enough for its automatic tipping device to deposit exactly 1.2 fluid ounces into a clean coffee can. That can with a clear plastic tube running through the bottom, would drop the exact amount onto the perpetually running, four-foot conveyor. The four filling stations, manned by some of the faithful, allowed just enough room for the worker to scoop the correct quantity, using a pie server or a trowel, into the paste jar, insert the paste brush, screw on the top and place it back on the conveyor. The end of the line would be the loading area where a laborer would wipe any excess off the jar, to affix a label and then placed into the cardboard box. Sam concluded the total elapsed time from mixer to box to be 32 minutes and 10 seconds. *Not bad,* thought Sam, *not bad.*

The next day was Sunday. Sunday's in Florida are usually pretty lazy and laid back. Those, so inclined, had been to church and back. They were changing into clothing a little more comfortable, many of them in bathing suits. More by accident than routine, they gradually drifted toward the pool and the old clubhouse. Mrs. Goldberg was a real sight. She still wore a one pieced suit but somehow it really looked different. It definitely was protruding. She had put on one of the new bras under her suit. She was the center of attention. And she was lapping it up like a puppy with his first taste of canned dog food. It wasn't only the robin egg blue suit and corresponding robin egg blue bra that attracted all the attention. She had dyed her hair a soft blue, had on blue eye shadow and even glossy blue lipstick. (She was a sight all right.) After the obligatory 'Hi, how are you?' to some of the easterners and assorted snowbirds, the group settled into their usual clique. When most of the gang was in attendance, Chip quietly told them they would all be needed the next day at the shack. They were finally going to do some real producing. Bert asked if he and Gert should wear their surveillance outfits, the 'camouflaged ones'.

"No," said Chip. "Your cut off blue jeans will be just fine."

The pool area was getting crowded. Chip suggested they get out of there, go somewhere where they could talk more openly. They all agreed except Mrs. Goldberg. She wasn't about to relinquish her status. She did, however, say she would keep an eye on the weather. They migrated behind building 87, the farthest from the pool. Chip was telling them of Sam's production plans. He explained they would need as much help as they could get. To avoid too much attention, he suggested they leave their cars home and ride the Coral Creek bus as far as the golf course. From there it was just a short walk to the shack the feeling in the air was electric. The anticipation was energizing. Now they had something to look forward to. They were going to be doing something, instead of just sitting around complaining about their aches and pains. They had a chance to be on the ground floor of this miraculous discovery. Not only would they enhance their own appearance, but also they might even make some money. (Let us count our blessings!)

ACTUAL PRODUCTION?

If there were any strangers waiting for the Coral Creek bus, they would have changed their minds, and taken a taxi. This assemblage was too, too much. Several ladies had packed picnic baskets. There was more than one cooler in evidence. The eclectic group was alive with excitement and adorned in a kaleidoscope of colors. Old baseball caps and newer style hats with advertising logos sat on top, and bodies sporting old style undershirts, T-shirts, polo shirts, blue work shirts, short pants, long pants, light colors, dark colors and although sneakers were the most prevalent, there were a few pairs of sandals, loafers and wing tips. (And that was just the men!)

The ladies' outfits were too diverse to even begin to describe. Most noticeable were the babushka's. It seems everyone was intent on going to work. All that is, except Mrs. Goldberg who insisted on "standing out". (And that she did.) The group was excited. Not only did they share something to look forward to but also they were going to have fun doing it. Talk about a bunch of school kids on a field trip. This was even better in that they didn't have to return to school.

They were trying not to attract too much attention, as the Coral Creek bus came to a stop in front of the complex. Four or five were standing at the bus stop. Three or four more were crouched in the hedges. Several others were standing in doorways, waiting to make a dash for it. There was giggling, laughter and guffawing from front to back. When the bus was finally loaded, the driver turned to ask where they were going. 'King Arthur' (remember him, the regal austere one?) stood up as straight as his 6 foot, 4 inch frame would let him, in such a little bus, and announced:

"On James, *on* to the golf course."

Everyone chuckled while the driver sat there nodding his head. By the time the driver got out to a main road and slipped it into third gear, "King Arthur" stood up again.

"Are you ready?" he asked, as he then went into his imitation of Lawrence Welk.

"A-one and a-two," as he started to sing, "Hi Ho, Hi Ho, it's off to work we go."

Arthur had a beautiful basso profound voice, or whatever you call that kind. The gang got with it in a hurry. But no sooner had they finished that one when Skeeter, who showed up wearing yellow swim trunks with tiny pink sea shells, an older style undershirt, (the kind with straps over the shoulder), a Gilligan type hat and shower clogs, starts to sing:

"How much is that doggie in the window?"

"Too much!" someone yelled from the back of the bus, *"Now sit down!"*

(You may recall that Skeeter had 100watt capacity but ran on 25watts most of the time.)

Chip wanted to sing, 'Hail to the Victors' but he was booed down immediately. Not to be outdone, 'Singin' Sam', he of the Italian heritage, got up.

"Okay, I got it," he announced. (Sam was the best tenor in the group. Come to think of it, have you ever met an Italian that wasn't a good tenor?)"Are you ready?" said Singin' Sam, as he tapped his foot to a moderate tempo. "One, two, three, four; ninety nine bottles of beer on the wall, ninety nine bottles of beer …"

The rowdy entourage joined in. By the time they got down to sixty-six bottles of beer on the wall, the bus pulled up at the golf course, not exactly in front of the clubhouse but off to one side of the entranceway. Chip handed the driver a walkie-talkie as he got off the bus.

"We'll call you when we're ready to go back," he offered over his shoulder.

They really did resemble a line of dwarves going off to work, old ones but the similarity was frightening. Once they all made it to the shack, Chip handed out the assignments. There wasn't enough room in the shack for all of them at one time. Chip explained that they would work in shifts. That way they could share the load and no one would get too tired. "Tee Shot Tom" and Skeeter finally got the generator going. The crowd let out a rousing: "Hip, hip, hooray!" Doc plugged in the cement mixer; it spit and sputtered a little, even missed a cog or two. But just like Old Faithful it jogged into motion.

"Hip, hip, hooray!" rose from the gathered throng.

This certainly was an exuberant group. Doc started gathering ingredients. The hedge leaves, (those miraculous ones), had been pre-washed and were spread out on the drying rack set up in the corner. It had been decided to change the work shifts to two hours. Even though they felt more chipper and certainly looked younger, there were some pretty old bones in this group. (Better not to push anyone too far.) Chip thought every thing would go better if he broke up the married couples so they didn't have to work with each other. As an example, instead of "Sexy Sam" and "Alluring Anita" working together, he paired Anita with 'Sly Eli'. That left "Audacious Audrey" to work with "Millie the Mermaid"'s husband, "King Arthur". She asked if Millie thought she could work with 'Sexy Sam'.

Why not," she replied, "wasn't it one of the singing sisters that named him 'Sexy Sam'? If she could do it, I can do it."

'The Lovely Lois', the levelheaded accounting person, was assigned to keep Skeeter out of trouble as production began.

The ingredients were poured in, the 30-gallon bag of leaves was added, and the conveyor sprang into motion.

"Hip, hip hooray," Arthur started, "99 bottles of paste on the wall!"

(It was sheer Utopia.)

The joint was jumpin', the machinery was hummin' and everyone not engaged in the actual production was asked to step outside. They congregated at the back of the shack where the saw grass had been trampled down. Chip stayed inside. He stood there, solemnly surveying the production operation. Miss Ellie walked up behind him.

"Why are you standing there with your hands behind your back and your fingers crossed?" she asked politely.

"I'm just hoping, honey, just hoping." Chip replied.

He just couldn't believe *everything was going this smoothly.* After about a half hour of furious mixing in the clankety-clank old mixer, Doc yelled out:

"Ready for the first batch!"

"Tee Shot Tom" shouted over the din of the noise: "Ready Mr. Dee?"

You would have thought you were on the back lot of a Hollywood movie set. 'Tee Shot' proclaimed himself the official: *"Dumpee"*.

The first glob slithered into the big funnel, then into the small funnel, found it's way into the sand pail, through the vacuum cleaner hose, up the Lionel sand loader. It magically dropped through the coffee can and thence onto the conveyor belt. 'Millie the Mermaid' and 'Sexy Sam' were ready at filling station one and two. 'Alluring Anita' and Sly Eli were eagerly waiting at station three and four, their pie slicers at the ready. The first jar was filled, returned to the conveyor on its way to the end of the line where the 'The Lovely Lois' and Skeeter were ready to place it in a box. As Lois reached for it, Skeeter started to pout.

"I want to do the first one," he mumbled.

"Okay, Skeet, go ahead," she said.

Skeeter hollered, "I did it, I did it. I made the first one!"

Another *hip, hip hooray* rang out through the shack. Meanwhile, the merry mob mingled making mayhem. Someone had dragged out the two old Army blankets to spread them on the ground. Several others had brought their own blankets or tablecloths. It's hard to believe the amount of bottles and cans that can be carried in those little coolers. Out they Came; the Bud; the Corona; the Puerto Rican rum; the gin and tonic; the olives, the vermouth and all of the appropriate mixers that you can imagine. Happy morning was about to begin. (It was too early for lunch.) They sat around swapping stories of the good old days. And of course comparing skin textures, wrinkles (or the lack thereof) were the main topic. They all agreed that Floragra was the greatest thing since sliced bread. And Mrs. Goldberg *strutted* her stuff. She was wearing her hot pants with matching spandex top. Even her toenails were painted for the first time in years.

"If only 'Old Abe' had lived long enough to see me now," she lamented.

Doc had taken a break from his mixing to step outside for a cigarette. (You would think Doc would know better by now, but old habits are hard to break.) As he looked over his co-conspirators, he warned them not to get too much sun. They still didn't know how the Floragra would react to the sun. Mrs. Goldberg piped up that she thought she would look great with a little tan. Time seemed to be slipping by so fast. Everyone was enjoying themselves immensely.

Skeeter had Belle Taco in his backpack along with a bugle. As he removed both items from the pack, the group 'Oohed' at Belle's smooth skin. It was close to high noon when Skeeter jumped up on the roof of the shack. He stood at attention as he raised the bugle to his lips. It was the signal for a lunch break. It sounded more like the call to the post at a horse race but everyone got the idea. The working crew poured out of the shack, glad for the break. As enthusiastic and energetic as they might be, they weren't used to actual work. It had been anywhere from five to twenty five years since any of them had real jobs. "Millie the Mermaid", (always the trendsetter), unrolled the short legged, rollup card table, set up the two canvas, folding chairs, put a linen table cloth on the table, placed two candles in the center and proceeded to ask "King Arthur" to: *"Please pour the wine".*

The balance of the clan sat there, staring in awe, with fascination and maybe even admiration. (The lady had class!) "King Arthur" spoke with a regal air about him as well, as he poured the wine into Dixie Cups:

"And here's to you, my dear." he proclaimed, "and to Floragra."

"Hip, hip hooray!" went up another shout.

Soon, the sandwiches, the pastas and the assorted sundry dishes were spread out. It didn't take long before someone stood up, "Who wants to trade a chicken leg for a peanut butter and jelly sandwich. Skeeter said he would. But he didn't have a chicken leg. The "The Lovely Lois" handed him one. He traded for the sandwich.

"I just love P B & J," he giggled.

Other trades were offered. *"Who wants to trade some macaroni salad for a fudge brownie?"* (Or you might have heard: *How about one half of a tuna sandwich for three olives and a pickle?*) After a few minutes of that, they decided to share it all. 'Sexy Sam' called it: *'an eat around'.* (Talk about a picnic, they we're having the time of their lives!) With their bellies full and the sun beaming down at a pleasant 82 degrees, some of the early shift participants felt a little groggy. 'Sexy Sam' was the first to poop out. He just lay down on the grass and proceeded to fall asleep. "King Arthur" wasn't far behind. The ladies were too ladylike to just sprawl out like that. They sat in the shade with their backs against the shack. Skeeter, who was always pumped up and never seemed to sleep, jumped on the roof again to blast the bugle call. Although it sounded the same as it did to start the lunch break he explained that this was the call to arms. They needed arms inside to bottle some more Floragra. The replacement troops were soon assembled. The generator was started and Everything soon began moving. Doc conferred with Chip.

"What do you think?" he asked.

Chip still with his fingers crossed behind his back, answered, "So far, so good."

He no sooner got the words out of his mouth when 'Beauteous Bev' ran up to him waving her arms.

"Stop the belt! Stop the machinery! Stop something!" she yelled.

"What's the problem?" asked Chip.

"Audacious Audrey and I can't keep up at the end of the line," she said. We can't get them in boxes fast enough. They're falling all over the place. We aren't exactly Lucy Arnaz and Ethyl Mertz at the candy factory, ya' know."

Doc stepped up to the conveyor. He stopped it with one hand. After all, it wasn't exactly an industrial strength conveyor. He had Chip shut down the entire assembly line. They decided 'Beauteous Bev' and "Audacious Audrey" must not be as agile as "The Lovely Lois" and Skeeter. They needed to make some adjustments. They couldn't do much with the machinery they had, so the change had to be in personnel.

"Do we need four filling stations?" Chip asked.

"Probably not," Doc answered, "what do you have in mind?"

"If we reduce the filling station down to two, we could put those two at the end of the line, packing boxes," suggested Chip.

"To fill is nil, we need flocks-es of boxes," replied Doc.

It was decided to pair "Tee Shot Tom" with 'Alert Gert' at packing station number two. The line started up again. With four packers, it ran smoothly.

So smooth in fact that Tom was screaming: "More!"

Soon he was flipping paste jars behind his back. He juggled two at a time, then three. (Man, he was good.) The ladies laughed and applauded. The more attention he got, the more he performed. He stepped back to shoot two pointers into the box. Once he moved all the way back to the door.

"Swish," he shouted as the jar headed for the box, "that's a three."

Chip put a stop to that before someone got hurt. By the end of the next hour, the last Floragra was tipped out of the mixer. It went flying thru the equipment, onto the conveyor and plop-into a carton.

As the machinery ground to a halt, Doc said, "Okay, let's get this place cleaned up so we can all go home."

They didn't have access to any water but thank heavens someone had brought a roll of paper towels. Doc used most of it to clean out the rickety old cement mixer. He expressed to Chip, that it would be nice if they could at least cover the opening of the mixer.

"We want to be sanitary, ya' know," he explained, (as if that would make any difference, under the circumstances.)

Mrs. Goldberg, who no longer considered herself a 'Moldie Oldie', said she couldn't help but hear their conversation.

"Here," she said, "Take my new blouse. This is the first time I've worn it so it should be sanitary."

"But you'll be almost naked," interjected Chip.

"Oh, that's okay. I don't mind," she said. "Besides, I have on one of my new bra s, the 38 short."

They put the sheer pink blouse over the opening of the mixer, tied the two arms together. Someone else took a bungee cord off of one of the coolers.

"There, that should hold it," said Doc.

Chip bellowed over the din of the crowd, "Okay, who's got the walkie-talkie?"

(Who else, but good old Skeeter?)

"What do ya' want it for?" he asked.

"We need to call the bus driver to come and get us," replied Chip.

"Ah'll do it, ah'll do it," drawled Skeeter.

(Sometimes he sounded more like Forest Gump than Forest Gump himself.)

"Hello, Mr. Bus Driver, we need you to come get us at the golf place," Skeeter said into the walkie-talkie. "Come in … Mr. Bus Driver?"

"Bus Driver here, who is calling?" came the reply.

"It's Skeeter-Skeeter-Pumpkin-Eater," said Skeeter.

"Oh it's you. That's neat, Skeet, be ready to meet," said the bus driver.

The group trudged from the shack to the entrance to the golf course. They were tired, but happy. They were exhausted but happy. They were weary but happy. They were just a happy flock. As long as the Floragra hedges held up, they would continue to be happy. The bus arrived shortly. One by one they slowly boarded. The driver asked them to hurry up and please step toward the rear. They all complied, all except Mrs. Goldberg. She wanted to stand in front, pink bra and all. The driver told her to sit down. She didn't until the bus went over the first speed bump at the entrance of the club. She may be a 38 short but she quickly realized she still had a lot of bounce to the ounce.

"I think I'll sit down," she said meekly

The mood on the bus ride home was in direct contrast to the morning ride. There was no hip, hip hooraying. There were a lot of drooping eyelids. More than one snore could be heard from the rear. The enthusiasm was waning a trifle, as one by one they realized they missed their usual nap. Arthur, Sam, Doc and Chip were mulling over their next step. The "Lovely Lois" reminded them that they hadn't put any labels on the jars.

"Audacious Audrey" and "Millie the Mermaid" chimed in, "Yeah, what about the logo we designed? We never did vote on it."

Chip asked Doc, "Why don't we vote now while we're all together?"

Okay by me," said Doc.

Chip tried to get everyone's attention. It was difficult to be heard over the snoring. Skeeter was only too happy to help out as he put the battered old bugle to his lips to blow something that resembled revelry. The group snapped to almost instantly. *What time is it? Where am I? Turn off the alarm and let me sleep.* It took a few minutes but they were soon all awake. Chip introduced the subject of the logo. *Where is it? We never saw it,* came the response.

Millie stood up, "I just happen to have a black and white copy in my purse. Pass it around but make sure I get it back."

'Splane it to us came the request from the front of the bus. "Audacious Audrey" wanted her five minutes of fame. She explained the wavy saw tooth line on the bottom would be mint green, representing the wonderful Floragra hedges. The round circle in the middle would be yellow denoting the Florida sun. The triangular shape, cutting through the sun, would be a Flamingo Pink pyramid, depicting mystical powers and the giant zigzag is like a thunderbolt of lightning signifying the rejuvenation of life. It would be passionate purple just for the affect. *Sounds good to us,* several of them replied. The vote was unanimous. "King Arthur" had regained some of his regal ness. He cleared his throat as he stood up.

"While we are all assembled, I would like to bring up another point," he began, resonantly. "This is too distinguished a group to keep calling ourselves a group or a bunch. Who knows, we could all become famous if the hedges hold out. Robin Leach may even interview us. What I'm saying is we need a name like a club or a real organization."

He went on, "You all know about *NASA* and that it stands for National Aeronautics and Space Administration. I propose to you that we should be known as *FASA*, which stands for Florida Agricultural Senior Association. What do you think?"

A rousing *hip-hip hooray* echoed through out the bus. Chip raised a hand to momentarily quiet the crowd:

"Let's take an unofficial vote on *FASA*. If you all agree, we'll have "Lean Jean", our resident legal eagle; check out any patent or trademark infringements. If everything is legal, she can file the necessary paper work to register both the logo and the FASA name."

They arrived back at the complex exhausted but satisfied. Satisfied that the mission had been accomplished and they had fun doing it. Whoever said growing old had to be boring? At least now there was more to life than shuffleboard and bingo.

MOLLY'S SUIT

Chip had just settled down with his afternoon Martini, wondering whether he should proposition the 'Merry Maid from Michigan' now or later, when the walkie-talkie squawked, *Yeh, security-one here, what's up?*

"Chip its 'Mrs. Goldberg'. Have you seen the weather report? I turned the TV on to check out "Windy Willy" but darn it he wasn't on today. Instead I got 'Melvin the Meteorologist'. He isn't nearly as cute as Willy."

"So what about the weather?" asked Chip.

"He said there would be a cloud cover over South Florida. We're gonna' get some rain. There might be a storm moving in. Then again, there might not. Melvin's not as sharp as Willy any way you look at it," replied Mrs. Goldsmith.

"Thanks Molly. Keep your good eye on the weather and call me if it looks serious.

Chip and Miss Ellie sat on the veranda sipping their high balls while discussing the day's activities. Chip decided to put off the proposition until later. Chip then told her about the weather report. He said it might not be such a bad thing as long as it didn't get too severe. Even though the hedges were watered daily there was nothing better than good old rain for natural rejuvenation. Besides that, they could use a break. Doc had mentioned he needed a haircut. A couple of people had doctor's appointments and Sam wanted to take his car in for detailing. (That's where they're supposed to clean the car inside and out but don't pay much attention to detail.)

For the next several days it was cloudy and a little breezy. There were a few showers off and on, but nothing to be concerned about. The interim period gave the group time to catch up on personal duties. Some of them replaced grocery supplies. Some got in touch with family or friends. Mrs. Goldberg, who used to use a walker, now hustled down to Lucille's without the slightest hint of a hitch in her walk.

"Lucille, ya' got time to take me shopping?" she asked.

"All depends where you want to go," she replied.

"To the flea market again. I need a new bathing suit," said Mrs. Goldberg.

"Oh, for God's sake, grow up," said Lucille.

"If I grow up any more, I'll be dead," she responded emphatically. I want to live a little."

On the way to the flea market Molly asked Lucille what size Mrs. Goldberg thought she would need.

"About a triple XXX, the way you been struttin' around lately," Lucille suggested.

"No way," blurted Mrs. Goldberg. "I think maybe a six or possibly an eight."

"In your dreams," retorted Lucille.

The flea market wasn't nearly as jammed as usual. They found a parking space near the front door.

"Okay, let's go," said Mrs. Goldberg, anxiously.

They found a swimsuit shop around the corner from the fast food aisle.

"Are you being served," inquired the clerk.

"No I'm not," replied Mrs. Goldberg. "Anyhow isn't that a TV show on public television?"

"Yes it is," replied the clerk. "I'm sorry madam, may I help you?"

"That's better. I'm looking for a whole ensemble, suit, matching cap and matching water slippers," said Mrs. Goldberg, proudly.

"I'm afraid we don't carry slippers to go in the water, madam," he replied.

"I don't want to wear them in the water. I just want to look great. And I need a suit, size six, to show off my tan," she said.

Lucille muttered, "If you get into a size six, you'll be showing off more than your tan."

"Jealous, are we?" Mrs. Goldberg replied. .

The clerk suggested that a six might not be the right size.

"Would Madam care to try on an eight?" he said.

"If you insist," she replied.

She took one into the dressing room. The eight might possibly cover her new firmer breast; however, she still had some hefty thighs and a roll around the tummy.

As she exited the dressing room, she said, "I don't care for this color.

Do you have anything in a silver lame, perhaps a size ten?"

She didn't care for that one either.

"I want to stand out," she added.

"You'll stand out all right," murmured Lucille.

The clerk showed her a knock out neon-green in size twelve, a Catalina something or other. A slight dip in the front, small cut over the hips but not sky high like some. The matching, mesh like, cap was made so that the brim could be worn down to look like an old whalers cap, could be folded under all the way around to resemble a shower cap or by leaving the front bill extended it almost looked like a baseball cap. (It was a very clever and cute design.) The matching water slippers weren't really slippers and weren't meant for water. They were rubberized but looked more like evening dress shoes than anything. She tried on the whole outfit. Can you believe the size twelve was a perfect fit? She stepped out of the dressing room to see what Lucille and the clerk thought about it. Lucille choked in disgust. The clerk explained that it was stunning. Several people stopped in the aisle to gawk. Some of the older men were astonished. And even gave her a wolf whistle. The younger ones just giggled. When Mrs. Goldberg saw the response, she said, *I'll take it!*

During the ride home Lucille called her an *egotistical idiot.*

"Well, you're a prudish old maid and a jealous one at that," said Mrs. Goldberg.

"I wouldn't be caught dead in that outfit," said Lucille.

"I'm sure you wouldn't. First, because you couldn't get it on and secondly, I doubt if there's a matching casket." The rest of the ride was pretty quiet.

But when they finally arrived home, Mrs. Goldberg said, "Thank you for taking me, Lucille."

Lucille answered, "You're welcome anytime."

(All's well that ends well!!)

MARVELOUS MARILYN

Chip took the time to contact his much older sister, 'The Marvelous Marilyn from Milford, Michigan'. She answered the phone on the sixth ring.

"What are you up to, Sis?" asked Chip.

"Oh the same old stuff day after day," she softly murmured.

"Marilyn, you're mumbling, chirped Chip. "Wake up and join the world," he added, enthusiastically.

"What for?" she says. "There's nothing out here."

"Well, I might have something for you to do. Do you have a color printer hooked up to your computer?" Chip asked.

"Yea, so what?" Marilyn replied.

"Do you know how to print some labels if I sent you the design?" said Chip.

"Piece of cake," she said.

He went on to explain how the Floragra program seemed to be working out just great. He told her how they didn't want to go to a professional printing company because they were trying to keep it secretive. In fact, he said, they had just completed their first full run. He would send her a jar with the sample logo design.

"That would be just great. I hope it's as good as you say it is. I got to go now and yes, I can do the labels, so long," she said.

"Wait, wait," yelled Chip. "What's the hurry?"

"I just got to go now," she pleaded.

"Go where?" he inquired.

"I gotta go, my bladder is working overtime. See Ya'" she said.

Chip was left holding a silent phone. He packaged up one jar of the miracle cream along with the intended logo and a short note about using the cream sparingly. He didn't tell her about Mrs. Goldberg. He didn't want his sister running around in a bathing suit like that!

TIME OFF

The next day was still kind of dreary with scattered showers on and off. The 'Lovely Lois', remember her, the chief bookkeeper, showed up bright and early.

She asked Chip if he had time to go over some figures.

"Heck, yeah! I've been trying to go over Miss Ellie's figure for three days now."

Lois gave him a little wink as she stepped into the apartment.

"You dirty old man," she teased.

Miss Ellie stepped out of the bedroom in her chiffon dressing robe and white, fluffy kitty cat slippers. She joined them on the terrace for coffee and bagels and then spoke to both of them:

"I have kept a very accurate log of our expenses and as close as I can tell, the Floragra cream cost us about thirty-two cents a jar. That's not figuring anything for labor and the free paste jars you found. Our stock on hand, of all ingredients, might produce another five hundred jars. Do we have five hundred jars before we need to buy some more? I think you should go over the figures with 'Sexy Sam', the manufacturing manager and Doctor Kenny Dee, the resident pharmacist. Then you can determine the selling price. In the meantime I'm going to leave this whole shebang with you while I take a short vacation back to Ohio."

"Is anything wrong back home?" inquired Ellie.

"No, not at all," she replied, "I just have an idea concerning Floragra that I want to try out. That's if Chip will let me take twenty four jars with me."

Chip told her there was no one in the world he would trust more than her. He was sure the secret of the hedges would be safe. Meanwhile, Skeeter had heard Doc say he needed a haircut.

"Ah'll take ya'," he said to Doc.

"And exactly how do you think your going to do that? Sure as hell not in Tiny Tim's golf cart. I don't need anymore tickets."

"No, not in the golf cart," replied Skeeter. "Doc, you can ride in the sidecar of my motorcycle, if you don't mind holding Belle Taco on your lap."

"That's a great idea, Skeet. Let's go, and I'll buy you a beer after we're done," agreed Doc. So off they went. Little Belle Taco looked so cute with her ears flopping in the breeze. They pulled up in front of Singin' Sam's Shear Shoppe. His name really was Dominic, but Singin' Dominic's Shear Shoppe, didn't sound right. Doc told Skeeter the guy was more of a butcher than he was a barber but he was fast, cheap and sometimes, pretty funny. 'Singin' Sam' was glad to see them. He hadn't had a customer all morning. Right off the bat he reads them the rules.

"I don't do dogs," he stated.

Doc sarcastically replied he didn't like doggie doo either! They were off to a good start, Doc no sooner settled in the chair, than the barber almost strangled him by pulling the cape too tight around his neck.

"So whatsa' new with you?" the barber wanted to know.

Doc advised him to *please shut up and cut his hair! He didn't feel like small talk today.*

"Oka Doka," Sam the barber said in a thick accent.

Then he broke out in song, some kind of *aria* or something. He was more loud than good. He was so loud that it seemed to bother Belle Taco's ears. The dog started to squeal. The barber sang louder. The dog squealed louder. Doc said he couldn't stand it much longer. "Okay, all done," says Sam.

"Thank God for that, I suppose you're gonna' charge me for the entertainment too," suggested Doc.

"Nope, not today, I *singa'* for you for free," he replied.

Skeeter tucked Belle Taco in his backpack as they crossed the street heading for the Flamingo Express. They stumbled up to the bar. It was pretty dark in the joint after coming in from the bright sun light.

"What'll it be, gents?" asked the barkeep.

Skeeter ordered a bottle of Corona. Doc said plain Seltzer water was good enough for him. He still had a small stash of liquid Floragra. He needed a fix.

"Anything for the dog?" asked the barkeep.

"Just a small bowl of water," replied Skeeter.

The bartender put the bowl on the counter.

"I doubt if anyone else will be in this morning," he noted.

Little Belle Taco lapped it up without spilling a drop.

"Good girl," said Skeeter, "want a *goodie* now?"

Skeeter reached into his backpack to pull out a sandwich bag of cookies. They looked a lot like chocolate chip cookies.

"Does your dog like chocolate chip cookies?" asked the barkeep.

"They aren't chocolate chip, they're taco chip cookies. I made 'em myself," explained Skeeter.

The bartender was inquisitive. Said he never heard of such a thing. Skeeter explained he made his own chips, added some Salsa and Tabasco juice before baking them. The dog loved them. Doc said he was *flabbergasted*.

"I know your dog is a Chew-wa-wa, but this is too much."

The bartender chimed in, "Wait till I tell some of my other customers."

THE SLOGAN

Chip was making overtures to Miss Ellie, over his Eggs Benedict, when the phone rang. It was Carmello. Carmello was still working in a pizza joint so Chip didn't know much about him.

Miss Ellie said, "Mellow Carmello was really a nice fellow."

That was good enough for Chip. Carmello said 'Lean Jean' the legal machine had kept him up to date. He wanted to know if there was some way he could help.

"Not at the moment," replied Chip.

"Incidentally," said Carmello, "have you seen the new weather lady on Channel 62?

What a fox! Who cares what the weathers going to be, she makes it sound good all the time."

"So what does she forecast?" asked Chip.

"Clearing tonight, better tomorrow, great the next day," replied Carmello.

"Thanks, Carm, for calling," said Chip, adding, "and say hello to Jean."

Chip thought it was time to get the whole group together again for a brains storming session. There were loose ends that needed to be tied up. Such as, how much could they charge, how they were going to market it, how would it be distributed, and so on. He made a few phone calls. He found out the club house was free that afternoon. No other meetings had been scheduled and no one would be using the pool, in this crummy weather anyhow.

Camille and Lucille made the calls informing them all to be at the clubhouse by one o'clock tomorrow. Chip made a list of items that needed to be addressed. By one o'clock, the clubhouse was jammed. Even 'Babs, the Blond Bombshell from Bristol' (Connecticut, that is) was in attendance. She had returned from

London only last night. Doc hadn't seen her yet. Thank God, she sat back in the corner or the meeting may never have gotten started. Chip stood up to quiet the crowd and start the meeting.

"Ladies and Gentlemen, thanks to all of you for coming," he said. "While this is not exactly a formal meeting, we do have a number of things to discuss. I need your input to help me guide the ship into the Sea of Good Fortune. This is the agenda we need to discuss."

A printed agenda was handed out:

#1.   *Our cost to manufacture.*

#2.   *Determine selling price to make a nominal profit.*

#3.   *Advertising and advertising slogans.*

#4.   *Distribution.*

#5.   *Open forum for questions and suggestions.*

He turned the meeting over to Miss Ellie, the 'Merry Maid from Michigan' who would give them their current financial status. She pointed out that Lois had conferred with them before she left and told them that the cost would be about thirty-two cents a jar. However, that did not include anything for labor, not even minimum wages, nothing for additional jars, if they needed any more and nothing for replacement machinery if anything were to break down. Chip asked if there were any questions? An old duffer in the back shouted, *why can't we get minimum wages? It's only a dollar, fifteen an hour, isn't it?*

Lucille stood up to answer the question.

"Where have you been for the last twenty five years, old timer? Besides with your retirement income, you don't need it."

Atta' girl, Lucy, you tell him, the crowd shouted.

'King Arthur', the suave one, was the next one to take center stage.

"Hrmpf," he cleared his throat. "Ladies, we need to rely on your experience," he started, "how much do you pay for a good face cream?"

A multitude of answers were shouted out, *$2.95, $6.49, $18.95 …*

"Okay, okay, that's enough," said Arthur. "Now, how much is a good facial at the beauty parlor?"

Several of *the girls* said they never had one. Several others thought they were around forty or fifty dollars. Mrs. Goldberg said she wouldn't need any more now that she had Floragra, however, a full facial including excess hair removal, could be as much seventy-five or eighty dollars.

"That's fine, ladies. Now we're getting somewhere," continued Arthur. "The next question is, if you had a choice of a very expensive perfume or face saving Floragra, for the same price, which would you choose?"

Every woman in the audience stood up shouting, *Floragra! Floragra!* They looked and sounded like a nominating committee at a political convention.

"Thank you, ladies, for your input. You have been extremely helpful," concluded Arthur who turned to Chip and Doc, "That should give you enough to set a selling price."

Advertising was next on the agenda. Chip had appointed 'Alluring Anita' and 'Millie the Mermaid' to share the advertising duties. 'Tee Shot Tom' was already marketing director and expediter. It was only natural that all three should work together. Millie took the lead.

"As you know," she began, "we don't have a lot of money to work with. And we won't have until we start selling some of this stuff. Therefore, let's hold off on the advertising budget and concentrate on a slogan that will easily identify Floragra."

'Lean Jean' interrupted, "We don't have final approval from the proper authorities and as far as I know, right now, we're legal in using the Floragra name, as well as the initials *FASA*. If we had a clever artist in the crowd, perhaps he could work *FASA* into a monogram."

'Alluring Anita' stood there, bashful and petite looking. She finally spoke up.

"Don't forget the logo we designed. We need a good slogan to go with it," she said.

'Tee Shot Tom' looked around the room to find Skeeter.

"Skeeter, what did you tell us about your little dog when Chip washed him with liquid Floragra?" asked Tom.

Skeeter didn't bother coming forward. He just yelled out:," I told ya' it was a smoother, that's what!"

Tee Shot stood there and said, "Alright folks, help us out here. What can we say about this stuff?"

They all seemed to blurt it out at the same time. Each one trying to be heard over the other: "*It's amazing! It's fantastic! It's a miracle in a jar! You'll wonder where the wrinkles went ... you can trust your car to the man with the Floragra jar.*" And some of them had memories that went way back. "*Double your pleasure, buy two jars.*" Finally Mrs. Goldberg walked toward the front of the room.

"I would like to say something," she said.

Chip, Doc and 'Tee Shot Tom' stood there wondering what was coming next. Chip raised a hand to quiet the crowd. The small clubhouse took on an almost church like atmosphere. Mrs. Goldberg started slowly, almost solemnly.

"You all know me as Molly Goldberg. You also know that I was somewhat of a recluse. I rarely left my apartment. Most of you used to refer to me as 'Moldy' Mrs. Goldberg, the crankety old broad in building ten. Now, I hear terms like Goody Mrs. Goldberg or Good Golly, Miss Molly," she said.

She was warming up. Her speech pattern was becoming quicker and her voice was raised a notch or two, and went on.

"Look at me now. Not a crease, not a wrinkle, not a crevice, not a crow's foot on my face."

"*Preach it, Mrs. Goldberg,*" some wisenheimer yelled out. "*Amen, baby.*"

Mrs. Goldberg continued: "You may laugh and joke but look at me now, and all because of Floragra. It's a miracle. I am living proof. And just look at these breasts. Have you ever seen anything so orbitally perfect in your life?"

She threw her shoulders back and thrust them out as far as they would go.

"*Take it off, take it off,*" came the cry from the rear from some sweet little old eighty five year old.

Chip interrupted, "Never mind that stuff, go on Mrs. Goldberg."

Mrs. Goldberg resumed speaking.

"I was tired of being a cranky old broad. I wanted to live again and I had a thirst for youth. I was *hungry to look younger.*"

'Tee Shot Tom' sprang up like a shot out of cannon.

"That's it ... that's it," he shouted, "There's our slogan: *THE HUNGER TO LOOK YOUNGER.* I love it."

Chip and Doc ran the phrase through their mental sensors. It sounded pretty good. A flurry of excitement permeated the group. Miss Goldberg broke back in:

"I'm glad I was able to contribute that although I hadn't planned on it. I'm also proud to stand before you today looking like this. I am living proof that Floragra works and I will gladly pose for the cameras anytime."

Chip thanked Mrs. Goldberg for her input and for helping them to find a slogan. They would definitely have to take it under advisement as they say in the business world.

The session was taking longer than Chip thought it would. He told the group he had two announcements to make.

"Number one, lets hold off on the distribution problem until another time because it was getting late. And number two, how many would like to go to the dog races tomorrow?"

"Hip-hip-hooray, atta' boy Chip, Get the bus!" came the reply.

It was decided that since this would not be a secret mission and the bus would pick them up in front of the building at eleven o'clock.

THE DOG RACES

The bus was packed. There were more colors than in a kid's kaleidoscope. There were vertical stripes, horizontal lines, zigzags, polka dots, solids and tie-dyed. There were more styles of caps and or hats than one could see in a New York Easter parade. Mrs. Goldberg stood out, as usual, wearing a huge yellow sunbonnet. She defended it by saying Chip had told her not to get too much sun on her face. The old fella was cute in his brown tweed Sherlock Holmes cap with the bill extending out of both the front and the back. The gaiety was spontaneous. They were ready for another good time.

Chip whispered to Doc, "If they only knew what liquid Floragra could do for them, there would be no holding them back."

The wheels on the bus went round and round until they reached the dog track. Skeeter was afraid to bring his Chihuahua. Not because he would be mistaken for a greyhound but because the greyhounds might mistake the dog for a rabbit with long ears. He left him home tucked snuggly in the sidecar of the motorcycle.

They emptied the bus in a flash. Chip asked the driver if he wanted to wait or would he like the walkie-talkie so they could call him later. The driver said he would stick around.

'Sly Ely' was leading the pack toward the gate.

"Who wants to be a millionaire," he bellowed. "Follow me, I got the system."

Most of the players bought a program. (You can't hardly bet on a dog if you don't know its name.) Most of them had never been to a dog race before. Therefore, they had no idea what to do. 'Sly Ely' was giving lessons.

"Just go up to a window over there and say you want to bet on number such and such," explained Ely.

Some old wisenheimer says, "I don't see 'Such and Such' in the program."

"Oh, drop dead," says Ely.

'Babs, the Blond Bombshell from Bristol', sidled up to Doc.

"Do I look like a taut?" she asked.

"You mean tout, don't you?" said Doc.

"Whatever," she replied.

Doc had to admit she looked pretty darn good.

'Audacious Audrey' confronted Ely.

"Okay, hawkeye, what's the system?" she demanded.

Several members of the clan gathered around as Ely expounded.

"If it's the lightest dog in the race, it should be able to run faster," he said.

"Not necessarily," Audrey said.

"Or if it's the youngest dog in the race, it should be able to out run the older ones," Ely said.

"Not necessarily," said Audrey.

Finally Ely said: "If all else fails, check the program to see how many times the dog finished in the money. That should be a good indication of what he can do."

"Not necessarily," said Audrey.

Mrs. Goldberg brushed the brim of her hat back.

"If a dog has four legs, it should be able to win," she concluded.

"Atta girl, Mrs. Goldberg."

Camillo and Lucille were sharing a program. Lucille said she liked "Drooling Devil" in the third race. He had been sired by, "Liver Lips" and "Sloppy Sue". They bet two bucks. The dog showed and paid $2.40. Bert and Gert were looking for a dog that was alert. Sometimes you could tell as they paraded to the starting gate. Gert asked why they were wearing muzzles.

"Ya' know how they yip and yap when they're in the gate?' said Bert. "If they didn't have the muzzles on they might communicate with each other. Something like: *You won last time. It's my turn today.* Or maybe, *if you bump me in the back stretch again, I won't sleep with you tonight.*"

"Makes sense to me," replied Gert.

'Sexy Sam' and 'Alluring Anita' were checking their program. Sam said he liked, "Step On It" out of "Dirty Shoes" and "Oh crap". Anita said she didn't like the sound of that one. She preferred "Toe Tapper" breed out of "Broadway Melody" and "Forty Second Street". Sam lost two bucks. She won $12.80. Mrs. Goldberg spotted one in the last race, "Lovely Lady".

"I don't care who the bitch was or any of that, I'm gonna' bet that sonnabitch anyhow," she said.

She won $8.80.

No one got rich. Most were lucky if they broke even. But they had a great time. On the ride back home there was a lot of chitchat about who won and who lost. The driver announced that he had won a hundred dollars.

"How'd you do that?" asked Sam.

"Ya' gotta' have a system," was his reply.

Lois asked if anyone was old enough to remember the old Spike Jones recording of Beetle Baum?

"*Sure, Heck yeah, Of course,*" several responded at one time.

"Isn't that the one where the guy announces a horse race and poor beetle Baum comes in last?" asked 'Tee Shot Tom'.

"*Yeah, cabbage moves up by a head!*" said some wisenheimer.

"Banana slips up in the bunch!" added Doc.

Chip chimed in, "It's underwear creeping up the rear!"

They all sang out, *"And Beetle Baum!"*

Skeeter was sitting next to Lucille, directly behind Miss Ellie and Chip. Skeeter blurted out, as he so often did, that maybe they should have a race dog that they could name 'Floragra Flash'.

"That's a great idea," broke in Chip. "But we need to make some money in the business first."

Skeeter continued, "Maybe we could race Chew-wa-wa's on a smaller circle. That wouldn't cost so much. Boy, wouldn't that be fun?"

The subject was dropped as the bus pulled up in front of the complex. As they exited the bus each one thanked the driver.

"Thank you folks," he replied. "I had a great time and I'm a hundred dollars richer."

That night, they all retired early. All that fresh air and a day in the sun had taken its toll. Besides, they had to allow time for their Floragra applications. Mrs. Goldberg used only a small amount on her bosom. No sense over doing a good thing. She was applying heavier amounts on her waist and thighs.

"If only I had someone to rub it on my posterior," she thought to herself.

That 'Doc Kenny Dee', slovenly as he was, was also looking better to her all the time.

THE PYRAMID PLAN

The next morning broke sunny and warm, the first nice day for about a week. All hands were ready and anxious for the trip to the shack. The 'Lovely Lois' had returned from Ohio.

"Chip, can I see you and Ellie alone for a minute?" she asked.

"Sure Lois, come on in," answered Chip.

Chip told Doc and Sam to take the group on without them. They would catch up later. Miss Ellie poured coffee out on the terrace.

"What's up Lois?" inquired Chip.

'The Lovely Lois' was usually very level headed and business like.

"I don't know where to begin," she said but then proceeded to explain.

"My trip to Ohio wasn't just to see my family. I did a lot of investigating while I was there. I've heard a lot about a company called Amway and another called Mary Kay Cosmetics. I found out that they have similar distribution strategies. I guess they're called pyramid companies. I've been thinking maybe we could do that with Floragra. Remember the twenty-four jars you let me take? Well I tried the pyramid thing on a very limited basis. Even though you didn't give me a selling price, I figured a jar should be worth $59.95 compared to the costs of a good facial. I knew our cost was approximately thirty-two cents. In order for the company to make money, we have to charge a distributor, five dollars. So I charged my sister five dollars and told her if she could find another distributor or agent to handle it, that she could make an extra five bucks. Do you see how the pyramid thing will work?" Lois went on, "I didn't have time to clear it with you so I went ahead and set up a separate company. I call it 'Florhio'. It's set up as a limited partnership. That way we pay the minimum in taxes and in case of failure, I don't get stuck with the whole debt myself. The possibilities are almost endless. We have enough people down here in Florida that are all out of stators, snowbirds, if you will. How about Florayork, Floravania, or Florianna? Floratucky, Floraenessee and Florasippi all come to mind. Each one would have a protected distributorship in their own state. Just think about it, no advertising, and limited bookkeeping. If the hedges hold out, and Doctor Dee holds up, there is no telling where this can go."

Miss Ellie and Chip were stupefied. 'The Lovely Lois' was so far ahead of the rest of them, it was almost unbelievable.

All Chip could say was, "Lois, I'm so impressed. I don't know what to say. It sounds like the answer to most of our problems. And it sounds like a real moneymaker. I think it's okay, the next step would be to recruit members from the various states.

Miss Ellie joined in, all excited.

"Just think, 'King Arthur' and 'Millie the Mermaid' could be Florajersey, 'Sexy Sam' and 'Alluring Anita' could be Floravania and we know a bunch of people that could handle Florafornia. Lois, you're the greatest!" she exclaimed.

The three of them were so excited they couldn't wait to tell everyone else. They borrowed Tiny Tim's golf cart and headed for the shack. As expected, half the group was inside, the other half, were lolling around outside. Chip asked Doc to turn off the generator for a while. He gathered the troops together outside.

"Folks, we have some wonderful news to tell you. Lois has a fantastic plan to tell you about," said Chip.

With that said, he turned it over to Lois. She outlined the pyramid plan to them but purposely held back on the Florhio Company. *Let them digest a little at a time*, she thought.

There was a lot of chatter, some furrowed brows and a couple of *"Atta' Girls"*. Someone spoke up, *"How much more is it gonna' cost me? I already have a hundred and ten in this thing and don't have anything but a smooth face."*

Mrs. Goldberg jumped up. "You idiot, don't you think your new face is worth every penny? Just sit down and listen."

Chip intervened, "There's a lot more to this that we can't reveal until 'Lean Jean' investigates the legalities of it. Suffice, for the moment, that we will all make some money."

Chip cornered Doc for a moment.

"What do you think will be the shelf life of a bottle of Floragra?" he asked.

Doc wasn't sure but he thought it would last at least a year, maybe longer. There wasn't anything in it that would spoil. However he was quick to add that they didn't have the equipment to run such a test. Whether it would lose it's potency over time, was anybody's guess.

"Why do you ask?" asked Doc.

"I'm thinking, if we could stock pile in a safe place, we should make as much as we can before the next hurricane comes along. We don't know if it will ruin the hedges or not. I don't think we should take any chances."

Chip proceeded to tell Doc about 'The Lovely Lois' Florhio idea. Doc listened intently.

"All the more reason to get maximum production out of what we have," said Doc. "I agree with your reasoning and salute Lois for an outstanding idea."

Whereupon he started up the generator and shouted out: "Okay, you dwarves, Hi Ho it back to work!"

After Skeeter tooted the lunch break on the bugle, which sound Belle Taco couldn't stand, they all moved outside to play pass the plate again. What a joyous group! They seem to be coming together as a tighter knit group more than ever. (Who says older folks can't get along or don't know how to have fun?)

After the lunch break, the inners became the outers and the outers went in. The generator was generating, the mixer was mixing, and the joint was jumping. But alas, about three o'clock they had to shut down because they ran out of the miracle leaves. After arriving back at the main gate to the complex, they all went their separate ways. A few of them donned their suits and headed for the pool. They received some very curious stares. *"Where have you been? We haven't seen you for a while."* The standard answer was that they had been keeping busy. At the super market 'Sly Ely' and 'Audacious Audrey' were aware of several dubious glances. They were asked more than once, if they had been to a spa.

"No," they replied, "Why do you ask?"

"Because you look fabulous, you must have both had plastic surgery!" said one of the residents.

"No, we're just healthy," replied Ely.

That evening 'Sexy Sam' and 'Alluring Anita' were dancing at one of the many jazz clubs in that part of Florida. They too, were aware of some dubious glances. As they tripped the light fantastic, another couple waltzed up to them.

"Where have you been, we haven't seen you out dancing in years and look at the two of you," said one of them. "Have you found the fountain of youth?"

After stammering the answer, "We've been taking some new vitamins," they then danced away.

Mrs. Goldberg was the most outstanding rejuvenation project. She was asked over and over again, what happened to her, 'Molly' would answer, in her indubitable manner, that she had found religion. She was a true believer. (She never let on it was Floragra she believed in.)

It was becoming very evident the group wasn't going to be able to hide the secret much longer. Chip asked 'Lean Jean' to drop all her other legal work for a day or so, to get some answers, ASAP and Chip stayed around the home front for a day or two to do some serious thinking. The phone rang bright and early one morning. It was Jean. *Could Chip bring Sam and Lois to her office for a conference? Would eight o'clock that night, be okay?*

Chip, Miss Ellie, Sam, Anita and 'The Lovely Lois', piled into Sam's Cadillac for the trip downtown. Since Carmello, that nice fellow, was Jean's husband, it was only right that he be there too. They convened in the conference room of Jean's plush office. Carmillo poured the wine in tribute to this auspicious occasion. He raised his glass.

"To Floragra," he said.

"Here, here," came the reply.

Chip had been mulling over 'The Lovely Lois' pyramid plan. Using some of 'Lean Jean's suggestions, he thought the plan could work to everyone's advantage if they followed a formula successfully used by several in-home demonstration companies. The two and a half once jar of Floragra, complete with application brush, would sell for say $59.95. An agency, such as the Florhio Company would purchase it from *FASA,* for say 30% off the retail price or approximately forty-two dollars. If Lois, as an example can recruit six more people, she would be considered a unit leader, which then entitles her to an additional 2% rebate. That would give her approx. eight dollars and forty cents extra on every jar sold in her franchise territory. If each of those six would recruit six more, Lois not only got the original 30% off and the 2% rebate, she would get another 2% rebate on the second tier of six, and so and so on. The company would still be making tons of money in which Lois would share because she was an original investor.

"Does that make sense?" Chip asked.

Doc, Sam and Tom all agreed it made sense to them.

"Where do we sign up?" they asked.

They would have to have a board of directors meeting as soon as 'Lean Jean the Legal Machine', could get the franchises ready. In the meantime, Chip suggested, they had all better head out to the shack to make sure everything was all right. The whole gang was standing around doing nothing. No one knew how to mix the potion or start the generator. Skeeter could start the generator but he wouldn't make a move without specific instructions. Chip took the time to remind everyone of their duties, especially Bert and Gert as they hadn't been reporting lately. They sure didn't need anyone stealing the formula now that they were so close to making some real money. He told Mrs. Goldberg and Carmello, they better start checking the weather more often. Molly said she wouldn't mind because 'Windy Willy' was back on the air. She stood up in a semi-rigid position and with a half salute.

"The only thing we have to fear is…. the weather itself," she proclaimed.

Someone told her *she was dating herself.*

The afternoon went well. (That's a pun; remember Skeeter said Floragra was a smoother?) Again, things went well enough that by 3 o'clock they called it a day. They kept running out of the miracle leaves. Doc said that was just fine. If they gathered too many, they would wilt and lose there power. Also, if they picked too many, the hedges would look bare which would arouse more suspicion. Later on that night, Skeeter, with Doc and Belle Taco riding in the sidecar, stopped by the Chip's place. It seemed like every time Chip was trying to proposition Miss Ellie, there was an interruption. Ellie answered the door. Skeeter had Belle Taco snuggly tucked in one arm.

"What's up guys?" Chip asked.

Doc replied there was nothing special and they only wanted to 'shoot the breeze'.

Skeeter said, "It's okay to shoot the breeze, but don't shoot my Chew-wa-wa!"

"Don't worry; Skeet, we wouldn't do that," replied Chip.

Doc said he had been wondering about *this Floragra thing.*

"Why, Doc, what's the problem?" asked Chip.

"No problem," said Doc. "But you know how you seem to have everything in place? I wonder what we're selling this for, how ya' gonna' advertise it?"

Chip interrupted, "What do you mean what are we selling it for, we're selling it to make money."

"Whoa, slow down Chip," replied Doc. "I don't mean, 'why' are we selling it, I mean 'what' are we selling it for? Is it a lotion, a potion, a notion or a solution to pollution, or what?"

"Oh, now I get you," said Chip. "What is it *good for?*"

"Now ya' got it," said Doc.

"Miss Ellie, made a list," said Chip.

"Okay, what do we know so far?" asks Doc.

Ellie butted in, "Would you fellas like a glass of sarsaparilla?"

"Sure," replied Skeeter. "Even if we don't know what it is."

She returned with four glasses on a beautiful etched glass, serving tray.

"I was thinking," she said. "We know the Floragra removes the liver spots."

"Okay, put that down, Number one," said Chip.

"Number two, it heals cigarette burns," said Doc, "and number three it takes the sting out of insect bites."

"Number four it grows hair," said Chip.

Skeeter jumped in, "And it's a smoother! Don't forget that."

"We got it, Skeet," notes Ellie, "that's number five."

"Number six, it enlarges breasts," said Doc.

They went on adding to the list. *"It does away; with wrinkles, it removes lines and crevices. It tightens the skin. It makes you look younger."*

"See, that's quite a list," said Doc. "Those are all things we know for sure, but how many more things could it be good for? We haven't had time to do much research or experimenting. I've been thinking, what if we ran a contest, just within our own contingent, to let them find other uses. We could offer a free dinner at Wishbone Willys to the winner. They would be doing the experimenting for us, in half the time and it wouldn't cost much."

Miss Ellie thought it was a wonderful idea. She added that there should be some visible proof of the accomplishment, and as in all other contests, the decision of the judges was final.

"Who are the judges?" asked Skeeter.

"We are, "she responded. "Just the four of us, and if there's a tie, Belle Taco gets to bark for the winner."

She was teasing, but Skeeter didn't catch on.

Doc reminded them of what happened when he added the liquid in his seltzer water. Just a small amount gave him a tremendous burst of energy. Unfortunately the Mrs. Butterworth bottle was empty. Seems he'd been nipping a little at a time.

"If we gave some of that stuff to my little dog, he could outrun them greyhounds," laughed Skeeter, who was always good for a laugh and never took anything seriously.

Chip suggested that Doc should make another batch of the liquid but to do it on the Q.T. They didn't need that kind of information to be known yet. The next day, at the shack, they announced the contest. All agreed it was a great idea. *"Hip, hip, hooray!"*

Doc suggested some possibilities might be that Floragra could be used as a shampoo (like Old Floragra). Some old wisenheimer yelled out *"Ya' can't use it under your arms if it grows hair!"*

"Yea, you're right. Cross out that possibility," Doc replied.

Chip took Doc aside for a moment.

"What if you changed the formula a little? Couldn't you make a depilatory to remove hair instead of growing hair?" he asked.

Doc didn't know but would check into it.

There was a buzz of undercurrent as they discussed the possibilities of winning the free dinner. Mrs. Goldberg, it turned out, was a phenomenon. Not because of what happened to her face and body but because of the short period of time it took. Some of the other ladies weren't quite so lucky. Oh sure the treatments were beginning to work but it would take time. The wrinkles and the creases were slowly disappearing and some of the 44 longs (some of which were extra longs) were beginning to shrink and regain some texture but none as quickly as Mrs. Goldberg. There wasn't a big rush to the brassiere stores at the flea market. But nobody was complaining. They had come a long way baby. To a sole, they were enjoying all the compliments. The whole tribe was trying the Floragra in different ways.

The entries started coming in. *"It's a shampoo. It's a conditioner. It's a great body wash. It's a moisturizer. It's a muscle relaxer. It eases the pain of arthritis."* Ellie, 'The Merry Maid from Michigan', kept track of who sent in what suggestion. She was sure there would be more.

ANOTHER CHAPTER

'Marvelous Marilyn from Milford, Michigan' monkeyed with her modem. She was amazed at the many moves mandatory to make so many models. She had promised Chip she could make the labels for the paste jars. She kept getting double lines on one thing or another. First it was the pyramid, then a double lightning jag. The circle representing the sun was more oval than round. She cursed her cursor. Then she cursed her brother. *"What a stupid design!"* she said out loud to her cat lying on a chair beside her. She finally got it all together. The labels came out perfectly. Even the correct colors were in the correct place. She called Chip.

"I got your dumb labels done."

"How many?" Chip asked.

"A millimeter of a million," she said.

"What the hell does that mean?" asked Chip.

"About three hundred," Marilyn remarked. "Do you need many more?"

"Maybe," he said.

"Hey, I moved mountains making this much, so don't get smart with me," she said.

Chip knew she liked to use the letter M. He teased her every chance he got.

"How soon do you need them?" Marilyn asked.

"I told you ASAP or how about UPS?" he quipped.

"Up yours too, buddy," she challenged, and then added, "Mom mumbled maybe you were moronic, now I know for sure."

She said the labels would be there the next day.

(Marilyn and Chip really did get along great. Better than most brothers and sisters, they just liked to 'play games', that's all.)

THE FLAVORS

Doc was riding in the sidecar of Skeeters motorcycle, hanging on to the little dog with its ears flapping in the breeze. Doc didn't mind because little Belle Taco sure was the cutest little thing. They got the generator started so there would be light in the shack. Doc went in. Skeeter said he would rather stay outside.

"Okee Dokee," said Doc.

Doc was pouring over some old manuals he had scourged from the trashcan of a local library. They must have been old if the library didn't even want them. He was making notes for future consideration. He thought to himself that there might come a time when they might want to use fragrances since *all the cosmetic companies seem to be doing it.*

He then started to review flavor names to himself, to hear how they would sound. *"How about Peppermint Pleasure in a green jar, or Vanishing Vanilla in a pure white jar? Perhaps Madam would prefer Very Cherry in a bright red jar? No?*

They maybe the sweet smell of Orange Blossom in, of course, an orange jar. If all else fails, try the Floragra flavor of the month, Rose Bud in the pink jar."

He had quite a conversation with himself. He thought they all sounded good and wouldn't be too difficult to produce. In fact the additional cost would be so minimal that they wouldn't have to change the selling price. Doc thought he had another great idea. He could put the five or six scent mixtures in a soda fountain dispenser. Instead of chocolate, cherry, strawberry etc., when you pushed the lever you get Peppermint, Orange Blossom or Rose Bud. Very clever, he thought to himself. Maybe we could put them in a pump bottle to sell over the counter.

In the meantime Skeeter and Belle Taco were still outside. Skeeter might not have all his marbles but he was wise about a lot of unusual things. As an example he had installed a cigarette lighter in the motorcycle. (What for, you ask, he doesn't even smoke. Aha! He could plug in his electric shaver. He could use it for a map light, if he had a map. He could plug it in a spotlight, which he occasionally did. He could even warm up Belle Taco's food if necessary, which probably never would be necessary in south Florida.)

However, on this particular occasion he was sitting in the sidecar with Belle Taco watching television. He picked up a five inch G.E. black and white TV at a pawnshop for next to nothing. (Who would ever want a B & W TV anyhow?) Skeeter did. The program was, "Who Wants to Be a Millionaire?" The question was, "What is a chew-wah-wah?"

A. *A chewing gum?*

B. *A baby in Chicago asking for water?*

C. *A Chinese dog?*

D. *One of the above.*

Skeeter almost lost his shorts scrambling out of the sidecar. Doc was hunched over, under a light, researching in a 1938 chemistry manual that he had picked up in a garage sale, trying to find out what was in a depilatory to make it remove hair. Skeeter burst through the door.

"I should be a millionaire!" he shouted.

Doc was stunned, "What the hell are you shouting about?"

Skeet explained the show on TV that the correct answer was, *None of the above*, and that was his final answer and he should be a millionaire.

"Yeah, you're right but you ain't on TV, so you ain't a millionaire, so forget about it," said Doc.

The next morning, on the Coral Creek shuttle bus, Mrs. Goldberg made sure she sat next to Doctor Dee. Doc was a little slow this morning due to working on the fragrances so late. The bus was equipped with two person bench seats. Mrs. Goldberg took advantage of the situation to sit as close as possible. Doc noticed it but didn't comment. He also took a second to scan the old girl from head to toe. Since the wrinkles had disappeared she didn't look too bad. The fact that the 38 short bra was so pointedly displayed didn't detract anything either. Doc thought, *She's no 'Babs the Blond Bombshell' but what the hell?* About midway through the ride, Doc noticed her left leg was rubbing up against his. He didn't think it was a nervous reaction.

Making small talk, she said, "Well Doc, what have you been up to lately?"

He explained without going into detail, that he had been working on some fragrances to enhance the Floragra.

"What kind of fragrances?" she asked.

"Oh, like peppermint, cherry and orange and ..." said Doc.

"Geez, Doc," she says, "Those sound so mundane. Couldn't you come up with something better than that?"

"What do you have in mind?" inquired Doc.

"Something more up to date, something, livelier," she said. "How about: "Passion Flower," or "Lust for Life" or maybe "Climax"? At least they sound more exciting."

"Food for thought," Doc said, "food for thought."

He was beginning to see where this was going. He took another glance. The face wasn't bad. The upper half of the body looked great. There was a small tummy. The outline through the short shorts showed a little flab around the thighs but not the saddlebags that had been there. *What the hell, she was no kid any more.* He started analyzing his own stature. *What the hell, he wasn't a kid either.* Before they got off the bus he noticed a red mark on his leg where she had been rubbing her knees. Once inside the shack there wasn't time for that kind of nonsense.

They got the generator started, the cement mixer was turning, and the production line was moving. Again they worked in two hours shifts, so no one would become too fatigued. Half were inside. Half were outside. Someone found the old radio and carried it outside. They found the older radio station. They were playing Spike Jones horse race song, "Beatle Baum." Skeeter said it reminded him of the dog races. Too bad his little Chew-wa-wa wasn't racing.

The next song was a slow Charlie Spivak number. 'King Arthur' asked 'Millie the Mermaid' if she would like to dance?

"Sure, you know I love to dance and I don't have anything else to do," she replied.

That was one of Miss Ellie's stock answers. It must be catching. Arthur and Millie kicked off their sneakers and danced bare foot in the saw grass. It didn't take long before 'Sexy Sam' and 'Alluring Anita' joined them. Next thing you know, there was Bert and Gert. That Foragra was amazing. It was making them look younger. It was making them feel younger. And it sure made them act younger. Not a creaking bone in the bunch. The two hours seemed to fly by as Skeeter sounded the bugle call for lunch. They did 'the eat around' thing again. It kept getting better every day. Not quite gourmet but closer. Mrs. Goldberg again sought out Doctor Kenny Dee.

"Doc, could you come here please? I can't seem to get the top open on my Coleman cooler," she said.

"No problem, Mrs. Goldberg, be right there," replied Doc.

Doc didn't notice anything particularly difficult in getting the top open. He played the game. Mrs. Goldberg thanked him and invited him to sit down for a sip of chilled wine. He obliged her, expectantly. She poured the wine into the Dixie cups.

"Classy, eh?" she said.

Doc didn't answer but he was watching. Wondering where this was going. She reached into her cooler.

"I got a surprise for you," she said, as she pulled out a couple of oysters on the half shell.

Doc's mouth fell open. "Mrs. Goldberg, this *is* a picnic."

"Picnic, shnicnic," she says. "No reason we can't enjoy ourselves. You should know about these things. Is it true oysters are an aphrodisiac?'"

"Only if they're raw," he said.

"They are," she said, "Have some more."

After the repast of wine, the oysters, and the crabmeat munchies and with the sun beaming down, Doc was feeling mellow. (Remember, it's the middle of the day, lunch hour, Mrs. Goldberg knew her way around all right. She had him right where she wanted him, at least for now.)

"Well Doc, what do you think?" she began.

"About what?" he says rather dreamily.

"About taking me out to Hot Doggies tonight for dinner and dancing?" she asked.

"What's a Hot Doggie?" he asked.

"You know, that jazz place where they have an impromptu band every night of the week," she explained.

"Okay," he replies, "What else do I have to do?"

The afternoon went flying by as usual. Everything was shut down, cleaned up and secured by four O'clock. As they stepped off the bus Mrs. Goldberg told Doc she would pick him up at eight.

"Okee, dokee," Doc replied.

Doc needed a long nap, badly. Mrs. Goldberg the 'moldie oldie' Goldberg didn't need a nap. (She was flying high, baby.) It had been years since she had actually been out on a date. She made plans to borrow 'Sexy Sam's Cadillac Eldorado. She showered. She shaved her legs. She body washed. She had her hair done. When she stepped out of the house, she looked like a movie star. An old one, but a movie star non-the less. Mrs. Goldberg was at least five years older than Doc but she looked five years younger. She pulled up at Doc's place at exactly eight O'clock. She brought Doc a corsage, a radish cut to resemble a rose. He was impressed. Doc, never known as a sharp dresser, did the best he could. His hair was combed, his face was shaved, and he wore an open collar sport shirt, over clean khakis and even shined his loafers. He took one look at Mrs. Goldberg. Then he let out a slow wolf whistle. She was quickly turning into a trendsetter. The shiny leather jacket was zipped down just low enough to reveal a hint of the black under-wire bra. The matching skirt was short, but not too short. The slit on one side was tantalizing. The dark hose were tucked into stiletto heel pumps. Not those big, clunky things the kids are wearing. The over all affect was fabulous.

They arrived at Doggies in time to share a slab of ribs before the band arrived. Doc ordered drinks while waiting for dinner. The lights were being dimmed to set the mood for the rest of the evening. Great ambiance but they couldn't find the spare ribs in front of them. The ten-piece band had been playing for a half hour or so. The after dinner drinks were replaced by the drinks of choice, for the rest of the evening. The band started playing that old Hoagie Carmichael hit, Stardust. Mrs. Goldberg couldn't sit still any longer.

"C'mon, Doc, let's dance," she said.

As she placed her arm over his shoulder and placed her hand gently on the back of his neck, Doc suddenly noticed she was almost the same height as he even with her high-heels on. She inched in closer. Doc could feel her (you-know-what) pressing against his chest. He kind of liked it. Hell. He liked it a lot. Doc hadn't been dancing in probably 25 or 30 years. He clumsily stepped on her feet.

"I'm sorry," he blundered.

"Don't worry about it," she said. "I step on them too."

"Maybe if you held me closer," she purred, "we wouldn't have that problem."

"Okee, dokee," he replied.

It took a few minutes before they got used to each other's style. They were finally getting the right rhythm, when the music stopped. Doc didn't want to let go. He kind of liked this cheek-to-cheek stuff. Mrs. Goldberg didn't exactly pull herself away either. The next number was the bands rendition of Buddy Morrows theme song *Night Train*.

"My God, how sensuous can this music get?" Doc thought to himself. He felt transported back to the thirties or forties.

The two were getting more in sync now a slow melodic movement. Good thing Doc didn't have a suit coat on because he was already beginning to sweat. They finished that dance and went back to the table for a sip and a short break.

"How do you feel?" asked Doc.

"I don't know," replied Mrs. Goldberg, "do you want to feel me to find out?"

"Not here, silly," he said. "I wondered if you're having a good time."

"Lovely, just lovely," she said.

Doc asked her another question. "Would you like to feel even better?"

"Sure, what do you have in mind?" she asked.

Mrs. Goldberg had about half a drink left. Doc says, "Trust me, you'll enjoy it" as he put one drop of liquid Floragra in her glass.

"Try that," he instructed her.

She didn't notice any difference. Not right away, anyhow. They sat there, in the glow of the candles, making small talk. The band had played another set. When they started up again she said, "Come on, Doc, I feel pretty good now."

They found their way through the darkened club to the dance floor. Doc didn't know it but this set was a trio of Latin numbers, a Samba, a Rumba and a Cha Cha. He had two left feet when it came to this kind of stuff. He stood there barely moving his feet. She danced around him. She swayed. She gyrated. She undulated. Doc thought maybe he shouldn't have put the drop of stuff in her drink.

"C'mon, Kenny baby, get with it, "she proclaimed. She had all the moves. Doc was content to shuffle a little and watch.

On the way back to the table she said, "I don't know what you gave me but I want some more."

Doc told her what it was. He explained one drop would last her all evening.

The band really warmed up on "St Louis Blues" "Memphis Blues" and "Blue Bayou." She couldn't sit still.

"C'mon, party pooper."

They next went through "One O'clock Jump" "Woodchoppers Ball" and "No Name Jive." She could do it all. Kenny couldn't believe it. She knew The Charleston, The Jitter But, The Swing.

Doc sat down in a chair alongside the dance floor. Molly was still doing her thing. Some of the other participants were stepping aside to watch. Molly grabbed the bandleader, "Hey do you know The Twist?" She demonstrated. The band caught on so they improvised a couple of numbers. Molly was the center of attention like she used to be those many years ago. She loved every minute of it. She did The Twist, The Crawl and The Swim. Wasn't there any step she didn't know?

A little after midnight Doc corralled her long enough to ask if she was ready to go.

"I've never been more ready in my life," she cooed.

On the way home, Doc was driving Sam's Cadillac. Mrs. Goldberg was teasing him by rubbing him on the inside of his right leg. The first time he went off the road wasn't too bad. But the second time was almost a disaster. He narrowly missed a palm tree. In his best Jack Benny voice, Doc said, "Now cut that out."

Doc thought they would stop at her place first. Later on, much later he hoped, he would drive the car back to Sam's, then walk home or spend the rest of the night in the clubhouse. He checked his pocket. He still had a key. As they passed through the main entrance, she sat so close she was almost on the other side of him. Doc's anticipation was sky high (not to mention anything else).

When the lights of the car turned the corner, they could see two strange figures at Mrs. Goldberg's front door.

"Is that someone trying to break in?" she shrieked.

"I don't think so but let's get a better look," Doc said.

He backed the Cadillac up a little, and then pulled straight ahead. The headlights out lined 'Sexy Sam' and 'Alluring Anita', just sitting there. Doc made sure he pulled into the parking space very straight. He didn't have the door all the way open before Sam said, "Geez, we didn't think you were ever coming back. Move over, I'll drive you home."

On the other side of the car Anita had Mrs. Goldberg engaged in a brief conversation. Mrs. Goldberg's reply to whether or not she had a good time was, "Lovely, just lovely-until now."

Doc was whisked away without as much as a good night kiss. He would never forget this night-so near and yet so far.

All Molly said, as she entered her apartment, was "Poop" or words to that affect. "Why didn't that dumb Doc have his own car?'

THE FLEA MARKET CAPER

The next day everybody was at the shack bright and early, except Doc and Mrs. Goldberg. Doc was missing because he didn't want to see Sam again so soon. Molly was missing because she was just plain tired. It had been an exhilarating but exhausting evening.

Chip rallied the troops by telling them what a terrific job they were doing, to keep up the good work, etc. and etc. Some old wisenheimer asked when they should turn in their suggestions for the use of Floragra in order to win the free dinner at Wishbone Willys?

Chip responded, "Well I guess you could turn them into Miss Ellie right now."

The suggestions came flying in. They found out it was used to cure Poison Ivy and Poison Oak. It relieved jock itch and athlete's foot it was great for diaper rash and cradle cap. It removed dandruff and ringworm. Was there no end to this miraculous ointment?

That night Ellie and Chip raised Doc on the walkie-talkie. "Doc, get your buns over here. You've done enough pouting for one day. If you're that bad off, I'll get you fixed up downtown."

They sent Skeeter over on his motorcycle to pick up Doc. Two beers were waiting for them when they returned.

"What's up?" asked Doc.

"We need to pick a winner in the Floragra contest," answered Ellie.

The four of them reviewed the entries.

"Golly geez, they're all good," said Skeeter.

Ellie started to smirk. "Wait, I've saved the best for last."

She took the folded entry out of her pocket.

The best use of Floragra is for 'puberty pimples', it read. It was signed by the old wisenheimer. Her laugh was contagious.

"He's well over eighty. He wouldn't know a puberty pimple if he had one in the middle of his nose," she said.

Skeeter said he couldn't quite *envision* that. They were soon all doubled over with laughter.

Ellie went on: "Even though we said we wanted proof, anyone with that much imagination shouldn't have to prove it."

The vote was unanimous; Wisenheimer was the winner.

The next day was cloudy again and humid as Chip met the UPS driver at the door. 'The Marvelous Marilyn' had a massive mailing. The note enclosed in the package read:

You might moisten the missive by intermittently moving your mangled mouth mainly on the manila message. (Translation: Lick the label on the back)

Signed: Much maligned Marilyn

Chip opened the package. The labels were beautiful. She did a great job. And the price was right. The only problem was that there wasn't any glue on the back of them. He thought about sending Skeeter over to the shack to get a couple of jars of paste that was still stacked in the corner but then realized all the newly filled jars of Floragra were over there already. Chip and Ellie rounded up a small crew to go to the shack for pasting duty. Miss Ellie brought along a thermos of water and some old dish clothes. She figured pasting labels on little jars could get kind of messy. Where would Chip be without her? They got the generator started in order to have power for the lights. Chip unplugged the cement mixer and the assembly line. As they opened the first of the jars of grade school type paste, they were amazed to find it was still pliable. It had been sealed up tightly for over fifty years.

'Sly Ely' and 'Audacious Audrey' were along on this assignment and it was Ely who devised the system they were to use. Place the label, upside down, on one of Doc's workbenches. The second person, Audrey, would take the top, with the brush sticking through it, and apply the paste to the label. The third party, probably Bert, would affix the label on the jar. Gert would then wipe off any excess and pass the jar to Lucille or Camille who would place it back in the box. However, as the first one was done, and before it was put into the box, Lucille held it up for all to examine. It was the most beautiful sight any of them had ever seen.

"Hip, hip, hooray." Then, someone yelled, *"Touchdown."* They felt they had scored a success.

The labeling operation went well, just as Ely thought it would. The three hundred jars were pasted, labeled, cleaned and boxed in nothing flat. It went a lot faster than the manufacturing and bottling operation. At this point, it seems to Chip that the only thing left to do was to set up the distribution channels. He would have to have a session with the snowbirds from the various states to see who was interested. No sooner had he thought of the distribution aspect, than an interesting thing happened. Lucille, dressed in her moo-moo or maw-maw, or whatever it was, and Camille, her long legs jutting out of short shorts, came knocking at Chip (the Dale's) door. Miss Ellie invited them in, asked what they would like to drink, and then announced that Chip was out on the veranda. Chip stood up to welcome the two ladies in.

"What brings you girls by?" He called all the ladies "girls".

It made them feel good.

Loquacious Lucille opened first.

"We want to rent a space in the flea market to sell Floragra and we want the thirty per cent off and we want to start tomorrow and we need twenty four jars right away," she said without taking a breath.

"Whoa slow down Lucille or you'll lose a wheel," piped Chip. "And what do you have to say about all this?" he inquired of Camille.

She answered meekly, "Nothing', she said it all."

Chip made the deal with Lucille and Camille. They all agreed the selling price should be $59.95, that the girls would buy it from FASA (the Florida Agricultural Senior Association) less the 30% and that any discounting at retail would come out of their own pocket. However, Chip was quick to point out; they had to sign a limited franchise since they were not authorized statewide.

"Okee dokee," he replied.

They left in a hurry, saying they had to get to the flea market office to secure a booth. They would be back for the stuff later. They were closing the door on the car when Skeeter pulled up.

"Where ya' goin'?" he drawled.

"To the flea market, want to go along?" asked Camille.

"Sure, I like to look at fleas," he said giggling. "But you gotta' wait till I drop my doggie off at Chips."

The trio found the manager right away. Negotiations went quickly. They were assigned booth number 111. Maybe that was a lucky number. The fee wasn't *too bad*; they later informed Chip and Ellie. There wasn't anything in the booth except an old glass front display that was too heavy for the previous renter to move. They stood there discussing what they would need, some kind of table and chairs, a receipt book or at least a cash register that prints receipts. If not a cash register, then a change box would do; and signs, lots of bright colorful signs. Skeeter chimed in that there was a card table and chairs at the dump and he could make some signs. Booth 111 was around the corner from the fast food restaurants and not too far from the main entrance. *Very convenient* thought Skeeter. The girls headed back to Chip's place to report on their booth and to pick up their supply of Floragra, Skeeter, and also to pick up little Belle Taco.

Skeeter stopped at 'Tee Shot Tom's' before heading for the dump. Skeeter asked Tom if he remembered where the card table and chairs were in the dump.

"I sure do," replied Tom. "Why? Do you need them?"

"I don't but Lucille and Camille need 'em for the flea market," said Skeeter.

He went on to explain about the Floragra booth.

"Gotcha' pal. Let's go look for them," said Tom.

The dump wasn't busy right then. Nobody was loading or unloading anything. Skeeter thought it was kind of neat the way the big trash trucks had to unload at the far end while the general public could throw their junk at this end. Skeeter liked to scavenge. Tee Shot got out of the motorcycle and made a beeline straight to the table and chairs. They really weren't too bad, either. A little skuzzy but a good cleaning with a strong detergent and Lysol would have them looking good in no time. Tom yelled back to Skeeter that he could only find three chairs.

Skeeter yelled back, "That's OK, they only need two."

Tom brought all three back to the bike.

"How we going to do this?" he questioned.

"No problem-o'," says Skeet. "If we got that there generator in here, we can get these things in."

He piled the three chairs on the seat of the sidecar and put little Belle Taco on the floor. Then he climbed in, sat on the now elevated chairs, turned to Tom and said:

"Hand me that table with the legs folded up and you can drive."

Tom was flabbergasted.

"Okee dokee," he replied

What a sight to see. Here were two idiots driving down the street in a sparkling, candy apple red motorcycle, with one guy holding up a card table like it was the main sail on pirate ship! The wind did jerk the table a couple of times.

Skeeter had to yell: "Slow her down, mate."

They made it all right. Lucille was pleased as punch. She helped them carry the stuff into her place.

"Put it in the bathroom," she directed.

As they left Lucille to cleaning the pieces up in her bathtub, they said they would check on some signs.

"Thanks a great deal," said Lucille.

Tee Shot recalled that it was 'Millie the Mermaid' and 'Audacious Audrey' that concocted the original Floragra logo. They went to see the girls.

"Well, yes, we have the originals," said Audrey. "What do you need them for?"

Skeeter told them the whole story.

"And that's why we need the signs," he explained.

Audrey said she didn't think their little sign would be big enough for the flea market. "*It wouldn't attract enough attention*". She suggested they go see that fine fellow, Carmello.

"He's asked to help out several times and he's a pretty good artist," said Marilyn.

"Thanks ladies, we knew you would steer us in the right direction," said Skeeter.

They found Carmello, on the porch, eating Jell-O. He gave them his best Jack Benny imitation of *"Jell-O, again?"* (Jack used to start his radio and TV shows with that line.)

Carmello invited them in. He said 'Lean Jean the Legal Machine' was at work. So he was just biding his time. They explained the whole story one more time. He said he would be delighted to help out. He could handle it. All he needed was some paint and a canvas. Well not a real canvas but something big enough to hang in the back of the display booth. He remembered he had done something like this once before using an old table oilcloth. Not a tablecloth with designs all over it but a real genuine, old-fashioned oilcloth.

"Hey, I know about those, Wal-Marts got em and they're rolling back their prices," said Skeeter. "Yippee eye yo."

Then he giggled.

Carmello said he would check it out and maybe he could get the paint and some brushes at the same time. He was already getting in the car when they left. Sure enough, Wal-Mart had everything he needed. He was back in half an hour. He spread the oilcloth out over the terrazzo tiles of the veranda. He had just started to outline the zigzag saw tooth shape of the miraculous hedges when 'Lean Jean' entered.

"What the hell are you doing," she commanded." I'll sue you for breach of cleanliness or something."

He got up off his knees, gave her a smooch on the cheek.

"Don't be mean, Jean, when I get through, I'll surely clean," he said.

They both laughed together as he re-told the story.

He had the painting done in a flash. (This stuff was a piece of cake.) He bought quick drying paint but just to hasten the drying time he turned the overhead fan on low speed. After a quick dinner they took the canvas over to Lucille's. As he slowly unrolled it, Lucille's eyes kept getting bigger and her mouth dropped wider.

"I can't believe it!" she shouted. She was as excited as anyone had ever seen her.

She called Camille on the cell phone.

"Get over here quick. You must' see this!" she practically screamed into the phone.

Then she called Chip and Ellie and repeated the same thing.

They all converged on Lucille at the same time. She wasn't used to all this commotion. She began to sweat and felt faint. 'Tee Shot Tom' and Skeeter came in, adding to the turmoil, each carrying a beer. Tee Shot took one look at Lucille. He stuck out his beer.

"Here, have a good swig," Tom offered.

"I couldn't do that," Lucille protested.

"Yeah, I know but you need it, so drink it," commanded Tom.

For a change, she did as she was told. She took a healthy gulp. Within minutes she had calmed down.

"Thanks Tom. That wasn't too bad," she said.

Camille was checking over the giant size banner. *"Wow!"* she kept saying over and over.*" Wow!"*

Skeeter came up with another of his unusual ideas.

"If we only had a blimp like that Goodyear one, we could really light it up, "he suggested.

"That's another great idea, Skeet. But we don't have one," replied Chip.

Camille jumped up excitedly.

"That gives me an idea!" She exclaimed. "Don't go away."

She made a quick exit out the door. Five minutes later she was back with a string of Xmas tree lights.

"Why couldn't we string these around the outside of the banner? They blink on and off to attract attention," she proposed.

Everyone agreed it was a great idea and worth a try.

Because they were now official exhibitors or vendors, they didn't have to cruise the parking lot looking for a parking spot. They backed up to the door at the rear of the building. 'Tee Shot Tom' and Skeeter helped them with the table, the chairs, the banner for the back wall, a change box (also from the dump) the scotch tape, the masking tape, an extension cord and a couple of lined spiral tablets. The box of 24 jars of Floragra was positioned in the display case. They would keep one out for demo purposes. The banner went up on the back wall. The lights were taped around the outside of it. They started blinking as soon as the extension was plugged in. They were ready. They were searching for youth.

They had the "Hunger to Look Younger." (They wanted the money, honey.) Neither one of the ladies had ever done anything like this before.

The first hour went by without a single person stopping. They were disappointed. Apparently they thought people would line up to buy it. They weren't thinking that this was a brand new product that no one had ever heard of it before.

A few of the vendors, in their immediate area stopped by to welcome them to the club: *"Why do you two want to get into this flea market thing? It ain't easy, you know. By the time the day is over, your bunions will have bunions."*

The girls didn't want to hear it.

A guy from a booth that displayed belts and wallets came over to see what they were selling. They started to explain all of the things that Floragra could be used for when he interrupted Camille.

"Ya know what?" he said, "My Grandad used to sell snake bite oil out of a covered wagon out West and nobody believed him either."

Something was wrong here. They took separate lunch breaks in the fast food area. Camille came back with some magic marker pens and brilliant neon poster board. She set them on top of the display to make a couple of signs. She was just making the first stroke when Carmello walked up. She explained to him what she was doing.

"I'll do that for you," he offered. "I'm good at lettering."

Camille told him what she wanted on the signs. He worked while he talked.

"I came by to see how the big banner worked out," he said.

"Fantastic, doesn't it look great? But we haven't sold anything yet," she whined.

"Like anything worth while in life, it takes time," said Carmello.

"Sad but true," she replied.

The signs were done. The one on the neon Hot Pink read: *"Soothes as it smoothes."* The lemon lime one spelled out: *"It soothes as you snooze."* She taped them to the front glass of the display case.

"I hope that helps," she sighed.

The afternoon dragged on. It didn't do any better than the morning session. They reported their sad results to Chip and Ellie. Lucille went home to soak her feet. Chip and Ellie discussed the problem during TV commercial breaks. Ellie said she knew there wasn't anything wrong with the Floragra. And the booth at the flea market seemed to be in a good location. The signs were certainly bright. She couldn't figure out what the problem was. Chip said he thought he knew the answer. He got up to make a phone call. The next morning Lucille and Camille were at their post-ready to try it again. 'Tee Shot Tom' and Skeeter lurked nearby. Ellie and Chip sat in the food galley drinking Cappuccinos.

The crowds were starting to build. The average vendor could expect a good day, but not the girls. No one even stopped to look. All of a sudden there was a commotion at the front entrance. There was a strange figure heading toward the booth. Who else could it be but Mrs. 'Molly' Goldberg! The group that followed after her was like the paparazzi after Madonna. The Floragra group could not believe their eyes, especially Lucille. Here was Mrs. Goldberg in living color, stopping in front of the booth.

"Hi girls!" she gleefully shouted out. "I brought you some customers."

Lucille and Camille quickly went into their pitch about all the things Floragra could do. They sold three jars, (all at $59.95 too with no discounts.) Of course not everyone bought. They were ecstatic over selling three. The crowd dispersed while Mrs. Goldberg sat in back of the booth catching her second wind. Ellie and Chip sauntered up. Camille told them about Mrs. Goldberg and how they sold three jars. Chip didn't let on that he was the one that put her up to it. Mrs. Goldberg stood up like she was going to conduct a seminar, which in a way, she did. She stood up straight for all to observe. The costume consisted of high heel shoes, shiny black trousers with a satin strip running down the side of each leg, a white pleated shirt, a red bow tie, a red and white striped blazer and a straw hat. She resembled Johnny Carson doing his Fern, using a pointer to indicate the Slawson cut off. The only thing missing was the false mustache. Then she started on the girls.

"You girls don't have any moxie, no savvy, and no chutzpah! You can't sit here and wait for people to come to you. You got to create excitement. Be enthusiastic and be energetic. Watch this," instructed Mrs. Goldberg.

She had fashioned a megaphone out of a large soft drink container and had the pointer ready.

"All right folks. Step right up. See and try the most sensational product ever created in your lifetime," she announced. "Do you have a thirst to look more youthful? Step right up for a demonstration and a free brochure. Do you have *the hunger to look younger*? Look no further. (She kept banging the pointer on the counter) I'ts right here, right now, how about you Mr. Baldy? Would you like a full head of hair? Like the TV commercials say, I guarantee it, ya' must buy it in order to try it. If you're not satisfied within 3 days, return it for a full refund. How about that? You can't beat it with a stick (Slap on the counter) okay, who's next? Look at these pictures folks. That's me using the walker. Look at me now.

I'm living proof. What more proof do you need? Step right up to step back in time."

Her throat was getting parched. She needed a drink. She looked for Chip to get her out of there. Lucille and Camille sold 10 more jars before the afternoon was over. Chip took the girls aside.

"You understand that Mrs. Goldberg did that as a favor?" he said. "We can't ask her to do it when there's nothing in it for her except the excitement of being center stage. I'm sure that within three days you will get referrals off of today's sales and in three days from then you will get more sales and so on and so on."

THE DEPILATORY

Doc didn't want anything to do with the flea market fiasco. He had more important things to do. He made a few phone calls to some of his old buddies inquiring about depilatories. They weren't any smarter than he was. (Not that Doc wasn't smart. He was smart enough, he just wasn't very knowledgeable.) He spent several hours in his "lab" at the shack going over his beat up old chemistry books. During a smoke break, he went outside to lean up against the back of the shack. He wouldn't allow any smoking inside. As he sat there, looking up at the cotton candy clouds, his mind wondered back to Mrs. Goldberg Goldberg and their night on the town. He very vaguely recalled that Mrs. Goldberg looked a little fuzzy in the chest area. *"Damn that Sam"* he cursed to himself, *"If he hadn't shown up to get his car, I might have found out if she was fuzzy anywhere else."* He was thinking of how her hips and thighs had been reduced and firmed up by using Floragra. It just stands to reason it will grow hair in other places, he thought. He had to make it into a depilatory.

Chip happened to stop by on a routine check. He filled Doc in on the flea market adventure. Doc immediately said he hoped the girls got names and addresses of the thirteen purchases for future reference. Doc explained that he was a little concerned about the stuff growing hair. Chip asked what Doc found out about hair removal.

"Without getting into the chemical lingo, like $H2O$, PDQ and XYZ, as far as I could tell we aren't far off," he replied. "You know the hedge leaves already contain folic acid. If we change the formula from paraffin wax to bees wax, add a little glycerin, pulverize some oranges for the citric acid that should do it. You wouldn't even need adhesive strips or any of that other junk to pull the hair off. I think I'll mix some up this afternoon. Maybe we can try it on Skeeters dog, Belle Taco."

"If what you say is all true," Chip interjected, "then what we have is 300 jars of stuff that will grow hair. What do we do about that?"

"Can't do nothin'," says Doc. "We sell it as a hair restorer. Think of all the bald headed guys out there. Not everybody wants to look like Telly Sevalles or Michael Jordan. That's also why I said I hoped the girls were keeping names and addresses."

"Oh, cripes," said Chip, "I better get over there to stop them from selling any more. Go ahead and make some new stuff. I'll be back."

Doc called 'Tee Shot Tom' on the walkie-talkie.

"Tom, I need a favor."

"Anything for you, bubba, what is it? he said. (He had been watching re-runs of Nash Bridges-bubba)

Doc told him to get some glycerin, some beeswax, a dozen oranges, a 12 pack of Millers and some Seltzer water and that it was going to be a long afternoon.

It wasn't long before Tee Shot showed up with Skeeter and Belle Taco. They carried the shopping in, put the beer in the cooler and asked Doc what they could do to help. Doc told them he wouldn't need the mixer and the rest of the paraphernalia as he only planned to make a few jars for experimental purposes. He would like them to stick around, however. What he didn't say was that he wanted Belle Taco. Doc had them add a little of this and that. The mixture was complete in an hour.

Doc poured a cup full of seltzer water, set it on the floor, then whistled for Belle Taco. The little dog came running in. He went straight for the seltzer water. He lapped it up like it was Mexican Salsa. Doc then scooped the pup up into his arms before Skeeter had a chance to realize what was happening. He quickly rubbed Skeeter's *chew-wa-wa* with the new mixture and handed him over to Skeeter.

"Whatcha' do that for?" asked Skeet.

Doc told him not to get his nachos in an up-roar and to sit tight for half an hour.

"Okee, dokee," he replied.

Skeeter carried the dog outside to be in the shade behind the shack. Doc and Tom cleaned the place up, and then settled down with Skeeter to drink a cold beer. They were discussing the flea market operation when all of a sudden, Skeeter jumped up.

"Look Doc, look what's happening. My dog is getting hair all over me," exclaimed Skeeter.

"That's great, exactly what we wanted to happen," replied Doc.

Skeeter seemed a little upset. Doc told him to look at the bright side. He wouldn't have to pay for any more clipping. And just think no more fleas either. But Doc thought he needed a second opinion. It worked on a dog, but how about a human? He went to see Mrs. 'Molly' Goldberg. She came to the door wearing a flimsy negligee outfit that was eye catching.

"Good golly Miss Molly, you look fetchingly jolly," gushed Doc. "expecting someone?"

"No, you fool, quit the drool and get in here," she answered.

"What can I do for you?" she asked.

"Well, Molly, I have a request but I don't know how to put it," said Doc.

"Spit it out. You're amongst friends," was her retort

"I thought you'd never ask," he said.

The robe was partly open when she answered the door. The rest came off swiftly but seductively.

"One lump or two?" she teased.

"Are you asking me about sugar in my coffee or what?" replied Doc.

"Don't be silly," she says. "Do you want to see one at a time or would you rather see them both at one heart-attacking time?"

"Shoot yourself. No, I mean suit yourself," his lips quivered.

She turned away from him. The robe dropped to the floor. She turned away from him. She turned slightly, peering over her shoulder. She turned a tiny bit more. Doc hadn't seen a globe like that in years. He kept reminding himself he was there on an experiment. She dropped the strap off the other shoulder. She wasn't wearing a bra. She pivoted, almost in slow motion. There they were, in live, living color! *"Oh, my God,"* he thought. The room was silent except; for Doc's rasping for air. She was still wearing the bottoms of her lounging outfit.

"Would you mind if I take a closer look?" asked Doc.

"Look but don't touch," she teased again as she swayed forward.

"I gotta turn on the light," said Doc.

"I expected something to be turned on but it wasn't a light, what's with you?" Mrs. Goldberg blurted out.

"Do you mind if I examine a little closer?" as he cupped a breast in his hand.

"Be my guest," she said.

He got out his magnifying glass and proceeded to rotate it completely around one breast, through the cleavage to the other orb including the nipple. Mrs. Goldberg could hardly stand it. She teetered first on one foot, then the other. She squirmed. She shuttered.

"Aha!" he exclaimed at last, "just as I thought."

"What the hell's with you?" replied Mrs. Goldberg. "Let's get on with it!"

"You have hair," he explained, "little, tiny, fuzzy hairs."

"So?" she replied.

"So don't you see? You'll be covered with hair where ever you've rubbed the Floragra," explained Doc.

Doc went on to explain the repercussions this could cause from all the jars already sold. He gave her a jar of the depilatory Floragra. He instructed her to apply it right away, wherever she had rubbed the original stuff.

"Would you like to apply it now?' she offered. "The sooner, the better."

Doc declined the invitation saying he had a lot of work to do. Poor Mrs. Goldberg was thwarted again.

THE RECALL

Doc hightailed it over to Chips and Miss Ellie's. He was almost screaming as he pounded on the door. Ellie answered.

"Where's Chip? Is Chip here?" he yelled.

Chip rushed in off the balcony as soon as he heard Doc.

"What's the matter, pal? What happened?" said Chip.

Doc blurted out, "We gotta do a recall! But I don't know how to do a recall, do you know how to do a recall, I don't know how to do a recall."

He sounded like a babbling fool.

"Now just settle down. Cool it. Nothing can be that bad. Tell me what happened," said Chip as he put his arm around Doc's shoulder.

Chip had alerted the ladies at the flea market. They had closed up shop early. Doc settled down long enough to tell them about Mrs. Goldberg's hairy chest and that he had given her a jar of the new Floragra. They hashed over the problem. Ellie, the 'Merry Maid from Michigan', spoke up.

"We have the names of the people that bought the 13 jars at the flea market. But what we don't have are the names of the people that bought the 24 jars that the Lovely Lois took to Florhio," noted Ellie.

"Geez, I never thought of that," said Doc.

"Not to worry," said Chip as he called Lois on the phone.

"Lois, I hope you're not busy, can you drop by for a minute?" asked Chip.

"Sure," she said. "Put the coffee on."

Before the coffee was brewed, she was at the door.

"Hi ho, everybody," Lois said cheerfully.

Chip explained to her what they had discovered so far and that Doc thought they needed a recall. 'Level headed Lois' came through again. She suggested that first they should figure out how to handle a recall. Then after that, she would call her twin sister.

Ellie spoke up: "I didn't know you had a twin sister. What's her name? Where does she live? Tell us about her, Lois."

Lois said there wasn't much to tell. They weren't identical. They only saw each other once or twice a year. She lives in Twinsberg, Ohio.

"While I'm known as short, stout and stubby Lois, she is known as long, lean and lanky Lynn. It was my Fathers idea to name us Lynn and Lois," she explained.

She went on.

"Did I ever tell you the story about Aunt Mabel and the twins? When my Mother announced to the family that she was having twins, Aunt Mabel asked what names they had picked out. Mom said she didn't know. One grandmother was Alice and the other was Dawn. "That's it," Aunt Mabel had said, "name one of them Alice Dawn and the other Mabel Twilight!" My whole family had a good laugh over that one," recalled Lois.

Lois called Lynn in Twinsberg to see if she kept the names and addresses of the 24 buyers. Yes, she had, and she was about to E Mail Lois for 24 more. Lois told her about the hair growing problem and that she would get back to her soon. *"See ya' twinny,"* she signed off.

Chip called an impromptu meeting of as many directors as he could locate. He explained the problem. He told them the mistake hadn't cost anything yet. There weren't any lawsuits, yet. But they better get a handle on it, post haste. He asked Lois to continue the meeting. She explained that since she had the most outstanding jars, she had the most to lose.

"And you know how I hate to lose at anything," she said.

She went on to say that they could have 'Beauteous Bev', the corresponding secretary, draft a recall letter, approved by Jean, of course. They would offer the buyers three options; 1. Return the unused portion for full refund; 2. Purchase a jar of the new; or 3.

"If they chose number 3," she said, "the customer would have one jar to grow hair perhaps for their husband and one jar that removes hair, perhaps for the Mrs. We want them to be totally satisfied whatever they decide. Does anyone object?"

'Old Wisenheimer' yelled out, "Will it cost me any more money?"

"Not a cent," replied Lois, who then added. "So you shouldn't wait. Do it."

The impromptu vote was unanimous. 'Beauteous Bev' rushed home to compose the letter.

F. A. S. A.

World Headquarters
Coral Creek, FL.

Dear Floragra User,
   The F.A.S.A. Company is committed to becoming the worlds' leader in facial and body cosmetics. In support of this commitment, we wish to advise you that your purchase of the original Floragra may not perform exactly as you expect. We hasten to advise the product will do everything we said it would. However, you may notice an increase in hair follicles.
   If your intent was to grow hair, please continue using our product.
   If you wish to derive many of its original benefits but also wish to remove hair we are offering you the following three options:

1. Return the unused portion for full refund.

2. Return the jar for exchange.

3. Purchase a jar of the new improved Floragra at half price.

   You may contact your sales' consultant, call us on the 800 number listed below or reach us at www.FLORAGRA. Com.

Sincerely,

CHIP N. DALE
F.A.S.A.

Doc settled down and was practically back to his old self now that Chip assured him that everything seemed to be under control. He recruited half a dozen helpers and headed for the shack. By noon they had about 50 jars that had been sold. Doc felt much better. In fact he offered to buy lunch if Skeeter would run over to the local Pizza Dome on his motorcycle. Skeet left little Belle Taco to play with his adopted family.

Meanwhile Chip and Miss Ellie cleared the contents of the recall letter with 'Lean Jean'. After getting her 'O. K.' they took it to the nearest *Kinko*'s to have copies made. The envelopes had been preaddressed and stamped by 'Beauteous Bev'. They were deposited in time for the 12 PM pick up at the post office. After a quick stop for a sub sandwich, they headed for the shack.

Lo and behold, the entire crew was there.

What a great group. They said they all were aware of what happened to Mrs. Goldberg and knew about Doc's new and improved Floragra. To a person, they wanted to do whatever was necessary to help this thing get straightened out a very close group of neighbors indeed. Chip was unsuspectingly checking each one over as he talked to them. He was looking for unusual hair growth. There wasn't any that he could notice. He whispered his findings to Miss Ellie. She concluded that no one else had used as much as Mrs. Goldberg. That accounted for the amazing results Mrs. Goldberg had that no one else even came close to but also why she was the only one to experience the hair problem.

"Miss Ellie, you're amazing yourself," Chip said.

"Aw shucks," replied Ellie.

They entered the shack to see how things were going. It was business as usual. The place was humming. Doc was in charge and lovin' every minute of it. The mixer was chuggin', the generator snorted occasionally but all in all everything was copasetic. Outside, behind the shack, Bert, Gert, 'Sly Ely' and 'Audacious Audrey' were setting up a croquet set. Bert had found two old mallets, which he repaired, then fashioned two more out of broomstick handles and 2X4's. He made the wickets out of old clothes hangars. They enlisted Carmello and Camille to also play. Bert tossed a coin to see who got the real mallets and who got the home made ones. Sexy Sam, he of the Italian lineage, brought his Bocce Balls. There was a rousing game going on over there. (Who needed to go to a fancy spa or join a sports club, they had everything thing they needed right here.)

The day's production was much greater than they expected. They now had a good supply on hand. Lois received the Email from her twin sister Lynn. (Believe it or not, not a single person wanted to return their purchase.) In fact she needed twelve more to fulfill the half off offer. And she would like an extra twelve to have on hand. Of the thirteen jars that Lucille and Camille sold at the flea market, ten of the customers took advantages of the half off offer. The F.A.S.A. (Florida Agricultural Senior Association) organization was up to date. The euphoria returned.

It had been approximately two days since Doc gave Molly Goldberg the new Floragra to remove the excess hair. Chip and Ellie decided to stop to see how she was doing. She invited them in enthusiastically. She was wearing her new spandex sports outfit, the purple one. Chip inquired how she was doing with the removal process. He wondered if she had any remorse about using Floragra

"Are you kidding?" she cried out. "Look at me. Can you believe it? Only two weeks ago I was using a walker and looked like an old hag. And now that Doc brought the new stuff over for me to use, everything tightened up that much more. I think I look fabulous and I feel great. When are we opening the flea market booth again?"

Ellie told her the girls were going to open again tomorrow, now that we have an ample supply on hand.

"That's great," she said. "I'll be there."

On the walk home, Chip asked Ellie if she knew what Mrs. Goldberg had in mind.

"Who knows? In Mrs. Goldberg's current frame of mind, nothing would surprise me."

THE COMMERCIAL

The next day was another knock out day in south Florida. The group had heard rumors that the flea market was going to film a commercial. Surely the Floragra booth would be in it because it was so close to the front door. And its proximity to the food court wouldn't hurt. The condo camp was abuzz with excitement. The whole gang planned to be there. Chip had to remind them, that Lucille and Camille ran the booth. The rest could hang out but don't interfere and don't get in the way.

Lucille put on her finest Sunday church finery. Camille looked stunning in one of those 'silky type' ankle length dresses with the Japanese floral designs. Neither one looked like a hawker in a flea market. Some of the other ladies were in their best bib and tucker. Each one was privately hoping they might appear in the commercial. The small cortege was standing at the door before the mall opened.

"I wish they would hurry, I gotta go!" 'Alluring Anita' said.

'Sexy Sam' told her to '*cross everything she had*'.

The door finally opened. The girls in the booth were ready. The signs were up. The lights were blinking. The crowd was huge. There was hustle and bustle, all over the place. A few of the older ones wandered over to the food area. It was pretty early for most of them. They hadn't even had their coffee. (Or prune juice either. Thank God.) An hour went by. Soon, two hours went by. No TV truck, no camera crew anywhere in sight. The booth hadn't sold a single jar yet. Old Wisenheimer said a couple of them should pretend to be customers and buy a jar. *"Nothing creates excitement like a busy counter."* He said he recalled the old medicine men had "shills" in the audience while they hawked their amazing elixirs.

They had just about given up on the TV thing when the loudest commotion any of them had ever heard was coming from the front entrance. The TV crew was shoving people out of the way; cables were being strewn all over the place, powerful bright lights were sweeping over the entire area. A TV cameraman was walking backwards. He was filming something in front of him. Ellie thought, *No, it can't be!*

Chip said, "Oh, yes it is, in living color."

Between the bright lights and the TV crew, the crowd couldn't see much at all. The rumors were flying. There were undercurrents whispered throughout the crowd. *"Was Marilyn Monroe reincarnated? Elvis was still alive? What was happening in front of the camera? Maybe it was Ricky Martin or Brittany Spears coming in.* The cameraman and crew kept backing up. As they did, the crowd separated further apart. There, savoring all her fifteen minutes of fame was ... Molly Goldberg!

There aren't enough adjectives to describe this woman. She's over 80-she's stunning. She's beyond reasonable life expectancy. She's vivacious. She's like nothing else in the world, in her age group. She was wearing a costume that consisted of the spike high heels, black mesh panty hose, a tight body hugging outfit that cut medium high at the hips, narrowing to the crotch without revealing anything. The low cut bodice revealed deep cleavage accentuated by the stiff under wire bra. (The camera guy handed her a piece of mesh to cover at least a little) The skinny top hat completed the ensemble. Someone said she looked like Judy Garland doing a routine in *"Give My Regards To Broadway."* Someone else thought she was a cross between Mae West and Angie Dickinson. No matter what they said she looked like, she was a knock out. The cameraman backed up past the Floragra stand. But Mrs. Goldberg stopped.

"Hi Ho, everybody," she beamed.

A guy with a microphone rushed up to her.

"Who are you and what is your connection to this booth?" he inquired.

(Talk about your Chutzpah, Mrs. Goldberg laid it on.) She told him about her walker, how she never left her apartment, that she was so wrinkled a steamroller couldn't have smoothed her out. She went on extolling the virtues of Floragra, how it changed her life and: "You couldn't beat it for only $59.95."

Doc jumped up on the counter, "Let's hear it for Mrs. Goldberg."

"Hip, hip, hooray, we want Mrs. Goldberg!" came the cheer. Then some old Wisenheimer yelled out, *"Mrs. Goldberg for homecoming queen!"* The FASA group couldn't have bought any better airtime. And no one could duplicate it for a commercial.

But a strange thing happened after that. The TV crew shot the rest of the commercial all right. But Mrs. Goldberg wasn't in it. Instead she appeared in a full five minute, segment on network news.

The phones started to ring. Mrs. Goldberg finally pulled her phone cord out of the wall. Chip and Ellie fielded as many calls as they could handle. Exhausted at the end of the first day of this mayhem, Chip and Ellie walked down to Mrs. Goldberg's. She was a jangle of nerves.

"Where is Doc when I need him?" she asked.

"What do you need him for?" Chip inquired.

"Well, he told me never to tell anyone, but he put a drop of some stuff in my drink one night that made me feel great," she said, "and I need some now."

Chip told her he would get some for her before the night was over. In the meantime they better discuss what was happening.

"I think you need a manager or at least an agent. Nobody expected this to happen," Chip said.

Mrs. Goldberg was perplexed: "What can I do? Can't Doc be my manager?"

They told her that since her appearance on TV, the Floragra orders were flying in. They were just about to run out of their supply and Doc was the only one with the formula. He sure couldn't handle both jobs. She started to sob a little.

"I wanted to be noticed but I didn't think it would be like this," she cried.

Just then there was a knock on the door. Whoever it was didn't wait for an invitation. The doorknob turned and in walked Doc. He looked at Mrs. Goldberg.

"Can I have your autograph?" he said playfully.

She perked up when she saw Doc.

"I'll trade you my autograph for a drop of your stuff," she offered.

"Somehow, I knew you would be in need of a little picker upper," Doc said.

He stuck his hand in a pocket and extracted a small vial. He warned her that one-drop would carry her for twenty-four hours. If he found out she was using any more than that he would take it away from her and never give her anymore.

"Aw, Doc, you always seem to know what's good for me," she said. "Why can't you be my manager?"

"I don't know, why not?" he replied.

Chip spoke up: "Because we need you to run the Floragra operation. You're the only one that knows the formula."

"Chip, my boy, I'm surprised at you. The miracle hedges are the only formula you need. I wrote everything else down. 'Tee Shot Tom' knows it and even Skeeter can make it," retorted Doc.

"It would seem our problems are solved once again," said Chip.

"Not all of them," replied Doc.

Doc went on.

THE BARBER SHOP

"I've given this Molly thing a lot of thought. She needs me and I need her. We also need an office that is more presentable than the shack and we need a telephone operator so these phones don't drive everyone nuts and I'm thinking, that crazy barber might rent us the back of his shop," Doc said. "I think I can convince him that it would attract some new business for him, too."

"That sounds like a plan," replied Chip. "Check him out tomorrow. I'll see what I can do about a phone operator."

The next morning Chip checked in with The 'The Lovely Lois'.

"What do you know about switchboard operators?" he asked.

"Not much. My sister Lynn used to be one but she's in Ohio. Why do you want to know?" replied Lois.

Chip explained the situation to her.

"What about Lucille, she ran a big PBX when she was younger," said Lois.

"I didn't know that," said Chip. "But what about the flea market store?"

"We'll pay her off on what she has coming and get someone else to work with Camille," Lois said. "As a matter of fact, she told me yesterday that her feet were killing her."

Chip said he would check it out. On the way home he stopped to see Carmello who said yes, he would like a piece of the action and he wouldn't have any trouble working with Camille.

Chip, next contacted Lucille.

"I hear you're having trouble with your feet", he said.

"Oh my God, yes! My feet are killing me," she cried.

Then he asked her if she remembered her switchboard days. She said certainly she did. That was like riding a bike, once you learn you never forget. Chip proposed the switch from the flea market to the switchboard. Carmello, or the company would pay her off, and pay her $5.15 an hour for her phone work. Before she could say no, he sweetened the pot with free Floragra for life or as long as the hedges held out whichever occurred first. She accepted the offer.

Doc made the deal with the barber. He agreed that they could set up two desks in the rear of the shop. They could use the beautician's old spot and the hair washing area. He didn't need that anymore. The nail filing table wasn't used either. And they could even use the last barber chair toward the rear. Doc told him they would probably have at least one secretary answering phones. He was sure she would insist that the floor be swept after every haircut. They were in agreement. Bell South was called to set up the phone system the same afternoon.

Mrs. Goldberg had her phone plugged back in. It never stopped ringing. The mayor of Coral Creek called to find out *"what the hell was happening"*. The airport called. They had some high level TV network people coming in to interview a Molly Goldberg of the FASA Company. They kept asking if the party wasn't sure they wanted NASA instead of FASA. Tom Brokaw called. Peter Jennings called. Sam Donaldson called. Barbara Walters left a message that she would call back. Leno and Letterman had people on the line. Oprah and Rosie were in a dead heat for an interview. Even Howard Stern wanted Mrs. Goldberg to show her boobs on his raunchy show.

Doc had taken command. He told Mrs. Goldberg they should listen to all offers. He felt they should get X number of dollars if she did a solo interview and twice as much if he was included since he was the primary principle in the development of Floragra. He made arrangements with the local super market to use their Fax machine. He explained to them that with this much exposure they might get some free advertising out of it.

'Tee Shot Tom' and Skeeter picked up a couple of old desk in a garage sale. They kind of squeezed them in an L shape around the barber chair in the back. Two phones, consisting of eight lines, were on the old filing table. Message pads were in place. Dominic, the old singing barber, told them they could use the mirror back there as a message center. Doc brought Lucille over early so she could get oriented. Everyone thought she might be a bit upset by the working conditions. She shocked them all by saying it needed a little work and a good cleaning but otherwise it wasn't too bad. Doc introduced Lucille to Dominic.

"Are you Italian?" said Lucille.

"Yeah Dominic, Mona celli," he replied. "Whatcha' think, I was, Irish?"

"You got an accent," she noted. "Where' ya' from?"

"East Coast, mostly New Yawk," he said.

"I would have never have guessed," she said.

"Me too," she said, "Ain't it a small world?"

The phones starting ringing a little after nine o'clock ... most people were polite in waiting that long. Lucille answered in her best Lilly Tomlin voice.

"Good morning," she sang out. "This is the Florida Agricultural Senior Association. How may I help you? I'm sorry, she isn't here, and may I take a message?"

With eight lines flashing all at one time, the answers soon became: *"Florida Agricultural, she isn't here but I'll take the message."* By noon, Lucille was answering: *"This is FASA, whad'ya' want?"*

She hadn't had a break all morning.

Dominic, who hadn't had a customer, yet asked if she would like some coffee and donut?

"That sounds great," she replied, "but first I gotta' go. Where's the bathroom?"

She asked Dominic if he would catch the phones for a minute.

"*Sho' ur*" he says. "No problem."

As she returned from the rest room, she heard him say: "Dominic, da singin' barbuh' heah."

It reminded her of home. Ten minutes later Dominic was back with coffee and donuts. She put all the lines on hold while they enjoyed their Dip-pin Do-balls and fresh coffee.

"Thank you, Dom. Do you mind if I call you Dom?" Lucille said.

"Nah, I been called worse," he replied.

They were getting along just great.

A local TV station found out about the barbershop. They sent a camera crew out to interview 'Molly'. Of course, Mrs. Molly Goldberg wasn't there. Lucille didn't let on right away. The camera guy shot footage of the front of the shop, then went inside for close ups of Dominic and Lucille. Apparently the young man thought Lucille was Molly. She didn't tell him any differently. The cutesy little interviewer arrived a little later. She interrogated Lucille long enough to find out who she really was.

"Come on guys, there's no interview here," she said.

As they were leaving, Dominic said, "If I had known you were coming, I would have had the quartet here." (Did you get that, as in, Barbershop quartet?)

SHOPPING

Molly asked Miss Ellie to take her shopping for some new clothes for her television appearance. They no sooner entered Molly's, than two or three sales people came over for her autograph. They recognized her from the TV show. By the time they got to the ladies department, the store manager himself was waiting to greet her.

"We are delighted to have you as a customer," he gushed. "We will accommodate you in the best way possible."

He sheepishly looked around for a camera crew but didn't see any. A well-dressed, matronly looking lady stepped forward.

"How may we serve you?" she asked.

Mrs. Molly Goldberg said she needed a couple of dresses, some *unmentionables*, pantyhose and new shoes. The matronly department head (no common clerks for this lady) snapped her fingers like the headwaiter at a high-class restaurant. Clerks from every department were falling all over themselves. Several young clerks brought out dress after dress. The department head for ladies shoes showed up. She thought they would be better off until a dress was selected.

Molly tried on half a dozen. She came out of the fitting room with each one to get Ellie's opinion. She said she wanted to look nice, but not too glitzy. A crowd was building up in the department. Every time she came out of the dressing room, the applause was a little louder. Molly reveled in the adulation. She selected a peach color, ankle length, and shimmering one; similar to the type younger Camille wore. The softly entwined, vertical lines of vines and flower, accentuated her newfound figure.

Molly told Ellie she thought Doc would like the peach colored underwear because it was almost flesh toned. She giggled when she thought about it. The shoe department lady found a perfect match in satin finished pumps. The outfit was complete.

"Could you please deliver it to such and such address?" she asked.

The store manager said it would be their pleasure, even if he had to deliver it himself.

As they got into Chip's beat up old Volkswagen Beatle, Molly sighed, "Geez, it's good to get back to normal."

She told Ellie she wasn't sure one outfit would be enough and asked if she would Ellie mind stopping at Burdines?

"At your service, madam," Ellie teased.

The scenario at Burdines was almost a duplicate of Macy's except the store manager wasn't around. She picked out a deep blue number (they called it Honolulu blue) adorned with a few silver sequins randomly running down the center. The matching blue shoes were a nice compliment. She looked sensational. (And yes, they would be happy to deliver it.)

When they got back to the complex, Doc was pouring over his notes. Goldie told him they had had a very successful shopping spree.

"That's nice," he said. "Now listen to this. I have you booked you for the Regis and Cathy Lee show on Monday, then on Thursday; we fly out west to do The Donny and Marie Show."

She said that was great but appeared a little disappointed.

"What's the matter, honey? I tried to get you on the most wholesome shows. None of that sleazy stuff where they want you to show everything," said Doc.

"Well what happened to 20/20?" she said.

"You want 20/20, we'll get 20/20. They said they would call back," she recanted.

Ellie detoured to the barbershop. She couldn't believe it. She found Lucille sitting in the unused barber chair eating pizza that Dominic had run out to get. All eight lines were on hold. Ellie noticed a plethora of messages Scotch taped to the mirror.

Lucille introduced her to Dominic: "He's been a big help," she said "Can you believe he's Italian and is from New York?"

"I would never believe it until you told me," replied Lucille.

Ellie headed for home, satisfied that everything was working out better than anybody could hope for. She found Chip sitting on the veranda, having a Pena Colada and sucking on yet another cigarette.

"Honey, you gotta' quit that," she sighed.

"Why, it's my first drink of the day," said Chip.

She thought to herself, *"He just doesn't get it."* She didn't want to nag but really wished he would quit the cigarettes.

She reported on the shopping trip and her visit to the barbershop. She asked how his day had gone. He told her the troops were making as much Floragra as they could. He told her that now the word was out, the other residents in the complex wanted to be included. 'Lean Jean' was going to be busy sorting out all the legalities. So far the secret of the miracle hedges was still a secret. He was going to talk to Bert and Gert to double their alertness. They were going to have to be extremely discreet in picking the leaves. He said he had been to the flea market. Carmello and Carmille were so busy they hardly got a break. Skeeter had to make some quick trips back to the shack to replenish their supply. Business was booming.

"Lets just pray that nothing happens to the miracle hedges," she added.

"Oh, yeah," Miss Ellie spoke up, "You better have Doc check the message center at the barbershop. There's hardly room enough to stick any more up there."

Chip kept trying to reach Doc on the walkie-talkie. But every time he did, Bert would answer. *"FASA. World headquarters, Bertrand speaking."* Chip, had to remind him, that he wasn't a telephone operator, that he was head of security and better start acting like it. He asked if Bert had seen Doc.

"Nope, not since I came on duty at 7:00 AM," he replied.

Chip told him he better start acting like he was on duty and quit answering like a switchboard operator. *"Okee, dokee-10-4, good buddy."* Chip was on his way down to Molly's when he met Doc on the sidewalk out in front.

"Where ya' been," he asked.

"I've been checkin' airlines and hotels to see where we get the best deals," Doc answered.

Chip told him it was a waste of time. He wouldn't have to worry about it, as the TV networks would make all the arrangements.

"Oh, really," Doc seemed surprised, "that'll save a lot of money."

"What did ya' want me for?" questioned Doc.

Chip said he better check the message center at the barbershop, that Ellie told him it was full. Doc said he had been so busy, he forgot about it.

"Wanna' go with me? We'll have a beer at the Flamingo Express," asked Chip.

They jumped in Chip's Beetle and headed toward the shop.

On the way Doc says, "Can I ask you a question?"

"Shoot," replied Chip.

Doc said, "I don't know what to do about a wardrobe. Molly's got all these fancy duds' to do the TV shows. I don't expect to be on any of them but I should have more than khakis, blue jeans and pharmacy smocks. I don't want her to be ashamed of me."

Chip thought some new clothes were a great idea.

"Why don't you ask 'King Arthur' to go with you?" he suggested.

"No," replied Doc, "I don't want to look like a royal highness. Would you mind going with me tomorrow?"

They set the time at ten sharp.

By the time they reached the shop, Lucille had already left for the day. The phones were still blinking. As they entered the shop they heard: *"Dominic, da' singin' barbuh heah."* He was having the time of his life. They decided right then that 'Tee Shop Tom', the expeditor, had better find an answering machine for after hours. Doc scanned the messages tapped to the mirror

"Holy Toledo!" he exclaimed.

He told Chip that Brokaw, Jennings and Donaldson all called back. So did Oprah, Rosie and Barbara Walters. Even National Geographic, thought there might be a story there, something about *the fountain of youth.*

"I can't believe this," he kept saying over and over.

He asked Chip's opinion as to what he should do.

Chip said, "I have to ask you one personal question first."

"Ok, shoot, we've been through so much together. I don't imagine anything you don't already know," said Doc.

Chip sheepishly asked, "Are you going to be sharing any of these hotel rooms?"

Doc was flabbergasted at the question. He fumbled an answer.

"I don't think so. I sure would like to but it wouldn't look right. We aren't kids anymore. If we were in a rock group, it might be different. What's that have to do with the TV shows anyhow?"

Chip went on to say that he remembered being interviewed, years ago, after a baseball game his team won, how nervous he got and that it exhausted him for hours afterward. With all this traveling, then making the rounds of the TV shows, not to mention the newspaper and magazine coverage, would take its toll on Molly. It would benefit the group if she could look as fresh as a daisy for every interview. A-N-D if doc was sleeping with her, the daisy could become pretty wilted.

Doc's simple answer was: "Geez, Chip, I didn't think of that, although I have thought of taking some of the liquid stuff along."

Chip said that was a good idea, if used sparingly. But not even liquid Floragra could make up for "picking the daisy" too often. Doc seemed to understand.

That evening, most of the clan members were having a confab at the 'Dale residence' where 'Sexy Sam' and 'Sly Ely' reported that everything ran smoothly at the shack, except that some of the mechanics seemed to be falling apart. (It cut into production time whenever they stopped to make repairs.) But Lucille could hardly wait to tell about her day. She repeated the messages from the networks. She went on and on. Finally, she was about to conclude, she said she thought she had two obscene calls. *"How so?"* someone asked.

"Well one guy said he was Donald Trump and he would love to meet this gorgeous creature. He even said he would send his private jet to pick her up. I didn't think 'The Donald' would even do anything like that, so I told him to 'drop dead' and hung up," explained Lois.

The group had a good laugh. *"What about the other call?"* someone wanted to know.

"Well, you won't believe it. This guy identified himself as Larry King and asked if *'the sexagenarian'* was there? He said he had seen her on a news clip and that she was 'Va va boom!' Can you imagine our Molly on the Larry King Show? I know he must be insatiable because he's been married so many times but this was ridiculous. I told him to shove it where the sun doesn't shine," explained Lucille.

The crowd roared with laughter. They had picked the right phone operator. Only Lucille could dream that one up. They finally got around to asking Mrs. Goldberg what she thought of all the messages. She said she was excited, she was dumbfounded, and she was flabbergasted. She was overwhelmed. She thanked everybody there, for their support, especially Doc and Chip. It sounded like an

Academy Award acceptance speech. *"That's Ok, Molly. If it hadn't been for your show at the flea market, we might not have sold so much so fast. Let's hear it for Molly. Hip, hip, hooray!"*

Doc quieted the crowd. He said he had a lot to tell them. Everything was happening so fast he, couldn't hardly keep up with it himself. He told them that they would be leaving for New York first class air for Mrs. Molly Goldberg, her manager, her "lady in waiting," and a bodyguard. Since he was her manager, he would be going. And Ellie was her "lady in waiting" while Chip would act as bodyguard. Not to be outdone ABC would pay their airfare home and supply them with front row seats to the Radio City Music Hall to see the *Rockettes*. CBS didn't want to appear cheap, so they agreed to supply limousine service for the entire stay plus their dining tabs wherever they wanted to eat, plus arrange for tours of The Statue of Liberty, The Empire State Building and the United Nations. It would be a whirlwind trip. He told them to mark their calendars for NBC news on Monday, ABC news on Tuesday; and CBS news on Wednesday. The Letterman Show was scheduled for Thursday night. They would all be home on Friday.

"Any questions?" asked Doc.

Wisenheimer wanted to know who would be in charge while they were gone. Doc said he thought Sam, 'King Arthur' and 'Tee Shot Tom' could handle anything that came up.

THE NETWORK SHOWS-NBC

The flight to New York was pleasant and uneventful. True to their word, the CEO limo met them at the airport to whisk them away to the Waldorf Astoria. They barely had a few hours to explore the immediate downtown district before they were due at the NBC studios. Molly said she would like something to eat before the program, but nothing too heavy. They could eat dinner later. Besides it was more fashionable. Chip called for room service. They shared two Waldorf salads. Doc informed the producer that Molly said she would be more comfortable with Andy Rooney instead of Barbara Walters. The producer said the old curmudgeon didn't do interviews. He just made dogmatic remarks. The interview with Barbara went great. She kept gushing over Molly.

"How old did you say you were?" said Barbara.

"Eighty plus," answered Mrs. Goldberg.

"Plus what?" asked B. W., anxiously.

Mrs. Goldberg said it didn't matter and that she noticed a few brown spots on Barbara's hands and arms.

"You know, Floragra could remove those in a day or two," she said. Then she asked Barbara if she had had 'facial surgery'?

"No, but I've been considering having a little taken off under the chin," replied Barbara.

Mrs. Goldberg responded, "Don't even think about it. Would you believe I had the biggest and the ugliest turkey wattle you ever saw? Now look at it, thanks to Floragra."

Mrs. Goldberg was becoming a fabulous spokesperson.

Mrs. Goldberg added: "Barbara, if you don't have the lust for life or the urge to splurge or the hunger to look younger; then you need Floragra."

Barbara couldn't believe it. Who was interviewing whom? She was so impressed she asked Mrs. Goldberg where she could buy Floragra. Mrs. Goldberg replied that she didn't think she should give the number out over the air because they were already back ordered. (Talk about a huckster that was one of the oldest plays in the book.)

The next morning, the trip to the Statue of Liberty was on the agenda. The four of them had seen plenty of ocean liners and yachts of all sizes in Florida but there was nothing like the New York harbor for shear excitement. The toot-toot of the tugs was like a half finished symphony. The tour of the Statue was breathtaking. Chip said he thought it was the greatest symbol of liberty and freedom that anyone could imagine. Doc was so awe struck that he got goose pimples.

ABC

The afternoon was spent resting up for the evening newscast. An hour before their departure to the studio a messenger showed up to inform Mrs. Goldberg that ABC would like her to wear the costume she had on during the flea market skit. Doc abruptly said no and besides she didn't have it with her. The interview went on as planned. Peter Jennings questioned her credentials, so to speak. He couldn't believe she was 80 plus. She must be lying. Mrs. Goldberg showed signs of becoming upset.

"I assure you, Mr. Jennings, I am who I say I am. I don't carry my birth certificate around with me but I'll submit to a lie detector test, if it would please you."

Doc, Chip and Ellie were all standing off camera motioning for her to cool it. She got the signal. She sedately sat down and crossed her legs, with the Hawaiian Blue skirt, rising just enough to expose well-shaped, firm legs. Peter Jennings was almost speechless. Mrs. Goldberg had resumed control.

"Gee, Mr. Jennings, I notice you're getting a little thin on top. Did you know the original Floragra can thicken up what you have and actually grow new hair? You should try it."

When the program ended, Mr. Jennings asked where he could buy some. They said they would send him some as soon as they got back.

CBS

CBS, which had been slipping a little in the news department, got wind of Molly's refusal to do the show in costume. Instead of sending a messenger, one of the producers showed up at the hotel in person. After a little cat and mouse sparing, he asked Molly how she would feel about wearing a real *Rockettes* uniform. She was thrilled at the thought. Doc was voted down. Three hours before show time, the quartet was chauffeured to the CBS studio. The entire staff had been alerted. The doorman almost tripped over himself when he saw Molly. She was whisked off to a waiting contingent of hairdressers, costume people, make up artists and every other kind of assistant you could think of. Ellie, Doc and Chip were shown to the famous Green Room where they were to wait until the show started.

Molly was treated like a movie star. She was primped, propped, pinned and pushed. The new undergarments held her firmer than ever. And that new bra was a real uplifting experience! She put on the dark mesh panty hose. Next came the real, genuine *Rockette* costume and the high heel shoes. The hairdresser made the final adjustments before spraying on enough lacquer to paint a car. She was ready. She stopped at the Green Room door to pick up the rest of her escorts. Chip asked if she was nervous.

"What's to be nervous?" she replied. "Underneath all this I'm still me. Like I said before, ya' gotta' have Chutzpah, baby."

(Boy was she ready.)

The announcer introduced her as the story of year, no, the story of the century and quite possibly, the story of the millennium. The green light went on. The stage manager whispered to her "NOW". She made an entrance that a newly crowned Miss America couldn't duplicate. Dan Rather was waiting with his mouth agape. He was stupefied. He finally managed to say how pleased he was to meet her and asked how she was.

"I'm fine now," she said.

"What do you mean now?" asked Rather.

"Would you believe three weeks ago I was using a walker and measured a 44 long? I'm fine now all because of Floragra," she said.

"What is Floragra?" asked Rather.

"I don't know and I don't care. All I can say is that it works. Got a wrinkle? Smooth it out. Gotta' bulge? Three applications make it disappear. Gotta' any kind of skin disease, Floragra can handle it. It's better than any Aloe or Herb," she said.

Dan Rather was tongue tied for the first time in his life. He finally got around to asking why she had on the costume. She felt like saying, *"to make your buggy eyes pop out of your head"*, but she didn't. She related the story of her appearance at the flea market to draw attention to the Floragra booth.

"Did it work?" he asked.

"I guess it must have because here I am. Incidentally, we may have to close the booth because we can't handle the crowds or the orders," she added.

Mr. Rather said, "Molly Goldberg, you are truly a phenomenon!"

The interview was over but not the excitement. Everybody on the set wanted to know where, they could get some. Doc and Chip took names and addresses. The CBS switchboard was going crazy. One of Dave Letterman's people stopped them on the way out. *Would she please accept his offer to appear on his show? He would even do a top ten reasons to use Floragra.* (But the only number one reason would be to look like Molly.)

Doc thought she should decline because ten reasons wouldn't do it justices there were a lot more than ten. Not only that, but he didn't want Letterman staring at her lasciviously which Doc was sure he would do. But the limo was waiting. They told the driver they didn't have much time before they had to be at Radio City Music Hall and could he recommend someplace to get a quick bite?

"Are you kidding?" he said. "At this time of night there is no such thing as a quick bite in New York, except at a deli."

That's fine," said Doc. "Pick one."

"Well ya' got two choices. "Either Katz's or The Second Ave Deli. Ya' might see some sport stars or celebrities at The Second."

Doc said they didn't have time for that. The driver deftly handled the big limo through the heavy traffic. He slowly drove past the front of the Second Ave Deli so they could see what it looked like. Then he made a right at the corner, another right into the alley.

Doc questioned, "What are you doing?"

The driver told him there was no place to park the limo. He added that he noticed Molly was still in costume and wasn't sure if she would be going in. Smart move they all agreed. They nominated Chip to go in for four corned beef on rye, four coleslaw and four coffees. What the hell, get one for the driver, too?

While Chip was in the deli, the driver told them parking wouldn't be any better around the Music Hall. So if they didn't mind they might be better off staying right there to eat their sandwiches. They agreed so he opened the portable bar, filled four glasses with ice and waited to take their orders. Doc and Molly decided to stick with the coffee. Ellie opted for soda pop but didn't know what Chip would have. Chip came out the rear door of the deli with a bag full of sandwiches and a tray full of coffee cups. They had a great time, eating while the driver entertained with exploits of driving in New York.

It was another unique Big Apple experience.

On the way to the Music Hall, Doc couldn't keep his eyes off of her. He stared. He leered. He ogled. Chip caught him out the corner of his eye.

"Look but don't touch," he said.

"Oh, s—," exclaimed Doc. "Give me a break."

As they pulled up to the front entrance, an attendant met them, holding a beautiful Caftan for Molly to put over her costume. Seems the driver had called ahead. The same attendant ushered them down the center aisle, to the steps on the side and up behind the curtain.

"Where are we going?" asked Ellie. "You passed our seats."

The attendant said, "No, they hadn't. They were to have the best seats in the house—backstage."

"Didn't they know Molly was to be introduced? It would be especially appropriate as she was still in costume.

"WOW!" Molly exclaimed.

They waited in the wings. There seemed to be much confusion. Dancers were running all over the place. Some were primping their hair. Others adjusted costumes. Still others were straightening seams. Molly didn't need anything except some fresh lipstick after eating her sandwich. Excitement filled the air.

Finally, the house lights dimmed, the band started playing, the huge curtain opened.

The Rockettes went through their routines flawlessly. The foursome stood there in complete rapture. The girls were fabulous. The settings were beautiful. The music was memorable. The glitz was astonishing.

They could tell the show was about to end. But Molly hadn't been called out. She wasn't sure what she was supposed to do even if she was.

Suddenly, the music ceased. The spotlights were trained on center stage. A voice came over the speaker system. ***"Ladies and Gentlemen, Miss Molly Goldberg."*** The dancer on the end escorted Molly to center stage. The music started up again, slowly at first. The girls parted just enough to wedge Molly smack dead in the middle. The dancers started, slowly, into their famous high kick routine. As the crescendo built, Molly thought to herself, "Why not?" She joined the famous *Rockettes* doing their most famous step. The audience started to stand. The applause grew louder with each kick. Maybe Molly couldn't kick quite as high as they did but she looked darn good. Never before had anyone that was 80 plus years ever danced with the *Rockettes*. Flash bulbs were popping all over. Camcorders were rolling. Even one TV station had a camera crew on hand just in case something like this happened.

Molly was called back for three encores. The crowd went wild every time.

Back stage, after the show, everyone wanted an autograph. Most of them asked how she could be that spry and look that young.

"Try Floragra, dearie, try Floragra," was her answer.

The rest of the stay went smoothly. They were treated like Royalty everywhere they went. Molly Goldberg was surely the woman of the hour. She attracted bigger crowds than Marilyn Monroe The trip home was relatively uneventful. Except when they got off the plane. Everyone from the condo complex was there to meet them. The terminal rang out with, *"We want Molly"* and "Atta girl Mrs. Goldberg." No limousine this time. They got on the Coral Creek shuttle bus along with everyone else.

BACK TO THE SCHOOL

Ellie, Chip and Doc were exhausted. And they didn't have to perform.

For Mrs. Molly Goldberg, Oldie Mrs. Goldberg, the end of the trip was a big let down.

She had been on a high ever since her debut at the flea market. She was disappointed too, because Doc had cancelled the west coast tour, thinking it would be too much for her. She started dropping hints like, "The Leno Show" would have been fun or too bad Johnny Carson isn't still on." Another time it was, "Don't you think Hollywood would be fun?" As her agent, Doc would say, "We'll give it some thought." As Doctor Kenny Dee, the pharmacist and longing lover, he couldn't wait to get back to work, back to the condo and back to a routine, which he hoped would include Molly. Bert, Gert and 'Tee Shot Tom' were waiting for them when they got home. Doc said he would help Molly unpack her bags. Chip and Miss Ellie went home. The trio followed them in. They were as nervous as three ants on a hot highway.

Bert started, "Chip, we got real troubles."

Gert chimed in, "yeh, real troubles."

Tee Shot said, "Now wait a minute. We don't know how much trouble we have. All we know for sure is that we got a citation."

Chip asked, "What kind of trouble?"

Ellie asked, "What citation? Where is it?"

Bert had the citation in his pocket. In his capacity as head of security, he didn't want to lose it. The citation was from the Florida FDA citing them for improper sanitation and sterilization. Bert asked what the FDA was. When Chip told him it was the Food and Drug Administration.

Bert said, "We ain't doin' nothin' with food and none of us do drugs unless the family doctor says so."

Chip agreed they had another stumbling block. He would talk to 'Lean Jean' about it first thing in the morning. After they left, Chip and Ellie settled down with a drink on the veranda. It was nice to be home even if there was trouble brewing.

The next morning they went out to the shack bright and early. There was a "NO TRESPASSING" sign on the door.

"This might be more serious than I thought," he told Ellie.

The notation on the door instructed whoever was in charge to report to the Coral Creek city hall.

Chip said, "I guess that's us. Let's go see what it's all about."

The city manager welcomed them and offered coffee. She explained the FDA as alerted to their operation by all of the publicity. They checked it out more out of curiosity than anything. Unfortunately conditions were so bad that they didn't have any choice but to close them down.

"However," she explained, "We were notified of the closing before it got filed with the state. Coral Creek is proud to be the birthplace of Floragra. We don't want you to leave. This is the greatest thing to happen to this town since ... well since I don't know when. Therefore, I have taken the liberty to set you up in the cafeteria of a near by school. Everything you need is there. And it's all stainless steel. The only stipulations are that you may only use it after 4:00 PM when the students and faculty are gone. Number two, that you leave it as clean as you found it. Number three that you make a donation of twenty-five dollars a week to the schools general fund. Do you think you can work under those limitations?" she asked.

Chip stood there like a schoolteacher had just reprimanded him.

"Yes, Ma'm, I think we can."

The city manager told them there was always a janitor on duty to let them in and out.

"Oh by the way," she added. "I don't think you'll need that generator or cement mixer any more, and no alcoholic beverages in the building. If you want to sneak out to your car, so be it. The kids do it all the time."

Chip and Ellie practically howled as they thanked her for all her help.

They rushed back to the complex to call a hasty meeting. Everyone showed up. There was no sense trying to hide it any more, except, they still didn't dare divulge the secret of the hedges. The crowd was delighted to hear the news. 'Lean Jean' wouldn't have to check into the citation.

Old Wisenheimer said, "Wow, we're goin' big time." And none too soon, it appeared. The shack had definite limits. Since Molly's stunning appearances hawking Floragra, production was way behind the demand. Lucille, 'Lucy the Lip', told them she had orders lying all over the barbershop. And Dominic had been so much help taking messages. He had them pasted up all over.

"Did you know he was Italian?"

At 4:30 sharp the Coral Creel shuttle bus pulled up in the school parking lot.

The comments ranged from: *"Look how big this place is." What a playground. Remember when all we had, was an old tire on a rope and the baseball field was really a field? Check the desk. Not an ink well in sight."*

Old Wisenheimer said, "Don't these kids study anything? They all have TV sets in front of them."

Bert spoke up, "Hey, stupid, don't you know a security monitor when you see one?"

'Sexy Sam' had to straighten them both out.

"They're computer monitors. They pretty much replaced the old blackboards."

Then Skeeter pipes up, "So I see, said the blind carpenter, as he picked up his hammer and saw."

The janitor showed them to the cafeteria. It was staggering. Steel, everywhere. 'Sly Ely' and 'Audacious Audrey' were impressed with all the utensils hanging from the ceiling-knives, forks, and spoons of every description, ladles and whisks. There were more toys than in a kid's sandbox. And bowls-they never thought there were so many sizes. Doc went berserk over the mixer and mixing tubs.

He said out loud, "Well, if your preparing lunch for a thousand students and faculty, I guess you better have the right tools to do it."

They brought the bag of leaves and all the other ingredients in from the bus. Doc quickly assigned workstations. *"You do this, you do that, and you stand here, and so on."*

The necessary ingredients were in the huge tub. Doc started the heavy duty, industrial strength mixer. It was all he could do to hang on to it.

"Whoa, stop the boat," he yelled.

He had forgotten to take the dough hooks off the beater and replace them with the regular ones. He started again. In no time the mixture was the correct consistency. Sure beat the old cement mixer! Because the lunchroom was set up as a cafeteria, all they had to do was fill the jars, put them on a tray and push them down to the next station. What a smooth operation. But again there wasn't enough work for all of them at the same time. The half that wasn't on the assembly line, found their way down to the gym. The last time Chip looked in on them they were playing volleyball! (Can you believe it? Don't forget, these were 60, 70 and 80 year old bodies acting like high school kids.)

The custodian stopped in the gym to sweep the floor. When he saw how much fun these old folks were having he changed his mind and joined them for a while. The next day he told the Phys. Ed. Instructor how good these old geezers were.

"That's nice but so what?" the instructor said.

"Don't you see the possibilities here?" said the janitor. "You could have a group of students play against them. Just think of the publicity. Think of the headlines in the paper. Not only that, but more than that, think what lessons the kids would learn from the oldsters. The exposure might help both sides. And don't forget they have Molly Goldberg on their side. Maybe we could even sell tickets."

Coach thought it over. The next day, during the gym classes, he asked if anyone would volunteer to stay after school to play volleyball with some older people. He kind of played on their sympathies, like *"We should be kind to old people. These old folks need their exercise, etc."* Some of the freshmen and sophomores thought it might be fun to really wallop a bunch of old fogies. Most of the upperclassmen thought it would just be a waste of time. Why bother? But coach rounded up enough volunteers to form a team. He told the janitor to set it up for after school the next day. The janitor informed Chip to have the group ready

Chip got the word out. Anyone interested in playing volleyball against the kids should dress appropriately and be sure to wear sneakers. That was no problem as most of them wore shorts and tennies' most of the time. 'Tee Shot Tom' came up with a great idea. Why not have t-shirts with our name on them? At least that way the kids will know they're really playing a team.

Wisenheimer says, "We don't have a name."

Chip asked for suggestions.

How about the Florida Funsters? How about the Floragra Flash? How about Fast and Furious? There were several others not worth mentioning. They finally settled on, *"The FASA Funsters."* (After all, isn't that what they were doing, having fun? And if it weren't for Floragra they wouldn't be there at all?)

'Tee Shot Tom' and Skeeter headed for that Utopia of bargains, the flea market. They found the t-shirt shop, which generally caters to mostly tourist. They ordered twenty-five shirts in assorted sizes but make sure at least one is small. Molly liked her clothes fitting very tight these days. They asked if they could get lime green (representing hedges) shirts with purple lettering (representing the flash of lightning in their logo).

"No problem," the clerk said. "We'll have them ready in two hours."

The clerk asked if this was an organized group because they; might be eligible for a discount.

Tee Shot said, "Heck yeh. FASA stands for the Florida Agricultural Seniors Association."

The clerk says, "Isn't that the group that had the Floragra booth and that woman Molly somebody that put us all on the map?"

When Tee Shot answered they were one and the same, the clerk said,"WOW, we'll be happy to do your shirts and give you a twenty percent discount."

Skeeter says, "Okey, dokey, we'll be back in two hours."

They ambled around for a while checking out sneakers. Skeeter asked Tom if he remembered the ones he had with the glow in the dark pink shoelaces.

"How could I forget? Whatever happened to them?" he replied. "My little doggie got hungry one day and I haven't found any more since then."

They lingered in the fast food area sipping on Cappuccinos. They picked up the t-shirts and headed back to the complex on Skeeter's motorcycle. Little Belle Taco was kind of crowded with all those boxes on the floor. They handed out the shirts as everyone was boarding the bus. To a soul, they informed Chip they didn't want to work that night. They either wanted to play or at least watch the big event.

"You deserve the time off. You've all done very well," he mimicked the phase from the TV show, "Are You Being Served".

When they got to the gym they found a rag-tag looking bunch of youngsters. Some in gym shorts, some in sweat suits, some in street shorts and a few in loose fitting blue jeans. When the kids saw the oldsters in their flamboyant tee shirts, they thought. *"What is this, some kind of joke?"*

The janitor said, "I tried to warn you. I told you to be ready to play."

"Yeh, sure, gramps," one of them laughed.

The teams shook hands before they lined up 'Alluring Anita' had been an Olympic hopeful in gymnastics and was still very agile. She would make the first serve, BAM! a line drive, barely over the net. Two of the kids smacked into each other as they went for the ball. It bounced away.

Point! *Hip, hip, hooray.*

'Alluring Anita' served again, another smash line drive, to the opposite side. A young girl stood there, looking very bored at playing these old people. The ball hit her in the face like a jet rocket.

Point! *Hip, hip, hooray.*

The kids looked at each other in amazement.

It's gotta' be some kind of fluke.

They can't all be that good.

Anita served again. This time she lofted one toward the back line of the court. An athletic looking youngster extended both hands. He managed to keep the ball in play. It traveled toward the front of the net.

He yelled, "Spike it spike it!"

The guy that was supposed to spike it hit all right, right into the net.

Point! *Hip, hip, hooray.*

The 'The Lovely Lois' said she wanted to serve. There were no objections on either side. The kids thought, *"What the heck can she do? She's barely five feet tall."* Lois had practiced her serves when they played the day before. She took a deep breath. Instead of throwing the ball up and smashing overhand, she tossed it up, then, with her palms up, she sent it to the middle of the kid's team. The ball went so high that when it drifted down it looked like it was in slow motion. The kids were stunned. They had never seen anybody serve like that before. A young girl in pigtails batted the ball up for a companion to play it. The second player manages to get to the front of the net. The tallest and perhaps the best player on their side, was ready. He thought to himself, *"Aha, we finally get a chance for a point."* He jumped up. He hit it so hard it almost knocked the air out of the ball. He was about to raise his arms in a victory signal when he noticed Arthur.

'King Arthur' had been standing around in a rather lackadaisical manner and had been watching the play. He straightened up all of his six foot four body. He met the ball at the very top of the net. He smacked it back at the kid so hard, that when it hit him, he almost fell over.

Point! *Hip, hip, hooray.*

The youngsters called for a time out. They needed to regroup.

During the break, there was a commotion out in the hall. A local TV crew was on the way in. It turned out that the clerk at the tee shirt shop had alerted them.

They were there to do a follow up story on Molly as well as a piece for a Short Sports segment. The kids couldn't believe it, a TV crew at their school? They didn't think it was fair either, because they weren't dressed in flashy shirts like those old people. The TV cameras were set up. The time out was over. The kids thought they were ready. Play resumed.

Point! Point! Point!

The score was 10 to nothing before the kids got their first point.

Chip, who had played a little volleyball in his day, was not so much a manager as he was a coordinator. He pulled 'King Arthur' out of the line up and put in 'Tee Shot Tom'. He substituted "Beauteous Bev" for the 'The Lovely Lois'. 'Millie the Mermaid' went if for Gert and Doctor Dee subbed for Bert. The kids were stupefied. *What is this with new faces and fresh bodies all the time? Wasn't there a rule about substitutions?*

The cameras were rolling as Molly, dressed in her lime green tee shirt (small, thank you) and matching spandex work out shorts entered the game. She didn't even have to do anything, just be there. However, when the first ball came her way, she femininely hit it to the player in front of her. When the second ball came her way she wasn't quite as feminine. The opposing players thought they had found a soft spot. The tall kid aimed one right at Molly. Instead of trying to set it up for somebody else to spike it over the net, she blasted that sucker like it was a giant mosquito! The tall guy missed it. The second guy missed it. The kid in the backcourt fell on his face lunging for it.

Another point and the camera caught the whole thing.

The game ended 21 to 10. They shook hands and agreed to play again some time. Molly again was the star of the show. No one objected because the exposure was priceless. The next day the kids told coach what had happened. He addressed them as a group.

"Did you learn anything from the experience?" he asked.

"The only thing we learned was that they're pretty good volley ball players," the pigtail one said.

Coach said, "You should have learned to always be ready for any challenge in life. You should have learned to never underestimate your opponent, no matter what the game of life throws your way. And you should have learned to respect your elders no matter what they look like or how old they might be."

Then he reminded them to watch the evening news because they might see themselves on TV. Molly, of course, was the lead story, how she had been so incapacitated and look at her now, etc. The Short Sport segment paid tribute to the school, it's Principal and its students, for the way they were treating the old folks. Both stories were well done and were a welcome relief to all the murders, rapes and violence, which dominated the evening news. As for the oldsters, they came away with a different opinion, too. As they got to know the kids a little better, they decided that not all kids were lazy, shiftless and aimless. If this bunch were indicative of today's youth, the country would be in good hands.

On the bus, they congratulated each other.

Old Wisenheimer said, "Guess we showed those young whipper-snappers."

'Sexy Sam' told him to sit down and shut up. He hadn't played and probably had no idea what a whippersnapper was.

EL ZORO AND EL ZORA

Back at the compound, everything was pretty quiet, except, Lucille. She had spent the day doing her switchboard thing. She said she didn't have time for frivolous things like volleyball. She had a stock of messages six inches high. Most of them were orders from out of state, generated by Molly's TV appearances. She was waiting for Chip to get off the Coral Creek bus. Dominic or Dom. as she was now calling him, waited with her. He had graciously given her a ride home. After giving Chip the messages, she introduced Dom to the group. Not all of them had been to the barbershop.

"This is Dominic Monacelli from New York City. Can you believe it? He's Italian!" said Chip.

Lucille asked Dom if he would like a glass of wine. It was the least she could do to thank him for the ride home. He followed her into her condo. Chip looked at the stack of messages. They seemed to be from all over. He showed them to Miss Ellie.

"This could present a problem," he told her. "We don't have franchises set up in half these places."

Ellie says, "So get them set up."

No obstacle was ever too big for Ellie to overcome. After all, she married Chip, didn't she?

'The Lovely Lois' and 'Lean Jean' were walking by on their way home when Chip stopped them to show them all the orders. He repeated his concern about not having franchises. The ladies looked at each other with a smirk on their faces.

"Not to worry, Chip," said Lois. "While you were in New York, playing games and having fun, we were hard at work. 'Lean Jean' had all fifty franchises typed up and ready. I guess we forgot to mention it."

Chip let out a big sigh. *Was this an amazing group of people or what?*

Jean told him all he had to do was fill in the correct name and address of the franchisee in that state. The 'The Lovely Lois' had the franchise for Florhio. 'King Arthur' and 'Millie the Mermaid' covered Florayork. 'Sexy Sam' and 'Alluring Anita' had Floravania. Marvelous Marilyn From Milford blanketed Florigan. 'Tee Shot Tom' and Beauteous Bev opted for Florajersey. Terrible Ter and Little Richard were all over Florexas. Camille said she had connections all over. She asked if her franchise could be for the Florabbean? No Problem. The west coast wasn't too well represented. They needed to find people for Florafornia, Floregon and Florington.

Chip handed out the Floragra orders to the respective representatives. He thought they might need to advertise for a few but that shouldn't be too difficult considering what an amazing product they had plus the heavy TV coverage by Molly, the Golden Oldie. Ellie suggested he talk to 'Babs, the Blond Bombshell from Bristol' (Connecticut, that is).

"She has a computer, you know. And she's connected to the Internet."

"What a great idea," he said. "But I haven't seen her in quite awhile."

Right on cue, she stepped out of the cab that had pulled up in front.

"Como teva?" she squeaked. (Translation: How are you?)

The cab driver was opening the trunk to get out her luggage. All eyes were riveted on Babs. She was wearing 'la espectaculo costuma." The full-length black gown had three layers of teal blue ruffles, trailing somewhat out the back. The waist appeared cinched around her middle. The back was cut very low, at least down to her waist. A thin blackstrap encircled her neck to support the tight bodice. Considerable cleavage was evident. The intricate design on the black lace shawl topped her lovely blond tresses and flowed seductively over her shoulders. Rita Hayworth, at her best, couldn't have looked any better. No one noticed the long, lean drink of water that got out of the cab on the other side. He stood up to stretch, easily looking over the top of the car. The intense dark eyes surveyed the scene. The gleaming white teeth were accentuated by the golden brown tone of his face, which in turn was enhanced by dark eyebrows and almost straight, jet black hair.

The cab driver had extricated the luggage. All eyes turned toward the tall, lean one as he moved to the rear of the cab. Miss Ellie, the 'Merry Maid from Michigan', stood there with her mouth open. 'Alluring Anita', who was all of five feet tall, was practically in shock. *"This guy must be six foot, six,"* she quickly thought to herself.

He was in full view now. A snug fitting black jacket similar to one a waiter might wear covered the white ruffled shirt open at the neck; the jacket was emblazoned with delicate scrolls of gold colored thread. The jacket, which ended at the waist, was clasped in front. Below that, were skin tight, black, leotard looking pants, ending just below the knees and held up from drooping by dainty black knots tied on the outside of each leg. The legs themselves were covered in shear white hose. The ballet type, black slippers completed the picture.

Babs said, "Allow me to introduce my friend, Juan El Zoro, the supreme matador de la Toledo."

Skeeter turned to Chip, "What did she say?"

Chip told him she just said this guy was the greatest matador in Toledo.

So Skeeter said, "I thought she went to Spain, not Ohio."

"Yeh, right Skeet."

Babs giggled a little as she said, "I am now Elzora, the female companion of El Zoro, Ole."

Elzoro bowed and kissed each lady's hand. He shook hands with the men, saying, "Eet ees for me a beeg pleasure that I should meet you."

He asked Chip where the nearest arena was. Chip thought maybe the circus at Sarasota might have one otherwise he would have to go to Tijuana. As El Zoro and Elzora entered her casa, he turned slightly, waved triumphantly.

"Hasta la vista." Elzora said, "He ees mucho beeg hombre, Si?"

The orders just kept coming in. The accolades and unsolicited testimonials were pouring in from all corners of the country. Barbara Walters called to say how pleased she was. Dianne Sawyer checked in. So did Katy Curic. Kathy Lee Gifford dropped a note that she would never have to worry about Frank again. They heard from Rosie O'Donnell. Even Oprah and Diana Ross were pleased. Sally Jesse was ecstatic. The list could go on and on. And it wasn't just the ladies that had the Hunger to look younger.

The big three network guys, Peter Jennings, Tom Brokaw and Dan Rather couldn't say enough. Regis Philbin wrote a long note saying if it hadn't been for Floragra he probably wouldn't have gotten the "Millionaire" show. Burt Reynolds placed on order for *"five jars of the kind that grows hair and five jars of the wrinkle remover kind."* (Please deliver to Jupiter, Florida.)

Mickey Rooney's order included a note inquiring if it would help him get taller. Pat Sajak only ordered one jar as the studio make up people were doing a good job of covering up, so far. Alex Trebek said maybe if he had heard of it sooner, he might have gotten the "Millionaire" show instead of Regis.

Floragra, was without a doubt, perhaps the greatest discovery in the past century.

There was no way this small group was going to keep up with the orders, no matter how dedicated they were. They quickly outgrew the schools facilities as well. They were going to need full-fledged production space and soon.

In the meantime, Doc had negotiated a deal with Dominic Monacelli, the singing barber. They agreed to pay him one thousand dollars a week, over and above his regular expenses, to rent the entire shop. He agreed only if Lucille would stay on. Overnight, the shop was converted into a modern office with stations for three switchboard operators. Lucille had her own glassed in office, complete with chaise lounge, coffee pot, microwave oven and a remote control TV set.

While the entire hubbub was going on, everyone seemed to forget about Mrs. Molly Goldberg, at least temporarily. When last seen, Molly, festooned in Caribbean Island garb, was on her way to the Calle Ocho Festival in little Havana. That's Miami's answer to the Mardi Gras.

Chip didn't forget the weather. 'Windy Willy' and 'Stormy Weather' could have taped the forecast and used it all week, *"warm, sunny, slight breezes, and temperatures ranging from high seventies into the low eighties. There may be a slight warming trend next week."* There didn't appear to be a storm anywhere on the horizon. So far, the Floragra hedges seemed to be holding up just fine.

Chip, Doc, 'Sexy Sam' and 'Tee Shot Tom' were sitting on Sam's patio having a beer. They were discussing everything in general but nothing in particular. Generally, they all seemed concerned about the same thing-where do they go from here with this project? Since the hedges held the secret and there was no way of predicting the next hurricane, it was an extremely risky venture. And even if there were another hurricane, would it ruin whatever the amazing ingredient is, through out all of Florida. It wouldn't take long for someone to figure out where the Floragra was.

The conversation seemed to boil down to two alternatives; one, they could add production people thereby working two or three short shifts through the night. Or two, they either buy or build the production facilities they needed. 'Tee Shot Tom', who seemed to keep his nose in everybody's business, said he didn't know of a kitchen type facility anywhere in south Florida that was big enough for their use, at least none that were available. Doc came up with a novel twist. His idea was that if they add the flavors, they could probably increase the price by twenty or thirty dollars. In that way, it might reduce the demand while at the same time it would increase profits. (These guys were learning to be businessmen, one way or another.) Chip interjected that he liked the idea of increased profits by adding flavors. However he doubted if it would decrease demand.

"After all," he said, "look at Viagra, the American public will pay almost any price if they think it will improve their lives."

"We would have to pay a little more for the colored containers too." Doc said, "What, maybe an extra ten cents and no more than ten cents for the flavor. So we add twenty cents to the cost while we add twenty dollars to the selling price."

"Not a bad deal," said Sam.

Chip told 'Tee Shot Tom', the expeditor, to check on the colored containers and get enough of the flavors for Doc to start production. Would you believe it, Tom couldn't remember the flavors? Or were they scents?

So Doc read him the list:

Green jars for Peppermint Pleasure

White jars for Vanishing Vanilla

Red jars for Very Cherry

Orange jars for Orange Blossom

Pink jars for Rose Bud

Doc also told him he could pick up the peppermint, vanilla and a couple jars of Maraschino cherries in any super market. Orange Blossoms and Rose Buds might be a problem. If he saw any along the road, just stop to pick them-if he got caught he could offer to pay for them. They could liquefy them in the blender.

THE BABY

They were just about to end the con-flab when Skeeter pulled up on the motorcycle. Little Belle Taco was fastened in the sidecar with his seat belt. Skeeter walked up to the guys carrying something wrapped in a big bath towel.

"What's up Skeeter? Whatchya' got there?" asked Tom.

Skeeter didn't say anything as he unwrapped the towel to show the cutest, new born, little chew-wa-wa you ever saw. *"Where did you get that?"* they wanted to know.

"Well, I ain't real sure how this happened, "he said. "Sometime ago I stopped to eat at a nice Mexican Place, *Los Amigo's* or somethin' like that. They told me I couldn't take Belle Taco in with me but the cook had his chew-wa-wa with him in the kitchen. They were sure he wouldn't mind keeping an eye on my doggie while I ate. So I said okee dokee. About an hour later, after I finished my Enchilada and the last Margarita, the cook brought my doggie out of the back room. He kept telling me what a frisky little thing she was and how his male doggie really liked her. I didn't think too much about it until I put her down to walk out of the restaurant. She kind of staggered a little like she was drunk or something. I thought maybe the cook gave her a drink of Tequila. Then a couple months later, I noticed her belly was a little swollen. Again I didn't think anything of it. I thought I gave her too much Spanish food, 'cause that's the only thing she eats. Then three weeks ago she starts acting like she's got gas. I figured I better not give her any more refried beans for a while. Then she pops four of these little devils out like they were Mexican jumping beans. I gave three of them away and kept this one. That's the whole story."

"Did you ever go back to tell the cook?" asked Tom.

"Sure I did. He got the other three," said Skeeter.

"So what did he say about that?" asked Sam.

"Boy, I'm proud of my Taco Grande', I guess he really is a Grande," replied Skeeter.

"So you kept the pick of the litter?" asked Tom.

"Yeah and I named him after Chip. You can have him if you want, Chip?" offered Skeeter.

Chip finally spoke up, "What's his name?"

"Well, since his mother is Belle Taco and his father is Taco Grande', I thought why not Taco Chip," said Skeeter.

"Ole' shouted Chip. "Wait till Miss Ellie sees this one. She'll love it."

Skeeter reminded Chip to feed him Mexican food.

"Oh yeah," say Skeeter. "I turn on one of the Spanish language stations once in awhile. She seems to understand them, must be born into them. And if you want to see something funny turn on one of those Flamingo dancers."

Chip said, "Don't you mean Flamenco?"

"Whatever," replied Skeeter. "Turn one on TV and my little doggie jumps all over the place."

And just as he thought, Miss Ellie fell in love with Taco Chip immediately.

THE HOTEL

'King Arthur' and 'Millie the Mermaid' stopped by Chip's residence later on that evening. They had just returned from a weekend in Miami and wanted to talk to Chip and Ellie. Ellie served coffee and bagels on the veranda.

Arthur couldn't wait to tell them what they had discovered. He started out by saying he knew the FASA group had outgrown all of its facilities and that major decisions were going to be necessary. To make a long story short, he told them he investigated an old run down hotel, in downtown Miami that seemed to be vacant. It seems that years ago it had been a favorite spot for politicians, movie stars and sports figures. However, as with many things, the glitter and the glamour wore off. The old favorites were long gone and the younger set established their own spots. Chip and Ellie sat there patiently as Arthur went on and told them the place looked a little rundown but that was mostly out of neglect. While they didn't get a chance to go inside, the outside looked in pretty good shape.

Chip finally broke in. "What does that have to do with us?"

"I thought you would never ask," Arthur said. "Chip, this could be a golden opportunity. I'm sure a hotel this size would have a huge kitchen and probably tons of storage room. I can just see the Art Deco lobby, the work out rooms and the pool. We could turn it into an old time, real honest to goodness spa. With all the retirees that live down here plus all the one's that come down for the winter, the place would pay for itself in no time. We could have the exclusive outlet for Floragra in Florida. I get all excited just thinking about the possibilities. I think we need a committee to investigate further."

He finally stopped to catch his breath.

It sounded good to Ellie. And Chip was sold. He told Arthur that it seemed strange that he would come up with something like that because they were just talking about possible sites. He didn't want to get too many people involved, so didn't say anything right away. He called Doc, the pharmacist, Sam, the manufacturing manager, and 'Tee Shot Tom', the expeditor, to join him and 'King Arthur', the distribution manager, tomorrow morning. Doc made arrangements to borrow Wishbone Willy's S.O.V., (remember, Same Old Vehicle). They piled in the old van and headed for Mee-yam-ee, as Skeeter occasionally called it. Arthur said he would drive since he knew exactly where it was.

It took a while to get through the heavy traffic. He cruised past the front of it so they could get a glimpse. He parked the car in front of the building. Of course it wasn't busy. From the looks of it, it had been shut down for a number of years. There was no way to get around behind it but they liked what they saw from the front. Sam stepped across the street to take several pictures. He even turned the camera on end so the wide-angle lens would be perpendicular. Arthur saw a small notice taped on the inside of the door, *'FOR INFORMATION-CALL ...'.* He called the number using his cell phone. The secretary that answered the phone said the broker was out however there was an agent in the office that might be able to help him. The agent could only supply some generalities but he would set up an appointment for them to get in to see it.

On the ride home Chip suggested that they not say anything to anyone, except their wives, of course. The air in the van was filled with garble like a Jerry

Springer Show. "Maybe we could do this and maybe we could do that." Doc was more concerned with the manufacturing facility than anything. 'Sexy Sam' wondered about the gym, the pool and the possibilities of a spa-did it have a sauna, a steam bath, access to the ocean, etc. 'Tee Shot Tom', trying to be frivolous to lighten up the conversation piped, up with:

"Gee, with all those rooms maybe we could hang a red light out in front."

Arthur gave him a big *hrmpf.*

"Are you forgetting how old we are or how old the ladies are?"

They met the broker at one o'clock sharp. The huge, old, brass door creaked as it was opened. They dusted the cobwebs aside as they entered the lobby. The broker was smart enough to bring along a half dozen flashlights. He apologized, saying the electricity hadn't been turned on in years. He cautioned them to watch their step because there was no telling what would be lying around. They made their way through the lobby, down several hallways toward the rear of the building. He took them out the service door. The main doors, which led to the old deck, where chaise lounges once lined the entire width of the building, were double bolted and chained. The beach hadn't been maintained in years. It was easy to visualize striped cabanas down to the water.

The broker told them they could check out the pool and get a closer look at the back of the building if they felt like climbing the ladder. "Hey, are you kidding? None of us are that feeble yet," said Chip. One by one they climbed the ladder, Arthur first, followed by Doc, Sam, Tom and Chip. They inspected the pool. It needed some work but was in amazingly good condition. Even the cement walkways around the pool were repairable. From this level, too, they could see the exterior of the rear a lot better. There were a lot of cracked windows but very few broken all the way out. The worst looking part of the building was the old canvas awnings. They had either rotted away or were blown away. The few shreds that remained flapped in the breeze like your Grandmothers underwear hanging on the clothesline. The group had seen as much as they could on this type of tour. They definitely had seen enough to be interested. They told the broker, Stan Sellemfast, to work up the figures for the selling price, down payment and interest. Naturally, they would have to confer with the rest of the group.

When they returned to the condo complex, they parted company, with each man commissioned to convince his mate that this was an exciting project. Chip virtually bounded up the stairs to tell Miss Ellie what they had found out. When he finally finished expounding, Miss Ellie spoke up.

"Sounds very interesting honey, but …"

"But what?" asked Chip.
"But don't you think you need a more thorough inspection?" she suggested.
"We-ell, yes, I suppose so," said Chip.

Chip said he thought they would have time for a thorough inspection, after they received the broker's terms.

The 'Merry Maid from Michigan' said, "Have you forgotten that you have a son that is a consulting engineer and architectural specialist? I'm sure he wouldn't mind a little Florida vacation."

Chip didn't answer. Of course he hadn't forgotten. He just didn't think they were ready yet.

Within twenty-four hours the entire group knew about the hotel adventure.

"I'll run the switchboard and reservation center," from Lucille.

We'll handle security," said Bert and Gert.

"I'll run the kitchen and dining room," said' Audacious Audrey'.

'Sexy Sam' volunteered to run the gym, the sauna, the steam room and specially the massage factor. If they seemed to be enthusiastic before, you should see them now. The Floragra was working wonders. They not only looked younger, but also felt younger and acted younger. Sure, there were minor little twinges, maybe even an occasional runny nose but that didn't matter. This was the happiest, most ardent group of geriatrics on the whole darn planet. They had a lust for life.

Ol' Stan Sellemfast, the broker, wasted no time in getting back to them. He had been in touch with the Japanese group in California that had owned the place for the last twenty years.

Stan provided a list of the terms:

Asking price:	20 Million
Land Contract:	10 years
Interest:	10 per cent
Down Payment:	25 per cent

Chip hit the ceiling. He started to rant and rave until Arthur grabbed him by the shoulders to calm him down. Arthur told the broker they would bring it up to the board of directors. He advised the broker to leave while he was still in one piece.

By evening, Chip had calmed down enough to be rational as he met with Doc, Arthur and Sam on Sam's patio. 'Tee Shot Tom' was playing a late round of golf.

The rest of the clan was slaving away at the school, trying to fill back orders. Arthur suggested they have a general membership meeting to get a consensus, check on their bank balance, then make a counter offer with a proviso for a professional inspection.

The meeting was called for the next evening in the school cafeteria. Every single person showed up including El Zoro and Babs (now El Zora). Lucille asked if it was OK to invite Dominic. Chip led off the meeting by reciting the terms they got from the broker.

Immediately, someone yelled out, *"Are you nuts?"*

"Exactly what I said," said Chip.

Arthur stepped in: "Now before you get too riled up, let's have the treasurer's report from 'The Lovely Lois'."

Lois said she couldn't tell them right to the penny because she hadn't received last month's statement yet but she was pretty sure the bank balance was around three million dollars. Again someone yelled out, *"You can't do much with 3 million, when you're looking at a twenty million dollar hotel!"*

Lois, who was generally pretty staid said, "Will you please sit down and shut up! Let us finish the proposal."

Chip stood up and said: "Here's what we think we can pull off. We make a list of everything that needs to be repaired or updated to meet the current codes. Then we offer 10 million, with more than half down, with a conventional mortgage over a period of ten years. Because of the age of the building, we think we can have it included in The National Register of Historic Sites. That automatically reduces the taxes. We may even be able to get government assistance for the restoration. And lastly we might be able to have the City of Miami give us tax abatements for all the new jobs we'll be creating. Are there any questions so far?"

Chip continued, "And if the demand stays this strong, we could increase the price again. Also, don't forget, this place will be a glamorous spa. If we administer Floragra applications, the sky is the limit. Who know what the *'Ritzies'* will pay to be pushed, pulled, powdered and pampered? I think the place will start making money within six months after re-opening."

Chip stood up again.

"But before we can make a counter offer, before we can go to the bank or before we can do anything else, we need to know where we stand; better yet, where you stand. We need an irrevocable pledge from each one of you that want to participate. This is a pledge of cold hard cash that you can get your hands on. We don't need a pledge like you make to the Public Broadcasting Station and then back out. Miss Ellie and Lois will write down your pledges."

Believe it or not, every single member made a pledge. Even Skeeter and Dominic, the singing barber, wanted a piece of the action. Chip asked Lois if she had a tally.

"Yahoo," she yahood. "We're over the top. If my figures are correct, that totals five million, three hundred seventy five thousand dollars."

Arthur sprang out of his chair. "That's just great! And if the treasury could kick in six hundred, twenty five thousand, they could offer six million dollars cash, as a down payment on a ten million dollar counter offer. Who would refuse?"

Chip added that before they made the counter, they should have the place inspected by an architectural expert so there wouldn't be any surprises later on.

Molly said, "But we don't know anyone like that. It would cost a fortune."

Chip said, "Oh yes we do and no, it wouldn't"

He went on to say that his son owns a firm like that back in Michigan. It was known as The BEST Engineering Co. They were a nationally recognized company and he was sure he could get the inspection done for a very reasonable fee. The clan gave him the go ahead.

The next day he called the BEST Engineering Co. and asked for 'Smarty Marty'. It was a rarity to catch him in the office. He was usually traipsing around the country solving problems. Smarty Marty picked up the phone.

"Ya, BEST Engineering."

"Hey Mart, it's your old man," said Chip. "I need some help."

Chip told him what was going on, and then asked how fast he could get there. Mart explained if they needed a fast job, he would need to bring along four or five men.

Chip asked why so many? Marty said he needed an electrical guy, a plumbing guy, a roofing expert and a foundation specialist. They could use someone local to do the Otis elevators and the Fire Marshall could cover that aspect.

"OK, when can you leave?" asked Chip.

He said no one was using the company plane right now, so if he could round up a staff, they could be there by 3:00 P.M. Talk about efficient. Chip borrowed Wishbone Willy's van again. He and Doc picked up the entourage at the airport, and then headed straight to the hotel where Stan Sellem was waiting for them. The inspection team was immediately impressed. It didn't look too bad from the outside. They carried the various testing machines and a variety of paraphernalia into the lobby. They only had a few hours to work before nightfall.

At this time it should be pointed out that the hotel is of an "art deco" design. Art deco can be loosely described as artful decoration. While not easy to describe it is generally referred to as modern or futuristic or curved or rounded. This particular hotel was one of the earliest and largest of that era. Most of the buildings have round corners. The majority, have a wide band of contrasting colors just above each row of windows. These are usually referred to as *"eyebrows"*. Our hotel was built in the late 1920's and 1940 when World War II ended production. The area has since been declared as the largest art deco community in the world and is protected from demolition by National Registry of Antiquities.

In addition to the rounded corners you would notice sleek curved lines and ovals through out the buildings. Glass blocks and neon lights are generously used. The interior designs are equally effective. If anything, could be conceived to be *"built in"*, it was attempted. Radios, as an example (remember there was no TV back then) were built into nightstands or dressers, which always had rounded corners. Art deco was the wave of the future. Unfortunately the future ended with World War II. However the so called *'modern design'*, which is the exact opposite of the sharp points or spires of a Gothic cathedral, can be seen in a modified style, in many of the newer buildings being constructed in south Florida.

Before giving the crew instructions, 'Smarty Marty' asked the broker if he had any of the original permits or blue prints.

"No I don't, but they might be on file at city hall. If I hurry I might get there by 5 PM and bring them to you in the morning," he suggested.

"That would be extremely helpful," Mart said.

Then, handing Ike several high beam flashlights, he asked him to take the Sonic Wave to the lowest basement to start on the foundation inspection. Al was to take the Infra Red Sensor and start working the walls. Tom was to begin checking the plumbing while Rick started on the electrical. Mart then asked Doc if they could contact an Otis elevator representative, call the fire marshal and then contact FPL to see if they could get a temporary permit to have the electricity turned on.

Chip mentioned to Doc, "Man, this kid doesn't fool around."

Doc answered, "Well you wanted a quick inspection. Looks like you're getting it."

The two of them left in the van to find a working telephone.

THE INSPECTION.

The inspection crew had gotten a good start before the broker told them they had to close up. He gave Mart hat blueprints and permits he could find at city hall. Doc had received a one-day permit, to have the electricity turned on from 7 AM to 7 PM the next day. The broker was to meet them at seven sharp. He wanted this deal badly.

That night the crew was to spend the night at Ellie and Chips. The three bedrooms plus the sofa sleeper could handle them for one night at least. Miss Ellie made a great spaghetti dinner. Later, as they sat around perusing the blueprints, Chip asked where this crew came from? Mart told him, with tongue in cheek, that they were all qualified people. Ike had poured his own driveway so why wouldn't he know about cement foundations. Al had built a chicken coop once so he obviously could do the wall inspections. Rick had worked in environmental water control in Texas so there was no doubt he could handle the plumbing. And Tom had re-wired a lamp one time and therefore understood the electrical. Chip looked at him like he was nuts. The rest of them were laughing their heads off. Chip found out later that they were a very qualified and experienced gang

The next morning everyone was up bright and early. It was warm and sunny by seven o'clock. Mart kidded that maybe they should go to the beach instead of doing the inspection. Doc pointed out that if the inspection went well and FASA bought the place, they would have their own beach. He offered that the guys, with their wives and kids, could come down for a week, FREE.

Mart yelled out, "That's it guys, lets go to work."

With the electricity on it was a lot easier to see what they were doing and made it much faster. Ike plugged the Sonic Wave gismo into an outlet. (Hooray- it worked.) The Sonic Wave is similar to the Sonar used in submarines. It passes through the concrete until it hits an obstruction, then bounces back. They are able to pick out hollow spots as well as check any steel girders within the concrete. The first couple of hours went very well. The Otis elevator inspector checked for rust on the cables and pulleys as well as any frayed lines. Amazingly everything seemed to be in good shape. (Nothing that some grease and oil couldn't correct.)

The Fire Marshals only complaints were that there weren't any smoke alarms and what sprinkler system there was, wouldn't be up to today's code. However, he thought that condition might be "grandfathered" in because of the hotel being built in the 1930's. The marshal also dropped a subtle hint that he did heating and air conditioning on the side. (Subtle enough to hand Chip, a business card as he said, "*call me anytime.*")

Al was making great progress with the Infra Red Sensors checking the walls and ceilings. He could find every imperfection, even every nail head. The only odd thing he picked up so far was the old razor blades that had been pushed through the slots in the old medicine cabinets. The plumbing was going to be a problem. The old galvanized pipe seemed to be all right in the upper residential floors but the basement was so damp from not being used that the connections appeared pretty rusty. Rick thought they could get by with new piping in the basement, and then replace the rest, floor by floor as money allowed or as renovations progressed. Tim checked in with the electrical report. Everything was fine but very, very inadequate. He pointed out that after all when this place was built there weren't TV sets, VCR's, dishwashers, microwaves or computers. He stated that it would be hard to imagine the world without those things now. He thought FPL (Florida Power & Light) could upgrade the system to handle just about everything.

By the end of the day, they concluded the old building wasn't in half bad shape. They had a *pow-wow* with the inspection crew that evening, back at Chip's place, to get their recommendations. Each guy had a written report of his findings. Believe it or not, there wasn't much of a list. No major structural damage was evident. They found a few cracks here and there, a few loose wires, a couple of drips in the basement, several leaking faucets, and a lot of broken glass but all in all not too bad.

'King Arthur' was the first to point out that they sure didn't want the Japanese sellers to know that. He asked the crew if they couldn't make the list of deficiencies a little longer by being more exact.

"We wouldn't want you to lie," he said, "just embellish it a little."

"We can do that," Smarty Marty said,

Before the inspection crew boarded there plane the next day the lists were completed and typed on official Shepard Engineering letterheads. As they waved goodbye, Chip yelled out, "Send us a bill."

"You can count on it," yelled Mart.

THE OFFER

By nine that evening everyone had gathered at 'The Lovely Lois" for their nightly nourishment of nonsense. But there would be no nonsense this night. Doc and Chip, and Tom, and Arthur were ready with answers. After they gave their report of the inspection, unbelievably there was only one question and that came from one old Wisenheimer: *"When do we make the offer, and how much is it?"*

Chip let Lois handle that one since she had all the figures.

"We will meet the broker, Mr. Sellem, first thing tomorrow morning when we will offer him ten million, with five million down on a ten year contract," she explained.

The question was raised, "why only 5 mil when we had agreed to six?" The answer was that some people might want to cut back on their pledges *and* they might not have to touch the treasury.

Arthur stood up to explain that even though the building was in relatively good shape, it would probably take from three to five million to renovate it enough to get it open. In fact they are thinking of asking the bank to finance eight million instead of five. Then, if they get the Historical designation and the tax abatements, they should be in good shape to just about remodel the whole ten floors.

"Here's where we stand right now," he said; hold out his convenient check list.

A. *The offer needs to be written and presented.*

B. *The offer must be accepted.*

C. *We talk to the bank.*

D. *We start renovating.*

E. *Three months from now, we open.*

"Also the kitchen area will be remodeled first, so we can transfer the Floragra production there," Chip. added.

Mr. Sellem looked over the offer. He was about to say *"Are you nuts?"* but Chip anticipated that kind of response. Before Sellem had a chance to open his mouth, Chip asked him how he would open the offer to the Japanese group, by phone, by FAX or by e-mail. In any event be sure to cover all the repairs first. Then point out they probably had depreciated down to nothing by now, therefore they had nothing to gain by hanging on to it. And don't forget to mention this would be their one and only offer. After all ten million in the hand was better than eight hundred gazillion yen doing nothing. Stan Sellem called Mr. Terri Yaki in California to tell him to turn his FAX machine on because an offer was coming through.

"Okee dokee" replied Yaki.

This modern age is amazing. Everything moves so fast. The offer was accepted, lock, stock and barrel, the bank loan was approved, all the pledge money was collected, the papers were signed and the key to the front door was turned over all within three days.

A NEW BEGINNING

It was a new chapter in the ongoing saga of the FASA Company. The immediate priorities were to have all the utilities turned on. Extra keys had to be made for the front and rear doors. And security was a big must. Bert and Gert said they could handle it. Ely The Deadeye, said that might be OK for a day or two but they really needed at least full time security guards at the front door. He reasoned that only Doc would probably use the back service door. Therefore, it would be closed most of the time. The front door was a problem; they didn't need any squatters or vagrants poking around. Chip suggested that Bert and Gert be in charge of all hotel security. They would be responsible for hiring the guards and outlining a plan for security cameras throughout the building.

They next decided that it would be cheaper and more expeditious to hire a cleaning company rather than buying mops, pails, brooms, sponges, etc. 'Audacious Audrey' was in charge.

It was recommended that a main floor meeting room become a temporary office. That is if there were enough volunteers to get it cleaned up. As usual, with such an excited group, there were more than needed.

While everyone else was yakking away, 'Tee Shot Tom' had reconnoitered the entire first floor. He located, not only the manager's office, complete with desks, filing cabinets, safe etc. but he found the storage room in the back of the building, adjacent to the kitchen. It was full of mops, brooms, pails, floor scrubbers, sponges, vacuums and cleaning supplies *'up the gazoo.'*

"Granted," he said, "they were old and stiff but most of it was useable."

So the gang cleaned out the main office instead of the meeting room. Chip kept looking at that humongous old safe. They didn't have a key and they didn't have the combination. He knew there was a locksmith in Lockport but that was too far away. Skeeter popped his head in the door.

"What's the matter, Chip?" he asked.

"Oh, I'm just trying to figure out how to get into this old safe," he said.

"Not to worry," squeaked Skeeter, "Let me at it."

"How you going to do it?" asked Chip.

Skeeter replied, "My Daddy taught me how to do this stuff before he went to jail. Remember, I got the lock open on the old shack?"

Chip said, "But this is different. This is a safe combination."

"Wait here a minute," replied Skeeter, "then just watch."

Skeeter came walking back in, undoing a roll of paper towel. He folded the sections neatly as he undid them. Chip stood there with a puzzled look on his face. Skeeter finally got down to the cardboard tube in the center of the roll. He knelt down in front of the safe, placed the tube against the door, put his ear up to the tube, then he slowly turned the dial. He told Chip to write some numbers down *nine-seventeen-thirty-two, etc.* Within five minutes the safe door swung open. It took him longer to unroll the paper than it did to crack the safe. If there was any hope of finding money or jewelry, those hopes were soon dashed. The only things in the bottom of the safe were some very old, dried out newspapers. They gingerly took them out of the safe to lay them on the desk. They read some of the headlines: "*1929-STOCK MARKET CRASHES-DEC7, 1941, JAPS BOMB PEARL HARBOR-1944-ROOSEVELT INAUGURATED, 4TH TERM-1945 TRUMAN ORDERS H-BOMB-1945 JAPAN SURRENDERS.*" There were several complete sections of a supplement to the Miami papers. There were called Rotogravure Sections, printed in a brownish color called sepia. None of the papers were of any value. However, they made for some interesting reminiscing to the geriatric group. On the very bottom of the pile were several autographed pictures of celebrities that had stayed there. (Talk about stirring up memories.) There was Clark Gable, Henry Fonda, Jimmy Stewart, Lana Turner, Rita Hayworth, Bette Davis and a few more that no one could recall. No great treasures but at least the huge, old safe would hold over a hundred jars of Floragra.

The cleanup was going well, both in the outer office and in the kitchen. Doc reported that he thought they would be ready to move all the equipment and supplies out of the school. Doc also found a walk-in cooler, not a freezer, but a cooler. He was excited about that. It meant they could store as many bags of Floragra leaves as they could pick, or as many as the hedges could yield without looking bare.

Miss Ellie left early in order to stop by the barbershop to check on orders and pick up messages. The three telephone operators had already left. As Ellie approached the door, she heard singing. She thought Lucille had the radio on. Boy was she wrong. She opened the door only to see Lucille sitting in a barber chair with Dominic on one knee in front of her. He was just finishing the last bar of *O Solo Mia*. He didn't hear Ellie enter so he continued singing. "*What a beautiful voice*" Ellie thought. Lucille was enraptured. When they realized Ellie was there, Lucille had a sheepish grin on her face and Dominic quit singing.

"Don't quit because of me," Ellie said, "I think you have a beautiful voice."

Whereupon Dom broke into *Santa Lucia* but he sang it as *Santa Lucille* again. Ellie thought to herself, "how touching. Chip never sings to me." Lucille had two piles stacked up orders for one only, the other of messages. Fortunately, the order pile was bigger.

When she got home, Ellie walked up to Chip, put her arms around his neck and said, "Sing to me, you lothario."

Chip responded with "Are you nuts? Have you been drinking Floragra?"

She put on her superficial pout by dropping her head and sticking her bottom lip out.

Chip gave in and said, "I'm sorry honey, come here and give me a hug."

Then she told him about Dominic and Lucille. They both had a good laugh.

In the meantime, Mrs. Molly Goldberg wasn't letting any grass grow under her feet either. She was the self appointed director of entertainment. She had remained in tough the several of the *Rockettes* since she had appeared with them in New York. She called on Trixie, Dixie and Pixie to see if they could come down to help her organize a show. *"No problem sweetie, when do you want us?"* Molly told them it would be a couple of months before thee place would be cleaned up enough to stay in. She told them of some of the plans for the grand old hotel. Everyone got excited. Trixie said they could probably bring *Rusty, Dusty and Busty* along. (Not their real names).

Molly had also made a few connections in Hollywood … California that is. She decided to tap her resources. She found out they would be happy to share some of their old movies. When she told them she especially liked musicals, they said great, they had some old *Ann Miller, Cyd Charise, Dan Dailey* and even *Donald O'Connor*. The old *Holiday Inn with Bing Crosby, Danny Kaye, Rosemary Clooney and Vera Ellen* was always a big hit as well as *The Glen Miller Story*. They even had a couple of what they called 'shorts' featuring the *Step Brothers and The Ink spots*.

There was a lot of retired Florida talent as well. Molly knew *Paul Cowan*, an old trumpet player with the *Duke Ellington* aggregation. And she knew the drummer with *Glen Miller*, Ray something, was still around. And *Harry Balzonia* had been with *Shep Fields, Rippling Rythym band. Kay Kaiser's* old singer, *Colly Flower*, could still carry a tune. Not very far, but he could carry it. *The McGuire Sisters and Jerry Vail* were making the geriatric circuit. If she was really lucky she might even get *Perry Como* for a couple of guest spots.

The more she thought about it, the more excited she became.

(Doctor 'Kenny Dee' might still be her manager but by golly, 'Miss Molly' was in charge.)

Doc was so busy getting the Floragra operation set up in the kitchen he didn't have time to keep track of Molly. Most of the equipment had been transferred over from the school. He kept running back to Chip.

"Have you seen the huge kettles we have?" he asked.

"Yes, I've seen them, old pot breath," said Chip.

Doc was ecstatic over being able to increase the production.

"We could double or triple our output," he exclaimed.

"That's great," said Chip, "but don't just stand there, we have no idea what will happen to the hedges. So, go man, go."

Bert and Gert had interviewed several protection agencies. They were looking for someone reasonable but that could also guarantee protection twenty-four hours a day, seven days a week. It would be helpful if the guards could get along well with elderly people. They finally settled on a company called I C U. No, that didn't stand for Intensive Care Unit. What really sold Gert and Bert, was the companies logo, a television camera with an eye looking out the lens and the V shaped somewhat like an eyebrow. I C U had experience in all phases of security. They even had some experience with the Super Bowl and the Latin celebration *Calle Ocha*.

It was determined that the most economical and by far the most efficient system would be with surveillance cameras. There was a room under the main staircase that would be large enough for the monitors. It was decided that a uniformed guard between the front door and the desk was needed more as a deterrent than anything. All the other guards including several specially trained females would roam around in street clothes. Bert noted that he wanted to keep his own walkie-talkie, so I C U would have to supply his own. Bert told them they only needed a couple of people to begin with, just enough to keep the gawkers out, while the renovations proceeded. Of course, after they opened they would want coverage at the pool, the work out rooms and a 24-hour guard at the rear door.

Every night around nine o'clock, the entire group would check into the manager's office, for a little nightcap. Chip was only too happy to oblige. (Wasn't this great everything seemed to be coming together.)? Doc had the Floragra production room humming. In fact, if things kept going the way they were, he might have to hire some help. Chip thought that was great but advised him not to do any hiring without talking to him first. Instead of hiring just any old body off the street, there may be some help back at the condo complex. Molly was busy, making more theatrical contacts. Bert and Gert were busy. 'Alluring Anita' and Millie the Mermaid were picking out the décor for the main lobby. They wanted it to be spectacular in an old art deco manner. 'King Arthur' and 'Sexy Sam' had their hands full over-seeing the gym, the pool and the spa renovations. 'Tee Shot Tom' with the 'Beauteous Bev' in tow, was just expediting things all over the place. Everyone was so busy, so excited and so happy; it was hard to hold them down.

Even Lucille and her singing barber, were taking phone orders so fast, they could hardly keep up. From time to time Chip accused them of slowing down for a little hanky panky. Then Dominic would put on a show about how fine Italian gentlemen don't to things like that to a fine woman like-a Lucille.

Doc was making such fantastic progress mixing the Floragra that he decided to ask Chip if he could set up a cot in the spare storage room. After all, mad scientists have been sleeping in their 'la-bore-a-tories' for years (especially in the movies). Chip didn't think anyone would object, so why not? Doc said if he had a small microwave and a coffee pot, he would be all set.

CONTEST IDEA

'King Arthur', who had the original hotel idea, was now wondering if they would be able to fill all the rooms. The more he thought about it and the more he talked to Chip about it, the more convinced he was that they would need more than just word of mouth. Mulling it over in discussions with 'The Mermaid', a plan starts to unfold.

"What if we had contests among the Floragra distributors in each of the states?" he asked. He answered himself. "We could sponsor bus trips to Florida as a prize."

"In fact, why not as a contest within a contest?" he said to no one in particular.

"First, we have a contest for our average everyday customer. The first ten people to submit their stories, in 300 words or less, of how Floragra changed their lives, wins a free trip to the hotel for them and their spouses, for one whole week. The local distributor, in that state, can do the judging," he proposed. "Secondly; we establish quotas for the distributors. The one that exceeds that quota by the highest percentage wins a trip for two to stay in the honeymoon suite for a week. Of course it may just turn out that they will ride on the same bus as the ten winners from their territory. The fact that they will act as chaperons, good will ambassadors and baby sitters for the more elderly will be strictly coincidental."

He finally took a breath.

"What do you think of that idea?" he gasped.

'Millie the Mermaid' was dumbfounded. She wasn't paying any attention.

"Oh. That's sounds good, Arthur, very good," she replied.

Arthur said he could hardly wait to tell Chip.

HOTEL HAUNTS?

Doc now envisioned himself as another Henry Ford or Tom Edison. Or maybe even Albert Enstein, nothing like being alone in your laboratory to boost the ego.

He worked late into the night experimenting with fragrances. After all, there were tons of weird smells and names already on the market. The name of the game in today's world was to keep coming out with new products or in many cases, the same old product with a new name or fragrance. By three A.M. he was beginning to get drowsy. *A couple of hours sleep on the cot would feel pretty good*, he thought.

He rolled a sweater up to make a pillow. Then he covered himself with an old tablecloth someone had found. As he closed his eyes he was thinking to himself "*What a strange feeling it was to be all alone in the magnificent old hotel. Boy, if these walls could talk, they could really tell some stories.*" He lay there in the quiet and dozed off.

"*Play it again, Sam.*"

Doc heard it loud and clear. He bolted upright.

"What was that?" he said. "Who's in here?"

"*Play it again, Sam.*"

There it was again.

"Hey, quit fooling around, who's out there?" said Doc. "Is that you Skeeter?"

There was no answer, just the stillness of the night.

He knew he had put in too many hours. He was exhausted. His mind must be playing tricks on him. He slumped down on the cot and was just dozing off, when he heard the voice again.

"Play it again, Sam."

This time the voice was clear and distinct. There was no doubt whose voice it was, *Bogart's!*

"Am I going crazy or is this place haunted?" he thought to himself.

His mind was racing. What should I do? I'm no hero. I'm a lover. His first thought was to turn on some lights. No, that wouldn't be smart. Why make himself an easy target. He suddenly remembered he still had his walkie-talkie. He buzzed Chip.

Chip answered drowsily. "Yeh, what doya' want?"

"Hey Chip. It's me, Doc. You ain't going to believe it, but Humphrey Bogart was here," he almost shouted.

"Yeah, I know that," replied Chip, "with Lauren Bacall back in the forties."

Doc yelled. "No, I mean tonight, like now. I heard him!"

Chip responded, "What the hell's the matter with you, calling me in the middle of the night with that preposterous story? Have you been smokin' those funny cigarettes again?"

"No man!" cried Doc. "Like I heard him, honest to God."

"Stick your head under a pillow and go back to sleep," commanded Chip. "I'll see you in a couple of hours."

Daylight was just beginning to creep over the horizon. Doc was calming down now. Perhaps he was only dreaming. He got up and made a pot of stiff, black coffee. When Chip finally got there, Doc could hardly wait to tell him what happened. Chip dismissed it by saying it was a bad dream. You better lay down to catch a little shuteye before the rest of the gang gets here.

As Chip entered the lobby area he could see most of the paid help was already busy. The cleaning and restoration was progressing smoothly. The window cleaners had moved up a couple of floors. He tried to remember their motto. "*Let us pane you?*" he thought it was. He chuckled to himself as he recalled the carpet people's slogan, "*We let you walk all over us.*"

Gallons of water and dozens of toothbrushes had already been used. The sponges were squishing, the mopping was flopping and the vacuums were sucking. What a beehive of activity. The best part was that the 'oldsters' were keeping up to the younger ones and in fact, were better and faster. Maybe they were more motivated. After all, it was their money that was paying for it. Also, the fact they were all using Floragra was pretty evident.

THE ARCHITECTURE

'Millie the Mermaid', 'Audacious Audrey' and 'Tee Shot Tom' had gathered for a mid-morning coffee. The conversation had finally turned to the exterior of the building. They concluded that with gentle sand blasting the entire exterior could be preserved. They didn't want to change the overall appearance. The building itself was pretty unique. All the buildings on Deco Drive were similar but each was unique by itself. The FASA building, as it seemed to be called more and more, was about ten stories high. (You may recall that FASA stands for Florida Agricultural Senior Association.) Porthole type windows in middle of each curve set off the smooth contour of the rounded corners. The bas-relief friezes, depicting palm trees and long legged Flamingos, ran from the top of the door to the roofline. As with most of the hotels built during that time, the quasi-lined columns on each side of the frieze, lent itself to making the structure look much taller than it was. The balconies or terraces jutting out on each corner were partially shielded from the sun by canopies that were generally referred to as "eyebrows."

The three agreed that the building would be outrageously attractive if the frieze was left neutral, the vertical columns were in Flamingo pink and the racing stripe, which went around the entire building immediately below the windows, was a soft purple-more like mauve.

That evening, the happy group gathered back in the old clubhouse (where the food fight had taken place). Chip remarked to Miss Ellie that he hadn't heard of an ache or pain in weeks. (Truly, a remarkable situation.)

An informal discussion was taking place when 'Audacious Audrey' and 'Millie the Mermaid' asked if they could throw out their color scheme for discussion. *Sure, why not,* they all agreed. The girls received a standing ovation for their idea especially after they explained that the colors were pretty close to the company logo.

One old Wisenheimer stood up. Everyone thought he was going to complain. Instead he said he had a further suggestion.

He went on, "That building doesn't have a finial or a topper like so many others. I've been thinking about that. I would like to suggest that we have the completed FASA logo mounted on the roof right over the front door. It could be outlined in neon lights, yellow for the sun, pink for the pyramid, green for the leaves at the bottom and purple zigzag for the lightning. They could be on timers so that each one flashed for a few seconds intermittently, then all at one time for a full minute before starting over. I can just see it!"

His suggestion was met with a thunderous ovation. (Was this a great group of young at hearts or what?)

FALDERAL

Doc, in the meantime, had regained his composure and was over seeing the production of more Floragra. Since most of the renovating and housekeeping chores were let out to private contractors, the geriatric group was more than willing to help out. (After all, what else did they have to do with their boundless energy?) Doc's main duties, at times like this was to keep giving out assignments to keep everyone busy. There was such a flurry of activity that no one noticed Molly Goldberg as she entered through the back door. Doc had a key made for her hoping they might rendezvous some evening.

Molly was resplendent in very tight fitting snakeskin, red pants, and a billowy see through blouse enhanced by a wired uplift brassiere. The red snakeskin high-heeled shoes completed the ensemble. She was a knock out. Most anyone would have taken her to be in her mid-forties. Certainly not the eighty plus which she no longer admitted. She sidled up behind Doc and gently blew on his neck. At first he thought it was one of those pesky Florida bugs. He whisked at it with one hand. The second time he felt it, he turned around thinking that maybe a spider had dropped from the ceiling. And there she was giggling like a teen-ager.

"Oh my; God," he exclaimed. "You look terrific!"

"Hi ya' big boy," she said in a sexy low voice.

"Where have you been? I've missed you," he said

"I flew out to Hollywood to round up some old movies. I picked up a few new outfits while I was there. How do you like this one?" she asked.

"Fantabulous," was all he could say.

They made plans to meet for dinner. After all the oohs and aahs from the rest of gang, Molly left to keep a few appointments. Production resumed with a chorus of, *"It's off to work we go, hi ho, hi ho."*

Chip walked back to the main office. His mind was racing like a centrifuge. There was so much going on, so much to do, so much to think about. He was thankful he had Ellie to keep him organized. He tried to keep a daily planner however nothing ever seemed to work out like he had planned. He thought he should remember to check with 'Lean Jean the Legal Machine' to make sure the names and logo's were protected. And there was 'King Arthur's idea of a contest between the Floragra distributors to think about. On the surface, it seemed to have some merit. But his mind was so completely absorbed that he didn't see the mop and the bucket in front of him. He kicked the bucket (so to speak), the water spilled all over the floor, while the mop handle sprang up hitting him in the head. Stunned, he looked around to see if anyone was watching. He sat the bucket upright, leaned the mop against the wall, and then, examined the spillage. Thank goodness the new carpet hadn't been installed yet. As he sat down at the old mahogany desk, he reached up to touch his forehead. *"Wow, that's a pretty good welt,"* he thought to himself. *A little Floragra ointment should take care of that.* He opened the safe where he knew they had stored a considerable amount. *Nothing. The safe was as bare as, Old Mother Hubbard's cupboard. What the hell is going on? Where is all the stuff? Had they been robbed?*

He paged Doc immediately.

"Hey, old beaker breath, can you come up to the office like pronto?" yelled Chip.

Doc ran past the bucket and the mop without even noticing them.

"What's up Kemo-sabe?" he said.

Chip swung the door of the safe open.

"Where is all the stuff?" he queried.

"It's gone, man. We shipped it all out and we still have back orders," was Doc's answer.

"Holy mole," he said. (He was thinking *Holy something else*, but this is not an X rated story.)

As he swung around in the big swivel chair, Doc saw the welt.

"Well, Miss Ellie finally got even, with you eh?" he remarked.

"Don't get smart. Where am I going to get some Floragra?" he asked.

Doc told him to come back to the 'lab-or-tory' where they just made a fresh batch.

After applying the cream to his forehead it only took about 10 minutes for the swelling to go down. (No wonder this stuff was in such great demand, it was good for a myriad of ailment.)

As Chip waited for the Floragra to work on the lump, it suddenly dawned on him that they hadn't seen Skeeter for several days. Just then the back door opened and little Belle Taco came bounding in. Everyone was so glad to see her that they hardly noticed Skeeter, who stood there, clad in a swimsuit with huge fins on his feet.

"Hey Skeeter, our pool isn't open, yet. Where you goin' with that outfit on?" asked Doc.

"I'm on the way to the car wash to give little Belle a bath. She gets frightened if I send her through alone so I go in with her," he explained.

"But why the swimming fins?" someone asked.

"Well you wouldn't want me to get my shoes all wet, would ya'?" he answered. (You just never know what to expect from Skeeter.)

The welt had gone down. Chip left them, laughing and fawning over little Belle Taco.

THE CONTEST IDEA

On the way back to the office, Chip bumped into 'King Arthur' and 'Millie the Mermaid'. They exchanged greetings as Chip invited them to come in and take a load off their feet.

"How's it goin'?" Chip asked.

Arthur spoke up: "We've been discussing the contest idea. The more we think of it, the better it sounds."

"I've been thinking about it myself and wanted to touch base on it. What have you come up with?" said Chip

Millie chimed in this time: "There are several things involved that we could do."

She went on to say that the contest within a contest sounded pretty good. Chip asked her to explain how they could work that out. She said they thought a quota idea for the individual state distributors would be weighted according to population. She mentioned that right now Lois' twin, Lynn, in Ohio, was going crazy and the California people were selling it like mad as sun tan oil. Almost all their orders were for the liquid instead of the cream.

Arthur jumped in to say there would be no voting in this contest.

"You either make quota or you don't. We don't want any dimpled chads, hanging chads or any other kind of chads. Make it or don't, plain and simple."

Millie continued. "The other contest could be just as simple. Entries would complete the sentence: *"I like Floragra..."* in 50 words or less. The board of directors can choose the ones with the most unique or unusual answers.

"And" said Arthur, "the biggest benefit of all, will go to us."

"How so?" asked Chip.

"The whole thing, air fare, bus fare, meals, lodgings, the whole magilla, is a write off to advertising or sales promotion, which increases our bottom line," concluded Arthur.

"Arthur," said Chip, "no wonder they call you King."

Just then 'Sexy Sam' and 'Alluring Anita' entered upon the scene.

Sam says, "I heard that last part about cutting expenses and increasing our net. I've got an idea for you to do the same thing."

He explained that some of the gang was starting to complain about not having time for any fun stuff. Even though most of them didn't put in any more than four hours in any given day and at the most it was 3 or 4 days a week, they felt they wanted more time off. Sam had investigated to see what could be changed. As it was now, they were shipping bottles or jars to each individual customer. Sam suggested they would save a lot of time and packaging expense by making bulk shipments to the distributors in each state. The distributors, in turn, could elect to make home deliveries, have it picked up at a central location or mail it themselves with their own advertising packaged in it. They would cut our costs considerably but more importantly they could cut packaging time in half, thereby gaining more fun time.

Chip was flabbergasted. These guys, and gals too, were simply amazing. He had never seen so much talent in one location in his whole life!

THE DATE

That afternoon Doc dismissed everyone early. He told them he had an important appointment. They all snickered to themselves. They knew what the appointment was.

He went home to shower, shave and freshen up for his dinner date with Molly. He was just exiting the shower, with a towel wrapped around his waste, when he heard the front door open.

Who the hell can that be? he wondered. *He didn't want to be late.*

As he came around the corner of the hallway, there she was.

"Good golly, Miss Molly, what are you doing here?" he exclaimed.

"I couldn't wait," she said. "And it looks like I'm right on time."

"Don't tease me, girl," Doc said. "Don't tease me."

Molly told him to slip into something comfortable. (Isn't that, the shoe on the other foot?)

"What about dinner, I thought we were going out?" asked Doc.

"Not tonight, honey. There's been a change of venue," she said.

She wasn't dressed for going out. Blue jeans, very tight but still they were blue jeans, a blue denim cowboy type jacket, with a few shiny baubles and red colored cowboy boots.

"I think I'll change into something more comfortable, myself," she suggested.

"If you insist," replied Doc.

Doc shaved and splashed some smelly stuff on his face. He had his Jockey's on and was scrounging for a decent pair of trousers. She snuck up behind him.

"Looking for anything special?" she whispered behind his back.

Doctor Kenny Dee, who was rarely at a loss for words, whirled around to face her. He let out a gasp and then held his breath. Here was this incredibly shapely woman, an octogenarian no less, standing there in a fabulous glittering lame' string bikini and sporting the old style, spike heel shoes. If you didn't know better, you would swear she had plastic surgery and liposuction. In his mind, he thought, she's got *Angie Dickinson's* legs, *Betty Grable's* derriere, *Marilyn Monroe's* waist *and Gina Lollabrigada's* bust. What a package!

"Wanna take a dip?" she muttered. (Talk about a double entendre)

He couldn't speak. She put her arms around his neck and softly purred into his ear. He was getting goose bumps all over. He finally regained his composure. He wasn't used to the female being the aggressor.

"I can't," he stammered. "I don't have a suit."

"I guess we'll just have to stay inside then and order dinner," she replied.

"Yeah, I guess," he mumbled, "seafood sound good?"

Doc called The Happy Crab. (There's a misnomer.) He knew they would deliver. While he poured the Merlot, she set the table. The shrimp cocktails were small but adequate, the crab cakes, tasty. The piece de resistance was the Red Snapper. Doc had an Uncle who lived in Puerto Rico whose last name was Mere.

In Puerto Rico, the Red Snapper is known as a Mero. Old George had a favorite restaurant that prepared the fish just the way George wanted it. It was featured on the menu as Mero ala Mero.

The snapper was exquisite. Their appetites sated, they sat back to relax. Another glass of wine and Mrs. Molly Goldberg stuck an old Glen Miller eight track in the machine. She started to swing and sway, she gyrated, and she undulated. Doc sat there just staring. *Geez, he was uncomfortably full.* She reached down to grasp his hand.

"I can't," he said. "I'm stuffed full."

She tugged on his arm. At that moment, as though on cue, he *flatulated!*

"Oh, for Gods sake, thanks a lot!" she screamed disgustingly.

She didn't bother to pick up her cowboy duds. She bolted out the door like a streak of lightning.

"What can I say? I'm sorry! I'm sorry!" he yelled after her.

Within minutes his head was hanging over the commode. (Must have been something he ate.) Doc was disgusted, disgusted with himself for missing the opportunity for a great evening, disgusted with her, because that wasn't the way he had it planned, and really disgusted with the food from *The Happy Crab*. After ten or fifteen minutes his stomach felt better. He decided to head back to the hotel. He figured the fragrances he was mixing would certainly smell better than it did around here.

HAUNTING

'Tee Shot Tom' had arrived back from his golf tour. After Doc entered the hotel via the rear door, he headed for the office to see how many new orders were posted. As he walked through the main lobby, he bumped into Tee Shot and Skeeter who were just about to leave. Skeet was showing Tom all the progress that had been made since he left. He was impressed and couldn't believe how much had been done in such a short time.

The three of them exchanged greetings; Doc patted little Belle Taco, and asked them to come back to the kitchen for a drink.

"Okee, dokee," says Skeeter.

Doc never one to shun a drink, reached for a beaker that looked as though it was part of fragrance experiment.

"I ain't drinkin' that stuff," spoke Skeeter.

"Don't worry," said Doc. "It's pure vodka, Smirnoff no less. I can't keep it in the original bottle or Chip would be upset. And by drinking vodka, he can't detect it either."

"You mad chemist are sly ones," expounded Tom.

"Don't give any to my 'Chew-wa-wa' he's Mexican, not Russian," noted Skeeter.

Tee Shot asked Doc what he'd been up to. Doc was still pretty disgusted as he started to relate the events of the evening. He got to the part about Mrs. Goldberg walking in the front door. He poured himself another drink. The other two had barely started on theirs. Doc was telling them about the string bikini when he reached for another. By the time he finished describing the food he was on his fourth. And when he got to the climax of the evening, which was no climax at all, he poured the fifth vodka. (No seltzer, no water, no rocks, just plain straight vodka.) Little Belle Taco was whining a little and scratching around. Skeeter said he thought she needed to go out. 'Tee Shot Tom' thought it was wise for him to leave too or they would all be in trouble. They told Doc he had better slow down and take it easy. Doc thought to himself, *"I couldn't take it anyway she presented it."*

After they left Doc looked around. There was so much to do or so much he would like to do. His head was beginning to spin a little. *"Oh, what the hell, I'll have another one just to get my head straight."* He weaved a little on the way to the John. As he stood there relieving himself, everything seemed to be spinning around and around and around. He felt like he was in the middle of a tornado. He made it to the cot before he collapsed.

Several hours later, in the middle of the night he thought he heard a noise outside of the door. He shook his head to clear out some of the cobwebs. He flipped on the rear floodlights as he peered out the door. He couldn't see anything except that he noticed a set of matches lying in front of the door. He slowly stooped to pick them up, slowly because his head was still woozy. The cover was written in Japanese. *"That's strange,"* He thought. *"I wonder how these got here,"* He didn't think too much about it. It hurt to think right at the moment. He turned off the lights before securing the door. He was exhausted. He shuffled back to the cot for more shut eye. He was deep into the REM's when he thought he heard voices again. Startled, he sat upright. **"What the hell?"** he thought.

"Hey, big boy." He heard.

"What? What do ya' want?" he said.

My God, was he talking to himself? he thought.

"Hey, big boy, come up and see me sometime."

He thought, *"It couldn't be Mae West. She's been dead for years. Molly, knock it off. I told you I was sorry."* Then he remembered some of the names they found in those old newspapers that were in the safe, Mae West had stayed here several times many years ago. The early morning sun was peeking over the horizon as Chip entered the back door.

"Doc, what's the matter with you? You're as white as a sheet. Did you see a ghost?" asked Chip.

"No," Doc replied. "I didn't see one but I heard one."

"You've been smelling too many fragrances," suggested Chip. "There's no such thing as ghosts."

"Chip, I'm tellin' ya' the place is haunted. First, there was Bogart, now Mae West. And how do you explain these Japanese matches?" Doc exclaimed.

"Doc, you're going coo-coo," said Chip. "First of all I think you dreamt everything you thought you heard. And secondly, the matches were probably dropped by one of the previous owners. Don't cha' remember, we bought it from the Japanese?"

"I still think the place is haunted," said Doc.

Chip advised him not to sleep there any more if he felt that strongly about it.

THE JAPANESE INVASION

Doc wasn't convinced that Chip was right about any of it. He would like to investigate further but he needed help. If only Molly hadn't left in such a huff. He had three or four cups of strong coffee. As he was changing into his laboratory clothes he thought to himself "*She wouldn't be doing it just for me. She would be helping the whole group. Maybe there's something going on that we should know about. What the hell, I'll call her.*

He called Mrs. Goldberg on her cell phone. She picked it up immediately, wondering whom it could be. Not too many people had her private number.

"Molly, don't hang up. It's me, Doc."

"Oh, I should have known," she said sarcastically.

"Listen," he began. "We got a problem; I don't mean you and me. I mean us, the whole group and we need your help."

She replied, "For you, I do nothing. For the group I would do anything."

Doc gave her a brief run down of hearing the voices and finding the Japanese matches. He said what with all of the new Hollywood connections, maybe she could get someone to do a little sleuthing on the Japanese guys that they bought the hotel from. Molly told him she had met *Tom Selleck* one time and he had been pretty good in Magnum P.I.

"See what you can do?" asked Doc.

Molly called *Mitzi Gaynor* whom she had met when she was checking out some of the musicals. No, she didn't know *Tom Selleck* but she knew someone who did. (Boy this was typical Hollywood. It was always not what you knew but whom you knew.)

"I'll have someone call you back this afternoon," explained Mitzi.

Molly was pleased with her new found status. At precisely three P.M. the phone rang.

"Hello, this is Molly Goldberg," said Molly.

"Mrs. Goldberg, may I call you Mrs. Goldberg? (That was Hollywood too, always sweetness and nice before you got stabbed in the back) this is Claudia Cohen." (Claudia was the gossip reporter that appeared regularly on *The Regis Philbin Show*.)

"What can I do for you?" Claudia asked.

Mrs. Goldberg explained the situation to her, all the while thinking *boy if anyone could dig up some dirt, and this was the right contact!* Claudia didn't think Selleck was doing that kind of thing any more but California was full of P.I.'s. She was sure she could find one.

A week went by during which time Doc and Molly mended some fences. It might be awhile before Doc got another opportunity like the one he blew, figuratively speaking, but at least they were talking again. In the meantime Bert and Gert were busy with their security duties. At the moment they only had two security guards from the I.C.U. Company. One kept on eye on the front door while the other one watched the closed circuit monitors.

There was a tremendous amount of activity going on. The painters, window cleaners, electricians, carpenters and plumbers were forever scurrying in and out. Bert kept telling the guards to report anyone looking suspicious. They couldn't be too careful. They didn't want any of the "stuff" to fall in the wrong hands. He even went so far as to line them up every morning, call them to attention, and then circle each one to inspect their uniforms. He must have been a drill Sargent during the big war.

Dominic and Lucille were still going strong. Lucille was supervising the operators in the conference room, off the main lobby, that had been set up as the communication center. That section was running smoothly although she told Chip she might need another operator and one more mail person because they were getting so many requests for literature.

Dominic, the singing barber, was busy setting up the tonsorial parlor. He insisted that it resemble the original, or at least what he thought was original, barbershop. Somehow he secured four old style barber chairs. You know the kind with the hydraulic hand pump on the side of the chair. None of this fancy foot power for him. These chairs also had the small headrest on the back. The kind you might see in an old Western movie. He had the shaving mug and brush etched into the glass door. And just for old times sake the red and white striped barber pole sat in one corner. And how strangely convenient the shop just happened to be next door to Lucille's phone center?

As Molly walked toward the phone center to tell Lucille she was expecting a very important call, she heard the dulcet tones emanating from the barbershop. She halted for a moment. First she heard the ending of *"O Solo Mio"* then a rousing rendition of *"You botcha' me, I botcha' you and everything goes crazy."* She had to chuckle to herself. *The guy can sing*, she thought. She alerted Lucille to find her as soon as the call from California came in.

Molly paused in the center of the lobby on her way to talk to Chip. She looked around. Boy the place was really shaping up. *Pretty snazzy*, she thought. The fluorescent lights hidden in the cove of the ceiling gave the room a nice, cozy feeling. Each corridor, leading off the lobby, had soft curved corners, which appeared to welcome any visitor. Come, explore me to see where I lead, they seemed to beckon. She wondered if they were going to have a fountain or waterfall. 'Audacious Audrey' and 'Sly Ely' were just getting up to leave as she entered Chip's office. They had just returned from a short Caribbean cruise. They were both tan as could be and looked great. As it was with the rest of the group, the Floragra was working wonders. They said, their ta-ta's, as Mrs. Goldberg sat down.

"Got a minute?" she asked Chip.

"For you, I got two. Hey, that rhymes," he noted.

"Are you aware that Doc asked me to help him investigate those phenomenons? she inquired.

"No, I'm not. He mentioned them to me. I think the only thing phenomenal is Doc. His imagination is bursting," replied Chip.

"That's not the only thing he has bursting," she said subtly, recalling the evening of a week ago. She looked up at Chip, "Maybe there is something going on that we should know about. Kenny doesn't shake very easily."

"Do what you can without getting hurt and let me know if I can help," said Chip.

As she strolled out of the office, she bumped into Mr. Sellemfast, the broker that negotiated the sale for them.

"How nice to see you again Miss Molly," he acknowledged.

"Yeh, me too," she flipped.

"Say, what was the name of the Japanese guy in California that we bought this place from?" she asked.

"Oh you mean, Mr. Terri Yaki. Very nice fellow to deal with," Sellum replied.

"Thanks a lot," she said, as she hurried off and making a beeline for the kitchen.

"I got a name, Doc! I got a name," she bellowed.

"Slow down, Molly or you'll bust your bra," replied Doc.

"I'm not wearing one, thank you very much," she huffed.

She told Doc about Terri Yaki. Maybe they didn't need a Sam Spade or a Richard Diamond after all. Why Doc couldn't call the dude and ask some question, she suggested.

"Not a good idea," thought Doc. "We don't want to raise any suspicions just yet."

Lucille came running in.

"I got the California call on the house phone. Where do you want to take it?"

"Right here," said Mrs. Goldberg, as she reached for the phone.

It seemed funny to be talking on one of those upright phones with the separate hearing piece you held up to your ear.

"Hi, Mrs. Goldberg, it's me Mitzi, Mitzi Gaynor."

"Mitzi, so good to hear from you, what's going on?" replied Molly.

Mitzi started, "I've got some news for you. I don't know if it's good or bad but at least it's something."

"Lay it on me," Molly said.

"Well I got a hold of Peter and explained your situation to him," she said.

"Whoa, wait a minute," said Molly. "Peter who, Peter Geer?"

"No, no, no!" cried Mitzi. "None other than Peter Falk, that's who, don't you remember how great he was in Columbo? Anyway," she went on, "he remembered investigating a shady Japanese organization years ago. He thought there was some kind of Oriental Mafia or something. I can't remember exactly what he said about that part of it. He did remember making friends with a Japanese guy who had a bit part in one of his shows. And sure enough this guy knew, or at least was aware of, *Mr. Terri Yaki*. He told Peter to be careful because the guy was bad news. Anyhow, Peter's contact shadowed Yaki to a Sushi bar one night. He claims he overheard Terri Yaki telling his drinking buddies how stupid Americans were. Seems he had recently sold them a haunted hotel for ten million dollars. How dumb, he said, wait till they found out. Then the best part was that after the Americans got the place renovated and got scared out by the ghosts, they would buy it back for the same amount. Apparently they had done the same thing in Europe. Anyhow they have an agent down there, named *Ota,* that's keeping an eye on the place."

Molly thanked her several times for all her help. She said she would let Mitzi know, if she wasn't afraid of ghosts, when they got the place open.

"And don't forget to thank Peter," added Molly who then quickly filled Doc in on the conversation.

Doc said, "Well you see, I'm not totally nuts, in spite of what Chip thinks. That also explains the Japanese matches. The guy has been right here spying on us. I think we should tell Chip."

After Chip, along with Miss Ellie, heard the story, he apologized to Doc for doubting him although Chip added that he still wasn't sure of the ghost.

THE SPIES

They decided the group had better do a little sleuthing on their own.

"Where's our security staff, where are Bert and Gert?" asked Chip.

Doc and Molly responded that they had just seen them heading toward the work out rooms with 'Sexy Sam'. Chip tried the walkie-talkie.

"Security two and three, come in please. This is security one, where are you?"

"Hey Chip, this is Bert. What do you want?"

"Listen, air-wave brain, what happened to the protocol? Aren't you supposed to answer as security two?" Chip admonished.

"Oh, yeah, I guess I forgot, this is security two, now what do you want?" replied Bert.

"Get down to my office ASAP which doesn't mean you're a sap, it means as soon as possible, got it?" replied Chip.

By the time Chip said *"got it?"* they walked in the door. They had been walking all the while they were talking. Chip told them the whole story with Doc and Molly filling in. He told them they needed some one to go under cover to find out about this Ota character.

"We can do some of our best work *under cover*," noted Bert.

Bert and Gert were ready for this assignment. They really got into this under cover, spying, and espionage stuff. They figured if they were going to do it right, they had better look the part.

When they returned from the flea market, they tried on their new outfits. Gert bought one of those new soft, silky long dresses with the slit on each side. It was a soft blue with a perpendicular muted vine of green and purple. It may have been a size or two too small. She no longer had the figure of a teenager and nowhere close to Molly's. Bert opted for a pair of black "chino" pants, a white knit sport shirt and a pair of straw type sandals. He was decked out with two cameras a light meter and a hand held flash unit. While Bert wore the typical sandals, Gert had on ballet slippers. Their headdress was a sight to behold. Bert spent two bucks apiece for a couple of pleated lampshades. He removed the harp portion from each. His fit pretty well even allowing him; to see through the rounded metal frame eyeglasses he had on. Poor Gert's lampshade was a little too large. She kept pushing it back on her head with her fan! They didn't want to give away; their disguises, so they slipped out the back door and headed for the nearest Japanese steak house. As she went to get out of the car Gert almost fell on her face. The tight little Japanese dress wouldn't allow her to stretch her legs out. She finally managed to stand upright. Then she tried a few steps.

"No wonder the Japanese women take such tiny little steps. These damn dresses won't let you move," Gert complained.

All the while, Bert was yelling, *"Come on. Hurry up!"* She had to pull the skirt up above her knees to catch up to Bert. They were met at the entrance by the maitre'de (the master of the house) with a deep bow.

"Good evening, lady and gentleman," he greeted, "what is your pleasure this evening?"

Bert replied they just wanted to eat.

"Ah so, you come quickly, your cook ready to start," he replied.

They were seated at the U shaped table with ten other guests. They barely had time to order when the knives started flashing. The rice was cooking, the mushrooms were browning, the soybeans were sizzling and the shrimp were dancing. About all that was missing was the meat. When the meat arrived, the cook, who was wearing the traditional three quarter length kimono tied with a black sash, quickly flipped the steak on the sizzling hot grill. Then he REALLY went into his performance. The razor sharp knives were flashing all over the place. Poor Gert, couldn't keep up with him because her lampshade hat kept slipping over her eyes. Every time she pushed it up with her fan the cook thought she was somehow applauding. He twirled the knives over his head, and then brought them down with lightening speed, to dice up some more meat. He even flipped the knives in the air, twirled and caught them behind his back. It reminded them of an act on the Ed Sullivan Show. (Man this guy was good!) They sat there dazzled by the show their cook was putting on.

Then Bert leaned over to Gert and whispered in her ear, "There's no other Japanese, in the place, we won't find out much here."

"Of course not, you fool. They don't eat here. This is strictly for tourist," she said.

They enjoyed a great dinner. The grill had been cleaned waiting for the next group. The dishes had all been removed. Bert was just about to relax with an after dinner drink when he got a bright idea. He told Gert to sit tight. He was going to ask if he could go back into the kitchen on the pretense of asking the cook a culinary question. The waiter thought it would be *okee dokee* and so escorted him through the swinging doors that led to the back of the building. Bert found the chef they had, having a beer and sucking on a cigarette. The chef quickly jumped up and bowed.

"Ah so," he said.

"Ah so, to you too," replied Bert as he tried to bow. (It wasn't easy after all he had to eat.)

"What can I do for you?" asked the chef.

Bert stammered. "I wondered if you ever cooked fish like that, you know on the grill?"

"Sure I cook fish like that, but you no ordered fish," he replied.

"Yeah, right," spit out Bert. "Maybe next time."

He wasn't sure where he was going with this. Then he thought, "What the hell, go for broke."

He turned away from the chef as though he were leaving. It dawned on him that he didn't want to expose his whole backside. He remembered those flashing knives and cleavers. With a quarter turn he half spoke over his shoulder.

"By the way, do you know a guy named Ota?"

"Ah so, yes, Mr. Ota's nice gentleman," he said.

Good, we're getting someplace thought Bert.

Our story now takes a quick look back at Gert whom we left sitting all alone. The dining room was empty except for the waiters and a few cooks waiting for the next group whose reservations weren't due for another half hour. One waiter said to the maitre d'..... .

Waiter: "Wanna' have some fun?"

Maitre d': "Yes, always can use laugh."

The waiter approached Gert: "Hi, my name is Yomamoto, what is your name, prease?"

"Gert," she replied.

"Ah, Missee Gertee, I thought your name Missee Sippi. You don't have drink?" he replied.

"No," Gert said. "I thought my husband would be back by now."

"*No probrum,*" said Yama, "*house-buy one for you.*"

He poured her a small glass of Saki. Gert was a little nervous about all this. *What the heck, she thought? What harm can it do? Besides, Bert should be here any minute.* She hoisted the glass.

"Here's mud in your eye, or whatever you Japanese say,"
She gulped it down like it was a shot of Canadian Club.
"Wow, that hits the spot," she exclaimed.
"Buy one, get one free," said Yama, as he poured another.
"Okee, dokee," says Gert. "Gee you guys aren't so bad."
She swallowed about half of it before her lampshade fell over her eyes. As it slid down, the waiter quickly filled her glass again.
"Missee-Gertee is feeling happy now?" he asked.
"Ah yes, very happy except for this stupid hat," she said.
"Prease do not remove hat. Un'rucky to remove hat in steak house," the waiter said.
"Oh, sure, I mean, Ah so or oh so or something," she muttered.
She downed another.
"Boy this stuff is good!"

We now shift back to the kitchen. The cook was answering Bert.

"Sure I know Mr. Ota, he in back room," said the cook.
Bert couldn't believe his luck-jackpot on the first try. The cook led him past the pantry, and the meat cooler toward a heavy looking windowless door in the far reaches of the building. Only a very small peephole in the door was evident. Not even a handle.
The cook spoke up: "Mr. Ota, you have visitor, prease."
There seemed to be a hidden microphone in the door because the cook was almost whispering. Bert could hear chains rattling and the slide of a bolt. He was beginning to wonder if this was such good idea. These guys didn't seem to fool around. The door opened part way. Bert could make out a little guy, about five feet three, dressed in a very expensive suit, complete with a silk shirt and a hundred dollar tie. Strange thing was, he was wearing a green eyeshade like you used to see in the movies of old gambling houses. Bert remembered the Japanese were great fans of old movies. When the viewer was satisfied that Bert looked harmless, the door opened slowly. (Mr. Ota, it seemed, was alone.)
"Come in, prease, takee seat," said Ota.
"Thank you," as Bert bowed politely.
Bert surveyed the room noting the décor.

Sparsely furnished, a Marilyn Monroe picture on one wall, no doubt, the safe is behind the picture, and the safe is always behind a picture, a racing form open on one table and the stock market pages spread out on another.

Bert picked up the real estate section off a chair before he could sit down.

(No wonder the guy was wearing an eyeshade, he was into a little of everything.)

Bert began, "Mr. Ota, my name is Bert and my wife is Gert. She is waiting for me by the grill."

"Ah so," said, the little Oriental. "Prease, do not have to call me Mr. Ota."

"What do they call you then?" asked Bert.

"Many people call me, Fung-yoo, but you call me Toy, okee dokee?"

"Okee dokee, Mr. Toy," replied Bert.

"No. Not okee dokee, Mr. Toy. My name Toy, like Roy, only it is Toy," replied Ota.

"Oh, now I get it. Your name is Toy, and your last name is Ota. So you are Toy Ota, right?" asked Bert.

"Okee dokee, now you got it baby," replied Ota.

Bert let out a long sigh. As he did, he pushed the real estate section farther back on the table. There, in full view, was a book of Japanese matches exactly like the ones he had found outside his door. His mind was spinning now. *What do I say? How do I get out of this?"*

He blurted it out: "Toy, what you know about a guy named Terri Yaki?"

The young Mr. Ota, who was perhaps in his mid-thirties, gave Bert a big grin.

"Ah so, you know Mr. Yaki? Everyone call him Yaki from Osaki. He, very unscrupurous," said Ota.

"But you do business with him, no?" asked Bert.

"Oh no Mr. Bert, I don't do business with that guy. All I do for him, I spy. Ho ho, very funny-old terevision show, *I Spy*. He pays me very well," exclaimed Ota.

"Then what are you doing around the FASA Hotel?" asked Bert.

"I just said, I spy, I keep track how you doing, I report to Yaki, he send money, quick," explained Ota.

"Oh, ho," said Bert as he formulated a plan on the spot, "why don't you come down there some day and I will give you a tour?"

"Good idea Bert, I give Yaki a full report, then Yaki send me more money."

Bert was thinking to himself. This guy will do anything for money. FASA's got money. Maybe we could turn the tables on Terry Yaki.

They agreed to meet at the hotel the following Tuesday. Bert made his way back through the dimly lit storage area. As he entered the main dining room, he heard billows of laughter. Standing on top of a counter was Gert, her makeshift hat, down around her face. She didn't see Bert at first. She was busy trying to do a Hawaiian hula while the staff was clapping out a rhythm, and laughing like fools.

Bert walked up to her and said, "Gert, get down from there this minute, what the hell are you doing?"

"Well if it isn't Bert baby," she replied. "What took you so long?"

She took one step off the counter top and landed right in Bert's arms.

"Hey, big boy, I'm glad to see you," she said, and then, passed out.

A couple of the waiters helped him get her into the car. They laughed hysterically as they walked back into the restaurant. As he pulled up in front of their apartment, Bert picked up the walkie-talkie.

"Breaker, breaker, good buddies, this is Bert and I need some help, pronto."

Chip heard the call. He picked up the unit and admonished Bert once again.

"You idiot, you're not on a C.B., you're on a walkie-talkie. Now what do you want?"

Bert told him he needed help getting Gert into the house.

"Why, is she hurt?" Chip asked.

"No, Gert is not hurt, she's just inert," replied Bert.

'King Arthur' and 'Millie the Mermaid' were just leaving when Bert pulled up. Arthur walked over to see what was wrong. Bert explained what happened, all the while tugging on Gert's legs trying to get her out of the car. 'The Mermaid' was standing there taking it all in. She saw the cone shaped thing lying on the back seat.

"What's with the lampshade?" she asked.

"Don't ask," replied Bert as he continued his struggle.

He finally got her into an awkward upright position. 'King Arthur' put one of her arms around his neck and attempted to support one side. Bert put her other arm around his own neck. They half dragged her and half walked her into the apartment. That wasn't easy either as Bert was about five foot six while 'King Arthur' was a good six foot three. Gert didn't know but she was listing badly. They flopped her on the sofa. It was then that Bert noticed the slit on one side of the slinky dress was torn up to her waist. He decided to let her sleep it off.

"Why don't the two of you come back to the hotel with me?" asked Arthur, "I'll explain the whole story to you and Chip at the same time, and boy have I got some news."

A REVEALING STORY

Chip and Miss Ellie saw them coming. They met them at the front door. Chip was ready to jump all over Bert again about his use of the walkie-talkie when he noticed Bert's disguised attempt at a disguise.

"Been to a masquerade ball?" he asked instead.

Bert ignored the question: then replied that he had a hellava' story to tell them and that he could use a drink. They called Doc and Molly, Lucille and Dominic. 'Sexy Sam' with 'Alluring Anita' plus 'Sly Ely' and 'Audacious Audrey' were there. Like the finale of a stage play, the cast of characters, were almost all there. The few missing ones could be filled in later. Bert said he felt like the lead actor on center stage. He started the story back with Doc's encounters, then Molly's Hollywood connections and finally got around to the undercover stuff. He described it all in great detail. So much so that Chip was becoming exasperated. He really laid it on when he got to the meeting with Mr. Ota.

"I stood right up to him and said, "Don't toy with me Toy."

Bert was carrying on like he was *Dirty Harry* or at least *Al Pacino*. He didn't tell him he almost dirtied in his Japanese "chinos". The group, were on the edge of their seats, half laughing at Bert's charade and half inquisitive. Bert eventually got around to telling them that 'Toy Ota' didn't really work for Yaki. He was doing the spy work for money.

Bert explained, "I think if we paid him a little bit more than Terri Yaki is paying him, we could get him to submit some false reports and thereby turn the tables on the whole damn group. Now here's the real kicker. Toy Ota is a professional ventriloquist and mimic! He was the one that dropped the matches outside the door … AND he was throwing the voices of Bogart and Mae West hoping to chase us out of the hotel. What doya' think of them bananas?" he said triumphantly.

Doc was the first to speak up: "I gotta' give ya' credit Bert. Thank God that proves I'm not Looney. See Chip, I tried to tell you."

They were congratulating Bert on his discoveries, pouring a few more drinks and patting him on the back. He acted like he just scored the winning goal in the Stanley Cup. Finally, someone, probably Molly, asked where Gert was all this time and where is she now?

Bert replied, "She was in the restaurant all that time, apparently entertaining the Japanese troops. Or vise versa, I'm not sure which. When I finally got of the kitchen, I found her doing the hula on top of the bar."

'King Arthur' spoke up, "We helped him get her into the apartment where she's sleeping off a good one. I think she deserves a medal for meritorious service above and beyond the call of duty."

"What about me, don't I get one?" asked Bert.

MAKING PROGRESS

Since this was the largest assemblage in quite a while, they decided to explore their options. 'King Arthur', probably the deepest thinker in the bunch, took the floor.

"As I see it," he began, "we have made tremendous progress since the amazing Floragra discovery. It would be a shame to give it all up now. Besides we're gambling on Mother Nature. Will the miracle bushes hold out? We don't know. Will we ever get this hotel finished? Should we explore Bert's idea of using Mr. 'Toy Ota' to thwart the Japanese in California?"

Chip interrupted, "There seems to be many questions. I'm sure we will iron them all out. However, I think we are over excited by these recent events. I propose we all take a week off to relax, and then reconvene with open minds. In the meantime the renovations can continue. We will need one volunteer to stay behind in case any problems come up."

Some old Wisenheimer, who had not been heard from lately, said *he could handle it.* The cheers went up, *"Here, here!"* Bert made his way back to his apartment. Gert was still zonked out. They disbursed and sent in different directions, although several climbed aboard the old school bus they had acquired for the trip back to the complex. They all seemed to walk past the hedges-just checking. The 'The Lovely Lois' decided to make a trip back to Twinsville, Ohio to see her twin, Lynn. A couple thought they would fly back East for a few days. Mr. and Mrs. 'Chip N. Dale' flew back up North to see 'Marvelous Marilyn from Milford, Michigan'. The rest of them just kind of hung around taking it easy. Several, especially the girls, could hardly wait to get to the pool. Not because they wanted to swim but because they wanted to show off their newly found bodies. It was like saying, *"Look at me, no lumps, no bumps, no crevasses, no creases and no wrinkles."* Apparently, the women weren't the only ones showing off. It was mentioned in a conversation later, that 'Sexy Sam' was doing jack knifes off the diving board. Doc remarked that what the heck, he didn't have any family to check on so he would just as soon stay to work on the fragrances. Besides, if Molly was going to be around, maybe he could make up for lost time. Even though, Skeeter wasn't exactly a charter member, he was so well liked that the group had adopted him. He told Doc he was going to use the time off to re pad the motorcycle sidecar for little Belle Taco. Besides, he would care of Taco Chip for Chip and Miss Ellie while they were away.

SMELLY?

By the end of the week the little coterie of geriatrics was chomping at the bit to get back to work. The time off had rejuvenated the whole group. One by one and two by two, they all made it back to the FASA Hotel to converge on Chip and Doc. Chip himself was eager to find out what Doc had come up with in the way of fragrances. They convened in the kitchen area. Doc was surprised they all came back at one time. However, he had been working feverishly all week. He was ready for them when they arrived. He had lined up little Dixie cups with samples. In front of each one he had placed a placard. The group was astonished that Doc was this organized. The presentation was worthy of an *"Oscar"* in the beauty business.

When everyone was crowded in, Doc began, "Ladies and Gentlemen, may I present: Tuity-Fruity followed by Oh, Baby, not to be outdone by WOW! And no fragrance line up would be complete without Kilroy, Poodleskirt and Hubba Hubba."

The applause was thundering. You would think you had just witnessed a fashion show in Milan.

(Fantastic Doc but how did you do it? How'd you come up with the names? If you were naming this product to make it more marketable, what would you call it?)

"Well," Doc explained,"I did a lot of research on beauty aids, hair shampoos, deodorants, perfumes and so on. Most of the names I thought of had already been used. There are hundreds of flower names like Passion Flower. There's a dozen Blue Lagoon type and another dozen names for gems. I got to thinking, how old is the market that is buying this stuff. You're right, most of us were born in the 1920's or 30's or maybe 40's. What do we remember most from our youth? I thought a lot about the war years, the big war that is. I considered 'Loose lips, sink ships'. Bu t we don't want to promote loose lips, we're promoting tighter, firmer lips. That's the story."

There was unanimous approval. Even Chip, who sometimes thought Doc was a dim bulb, was impressed. Wisenheimer asked if Doc had thought of food names *like Champagne or Caviar.*

"No," Doc replied. "I did have fun with one other, though I mixed up some Flame Red and I thought of calling it *Fire Hydrant*. But then I thought, no if you had it rubbed on your body, you might have a problem with dogs as you walked down the street."

That gave everybody a good chuckle. They settled down for happy hour. Chip spotted 'The Lovely Lois' in the crowd.

"Are your books up to date?" he questioned.

"Sure are," she said.

Chip quieted the gang down long enough to see if they could have an unofficial accounting by the various department heads. He thought they should all be brought up to date since most of them were there.

Lois, the treasurer, gave the first report. They were in great shape. They had so much money in the treasury that they could pay off the mortgage if they wanted to. She thought if they added the fragrance line, and it sold like they expected, each and every investor would have their money back within a year … *'oohs and ahs and applause'*. (There's nothing this group liked better than money, except, their youthful looks!)

One by one the department heads reported their area of expertise was completed or would be in another week. The beach had been dragged, grated and new sand brought in. The cabanas, with the special roofs that looked like palm fronds but could stand up in a stiff wind, were done. The pool was ready to be filled. The dining room was complete. The coffee shop/grill was done. 'Tee Shot Tom', the expediter, reported he had located a manufacturer in High Point, North Carolina, that was duplicating the Art Deco designs of the furniture for the suites. They should be here next week.

The biggest hang up appeared to be the carpet for the lobby. This was the biggest order the company had ever received for a custom floor cover. They were used to making area rugs of 6' x 8' or 8' x 10', but never one like this. They weren't sure how to get the Floragra logo, with shrubs at the bottom, the pyramid over the sun and the lightning zigzagging through the apex of the pyramid. But 'Sly Ely' told Chip it shouldn't be a problem. He knew a guy back east that had the cutter and the embossing shears to do the job. Either give the job to that guy, hire him to supervise the carpet company or rent the equipment from him. Chip told him to work it out-pronto.

The finial or topper had been installed and wired up on the roof. No one had seen it lit up yet. They were waiting for the grand opening. All in all, it seemed everything was going great. They were way ahead of schedule.

THE JAPANESE PROPOSITION

As the group broke up, Bert and Gert, (yes she was still alive and well) sauntered over to Chip and Doc.

"What are you thinking of doing with the Japanese group in California?" asked Bert.

Chip asked Doc, if he had noticed anything suspicious in the past week.

"I haven't heard any more ghosts but I have had the feeling of being watched. Every time I walked up to your office or looked out the front door, I thought I say someone jump into a car that sped down the street. Maybe it was just my imagination," said Doc.

"I don't think so," said Bert, "these guy's mean business. These aren't kids we're fooling with. This 'Toy Ota' guy is one tough Oriental cookie. We wouldn't want a shady character like that hanging around after we're open," he said.

"What do you suggest we do about it?" asked Chip.

"Like I said before," answered Bert. "We hire this Ota character to give Terri Yaki a false report. Case closed. They're off our back."

"Ok," said Chip, "you make an appointment for Ota to come here. Do not make any deals. Just set up the appointment."

Bert asked Gert if she wanted to go along.

"NO THANK YOU!" she exclaimed. "I still hurt. I don't know what happened that night and I don't want to ever know what happened that night. I'll never go near that place again, especially wearing a lamp shade."

Bert was on his own. He got into see Mr. Ota without any problem. He did, however, detect a few snickers from the wait staff as he walked through the restaurant. The meeting was set up. Mr. Toy Ota said he could be at the FASA building about 1:30 the next day. Upon returning to the hotel to set it up with Chip, Doc and probably a few others, the first thing he did was alert the security guard at the front entrance.

"Now tomorrow, we are expecting a visitor. A little Oriental guy dressed like a New York mobster out of an old movie. Don't be alarmed but frisk him at the front desk," he instructed.

Chip invited Doc, 'Sexy Sam' and 'King Arthur' to attend the meeting. Mr. Ota was on time. He was frisked without incident, was escorted to the office and offered a seat. But before sitting, he bowed in front of each one, extended a hand, and muttered *"Ah so"*. Chip outlined their plan, emphasizing that they would pay him more than Mr. Yaki was paying him. That got his attention.

"What I have to do?" he asked.

"Just the opposite of what you're doing now," said Arthur. "You say in your report that everything is going fine, we don't have any problems, that we will be open for business in one month and that, in your humble opinion, we will never sell the hotel at any price."

"That a lot of lying for ten thousand," Toy said.

"Ten thousand, my eye," spoke up Sam. "That Yaki guy isn't paying you anywhere near that kind of money."

Ota spoke up, "What is that figure on top of building?"

(Clever, these Japanese, never answer a direct question. Always evade the truth. Parry and thrust. Change the subject. Before anyone had time to remember that the Japanese evasion the Japanese ambassadors carried off in the white house on Dec. 7th, 1941.) Doc blurted out that the figure represented the Floragra logo.

"What is Froragla?" Ota asked.

At that point, it dawned on Chip that this guy didn't know anything about their little group. He asked for a short recess to use the men's room and to order some beverage. He instructed Mr. Ota not to wander out of the lobby. (They didn't want him stumbling on the manufacturing area.) They told him he would be on their 'Candid Camera', if he did. The four guys headed for a conference room.

"Doc, you got a big mouth," Chip admonished.

"I'm sorry Chip, I didn't think," replied Doc.

Chip asked if anyone had any suggestions: "We don't want to spill the beans on the whole operation. Where do we go from here? What do we tell this guy?"

Big 'King Arthur' gave a "hrmph", cleared his throat and replied that he didn't think they had a problem yet: "We tell him the sign is our topper on the building, that it is the logo for FASA, The Florida Agricultural Senior Association and let it go at that."

Chip was relieved, "Good thinking, Arthur, but what about the Floragra slip?"

Arthur thought for a moment. "Let's get those drinks, I need one."

All the while they were setting up the drinks for themselves and for Mr. Ota, Arthur was thinking:

"Let me handle the negotiations from here. I've dealt with these kinds of people before. If worse comes to worse, we can tell him about Floragra but don't have to tell him where we get it. Take it from me, there's only one thing these guys appreciated more than money and that's sex. If we have to, we give him a small sample of Flora-

gra, tell him it's an aphrodisiac and go from there. Once he's hooked, he'll keep coming back like a drug addict."

They agreed that was as good a plan as any. They found Mr. Ota eyeing up Lucille at the switchboard. They regrouped in Chip's office along with an assortment of beverages.

When everyone was seated 'King Arthur' said, "Mr. Ota, we are prepared to offer you five thousand dollars to correct your reports to Mr. Terry Yaki. I figure that's five times what he's paying you."

"I'll take it," Ota said without hesitation. "However, you still haven't answered my question about the sign on the roof. How can I turn in a report if I don't understand what you're doing?"

Arthur went through the FASA explanation, which seemed to satisfy Toy, for the moment and the meeting disbanded. The four members were escorting their guest to the front door.

Toy Ota stopped at the door, "Suppose Mr. Yaki no believes my report?"

'Sexy Sam' spoke up, "You make sure your report is very believable and we will make it worthwhile beyond your imagination."

"How you do that?" queried Ota.

"Never mind how just believe old Sexy Sam that you will feel younger, more virile and sexier that you were as a teenager."

"Okee, dokee," said Ota, and out the door he went.

A CARPET PROBLEM

With a sigh of relief, the four guys went back to the office.

"Another obstacle over come," said Chip. "However, I would like to bring up another one."

"What's that?" asked Doc.

Chip went on to say that now that they were so close to getting the place opened, he felt there was a lot more organizing to do than any of them had the experience to perform. He was thinking they needed to hire a full-fledged hotel manager. One that could over see the beach, the pool, the dining room, the guest rooms, just everything in the day to day operation of a first class hotel.

"What do you think?" he asked.

Doc and Sam seemed surprised. They had never thought about it. 'King Arthur' said he wondered when it would come to this. He interjected that there was a lot of other things to be considered like the Floragra production, the various contest, coordinating the contest winners, the musicians and the entertainment in the ballroom, and on and on. Arthur said he thought it would be wise to have a general membership meeting to see how everyone felt and then they could also bring everyone up to date.

While this was going on, 'Tee Shot Tom' and 'Sly Ely' were taking charge of the carpet problem. First, they contacted the local carpet guy to do a little negotiating. They made a deal to pay him close to the original price to install carpet in all the rooms and hallways if he would relinquish that portion of the contract that dealt with the lobby and that blasted logo.

"Glad to," the guy said.

Tom and Ely picked up the rolls, in various colors and loaded them in the U Haul. They stopped at home long enough to tell their spouses what was happening. 'Beauteous Bev' wanted to know how long they would be gone. Tee Shot thought it might take a week.

"Why can't we go along?" she asked. "Ya' got an extended cab, don't cha'?"

"OK with me if it's OK with Ely." Said Tom.

Bev phoned 'Audacious Audrey', to *'see how she felt about it'*.

"I just said the same thing to 'Sly Ely'," she replied.

The four of them phoned Chip to fill him in.

"Be back in a week," they said, and away they went.

As soon as they arrived, they made the arrangements with Ely's carpet buddy, and then decided to take in some of the sights. None of them had been back to the Big Apple for thirty years or so. The buildings were all in the same place but things had changed. Most of their old haunts had moved or gone out of business. None of the dance halls they so fondly remembered were open any more. *"What happened to Toots Shores or The Copa? What about this or what about that?"* By the end of the week they were more than happy to head back to sunny Florida.

The carpet arrived the day after they returned. Four men were sent to install it in the lobby. It was absolutely gorgeous. The sculpturing was done so well that if you didn't know better you would think it was inlaid tile. It rivaled some of the ancient Roman mosaics. No one walked on the logo except Skeeter.

DECISIONS

The general membership meeting was called to order in one of the conference rooms. Each department head, once again brought them up to date. Each one had a glowing report of his progress and thanked all the helpers. Doc gave a brief summary of the Floragra production. His one big concern now was what happens when the kitchen opens for business? How were they going to keep things separated? Who was going to be the head chef? Was it someone he could get along with in sharing the kitchen? Chip suggested they hold off on that for a little bit to give it some thought. Chip called for some of the other reports. 'Sexy Sam' reported that the pool people he had contracted would begin filling the pool the next day. They estimated it would take five or six days to get it filled and bring it to the proper PH level. They estimated if all goes well, it could be open by next weekend. Since Sam had also been in charge of the beach area he said he had an important question, "What were they going to do for life guards?" He felt they needed someone that not only was a strong swimmer but someone trained in revival techniques. He thought maybe *Johnny Weissmuller or Esther Williams* would be great but he didn't know if they were still alive. If not, then maybe *David Hassellhauf from Baywatch,* would be interested. Chip again suggested that they hold off on that for a little bit to give it more thought. What he was really doing was holding them off until he told them about hiring a hotel manager.

Lucille was next up. She gave a detailed report of the calls coming in for new orders, how many for reorders, how many were inquiries only, how many were for samples and on and on and on. She ended up by saying the last operator they hired was doing a good job but she was already complaining about the overload. Lucille wondered if they could hire *Lilly Tomlin*?

Chip said, "Let's hold off for a minute."

Mrs. Molly Goldberg really didn't have a progress report. She said she had a lot of talent lined up but couldn't make firm commitments until she knew when they were going to open. She informed them that she had made contact with *Jerry Vale and Al Martino* who was down here doing the Medicare circuit. They both assured her they would be happy to be part of such a wonderful undertaking.

She added "And don't forget Burt Reynolds and Perry Como."

She took a breath before continuing. (God, she looked great. More like Angie Dickinson every day.)

"I have a suggestion to make," she said. "I think we should have a pre-grand opening just for the FASA group. We could call it a Revival Meeting by reviving the good old days or just a sock hop. All of you have old 78-RPM records, or 45's or at least 8 track tapes of some of the old bands. If you would bring them into me, I'll find a disc jockey to line up a program. We'll open the kitchen for hot dogs, hamburgers, chocolate malts, banana splits and cherry cokes. I think we would have a great time and maybe iron out a few bugs in the process."

Molly received another standing ovation. She was getting used to them. Chip didn't have much choice in this one. He was outvoted a hundred to none. He voted for it himself. The date was set for two weeks from Saturday. Before he could get them settled down there were shouts of *"I got Glen Miller, I got Tommy*

Dorsey, I got Duke Ellington." Molly said she had a DJ in mind that would knock their socks off (But she wouldn't say who it was). When order was finally restored (man they were rambunctious) Chip said he had an announcement to make. He told them why he thought they needed an experienced hotel manager. The announcement left everyone surprised. There was an undercurrent of buzzes. *What were they going to do? There wasn't anyone any better than Chip N. Dale, not in this group anyhow.* 'Audacious Audrey' raised her hand to stand up.

"How about, *James Brolin*, remember how great he was in Hotel when it was on TV? I bet he could do it without *Veronica Hamill*. Besides he doesn't have much else to do these days."

Chip said they would take that under advisement but he doubted if Streisand would let her husband do anything like that. He told the group that if they knew anyone that might qualify to let him know. (It was the end of another exciting day for the Floragra founders.)

THE SOCK HOP

The next week, The Salvation Army, The Goodwill, The Purple Heart and every resale shop in South Florida couldn't figure out what was happening. There was a run on saddle shoes, penny loafers, poodle skirts and white T-shirts. Doc didn't need to go looking. He never got rid of his. In fact, he wore half of the stuff every day. Molly didn't need much either. She was thinking of showing up in her Rockettes' uniform. That style hadn't changed much in the last 50 or 60 years. Besides, she was busy accumulating the record and tape library. She started to make a list and was amazed at how many big bands had been around in the 20's, 30's, and 40's. She was having a ball assembling all this stuff. Every time she ran across one that jogged her memory, she would put the record on her old RCA. Then, singing along, she danced around the room with her kitchen broom for a partner. She was traveling back in time when it dawned on her that, hey, she felt almost as good now as she did thirty or forty years ago … thanks to Floragra. Oh, this was going to be so much fun.

She called Doc, "Hey big boy, I don't have a date for the prom."

"What the hell are you talking about?" was his response.

"The big ball, the pre-opening, the revival meeting, the sock hop that you are planning on going to, isn't cha?" she said.

Doc said, "He supposed so, but hadn't given it much thought."

"Well think about it, Dearie, you and me dressed to the nines and be hopping' all over the place. Also think about transportation. We don't want to go on the bus all dressed up, do we?" she added.

Doc guessed *he'd better get cracking' on this thing. He could see she was all wound up.*

Years ago Doc had restored old cars as a hobby. He made a few calls up North to some of his old car buddies. They quickly got back to him with the names of several car clubs in South Florida. Most club members were more than happy to show off their cars. It doesn't take long for the word to spread among car clubs. Many guys belong to more than one club. For instance, you could belong to the *Model-A Restores Club* and *The Corvette Club* at the same time. Soon, Doc was getting calls from all over Florida. The restorers would use any excuse to show off their cars. Doc decided, what the heck, they might as well all arrive in vintage cars. He made arrangements for about twenty-five cars to show up at the condo complex and then parade them all to the hotel.

Doc and Molly were to be driven in a *'32 Ford Roadster*-with the top down. 'King Arthur' and 'Millie the Mermaid' fittingly, chose a *Rolls Royce Silver Cloud*. Chip and 'Miss Ellie the Merry Maid from Michigan' picked out a really sharp '32 Coupe, with flames on the hood. They would ride in the rumble seat. Ellie thought it would be fun to stand on the running board. Chip didn't think they could get away with that in downtown Miami. The rest of the entourage consisted of *Chalmers, Studebakers, Terraplanes, Marmons, Packards* and even a *Stutz Bearcat* and a classic Auburn. What a night this was going to be!

Chip had been in contact with his sister, 'The Marvelous Marilyn from Milford, Michigan'. He E-mailed her to check on a place in downtown Detroit; he thought it was on Bates Street that specialized in antique stage costumes or old theatre memorabilia.

"Have you flipped your wig again?" she E-mailed him back, what's up this time?"

"I'm looking for a complete Soot-Suit. Remember those? I need the whole thing including the wide brim hat and the two-tone shoes, size 8. Call me if you find one, I'll need it UPS'd overnight," he said.

As usual, she came through. The package arrived the next day. Chip was in the master bedroom, trying it on when Miss Ellie walked in. She broke out laughing. "Hubba hubbaaa," she strung it out.

The pants were pegged as tightly as they had been when he wore the bicycle clips to keep them out of the bike chain. The waist ban was half way up between his naval and his pectorals. They were sharply creased. The shirt was adorned with Mother of Pearl buttons. And the coat was almost too much to describe, a brilliant yellow and blue (indicative of the University of Michigan colors) plaid padded wide shoulders, rolled lapel with a single button. And long. Of course, everything Chip wore was long. He was only five foot three to begin with. The fedora was a yellow wide brim with a wide blue band around it. The shoes, size eight, were brown wing tips with a white panel on top. He slipped them on to show Ellie his *Fred Astaire* moves.

"What about the watch chain or whatever it was called? Ya' gotta' have a big long watch chain," said Ellie.

He remembered that back in his youth, he had a gleaming gold chain about three feet long. He didn't remember anyone attaching them to a watch. It clipped on your belt, draped down to your knees, then up to a pants pocket. Most guys clipped their car keys on it, although once in awhile someone got caught with a penknife on the end. He even knew one ritzy guy that had a money clip on his. He thought they might find something at the flea market that they could fashion into one. He looked at himself in the mirror. With a wry smile, he muttered, *"Not bad for an old duffer."* She was still laughing when she left the room.

A CHANGE AT THE TOP

The main thing on the agenda right now was to hire a hotel manager. Chip had done pretty well up till now but he knew what needed to be done from here on was more than he could handle. He summoned 'Sexy Sam' and 'King Arthur', who both had some managerial experience. Chip explained what he thought they should be looking for: pleasant personality, good sense of humor, patience (especially with the elderly) and good salesmanship.

Sam spoke up immediately: "I know just the guy, why didn't I think of this sooner?"

"For God's sake, Sam who?" came the reply.

"Another, Italian," Sam boasted. "He has at least three of the traits you're looking for, a dynamic personality, good sense of humor and, Lord only knows, he's a salesman. He almost single handedly saved Chrysler Corporation at one point."

"You're not thinking of *Lee*, are ya'? asked Arthur.

"Yeah why not, I'm sure he can do it. My only reservation is that Italian temper. Maybe he's mellowed in his later years," said Sam.

Chip wondered how they could get in touch with him and what would they have in common to talk about, although Chip did own a Dodge Caravan mini van up north.

Sam said, "Well ain't I, Italian? I'll talk to him."

They decided to call him. The operator tried Bloomfield Hills and all the Grosse Pointes. No Lee Iacocca was listed. She left a message at the Chrysler world headquarters in Auburn Hills, Mich. An hour later, one of the VP's called back. He understood that Mr. Iacocca was deep-sea fishing somewhere off the coast of Florida. The company didn't keep track of him much any more.

Now what do we do?, the threesome wondered?

'King Arthur' had an idea.

"Let's get a hold of Mr. Toy Ota," he suggested. "He's supposed to be such a supper sleuth. Maybe he can track Iacocca down through one of the marinas. It's worth a try."

Sam jumped in: "That's a great idea as long as Toy Ota doesn't tell him his name. You know how Iacocca felt about Japanese car manufacturers."

Bert made the contact with Ota again.

After explaining what they needed, he left him with one final instruction, "Don't' tell him your name, lie, if you have to."

It didn't take long for Ota to track Iacocca down. He made a few calls to some of his sleazy connections. Bonefish Willy, it turned out, had seen the fishing party leave early that morning. If they had any luck he guessed they would return around three or four that afternoon. Toy Ota took off hoping to catch Iacocca at the dock. He had changed into his dockside clothes so as not to be too conspicuous. When Iacocca's boat pulled in, Toy Ota was right there to help tie up. He cheerfully asked if they caught any.

Iacocca said, "Are you kidding, we got so many, we had to throw them back."

"Mr. Iacocca, my name is 'Cam Rhee' (he didn't think Iacocca would get the connection) and I have been hired by some people that desperately want to talk to you today or tomorrow at the latest."

Of course, Iacocca was surprised. He wanted to know who these people were and why would they want to talk to him. Were they looking for money like everyone else? Cam Rhee told him the people were the top management of the FASA Group, they were all pretty well off and other than that, he didn't know what they wanted. Iacocca pondered for a moment. He vaguely recalled hearing about FASA. He thought to himself that this *could be a very interesting turn of events.* Cam Rhee gave him the address of the hotel and suggested he be there around ten o'clock. He only suggested the time. No one ever commanded or instructed or directed Mr. Iacocca to do anything. At least nowadays they didn't. However, the next morning, at ten sharp, Mr. Iacocca entered the hotel lobby. The first thing he noticed was the Floragra logo in the carpet. He was impressed. *"Wow,"* he thought, *"these guys aren't fooling around."*

Chip shook hands and invited him into the office.

"Gentlemen," he said to 'Sexy Sam' and 'King Arthur', "let me introduce Mr. Lido Anthony Iacocca."

Iacocca interrupted, "Please, just call me Lee."

Chip introduced the other two as Sam and Arthur. Lido was dressed in his Palm Beach seersucker suit, blue shirt with white collar, a spiffy, resort type tie and wearing white, woven loafers. Chip asked if anyone wanted a morning picker upper or was coffee okay.

"Kind a' early for a beverage, coffee's fine," said Iacocca.

(When in Rome, the old saying goes.) They all had coffee. After the initial dancing around, Chip got right to the point.

"We're looking for a good hotel manager," he said.

Before he got much further, Iacocca interrupted: "First tell me what FASA stands for, what is Floragra and what are you attempting to do here?"

Arthur gave him a run down of the Floragra story, how FASA came about and that they originally thought the hotel would be a good write off. Sam told him, they were making more money than they ever dreamed of, that Floragra made them all feel young again and they were having the time of their lives.

"I have to say I'm impressed. Not a one of you looks over fifty. I've heard stories about this Floragra stuff. Now I believe them," said Iacocca. "May I have a tour of the place?"

"Absolutely," said Chip, "There's not much to see, but what you see is what you get."

The lobby looked great as they crossed through it to the barbershop. Lee met Dominic.

"Ah, Paeson."

That was a good start.

'Loquacious Lucille' and the rest of the girls were manning the phones. Mr. Iacocca was overwhelmed with Bert and Gert in the security room. Especially when Bert asked him what his "handle" was. They showed him the kitchen and the walled off section for the Floragra production. Doc was nowhere around. In fact, the whole section was void of any activity. They used the rear door to show him the pool, the volleyball court, shuffleboard area, the cabanas and their own little stretch of beach. They walked back up from the beach. The striped awnings looked just like the originals. He was as impressed as though he had just envisioned an 1964 Mustang. Chip asked him is he would like to see some of the guest rooms.

"Not right now," Lee replied, "however, I'm curious as how just the three of you got all of this accomplished?"

'King Arthur' spoke up: "Are you kidding? We're good but not that good. There are probably fifty more people involved."

"But I don't see anyone else around," noted Lee.

Sam proceeded to tell him about the sock hop coming up on Saturday and that the rest of the gang was probably out looking for costumes. He explained it should be a real fun evening and Iacocca was invited to come where he could meet the rest of the group.

"Bring a date, if you want to," said Sam.

He said he would *be delighted*. He hadn't done anything like that in years. He explained that he should be leaving because he had a late tee off time, but maybe they could get together for dinner. That was fine with the three of them.

"However, before I leave, I have one question," he added.

"What's that?" asked Sam.

"How did you ever get the name 'Sexy Sam'? You don't look so sexy to me," said Lee.

"I certainly hope not," replied Sam.

Then he went on to explain that he was watching a sister's act that was playing the Medicare Circuit. The lead singer said she needed a sexy guy out of the audience to sing to.

"I got picked because I was closest to the stage. First she asked my name, then, introduced me to the audience as '"Sexy Sam"' and it stuck with all my smart aleck buddies in the crowd," said Sam.

Iacocca said he always thought he was the sexy Italian but now he knew better.

"The only nickname I ever had was "Gypsy Rose" also from some smart alecks."

Sam said he didn't get it.

"*Gypsy—Rose-Lee*, now, do you get it?" he asked.

"Oh yeah," sputtered Sam.

After he left, the three of them let out a big sigh. They seemed to think the initial meeting went pretty good. They had decided to meet at one of the more affluent restaurants in town. 'King Arthur'; 'Millie the Mermaid'; 'Sexy Sam' and 'Alluring Anita', all rode together in the King's Crown Imperial. (Is that appropriate or what) Chip and Miss Ellie drove SOV. Mr. Iacocca was already seated by the time they arrived. Seated next to him was a devastating blond, about twenty-five years younger than him. They were sipping Asti Spumonti. Doc and Mrs. Molly Goldberg were the last to arrive. Molly, of course, had to make a grand entrance. The usually sloven Doc, looked nice. He even wore a shirt and tie and a sport coat. As they used to say when wash and wear clothing first came out, *"he washed up well"*.

Molly sauntered in: "Hi, ho, everybody."

Every eye in the entire room was directed at her. She had on her wired, push 'em up, squeeze 'em together harness. The basic white, clinging dress was covered with Mother of Pearl sequins. It wasn't quite a wrap around. However, the folds went straight down between her bosoms then rounded off to each side approximately at the knees. That tended to expose considerable leg, which was set off by silver, high heeled, ankle strap, evening slippers. Her hair had been perfectly coiffed, a little puffy at the top, very short, curly bangs, cut and shaped toward the rear similar to what used to be called a "ducks ___" tail.

She looked fabulous.

Chip was about to make the introductions to Mr. Iacocca and "Baby" when Molly rang out, "Gypsy Rose, it's me, Gypsy Molly!"

"Don't you remember, you told me I was sexier than the original Gypsy Rose Lee when I met you at the stage door after appearing with the Rockettes in New York City?"

Iacocca closed his gaping mouth and said, "How could I ever forget? How have you been? You look fantastic. Here, sit next to me, on this side."

Chip looked at Arthur and Sam and whispered, "I think we're in."

The light dinner conversation was pretty much dominated by Molly telling Lee about her exploits in New York, the television shows and her connections in Hollywood.

"And I owe it all to Floragra."

Iacocca wanted to know more about this stuff.

"Don't ask me. Ask Doc here. He's the master mind."

Molly had received so much attention, that Doc was getting jealous. He had fallen into a sullen mood.

"I can't tell you about it sitting here. Come by the laboratory sometime and I'll explain it to you," said Doc rather coolly.

Chip thought to himself, "Oh, oh, there's trouble ahead."

They were just finishing dessert when the orchestra started to play. The first set was *Moon over Miami, Red Sails in the Sunset* and *Caribbean Moonlight*.

Gypsy Rose Lee asked 'Gypsy Rose Molly' if she cared to dance.

"I'd love to," she squealed. "Doc doesn't dance much anymore."

They could see the scowl on Doc's face. Chip tried to think of something to say.

"How are the orders going, Doc? Are we caught up yet?"

Doc replied, "I don't know and right now I don't care."

He was no longer sipping the Asti', he was gulping it. He ordered a boilermaker. No sooner, was it brought to the table, it was gone. He ordered another. The boilermaker mixed with the wine, and combined with his inner rage, was working fast.

"*What the hell,*" he thought, "*why not?*"

"Hey baby, wanna' dance?" he asked.

"Why not, I don't have anything better to do," she answered.

The next set was more upbeat and included, *Opus One, One O'clock Jump and String of Pearls*. Lee and Molly decided to sit this one out. After all, Lee hadn't been exposed to Floragra yet. He didn't feel nearly as young as Molly. "Baby", whom we told you was at least twenty-five years younger than Lee, and we assume Doc, was no match for Doc. The combination of the booze, the Floragra and the mood he was in, combined to turn him into a real *Bo jangles*. He could swing, he could sway, he could spin, and he could boogie. He was doing it all. He kept glancing at Molly and she could see it in his eyes, *"You can't dance much anymore, huh!"*

When everyone returned to the table, 'King Arthur' suggested they call it a night. They had a busy day tomorrow. The next morning some of the guys were in Chip's office trying to cheer up Doc by boasting his ego.

"Boy, Doc, none of us knew you could dance that well. We were impressed."

"Only when I'm snockered," replied Doc, "besides, Molly wasn't too impressed, not with me, anyhow."

Wise old Arthur spoke up, "Oh, I don't know, you may have impressed her more than you know. I saw her watching you with that young babe."

"Really?" interjected Doc.

Just then the phone on Chip's desk rang. It was Iacocca.

"I'll take the job on one condition, "he said.

"What's that?" asked Chip.

"I want to buy into the FASA group so I'm guaranteed a steady supply of Floragra," Lee responded.

"But we haven't discussed salary or anything like that," said Chip.

"I don't need any salary. Besides you said I could play golf or go fishing anytime I wanted to as long as the hotel was running smoothly," said Lee.

Chip told him he would run it by the board of directors and get back to him later in the day. He had the speakerphone on. The guys heard the whole story. Sam said he thought the rest of the group would abide by whatever decision they made. They hadn't received any complaints so far. Arthur said the only problem he had with the whole arrangement was that they didn't need any more money. He didn't think Iacocca should buy in. He thought maybe 'Lean Jean', the 'Legal Eagle', could figure out a way to make him an honorary member. Doc had only one thing to say.

"He better keep his Italian pinkies out of my laboratory!"

Chip assured him that the contract Jean would draw up would specify Iacocca would run the hotel only and would have nothing to do with the Floragra production. Chip called Iacocca back around four o'clock.

"We got a deal," he announced.

"Deal," said Iacocca.

THE SOCK HOP

The antique cars were lined up in front of the condo complex. The police escort would lead the parade, with Skeeter on his motorcycle and Belle Taco in the sidecar, immediately behind them. Chip and Ellie were first in the *'32 Ford Coupe* with the flame job, followed by Sam and Anita in the *1923 Baldwin* then Arthur and Millie in the *Rolls Royce* and so on. Do you get the picture by now?

The police escort wended them through the traffic lights on all the side streets. They were careful to stay off the expressways for fear of tying them up. Heck, most of these cars had never been on an expressway. As they entered the now historic art deco district, the throngs of pedestrians cheered and waved like it was the end of World War II. The first six who were in the three lead cars decided to go in first since they would be the welcoming committee. Because parking was at a premium in the old district, the drivers had to park them in a nearby parking garage and then stay with them to protect them. Skeeter was to zip over on the bike to alert them when the party was over.

'The Galloping Gourmet' was busy in the kitchen. The smell of hamburgers and sizzling onions permeated the ballroom. The half dozen soda jerks were ready, dressed in typical uniforms of the day, black loafers, black pants, short white, and waist jackets, topped off by a white cap trimmed in black that was shaped somewhat like a kayak. The soda glasses sparkled in rows next to the banana split dishes. The dispensers had been filled with chocolate, strawberry, cherry and pineapple toppings. The kitchen crew was ready. (Of course, dear reader, you know Molly will make a grand entrance. However, she had been a busy little beaver with her show business connections.) Among the "guest" waiters and waitresses were *Betty White, Bea Arthur, Rue McCalahan and Estelle Getty*, all from the *Golden Girls* TV show. *Paul Newman* looked handsome in his waiter's uniform. *Elizabeth Taylor, Debbie Reynolds, Shirley McClain and Joan*

Collins, all stopped by to join the festivities. They were in town promoting their new movie; *"These Old Broads".* (If they had known about Floragra sooner, they wouldn't have had to make a movie by that title.) *Perry Como and Burt Reynolds* didn't have too far to drive to get there. *Edd Byrnes, Kookie, from the old 77 Sunset Strip* show looked the part in his waiter's uniform.

The crowd gathered quickly. Molly had informed Chip that she had a few surprises. Who should come walking in, but *Ed McMahon?* He was to announce the arrivals. After a short beer, which Doc kept hidden away back in his cooler, the resonant one was ready.

He cleared his throat and began: "Ladies and gentlemen: May I present, 'Tee Shot Tom' and 'Beauteous Bev'. Ladies and Gentlemen, presenting 'Sly Ely' and 'Audacious Audrey'. Ladies and Gentlemen, may I draw your attention to 'The Lovely Lucille' and 'Dominic the Singing Barber'?"

(God, he was a great announcer. He made them all feel like royalty.)

There was a slight lull, Ooh's and ahs could be heard emanating out in front of the building. The assembled masses thought surely it was Molly, getting ready for her grand entrance.

"Wow," exclaimed McMahon.

He fumbled a little but finally gained control.

"Presenting 'Babs the Beautiful Bombshell from Bristol' (Connecticut, that is) also known as 'El Zora', escorted by none other than 'Senor El Zoro'. No one had seen Babs for some time, busy on the 'Continent', you know. Apparently she had just arrived home that afternoon and wasn't aware of the sock hop theme. She was outstanding in her toreador outfit as was El Zoro, but Babs was the showstopper. The commotion simmered down before the next couple entered.

"Ladies and Gentlemen, here are 'The Lovely Lois' and her escort, Mr. Wisenheimer."

Molly and Doc met *Mitzie Gaynor* out front. Molly said she didn't want to upstage Babs, so they snuck in through the side door. Mitzie had gone to the old wardrobe department of MGM to find Mrs. Goldberg's complete outfit. She looked sensational. Not only was she wearing a poodle skirt, but also the poodles were padded before they were appliquéd!

McMahon once again cleared his throat, "Folks, I humbly present Mr. Lido Anthony Iacocca and Whatta' Babe," he then added, "Entering the hall now is couple number thirty-two, Bert and Gert."

This sounded like one of those ballroom dance contests. Bert was truly a sight to behold in his striped pants, plaid jacket soot suit. He gave Gert a little spin as they entered. Anyone of any significance was now there. A few stragglers were bound to show up. As Lee and Babe circulated through the room, he couldn't believe how many beautiful young looking women there were, and most of them were as old as he was. There was growing anxiety in him. All of a sudden he had, 'The Hunger to Look Younger.' There was electricity floating through the crowd. Comments ranged from, *"You look great, to where have you been for the last fifty years?"* to *"Hubba hubba!"*

The temporary soda fountain, which Tee Shot Tom had appropriated, was doing a booming business. Cherry cokes and chocolate shakes were all over the place. What a sight. No Hollywood movie ever made could duplicate this affair. It's relatively easy to describe the "girls" costumes, saddle shoes, bobby sox, poodle skirts, white tee shirts and pink ribbons in the hair.

The Zoot Suit, on the other hand, is difficult to envision.

The top of the pants were worn three to six inches above the navel, generally held up by suspenders. Although in some parts of the country, a thin belt was preferred. Normally the pants consisted of one or two pleats. Again, depending on your section of the country, some guys preferred the straight front complimented by a very sharp crease. The pants ballooned down past the knees where they began a taper to the ankles, which was so small that you struggled to get your feet through the opening. The coats, ah the coats, were usually called coats instead of jackets because they were more like outerwear than dinner jackets. Extremely padded shoulders, set off by draping lapels, rolled down to a single button. And the hats, yes, men wore hats back then. The hats had excessively wide, stiff brims with a wide band around the crown. The shirts were whatever you could afford from broadcloth to oxford cloth to silk. Although most guys preferred the good old white tee shirt for greater flexibility. The taller you were the better you looked in a Zoot Suit. 'King Arthur', one of the tallest in the group, was absolutely resplendent in his threads and 'Millie the Mermaid' was not to be outdone by anyone. The party was well under way before Molly took the microphone on center stage.

"Ladies and gentlemen and be-boppers of all ages, I have a surprise announcement to make," she bellowed into the mike.

"What, are ya' pregnant?" heckled some old Wisenheimer.

That got a chuckle out of the crowd.

"Not yet," she replied.

(Molly was always ready with a quick come back.)

"Are you ready for dancing?" she asked.

Yells and cheers rang out.

Molly continued, "Ladies and Gentlemen, you're D.J. for the evening ... the one and only ... *Mr. Dick Clark!*"

Dick made his entrance amid an enthusiastic applause. The house lights dimmed. Barely audible but building to a crescendo was his old theme song, *"Band Stand Boogie"* played by *Les Elkhardt*. The crowd went wild-like teenagers at a Sinatra concert. Some of the older ones remarked that the radio show, which, preceded the 1954 TV show, started with *"It's Make Believe Ballroom Time, MC'd by Martin Bloch.* Several old phonographs, record players and eight track decks were displayed on the stage. He wasn't using any of them. Molly took the time to have all the music put on digital discs. Clark announced that he thought they should begin the evening with an appropriate little number entitled: *"Sentimental Journey by Les Brown, sung by Doris Day".* About half way through the number, most of the group quit dancing and moved in toward the stage. *"Gonna' take a sentimental journey, to renew old memories,"* they sang. Appropriate, indeed. When the number finished, Dick Clark stood up.

"Enough of that slow stuff, are you ready?" asked Clark.

A rousing cheer went up. The next three in the set were: *"Little Brown Jug", "Opus One", and "Sing, sing, sing".* (Oh, man, they were ready!) The Zoot Suits were zooting, and the poodle skirts were poodling. Talk about Jivin' Geriatrics, they were groovin'!

The evening turned out to be one of those unforgettable events like a senior prom. By eleven thirty, they began to slow down. Their marathon dance days were over. Chip announced the last call for the soda bar and he suggested everyone get one last beverage for a special toast. *"What now?" they thought, "What could be any better than this?"* When he was sure everyone had a beverage in hand, Dick Clark announced, "Clear the ballroom, everybody outside."

They wondered what was going on as they wandered out to the sidewalk.

Chip said, "Now pretend you're in Times Square on New Years Eve. Help me count down. Ten", he started, "nine, eight, seven ..."

'Tee Shot Tom' was still inside the building, listening intently. When he heard "One," he threw the switch. The night sky lit up as the neon sign on top of the building came alive. *"Oohs, ahs and wows",* were heard as everyone saw the Floragra sign for the first time. (What a way to end the evening.)

CHANGING OF THE GUARD

The next day, a Sunday, started off rather leisurely. There were a few churchgoers but most of them opted for breakfast on the patio, reading the paper and letting the bones recuperate. Thank the Lord there weren't any hangovers, not from chocolate shakes, anyhow. It was another gorgeous Florida day. Temperature expected to hit the mid 80's, low humidity and a soft breeze gently swaying the potted palms.

They began straggling in about noon or so. Lee Iacocca was already in Chip's office to reconfirm his responsibilities. They agreed that Lee would have absolute and complete control of the hotel operation but was to have nothing to do with the Floragra production. That was 'Dr. Kenny Dee's' domain, and his alone. Both men were to be restricted only by the board of directors. Everyone seemed satisfied with that arrangement.

Chip handed over the keys to the office.

"It's all yours now baby." he said. "And don't lock the safe because the only one that can get into it is Skeeter."

Miss Ellie and Chip headed back to the kitchen for a coffee. Half the group was there, having a snack and discussing the previous night's activities. They all agreed that it was a night to remember. And that Mrs. Molly Goldberg was the star of the evening by bringing in Ed McMahon, Dick Clark and the cast of stars emblematic of a Hollywood production. They cheered Chip and Ellie as they entered the coffee shop. *"Hip, hip, hooray"* the finale was fantastic they all thought. *"Long live FASA."*

Iacocca had the reputation of being very organized. Within an hour he had a list on his desk as long as his arm. He needed to hire a wait staff, a kitchen staff, cleaning people, chambermaids, pool personnel, and maintenance men and grounds keepers. Chip had informed him that they would like to open in one month. That wasn't a lot of time.

Lee looked at his list. A lot of the jobs could be contracted out, especially the pool maintenance and the grounds keepers. He felt he could steal some of the top people from *The Fountainbleu, The Eden Roc or even The Diplomat.* The excitement would be that no one else had Floragra as a fringe benefit. He picked up the phone to call "Babe".

"Hi, Babe I need same help," he said.

"I'll help you any way you want me, as long as it doesn't involve that dolly, Molly," she answered.

He told her he needed a personal assistant. There might be a little typing but she could handle that on a computer. She agreed without ever discussing wages. She knew he would take care of her one way or another.

His first directive on Monday morning was sent to each member of the FASA group. It advised them to start using the rear door. They were welcome to use any of the hotel amenities but loitering around the hotel lobby wouldn't look too professional. It also advised that a bank of lockers had been set aside in the work out area, with the letters FASA on each one, for the exclusive use of the members. He pointed out that, as great as some of them looked, it wouldn't be proper to be going in and out of the lobby in a bathing suit. 'Sexy Sam' was to assign numbers and keys. They were also advised that there would be no dogs or animals in the hotel. However, there was a large space set aside, under the stairway leading to the pool, for Skeeter to keep his motorcycle and a comfortable spot for Belle Taco and Taco Chip. Then he had to take off for a golf date.

He also had another pre-arranged date for golf on Tues. morning. Babe was already there by the time he arrived. She had been roaming around getting to know the place when she stumbled upon Doc in his laboratory.

"Well, hiya' Beau, ben' danc'n lately?" she asked.

"As a matter of fact," he replied, "yes I have, and what's with the Beau?"

"You know," she said coyly, "like in Beau jangles."

"Oh, that. I guess I had a little too much to drink," he said.

"What are you doing here?" Doc inquired.

"Oh, I guess you haven't heard. I'm Mr. Iacocca's new personal assistant," said Babe.

"I could use one of those myself," Doc said.

"What are the benefits, I might be available," she replied.

"Lets' just drop it for now. But don't give up. Who knows what the future brings?" said Doc.

He excused himself to go check on one of the vats.

Over the next several weeks, the joint was humming Lee Iacocca, who had a reputation as a pretty good negotiator, contracted the local unions, (Chip was glad he didn't have to do it). Contracts had been reviewed by 'Lean Jean', the Legal Eagle, and were signed for cleaning help, the wait staff and all of the kitchen personnel. He emphasized that this was to be a first class operation, not a training station. They wanted only experienced people that spoke American. There is considerable difference between American English and 'English, English.' Accents were acceptable if the American could be understood.

The pool maintenance people were already on the job as the FASA group, were using it almost every day. The ground crews had the exterior looking fresh as a Florida morning. There was only one thing left to do. Molly had made a suggestion, and who could ever turn Molly down, that she thought the soda fountain theme was so successful on the sock hop night that it should become permanent. 'Tee Shot Tom' told Lee that he would handle getting it installed.

Molly thought it should stay right where it was if possible. It would be a great meeting place because it was adjacent to the hallway leading to the pool and the beach. And it was only a few feet away from the elevators. She reasoned that if someone had a bathing suit on, they wouldn't want to meet in the lobby.

"*I'll meet cha' at the soda bar,*" sounded good to her.

'Tee Shot Tom' said it was no big deal because it was already in place. It wouldn't take much to hook it up permanently.

He said, "Too bad we can't think of a good name for it."

Skeeter, the ubiquitous one, spoke up, "Why not call it: 'The Hunger Room', like, it is a place to eat and it goes with The Hunger to Look Younger."

(God bless Skeeter, you just never knew what might come out of him.)

Lucille came over from the telephone center. She told Lee that the operators had reported an increase in calls inquiring about room rates. One girl reported that a caller asked if he could stay a month while another said she had a call inquiring about hourly rates. She didn't think too much of it at first but the calls, were becoming more frequent. Iacocca said he would talk to Chip about it. 'Sexy Sam' and 'King Arthur' walked by. It seems they had appointed themselves custodians of the neons. There were plenty of them, inside and out. After all, what good was an Art Deco hotel without neon?

The grand opening was now less than a week away. Everything seemed to be in place and in order. Every evening the "jive 'n geriatrics" gathered around the pool or back at their old clubhouse to discuss the events of the day. Somehow the ladies always returned to the same topic, "*What are you wearing to the grand opening?*" It was generally decided that the sock hop was great but it was over. This is to be a momentous occasion, formal wear would be much more appropriate. Molly hinted that all the major TV networks, the wire services and several newspapers would cover the event. She also remarked that she had an evening dress she was dying to wear. El Zora said she didn't have any problem with that. She might have a tricky little number of her own. And Babe chimed in that she would finally get a chance to dress up. These little chitchats got the adrenalin flowing again. You could feel it in the air. The excitement was building.

Later on that night, Miss Ellie mentioned to Chip that she hadn't bought a new evening gown in many years. She knew the three "queens" would be vying for attention. She told him she really wanted him to be proud of her but at the same time she would like to make a fashion statement of her own. Chip didn't say much. He sat there nodding his head. There was an occasional grunt that sounded like, "*Ok, honey.*" He was busy thinking about the unusual phone calls

Lucille had reported. *"Very strange,"* he thought, *"seeing as they hadn't done any advertising or not even put out a press release."*

Of course the BEST gang had been invited. (Remember them, the guys that did the inspection before FASA bought the building? FASA never did receive a bill for services rendered. You wouldn't expect Marty to bill his own father, Chip, would you?)

The nomadic shepherds hopped on the company jet and headed for Houston first, to pick up 'Tricky Ricky and Terri Berri.'. 'Marvelous Marilyn from Milford' had met them at the airport. This whole group worked hard and played hard. And this was playtime. When they landed in Florida, 'Smarty Marty' and 'Chaquita Anita', 'Big Al' and 'Little Jer', with 'Tee Off Tom', and 'Starlight Stella', were met by Chip and Miss Ellie.

Chip said, "Who's drivin' this thing?"

Just then Ike and Mike, who's name was really Michelle, but Ike liked Mike better, emerged from the plane. Ike was flying, (well it was his plane.) Greetings and hugs were exchanged as they piled into the limo for the ride to the hotel

After introducing them to Lee Iacocca, who was told by Chip to give them VIP treatment, they were to have the top floor for themselves. After freshening up, they were given the deluxe tour. The gang was really impressed with the way the old hotel looked.

'Smarty Marty' said, "What did' ga' do wash the whole thing down with Floragra? It looks fabulous."

THE GRAND OPENING

Lee Iacocca was like a whirlwind, a human cyclone. The big day had finally arrived. He split the regular hotel staff into two, one half to report early, the other half later so they could work into the next morning. As each shift reported he had lined them up for inspection. He was a perfectionist by nature but this day was special. Everything must be perfect. He called the caterers again to make sure they would be there on time. He checked the bar and the bartenders. He looked in on the pool boys. He walked out to the beach to make sure the cabanas were ready. He barked orders. He pleaded and cajoled. He begged and complimented. He appeared when necessary. He was the master mechanic and all the pieces had to work together perfectly.

The huge searchlights were to be turned on just before dusk. The Tiki lights on the beach were to be lit at sundown. The Hawaiian family he had flown over had the pig for the luau cooking in the pit since noon. He checked with Chip and Molly over and over again. Molly told him that TV crews and newspaper people would be there in plenty of time. Chip told him the *Goodyear Blimp* with the Floragra logo flashing, was scheduled to circle overhead for two hours after dark. The twin pianist in the lobby, were to play "cocktail" music from five o'clock until the band started. Iacocca asked them about six times if they were sure they knew *"In A Small Hotel"* which they were to play every half hour. Lee reiterated to the Floragra group that the hotel was limited to four hundred people. They didn't want any trouble with the fire Marshall so would they please help him steer the overflow out to the beach.

Last and of utmost importance were the tour guides. The U.S. Honor Guards didn't go through any more spit and polish than this group. Both male and female had to be perfect. He informed their leader that he expected at least six greeters at the front door. They were to welcome the visitors to the FASA Hotel. Then graciously hand each woman a miniature orchid, in the small vials.

Iacocca had commissioned 'King Arthur' to order gift boxes from Russia. These were small, round, wooden boxes with a removable lid, highly lacquered. Even empty it would have been a beautiful keepsake. But with the Floragra logo embossed on the lid and a free sample of Floragra inside, they were almost priceless. The tour guides were told that the orchids would be on one table and the gift boxes on another.

"Make sure everyone gets a gift but also make sure there's only one to a customer. This stuff is expensive and we're hoping they will buy some after they have tried it," said Lee.

(What grandeur, what pomp, what pageantry, what else could anyone ask for?)

Chip, Sam and Arthur followed Iacocca to make the rounds one more time. They switched on the mirrored ball suspended from the ceiling in the ballroom.

"It's revolving," reported Sam.

They checked the stage lights and microphones.

"Testing, one two three," Arthur's deep voice said.

They tried the champagne as they checked out the bar. "Not bad," said Lee, "not bad."

One last check out in front, showed not a speck of debris, or a blade of grass out of place. The finial was set to light up at dusk. The five-piece Red Garter Band was ready, off to one side. Their job was to put everyone in a good mood, while they were waiting to get in. No matter how hard they tried, Iacocca figured there would be a line up at the door. The Red Garter Band was to shift to the beach when the big band started up.

The police had the 'no parking signs' up in front of the building and were standing by to maintain law and order, mostly order.

The ladies spent most of the afternoon and early evening getting dressed. The five or six of them were to arrive by limousine. In fact the entire group probably had their own limousines or shared one among the several couples. The men, that had stayed behind to follow up on last minute details, had stored their evening-wear in the gym lockers.

The piano duo, were tinkling softly in the lobby, reminiscent of a fine piano bar of years ago. At five PM. the BEST group exited the elevators. They were much younger than the geriatric group and were preparing for a long evening starting with happy hour. (What a fine looking group they were.)

At six PM, the first of the TV and newspaper crews began to show up. They figured if they arrived early enough, they might get a snack and a beverage. By seven PM, the gentlemen had changed into their best bib and tucker. They were sipping champagne near the front entrance, waiting for their ladies to arrive. Shortly after seven, the first limo pulled up in front. Out stepped Whatta' Babe, as she was becoming known since Ed McMahan's exclamation, along with 'Alluring Anita' and Beauteous Bev.

The TV helicopter, circling overhead, reported a string of limos coming in from the airport that looked like a presidential cavalcade. Some of the limos and courtesy vans from the surrounding hotels and motels were beginning to line up. The searchlights were prowling the night skies, pointing the way to this fantastic event. The gawkers were filling up the sidewalks and street. The police were busy trying to keep them out of the street.

A sleek, black, Lincoln Continental stretch limo eased up to the front door. Out stepped Lucille with Dominic, the singing barber, along with Babs and El Zoro

'Babs the Blond Bombshell from Bristol' (Connecticut, that is), European traveler that she was, was well acquainted with the fashion capitals of 'The Continent.' (You may recall that no one knew for sure where or how she derived her money but she always wore, if not the latest, at least the greatest of startling fashions.) And so it was this evening. A lady's tuxedo just a cut above anything else likes it. The short, black Eisenhower type jacket had shiny, satin lapels of moderate width. The jacket neatly held together by two satin covered buttons. She wore no blouse or undergarment of any kind. She created the *Jennifer Lopez* illusion but on a classier scale. (Of course she was a lot older than Jennifer) The bottom half of the tux consisted of very short, short shorts, and covered by a short skirt, which didn't quite surround her body. While the back was completely covered, the skirt ended just in front of each hip thereby exposing the short shorts and the shapely contour of her legs. The black satin stripes on the skirt were centered at mid-hip on either side. The skirt had a unique innovation. Because it didn't go all the way around, fastening it or holding it up could have been a problem. However, the designer had sewn a metal, spring belt into the waist hem that could be spread to put it on or take it off. Although she didn't need it the red bow tie drew attention to the bosom area. The soft blond hair, which gleamed in the lights of the ballroom, was done in a Lana Turner style. (She was knockout to be sure.)

The scene might remind you of the celebrities arriving at the Academy Awards.

So far, at least, the greeting crew was keeping up passing out the orchids and the Floragra mementos. 'King Arthur', who had stayed behind with Chip, Sam and 'Tee Shot Tom,' was wondering what happened to 'Millie the Mermaid.'

"I hope she gets here soon. I don't want her to miss half of it," he remarked to Chip.

"I'm a little concerned about Miss Ellie, too. I'm sure they'll be here soon," said Chip.

As the doors to the next limousine opened, out stepped 'The Lovely Lois' and her twin, thin Lynn. Then, who would be seen, practically pouring out the door, was none other than 'Millie the Mermaid.' Arthur didn't know she could be that *slinky*. However, in fairness to Millie, considering the outfit she had on, that was the only way she could disgorge herself from the back seat.

'King Arthur', rarely at a loss for words, stood there with his mouth open. She looked as beautiful as ever, not a wrinkle, not a blemish, just fantastic.

"What kept ya'?" he finally sputtered.

"I had a helluva' time getting into this thing, but doesn't it look great?" she replied.

MILLIE'S DRESS

'Millie the Mermaid,' another of the beautiful women that Lee Iacocca admired, was absolutely breathtaking when she entered the ballroom. Her gown was custom made, one of a kind. The dressmaker had cut each individual sequin into the shape of a fish scale. Then, putting them into small clusters of three on top, two in the middle and one on the bottom, each cluster creating sag, outlined with a fine metallic silver cord. Each row then overlapped the next and so on, a little like a chain mail suit of armor back in the Roman days. A very plain collar line circled the back of the neck, circled around toward the front where it draped into a plunging neck line, overlapped just slightly at the midriff, then separated just above the knees, only to extend toward the ankles on the way to the rear. There, it swooped into a fantail, which was long enough to resemble a mythic mermaid tale but short enough not to hinder her dancing. The blue/green, yellow/orange phosphorescent shimmied as she walked. If a fish could swim vertically and still look graceful, that's what she looked like. To complete the picture, she wore a blond hairpiece, shoulder length, slightly curled on the ends. The hairpiece covered the plain neckline. She was gorgeous and 'King Arthur' never was more proud. They didn't call her 'Millie the Mermaid' for nothing!

Most of the regulars were now there. A huge crowd was in the ballroom after getting a tour. The same conversation seemed to be repeated over and over again about how great the old hotel looked but more than that, how great the main participants looked. *"They all look so young and seem so vibrant,"* was heard many times over. *"I'll have to try that Floragra stuff ... Me too, if that's what it does for you."*

Chip was getting antsy. *"Where could she be?"* he wondered.

Most of the cars were emptied and gone. There were still two or three lined up but they no longer stretched around the block. All of a sudden, here came Skeeter on his motorcycle flying around the corner. He came to a screeching halt at the front door. Chip had stepped outside to see what was happening.

"Hi Chip. Look who I got," yelled Skeeter.

"Oh my God," said Chip. "Miss Ellie, what are you doing in the side car?"

She explained. "Everyone else went ahead without me. I was just going to call you when Skeeter showed up."

She handed little Belle Taco to Skeet as she began to untangle herself from the sidecar. Chip gave her a hand.

"I can do it alright. Here hang onto this hat box," she said.

"You're wearing a hat tonight?" he asked.

"No, it's my hair piece. Open the box and help me put it on straight," she instructed.

As usual, Chip did as he was told and by now many of the sightseers rushed over to see what all the commotion was about. And what was a motorcycle with a sidecar doing in the line of limos? Thoughtfully, Ellie had put a mirror in the lid of the hatbox. Chip held the lid up for her. In a moment, a wig of jet-black straight hair covered her naturally blond hair. The short cut revealed the tips of her ears in which she had inserted the black onyx, dangling earrings. The bangs across the forehead were perfectly straight. She had used the eyebrow pencil to give the eyebrows a slight Oriental slant. The eyeglasses too, were shaped with points at each temple, which added to the affect. The Chinese red, satin gown was outstanding. The Mandarin collar didn't quite come together. The first cloverleaf button fastener, was located approximately at mid-bosom, Chip liked the cleavage. The material clung to her shapely body like a plastic wrap. The one-piece dress cascaded down to her calves. The slit on each side of the skirt was highlighted by an onyx clasp, which matched the earrings. She wore no hose. The Floragra smoothed legs were tantalizing. The black, high heeled, shoes with ankle straps completed the picture.

"*Isn't it strange,*" thought Chip, that *his old high school colors were red and black, although a slightly different red? How appealing could she be?*" Chip told her she looked like an Oriental lollipop and boy what he could do with one of those.

He had pinned the black orchid on her before they got to the ballroom. As they entered, there was a hush. All eyes turned toward the couple. There was no doubt Miss Ellie was the queen of the ball. Chip, in his white summer tux, gently held her elbow as they made their way through the crowd. Talk about grand entrances, first in the motorcycle and now in the ballroom. Chip recalled how lucky he felt to have found this woman at this time in his life.

The eighteen-piece band was in place by nine o'clock. They had many of the original arrangements of some of the great oldies such as *Moonlight Serenade, Deep Purple, Getting Sentimental and Hoagy Carmichel's, Stardust.* This wasn't, *Make Believe Ballroom,* this was the real thing. *Lester Lannin* and his great "society" orchestra couldn't have done any better. There was reminiscing of Glen Miller's "something old, something new, something borrowed, something blue" emanating from the Grand Island Casino.

In the meantime, Mr. Lee Iacocca was as busy as the proverbial one-armed paperhanger. He was all over the place. He barely had time to notice Babe, yet alone dance with her. He rushed up to Chip. He was out of breath as he told Chip he had just returned from the beach.

"What are we gonna' do?" he said, practically exhaling the words. "We have two separate parties going on, one in here and one on the beach. The beach crowd is overflowing. The Red Garter Band has everyone jumping and jiving. They're not all wearing formal gowns and tuxedo's either, they're dancing barefoot in the sand. I'm afraid they'll get out of control. And they still keep coming."

"Don't panic," said Chip. "Bert and Gert are right there in front of the stage. I'll talk to them."

Bert, the ever alert, head of security, hadn't noticed the problem. As soon as he was informed, he jumped into action by alerting the watch commander of the

ICU Company, who in turn walked out to the front of the hotel to confer with the local police.

The Captain in charge called in for reinforcements. In the blink of an eye, there were six police cars, lights flashing, sirens screaming, pulling up in front. The Captain told them they were not to allow any more people in.

"Be polite, we don't want to break up the party, just control it. By circulating around the premises, we can kind of hold it down, just by being here," he directed.

The local police department didn't need any more bad publicity. A short time later Chip bumped into Iacocca again.

"Not to worry, everything's under control," said Chip.

(Another dilemma, overcome.)

Doc hadn't seen Molly all evening. He wasn't too disappointed, even though it was his birthday, because with Iacocca being so busy, it had fallen upon Doc to entertain, 'What ta' Babe.' After all, they had danced together before and hadn't she tried to come unto him in his own laboratory? Besides, she was one hell 'uva dish.

About ten O'clock the music stopped. The drummer snapped off a drum roll. The stage lights dimmed. One lone spotlight was trained on the microphone at center stage. The crowd fell silent. Entering from the left wing, all anyone could make out was a pink gown, which seemed to float toward the mike. A low. throaty voice began, "*Happy Birthday to you—Happy Birthday dear Doc.*" (Oh, my God, it was Marilyn Monroe and President Kennedy all over again ... no, it was Molly Goldberg singing to Doctor Kenny Dee!)

Molly had Mitzi Gaynor resurrect the original pink Taffeta gown from the studio archives, just for this occasion. She even had the Marilyn hairdo and the gloss lipstick. She looked absolutely radiant. The crowd yelled, "*One more time.*" It turned out to be four more times. Doc was flabbergasted. Molly raised her hands to quiet the crowd.

"And now Doc, a special treat just for you!" she announced.

She disappeared from the stage as the first of the *Rockettes* made her entry. The stage was quickly filled with high stepping, leg kicking *Rockettes*. There were a few current ones that flew down from New York but most of them had retired long ago. (Once a *Rockette*, always a *Rockette*, the saying goes.) Age had not diminished their ability. Pixie, Trixie and Dixie were on the right side, Rusty, Dusty and Busty were on the left. They went through several of the old routines. Most of them were now in their 50's or 60's. They were doing that rotating star routine where one girl is in the center and the rest fan out into four lines opposite each other. When the lines broke out to again form one line of high steppers across the stage, there was Molly, right smack dab in the center. Complete with the official *Rockette* uniform. The whole place went absolutely wild. The chant started slowly in the rear of the ballroom. It soon worked its way up front, much like the "wave" at a sporting event. *"For she's a jolly good fellow, for she's a jolly good fellow. Let's hear it for Molly!"* Someone cried out, *"Hip, hip, hooray-hip, hip, hooray."*

The dancers were brought out for three encores. Needless to say, Doc was over whelmed. Closer to midnight the crowd thinned a little. There was more mingling than dancing. Many of the non-Floragrians were beginning to leave, especially the beach crowd. The pig and poi (sounds like an English pub) were all gone. The hotel kitchen staff was still hard at work, more Hors D'oeuvres, more finger sandwiches, more of everything. The bartenders hadn't let up either.

Ted Danson and Tony Danza staged an impromptu song and dance. *Eddie Fisher and Phyllis McGuire* had done a duet. *President and Rosalyn Carter* took a swirl on the dance floor. *Ted Koppel* told Iacocca that *Sam Donaldson* couldn't make it but to be sure to bring back enough Floragra for both of them. *Regis Philbin*, accompanied by his new co-host, *Kelly Rippa*, also asked about the new miracle product. His producer, Gelman, had mentioned that fifteen or twenty shows a week was beginning to show a little. The *Golden Girls, Bea Arthur, Betty White, Rue McLenahan and Estelle Getty*, said if the sample they received did anything, anything at all, the Floragra people would be hearing from them. There were just too many notables, movie stars and celebrities to mention them all. The newspaper people were busy jotting down names all evening long. One reporter was seen in a corner listening to *Johnny Carson, Dom Deluis and Don Rickles* recall the good old days. They, incidentally, had all placed orders for Floragra. Carson even booked a suite for a week next month.

It was well into the wee hours of the morning before the last guest left. Fortunately for our group, they were all staying at the hotel overnight. Iacocca had thoughtfully assigned rooms to all of them. All in all, they resoundingly agreed the grand opening had been a grand success. *USA* ran an extensive article. *The Miami Herald* headlines were unique. Instead of *"NASA launches another rocket"* the headline read, *"FASA launches new hotel"*. The article extolled the renovation for making it look as good as the old one but with so many modern amenities. One of the local TV stations headlined their show with "A new dive on Deco Drive".

Needless to say, all the publicity didn't hurt business at all. The very next day, a Sunday, Lucille checked the answering machine. Someone had enough forethought to add a second machine. Lucille reported that both machines were full. She needed more help and more phone lines. The calls were not only for Floragra orders but for hotel bookings as well. It seems one of the TV networks showed about one minute of Molly and the *Rockettes*. The phone number had been given in the telecast. This whole adventure was nothing short of phenomenal. Even a Hollywood scriptwriter couldn't have thought up this one.

The general membership meeting was held that afternoon in the ballroom. Most all of them were present or accounted for. You would think there would be a big let down after such a momentous occasion but not with this group. The whole gang was moving around congratulating each other on how successful the grand opening had been and how great each one looked. Old Wisenheimer jumped up on the stage.

"I would like to propose a toast to Lee Iacocca for his fantastic organizing skills in making the evening absolutely perfect," he began.

The crowd responded, *"Here, here."*

"I would also like to propose another toast to Mrs. Molly Goldberg, whom, I think we all agree, was the star of the evening," he added.

Again, the group responded with *"here, here"* and a huge applause. Old O.W. waited for the din to quiet down.

"Lastly," he said, "I feel we should give recognition to the most outstanding person at the ball, Miss Ellie, 'The Merry Maid from Michigan'. The applause and clamor left no doubt that the crowd agreed.

Lee finally took the stage. He informed them that the fun and games were over, for a little while at least. The hotel would start taking bookings the next day. He reminded them that from now on they were to use the back entrance and to please not hang around the lobby. He also alerted them to keep their eyes and ears open because the telephone operators had received some unusual calls.

He went on, "I assume by now you have all vacated your rooms, so the cleaning crews can get them ready for business. And one last thing," he added, "I want you to know what a pleasure it has been to work with this fabulous group of people. Ya' know what's so special about it? There are no little cliques. You are all part of the Floragra family who look after each other and enjoy each other's company. I thank you for allowing me to be part of it."

After another round of applause, Lee yelled out, over the noise, "Now I'm going out to play a late round of golf!"

They dispersed to let the cleaning people do their job. By the end of the week, the hotel was booked solid for months in advance. With the conference rooms also booked so far in advance, at least the kitchen staff would have an idea of what to have on hand.

The FASA hotel was new and exciting. Everybody wanted to be part of it. And Floragra was the star of it all. The group said a special prayer that Sunday that the miracle hedges would hold out.

THE DROUGHT

The heat was on! Not on our happy little group but on the hedges. Skeeter was the first one to notice. He was out picking his daily quota of the miraculous little green leaves when he noticed they were kind of droopy. They didn't have that healthy snap as he pulled them off the hedges. South Florida was in a major drought. Water levels were dropping fast. Most communities had already placed a ban on lawn watering, car washing or any other excessive use of water. Some, if not all, of the dams controlling Lake Okeechobee had been closed, thereby stopping the flow of fresh water to the Everglades. That allows the possibility of ocean salt water to enter the system. Who knows what that would do to the ecology? The area in which the hedges were growing have had less than one inch of rain in the past four months. No wonder the precious hedges were beginning to droop. Chip, as usual, was sitting out on the veranda when he noticed Skeeter spraying a small section with an old window wash spray bottle.

He yelled down, "Hey, Skeet, come up here for a minute."

"Okee, Dokee, Dominokee," replied Skeeter.

Miss Ellie had his coffee poured by the time he got up there.

"What are ya' doin' with the spray bottle?" Chip asked.

"I'm watering the hedges. Dontcha' see how droopy they're getting?" he replied. "And there's no rain in the forecast for a least a week."

Chip said, Wow, what a good idea, Skeeter. Maybe we should all being doing that?"

Skeeters mind bulb became considerably brighter.

"I'll go tell everybody," And on that, he rushed off.

That evening, after the dinner hour, Chip and Ellie went out with their spray bottles. They were quickly joined by roughly twenty-five more people, all wielding spray bottles. It resembled a company of the old fire brigade passing buckets of water. 'Sexy Sam' took charge.

"Okay, you spray this section. You spray that section."

And so on. It didn't take long for the bottles to empty. Sam told the first five to go in to refill their bottles. Then wait outside before spraying. Then the next five were to do the same thing until they were all refilled. His thinking was he didn't want the water monitors to notice any unusual consumption in this part of the complex.

When they were re-assembled and at their respective posts, Sam gave the orders:

"On the count of four, shoot. Ready on the right, ready on the left, ready on the firing line.... Ok, one, two, three, four, shoot! You weren't all together ... let's try it again," he said. "One, two, three, four, shoot! You weren't all together. Let's try it again. One, two, three, four, shoot!"

Now they had a rhythm going. It looked more like a *conga line* than a firing line. (This gang could have fun no matter what they did.) When they were empty they stood around talking. Ole Wisenheimer brought up the point that they couldn't keep stealing water like that without being caught. 'King Arthur' brought up a point. Instead of using the dishwasher every day, why not wash by hand and save the dishwater for the hedges?

The next night, instead of spray bottles, there were twenty-five people out with buckets, pans and plastic five-gallon containers, all full of dishwater. The hedges perked up a little after that. But was it enough to save them? Windy Willies weather forecast didn't show any rain for at least the next ten days. The situation was bad. They had too much to lose. This called for even more drastic measures. Again, it was Skeeter with another bright idea.

"Ya' know how much water goes down the drain when ya' take a shower? Why don'tcha' put a kiddy pool in your shower to catch the water?" he suggested.

Bert says, "That's a good idea but how do you carry it through a doorway and out to the hedges?"

Molly spoke up. "Sometimes your bulb doesn't burn too brightly either. You take a sponge or a mop or a cup or a towel or whatever to wring it into a bucket."

"Oh, yeah," said Gert.

The next day both Wal-Mart and K Mart ran out of kiddy pools. Because the water department people couldn't tell them not to take a shower, they all decided to shower two or three times a day. They faithfully followed this routine for almost two weeks. The weather was the most dominant thing on their minds. Molly no longer cared what Windy Willie looked like on TV any more.

"Just bring us some rain," she implored.

Finally one afternoon, there was a huge dark cloud way off in the distance. Several of Chip and Ellie's neighbors could be seen outside, staring up at the sky, as if they were in prayer.

Tee Shot Tom could be heard muttering, "Come on you coward, come over this way."

Ever so slowly the dark mass edged in their direction.

Then ... *"I felt a drop. So did I. Me too."*

Skeeter yelled out, "Get the kiddy pools out here to catch it!"

Talk about a beehive of activity there quickly were twenty-five kiddy pools stretched out on the driveway. It barely rained hard enough to cover the bottom of the pools. The cloud drifted away, the sun came out and four of the guys were emptying all of the pools into one.

Old Wisenheimer said, "I guess we didn't pray hard enough."

However, the next morning, they all woke up to an overcast sky, not exactly foreboding but more ominous than they would have liked.

Chip called Doc, "Have you looked outside yet?"

"Yes, I have," said Doc, "What do ya' think?"

"Let's hope it's just a good hard rain. It's too early for a hurricane and there wasn't any in the forecast," replied Chip. He was just hanging up the phone when he heard the first clasp of thunder.

Miss Ellie yelled at him from the veranda, "It's here, It's finally here!"

It rained fairly hard most of the morning. About noon it began to let up. Chip gave a sigh of relief. At least it wasn't another hurricane like Andrew that started this whole thing in the first place. They could almost see the hedges perk up as they watched.

The next couple of months went just as smoothly as a hot fudge sundae. Lee Iacocca had the hotel running as efficiently as a '64' Mustang. And Doctor Kenny Dee kept finding new ways to increase production but they were still back ordered. This truly was the discovery of the millennium. The general membership of the FASA group had decided that there was no need for a contest. And there was no need for flavored Floragra unless they just wanted to make more profit. Doc could just hold that idea in abeyance for the time being.

Several members of the constituency were in the soda bar/malt shop, or Hunger Room, as Skeeter named it, when Lucille walked in with a big stack of messages. The big half, were for more orders that she handed to Doc. The smaller half, were mostly for Mr. Iacocca or Chip. Chip said he would take them up to the office. Iacocca was hanging up the phone when Chip walked in.

"Whatcha' got? he asked Chip.

"Not sure," replied Chip. "I never heard of most of these people."

Iacocca said, "Tell ya' what, you take half and I'll take half. Let's see if we can find out what this is all about."

It didn't take long for them to see a pattern in the phone calls. There were calls from *Cheesbrough Ponds, Smith/Kline, Maybelline* and *Pfizer*. Everybody wanted to buy out FASA. Even *Kellog and Post* thought they could corner the cereal market if they could enhance their products with Floragra. Chip told Lee he could see something like *Wheaties* advertising <u>The Breakfast of Older Champions</u>.

One of Lee's calls was kind of interesting. The guy said his name was Bruce Easily from *Eli Lilly* and he was interested in their agriculture company.

Lee said, "What's your name again, Ely what?"

The guy said his name wasn't *Eli* anything. He said he was <u>Easily</u> with the *Lilly Company*. Iacocca told him he was easily with the Floragra Company. Then Lee told him they didn't sell lilies, it wasn't that kind of agriculture and they didn't need any lilies so please don't call back.

The calls were coming in from all over the world, Germany, France, Japan, China and even Brazil and Cuba. You can imagine what they told Castro! But Chip had a call that was really confusing.

"Mr. Dale, my name is Bird, J. L. Bird and I'm with Oil of Olay," the caller stated.

Chip says, "Are you saying Olay or Ole'?"

The man says, *"Oil of Olay, sir."*

Chip says, "I know there's oil in Kuwait but I didn't know there was much in Spain, Ole!"

Mr. Bird said, *"he wasn't selling oil, but that he was in body lotions and fragrances."*

Chip says, "These hedges don't have any fragrance and we already have a fragrance line up so I don't think we can help you. Thank you for calling."

The calls went on for several weeks. (Could there be anyone left that hadn't called?) Then one afternoon the reservation clerk strolled into Lee Iacocca's office.

"I just made a reservation for a guy that I think you should know about," she said. His name is Dewey; he'll be checking in by ten O'clock and would like a meeting with you and the top management of the FASA Company, if it could be arranged.

Iacocca turned to Chip and said, "Now here's a man that's not fooling around with phone calls. He wants to get right down to business. Can I arrange a meeting with you, Doc and this guy, say noon in one of the conference rooms? We'll see what he has to offer."

Chip made the arrangements. At twelve O'clock sharp, Mr. Dewey stepped out of the elevator. Iacocca made the introductions. Mr. Dewey said he was with the law firm of *Dewey, Cheatum and Howe*, representing one of the Trump companies.

Mr. Dewey explained, "We are extremely interested in your Floragra product. However, since you are not listed on any of the major stock exchanges, it is difficult to get any information. May I ask where you derive your raw material, how many people are in your company and are you interested in selling at a tremendous profit?"

Lee Iacocca was used to these slick operators but this guy was good. Lee was impressed with the way the guy cut to the chafe, got right to the point.

Iacocca shot back, "It's none of your business where our raw material comes form, there are twenty five owners of the company and no we don't want to sell."

"Please don't get upset," he explained, "I'm here strictly on an exploratory mission. I realize how busy you gentlemen are, so I thought I would save you some time by getting to the point. Allow me to state our position. Then take your time to think it over. We are offering twenty million for the hotel, five hundred thousand each for every member of your group plus an unlimited supply of Floragra for as long as it last. I will be staying here at your fine hotel for three days. I hope to get in some golf and a little deep-sea fishing. With that said, I bid you gentlemen good afternoon. I'll be in touch."

"Holy Toledo!" said Doc.

"WOW!" was Chip's exclamation.

"Now what?" asked Lee.

The three days seemed to fly by. They hadn't seen Dewey at all. He was gone bright and early every morning. About an hour before he checked out, he went into Iacocca's office.

"Well sir, have you made a decision?" he asked.

"No, we haven't. We haven't been able to get a quorum together to even present your proposition. However, the three of us have discussed it at length and we believe it deserves consideration. We'll get back to you, one way or the other, within a week or so. We want to thank you for staying here and hope you enjoyed your visit."

"Immensely," was Mr. Dewey's reply. "I'll certainly recommend it to my partners Cheatum and Howe. And believe me; Mr. Trump will get a very favorable report."

It took several days before Iacocca could get the entire membership together.

Meanwhile, the hotel was doing a fabulous business, the FASA Company was doing a fabulous business everything was fabulous. At least it was until they heard from Mr. Essence. Herb L. Essence, that is, with FDA. It seems the Food and Drug Administration had gotten wind of the Floragra group. Mr. Essence hinted that their seemed to be several FDA violations, the least of which were lack of the proper authorization, improper manufacturing facilities and incomplete disclosure of ingredients. (Isn't that just like the government to kill a good thing?) Lee Iacocca was about to get his Italian temper up when Herb L. Essence politely asked if Mr. Iacocca would mind answering a few questions. Iacocca had been through these government things many times before. He was sure he could handle this guy.

"Don't mind at all," he stated. "Go ahead, pal, shoot."

"First of all, I need a sample to take back to Washington. Secondly, we know from the various TV newscasts, what you claim it will do, we just need to find out if the claims are true and what's in it. Thirdly, your government thinks this is a fantastic discovery. If you will comply with the proper regulations, we will allow you to continue operations."

He continued, "We know you are using the leaves from hedges that our research tells us are of the ficus strain. What we don't know, is why it works the way you say it does. We think, with extensive experimenting, we may be able to propagate the hedges or duplicate them scientifically. If the government can do that, just think of the possibilities? We could change the social security age to at least seventy-five, thereby saving billions of dollars. We could practically cut out Medicare and Medicaid, saving billions more. We could use that money instead to build government run homes for the aged, giving them a much better quality of life in their declining years."

Iacocca finally got a chance to interrupt him.

"Wait just a cotton picking' minute. We'll apply for the proper permits. We'll give you the samples, not because we want to, but because we almost have to. But we don't agree with the government cutting back on the few services it already has in place and we sure as hell don't agree with any government run institutions. We happen to think private enterprise is a great thing and competition, especially with the government is even greater. So Mr. Herb L. Essence, we'll have your samples ready within an hour. Good day, sir."

Doc and Chip never opened their mouths.

As soon as the guy left Lee said, "I can use a drink."

They went back to Doc's private stash. During their discussion, they agreed they needed to consult with 'Lean Jean the legal machine' and maybe 'King

Arthur' would have some ideas. Early the next morning, they convened in the office. They filled Jean and Arthur in on the details of the meeting with Herb L. Essence of FDA. Jean was about to speak when Chip interrupted her.

"Before you say anything, I think you should be aware of the rest of the equation," said Chip.

Iacocca filled them in on the offer Donald Trump made through Mr. Dewey. They all sat there, in silence, for several minutes. 'King Arthur' finally broke the silence. Always the gentleman, he said,"Jean, I think you should give us your thoughts first."

"I don't know what to say about the Trump offer but I can tell you we don't have the expertise or the manpower to fight the U. S. government, or the time," she noted. "But if they decide they want the hedges, they will eventually get the hedges even if they have to exercise the right of *eminent domain*. It may take ten or twenty years but most of us don't have that much time."

Arthur stood up. "Gentlemen and madam attorney, first of all we have to run this entire scenario before the group. Since we would be ill advised to take on the United States government, I suggest we look at our alternatives, particularly the Trump offer. The only thing I can see wrong with it is that some of our people have more invested than others. We're not making a ton of money on the twenty million for the hotel. It would be a shame to take the heavier investment money out of that. If the group agrees that this is the way we go, I think we should counter offer at twenty for the hotel, plus the five hundred thousand each, plus the lifetime guarantee of Floragra, plus the exact amount of each individual investment. Also, may I point out Mr. Trump just spent forty million to open a golf course here in south Florida. He knows more about us than we do of him. In fact, I'm curious how he knows so much."

Doc, Chip and Lee agreed they needed to discuss the whole thing with the rest of the group. The meeting would be held in two days. That gave them time to think things out and get somewhat organized.

The next morning Lee was in his office when his buxom assistant walked in.

"Hey, I gotta' talk to ya'," he said. "I want to be fair with you so I'm going to tell you something that you must promise me you will not repeat until I say so."

"Ok, boss, whatever you say," she said. "Now I'm, curious, what is it?"

Iacocca told her the whole story.

"The reason I'm telling you is that if we sell to the Trump people, you will be out looking for another job," he pointed out.

"Oh, I don't think so," she says.

"What do you mean by that?" Lee asked.

"Well, now that you're being honest with me, I'll be honest with you," she continued, "I already have a job. I have been working for, 'The Donald' ever since I met you. That was no accident. I've been reading all your messages and listening to conversations all over the place. You might say I'm an undercover agent. Mr. Trump knows everything that goes on here, including the formula. He's as anxious to get a hold of Floragra as anyone else is."

"I'll be damned," sputtered Iacocca. "I'll be damned!"

With that disclosure, he dismissed her and went back to Doc's lab for a drink.

The meeting was called to order. Iacocca told the group the whole story, including the part about Trump's spy. (Whatta' Babe.) It took about fifteen minutes for the whole thing to sink in.

Finally Old Wisenheimer said, "Whatta' we gonna' do?"

Chip quieted the crowd as he stood up.

"Knowing what we now know about undercover agents etc. I think we should make the counter offer that Arthur pointed out. Trump will jump at it. We wont have to worry about government intervention, or any conglomerate takeovers or any Japanese trying to get the hotel back. We each get our initial investment back plus five hundred thousand. That makes us twenty million dollars ahead, which I suggest we put into a yacht and crew big enough to take a world cruise. Think about it tonight. We'll take a vote at 3:00 PM tomorrow."

The next morning, 'Tee Shot Tom' was riding in the sidecar of Skeeter's motorcycle as they headed for the yacht basin. Walking along the dock they could see several nice boats. Tom kept asking questions. He finally ascertained that in order to comfortably accommodate twenty-five people the boat would need to be at least two hundred feet long and would require a crew of eighteen to twenty. They could get a pretty nice one for about thirty million.

Skeeter kept asking, "Yeah, but does it have a dinghy?"

One vendor really hit their hot button. He said he had a two hundred and ten footer that had been only used once by some sultanate or a Greek shipping magnate then traded it in for something larger. They could probably get it for around twenty million.

"Yeah, but does it have a dinghy?" asked Skeeter, once more.

They scooted back to Chips ASAP. Ironically, Skeeter had never been on a boat and Tee Shot was never in anything longer than twenty feet. They got back to the hotel a couple of hours before the meeting was scheduled for the votes. They filled in the guys on what they found out.

'Tee Shot Tom' said, "Man, the thing is beautiful. It's already in the water just waiting for us."

THE FINALE

The meeting started promptly at 3 P.M. Chip asked Miss Ellie to take a roll call. He didn't want to leave anyone out.

"All present and accounted for," she reported.

Chip asked if there were any questions or if anyone cared to make a comment.

'Bab's the Blond Bombshell from Bristol' (Connecticut that is) stood up: "No matter what we decide, I just want you to know that El Zoro won't be included. He's already on his way back to Spain. Thank you."

Then Old Wisenheimer (no one was sure exactly how old he was, most estimates put him over ninety) stood up: "First, I want to say what a great pleasure it has been associating with this fine group of people. I regret, however, that I must bow out. Certain duties have called me elsewhere. Therefore, I will not cast a vote. However, if I were to vote, I sure wouldn't mind a cruise."

A strange hush fell over the group, it was now time to make the decision ... stay on, comply with the regulations or accept the Trump offer. The vote was unanimous to take the Trump offer. After the roar died down, Lee Iacocca stood up. He thanked everyone for his or her cooperation, etc. but mostly for friendships. He told them he didn't think he could play much golf aboard ship so he was going to stay behind. He would stay on until the Trump group took over. His only concern was his lifetime supply of Floragra, which could be worked out.

It took about eight weeks or so for everything to be worked out. In the meantime they each had an inspection of the yacht. To a person, they were tickled pink. (And why not, the staterooms were more like fancy hotel rooms.) Each suite was complete with a TV (with satellite reception) a VCR (with tons of movies, thanks to Molly), compact disc player (with loads of big band music) and a small microwave (for midnight snacks).

'Tee Shot Tom', who was younger than most of the group, used the time to get his helicopter pilots license. (What good is a helicopter on board if no one knew how to use it?) Skeeter was learning how to operate a dinghy. The last thing to be loaded before departure was the five-gallon drum of Floragra.

As we watched them take off into the setting sunset, we could see the name emblazoned across the stern: ***FICUS MIRACULOUS***

978-0-595-46737-2
0-595-46737-7

Printed in the United States
114574LV00001B/61-108/A